Shadows of Leonardo

Will Ottinger

Black Rose Writing | Texas

ISBN: 978-1-68433-624-1
PUBLISHED BY BLACK ROSE WRITING
www.blackrosewriting.com

Printed in the United States of America
Suggested Retail Price (SRP) $19.95

Shadows of Leonardo is printed in Garamond

*As a planet-friendly publisher, Black Rose Writing does its best to eliminate unnecessary waste to reduce paper usage and energy costs, while never compromising the reading experience. As a result, the final word count vs. page count may not meet common expectations.

To my wife Sandra, as always and forever.

Acknowledgments

My thanks and gratitude to those whose advice and assistance helped smooth the road. A special thanks to Jon Harbuck, K.C. Curtis and Julie Elb for their cover-to-cover proofing and encouragement, and to Jerry Weiner, Ray Dan Parker, Mel Coe and David Kruglinski who endured repeated drafts, pointing out where I occasionally got off track.

And there are few things more appreciated than the consistent critic and proofreader who endures multiple readings of my efforts – my wife, Sandra. Her vast knowledge of mysteries and suspense novels adds fresh perspectives, while also possessing an editor's unrelenting and merciless eye. Any other errors or oversights are entirely my own.

Shadows of Leonardo

Chapter One

Western Border of Russia
Dosevski Railroad Station
January 3, 1945

The gaunt officer glared at the swirling flurries. He detested every flake despite the snow's efficiency in hiding the mass graves. More than anything, Anton Weisser craved an end to the relentless Russian winter. Shivering on the decaying train platform, he surveyed the boundless white landscape, exhausted beyond his thirty years, the cold attacking his left hand more fiercely than ever.

Ignoring the pain, he scanned the hazy horizon for Russian tanks and spat over the edge of the train platform, watching the spittle harden into ice. Why, he wondered, had some witless Bolshevik constructed *anything* in the exact center of nowhere? For days he'd seen no signs of life other than protesting crows and solitary owls.

The bombed-out railway station squatted like an abandoned orphan in the snowdrifts, a monstrous iceberg in the white wilderness. Snow-covered mounds lay like graves around the structure, but the dead no longer mattered, not in Russia

Turning his back to the icy wind, the SS *Sturmbannführer* lit the cardboard tube that served as his last cigarette. The Russians, he long ago decided, were incapable of producing a decent cigarette. This one smelled like a Turkish outhouse, but the bastards produced tanks like a bitch birthing pups.

A battered truck sat a few meters from the parallel rails, its chassis sagging on worn rear springs like a gut-shot stag. Inside the Russian GAZ's cab, the last three members of his SS *einsatzgruppen* unit huddled together like lost children, their skills no longer required. Hopefully, they wouldn't need to build a fire beneath the truck's engine to thaw the oil. He'd watched Luftwaffe mechanics perform the trick on grounded Heinkels and Focke-Wulfs, desperate to get a few frozen bombers and fighters airborne.

Weisser drew on the noxious cigarette and frowned at his reflection in a smeared window pane. No raven-black uniform now, he thought, no polished riding boots or waving flags. Only layers of rancid clothing and a peasant's boots. The stubble of an unkempt black beard covered his cold-bruised skin, the stiff bristles matching the color of his hair. He leaned an inch closer to the glass and gave a humorless smile. He lacked a recruiting poster's depiction of the true blond Aryan, but purity of the blood had assured his admission into the SS.

He tossed away the cigarette, startled as a shrill whistle pierced the stillness. Squinting through the haze, he watched a squat black locomotive plow a bow wave of snow toward the station. Trailed by a toy-like coal tender and a single boxcar, the driver wheels groaned to a halt beside the platform as though too weary to perform another revolution.

A pair of round goggles and a muffled face peered down from the engineer's compartment. The boxcar door rattled open and Weisser stepped off the platform, his straw-filled boots squeaking against the snow. Flickering light back-lit a boyish face in the doorway. A Russian PPS submachine gun slung over the one shoulder, only the figure's soft *Wehrmacht* cap provided any clue he was part of the German Army.

Hell, Weisser thought, the entire army looked like Russian conscripts.

The over-coated figure jumped to the ground, saw Weisser's rank and saluted.

"*Leutnant* Rothmann," he said, his grin relieved. "Good to see a friendly face, sir."

Weisser returned the salute as the boy jerked a thumb over his shoulder at the bundled figure in the train cab who raised his goggles. "I found this old sweat sneaking around the rail yards at Lovinsk, trying to figure out how to steal a train," he said. "He's a railroader from the Munich-Berlin run."

A flurry struck the boxcar and when Weisser didn't reply, the lieutenant dragged a cigarette stub from his tunic. He turned his back to the demolished station and managed to light up after the third match. "Never expected to find anyone here," he said, cupping the cigarette. "We've got shit for a Russian map that doesn't show a station here."

An icy gust struck the two men who faced away from the wind. Weisser looked at the truck and back to the unexpected arrivals. The boy and engineer were complications, but might prove useful in a firefight if they ran into partisans.

"Your unit, *Leutnant?*"

The boy pulled himself up. "Twenty-Ninth Panzer Grenadiers. What's left of them."

"So, you decided to take the train home."

"No, sir. I'm following orders."

"Orders." Weisser had heard such tales before.

The boy nodded. "We're almost out of coal. I told Johann anything worth stealing was gone long ago, but we saw your truck and I knew God sent us a signal."

Weisser suppressed a smile. The fool believed God existed in the steppes. "Did your orders require you to steal a train?"

"No sir. Well, actually, yes." Rothmann's face lit up with pride. "I built a fire inside to keep the crate warm. They told me the contents would be ruined if they froze."

"A single crate?" What was he talking about?

Weisser looked through the open door. A smokey haze filled the empty car, obscuring a single four-by-four wooden box lodged in one corner. How many fools did the army have left?

"I found a cauldron in the train yard," Rothmann said. He patted the boxcar's wooden slats. "This is an old cattle car and I'm burning cow chips to keep the interior warm."

"What's so important to warrant an officer and a train?"

"The crate's for *Reichsmarschall* Göring."

Now it made sense. Fat Hermann's lust for booty remained unabated while the world collapsed around his piggy ears.

"What's in this crate of yours?"

"No one told me, sir. I'm supposed to deliver it to Berlin."

"Berlin? Our engineers are blowing up the tracks down the line. You'd be lucky to make another ten kilometers."

The lieutenant lifted his chin. "I have my orders."

A zealot, Weisser thought, or useful nitwit some higher-up believed would make a convenient scapegoat if the cargo disappeared.

Rothmann walked to the locomotive and motioned the engineer from the cab. Ice pellets hissed against the steaming engine's boiler. The approaching night intensified the cold as he and Weisser sidled closer to the tracks, grateful for the locomotive's warmth.

Weisser thrust out his gloved hand. "Your orders."

He scanned the pages. No details about the cargo, but the orders were typed on Göring's personal stationery. Typical, Weisser thought. The drug-addicted *Reichsmarschall* cared more for looted antiquities than his dying air force.

"I need to check the crate's contents."

Rothmann stiffened. "My orders prohibit…"

"I don't need a reason, *Leutnant*, but if your cargo's valuable, I'll make room in our truck."

Weisser hoisted himself into the boxcar. The frigid air stank of scorched cattle dung. He warmed his hands above the blackened iron kettle. His curiosity overcoming the stench, he turned to Rothmann.

"Let's have a look inside."

"My orders state the cargo is not to be opened."

"New orders. Open the goddamn crate."

Rothmann hesitated only a moment before he produced a crowbar. Weisser's three men appeared at the boxcar's sliding door, but he ignored them as screws popped and boards splintered. Rothmann pried off the lid and stood back.

Five cloth bundles huddled against one another. Weisser lifted out one of the rectangles and removed a blanket.

Rothmann gasped and stared at the gilded frame. "That looks old."

Mesmerized by what he held, Weisser re-wrapped it and placed the bundle inside the crate. He ordered Rothmann to reseal his cargo, watching as the lieutenant hammered the lid closed.

He could not take his eyes from the crude box. Impossible, he thought. Not in a stinking Russian boxcar, meaningless in a freezing wasteland. The unfairness of the discovery in a filthy boxcar left him faintly nauseous. Why now?

But to hold such a treasure…

Oblivious to the stench of long-dead animals, a vision emerged, unfolding like a detailed nautical chart. Weisser stared at the crate as the outrageous idea crystalized with astonishing clarity. It seemed the plan had lain dormant his entire life, waiting for the moment. Insanity to be sure, but the audacity intrigued him. It might be the last mistake of his life, but odds were he'd end up dead, anyway. He'd always thought himself a gambler, so why not a final toss of the dice?

He laid a fatherly hand on Rothmann's sleeve. "Let's load your cargo onto the truck and I'll give you and your engineer a lift."

His men lugged the crate to the truck. Rothmann and the engineer watched it loaded onto the truck bed. A beefy corporal with a reddened face jumped down from the canvas enclosure and slammed the tailgate shut, swiping at his runny nose.

"What's in it, Major?"

Weisser drew his Walther from its holster. "Evidence. These men are deserters and looters."

Rothmann, walking back to the train for his gear, stopped short. The engineer bumped into him and looked back at Weisser.

"Sir?"

Weisser raised the Walther and shot both men.

For a moment, no one moved. Rothmann sprawled on his back. His mouth hung open as though protesting his innocence, the engineer face down beside him. His companions rummaged through the dead men's pockets. The corporal grinned and began tugging off the lieutenant's fur-lined boots.

"You want any of this stuff, *Herr Sturmbannführer?*"

"No, take what you want."

A private ripped open the bloody coats. "No fucking cigarettes."

The corporal sat in the snow and began removing the remnants of his own boots. Weisser reached over the truck tailgate, checked to make certain Rothmann's weapon was loaded and killed all three with a long burst.

The vastness and heavy snowfall swallowed the sound. He stared at the five bodies for a long moment before turning away.

Now begins the hard part, he thought.

Retrieving Rothmann's food and extra ammunition drums, he double-checked several cans of extra gasoline stored between the cab and truck bed. Last he'd heard, Königsberg and Danzig were ice-free. Joining the general retreat only meant more fodder for the sausage grinder, but if he made it to the sea, he'd free himself from a lost war.

He settled behind the wheel and savored an odd sensation of newfound freedom. Two sacks of gold rings and loose diamonds sat on the seat beside him. Neither meant anything to their former owners, whose corpses rotted in shallow trenches. He looked through the dirty rear window at the crate and savored his discovery again. All the jewels and gold were baubles compared to its contents.

"Right man, right place, right time," he said to the snow-dusted windshield.

His plan bordered on insanity, but the Allies had surely discovered the camps by now, readying a hangman's noose for the faithful who had carried out their mission. A loyal soldier who did his duty deserved a better fate than an anonymous death in a frozen wilderness. Göring's orders were an ironclad passport to the coast. With the crate's contents, he could cheat the victors' revenge. He'd bribe passage aboard a neutral ship and create a new identity. Maybe a Swedish one. The Swedes had played it safe during the war, neutral again. He grinned and relished the thought of playing the unfortunate refugee in the land of sympathetic blonds. If he could remain alive.

He pulled the Russian weapon within easy reach, held his breath and punched the starter. The engine clattered to life. He engaged the clutch, jamming the floor lever into low gear. A gust of wind rocked the slab-sided relic, but the tires took hold and the truck trundled past the five bodies vanishing beneath the snow.

Weisser smiled despite his cracked lips. What he'd found in the reeking cattle car would transform his life forever.

Chapter Two

New York City
Gallery Britannia
Spring Evening 2018

"Do I know you?"

I turned to the overweight man in a Brioni tuxedo, trying not to stare at his garish red cumberbund. Clutching a flute of champagne, he tottered beside me, inspecting a Jamie Wyeth oil that glowed under a Halogen spot. My tipsy friend was the first guest at the gallery opening who had spoken to me.

"I don't think so," I said. "I've got one of those faces that's described as common, particularly by attractive women."

The jowly art-lover tossed back his free champagne and laughed. "Life's a bitch." He inspected me more closely, taking in my tux that didn't quite match his tailored ensemble. I'd lost a little weight since the van Gogh travails and my I needed a haircut, but I saw no hints of gray among the black and imagined I still looked younger than my late thirties.

My companion snapped his fingers soundlessly. "I know you. You were all over TV and the newspapers. Barrow. Adam Barrow, right? The guy who found the... what was it?"

"A van Gogh."

"Right. You get rich?"

"No."

"Another bitch," he said with a lopsided grin.

My boozy companion wandered back to the bar. My ego sufficiently dented, I drained my glass and looked for one of the roving servers. Fame, I learned, was smoke, and smoke didn't linger in the world of electronic stimuli.

A year earlier, I'd rescued a lost van Gogh. It created a sensation in art circles, but too many people died to declare its discovery a national holiday. The startling image of the young girl now hung in the Getty, her glory secure until the museum shipped the massive painting to the Louvre. I lost the ownership wars after claims and counter-claims declared the painting had been stolen from France at the outbreak of World War II. An international court upheld the decision and denied my appeal, leaving me where I'd started, the struggling owner of a small gallery in Chicago.

I'd also lost Katia, who deserved equal credit for the discovery. God should have spared her life, but he didn't. No matter how I dissected her death, she died because of my obsession with the dead Dutch artist. My discovery of the van Gogh might warrant a small footnote in art history, but I'd trade everything to have her back.

Now I worked for Phillip Dansby, an old friend of my father and one of the richest men in the world with an art collection to match his success. The ex-pat British billionaire somehow decided my discovery revealed hidden talent. Either that or he had a weakness for lost lambs. Unable to resist the possibility of unearthing another lost treasure, my life's goal shifted from a small gallery owner to a tracker of lost art, joining him in New York after he agreed to keep my Chicago gallery afloat.

One of the downsides was tonight. He'd set me adrift in a sea of strangers. The throng appeared in high spirits despite the spring storm that washed Soho's streets in headlights and oily neon rainbows. Gallery Britannia vibrated with conversation and laughter, many of the city's wealthiest patrons preening for one another. My two art degrees meant I could hold a short discourse on any artist on the walls, but art discussions took second place to the see-and-be-seen partygoers.

Bored with the crowd and the string quartet, I headed for the bar when a heavy arm fell across my shoulders.

"Adam, you enjoying the festivities?"

Dansby appeared mildly drunk, but one could never tell when his good humor showed itself. Flushed with the gallery's success, he carried his advancing years with disarming ease and charm, a wily sixty-year-old British army veteran who looked forty. If one looked closely, only his face carried telltale traces of his age, the character lines carved by time and decisions. Several inches taller than me, his cropped grey hair failed to conceal two livid scars across his scalp that he jokingly claimed were souvenirs from a jealous husband. He remained an enigma in the art business and I never mastered separating his *bon vivant* mask from the real Phillip Dansby. No matter which face he showed the public, those who underestimated him paid a steep price.

Pulling me away from the Wyeth, he waved a hand at the canvas. "Jamie's a lucky sod," he said. "Didn't need to die to become famous." Dansby raised his glass to the painting. "Welcome to the Famous Living Wankers Club, old boy."

"Are you famous, Phillip?"

"Infamous, actually."

"Phillip, the champagne's great, but I don't know a single damn person."

He smoothed his navy and burgundy cummerbund, a less-than-subtle reminder that he was late of Her Majesty's Guards and Special Air Service. Cashiered for a series of unspecified indiscretions, he still considered himself a cut above those who never served a monarch.

"Just consider this evening's festivities what you Americans call a perk," he said. "Having you join me tonight is meant to establish your bona fides as a highly valued associate." He looked around the lavish space, newest addition to New York's poshest art district.

"You'll likely end up associating with one or two interesting people. A few are here tonight and I want you to mix and mingle, carry my banner, as it were." As we talked, he guided me into one of the alcoves and changed the subject.

"I need a favor," he said, lowering his voice.

"A favor."

"Just so. There's an auction scheduled at Delaudier next week. A pen-and-ink study by Leonardo that supposedly depicts Christ as a younger man. The world's never seen it, and it's attracting tremendous attention. I inspected it last week with Jean-Henri, and he's convinced. You'll bid on it for me while I'm in London."

I started to protest when he held up his hand.

"I'm willing to go $40 million."

I blinked. "$40 million? You're throwing me in the deep end."

"Time for you to swim in deeper waters, dear boy. You'll be my registered bidder. Just keep raising your paddle. If the bidding exceeds the $40 million mark, then I'm out."

"What did the drawing bring last time it was last offered?"

"It's never been shown. Delaudier won't say how he acquired it, but two sets of experts inspected it and I'm willing to overlook provenance in this case. An unknown da Vinci is a major find."

Forty million dollars. A waiter with a tray of champagne appeared. I handed him my empty and grabbed a full glass.

"You'd stand a better chance if you were there," I said. "People might drop out if they see you bidding."

"Can't do it. I have a business conference in London, and I don't do telephone bids. You can have a go at this one yourself." He smiled and scanned the crowd for his date. "I'm taking Haley with me."

Haley, a wide-eyed Broadway blond with a very Broadway body, I'd watched her wandering the room looking lost, drawing male appraisals and stares from women. I'd met her earlier in the evening and confirmed Dansby preferred women with obvious physical attributes, a condition which Haley fulfilled in spades.

"These aren't my people, Phillip," I reminded him.

He lowered his voice. "Mine either, but you never know when one or two might prove useful."

He missed the point. "I haven't had a genuine conversation with anyone tonight."

"Not to worry." He surveyed the room as though assessing subjects in his realm. "Most are wealthy lumps mixed in with frauds and pretenders."

"Okay, but I'm more interested in the Delaudier auction."

"Just do me a favor and don't bid on another dead acolyte. I don't want work by some student who mixed paint for Rembrandt or a clever chap who painted copies of Degas."

The Degas quip cut deeply. In the year I'd worked for Dansby, I'd uncovered nothing but a clever fake. I'd chased the ersatz Degas to Paris and back, spending Dansby's money like a drug lord, hungry to prove the Van Gogh hadn't been a one-off stroke of luck. He had the patience of a racehorse breeder, but I felt pressure and didn't kid myself about him. He'd thrown me a lifeline after the van Gogh and I'd almost snapped it from the start.

"Remember, if you spot something else of interest in the catalog, talk with Jean-Henri," he said. "The old French frog's never failed me."

"I hope he never hears you call him a frog."

Dansby laughed. Jean-Henri Bonnet was Dansby's artistic hit man, confirming or disparaging art that caught Dansby's attention. The term "specialist" didn't describe the Frenchman's talents. I might be the hunting dog, but Bonnet decided what to kill. He and his partner Gerry lived the good life in New York, enjoying an elevated status in the city's upscale gay community. I'd spent six intensive months trying to absorb a modicum of his knowledge. Relegated to the bottom of the heap after I touted what was an expertly forged Degas, we formed an uneasy truce.

I admired his knowledge, but the irascible Bonnet wasn't God, although he saw me as a threat, the new boy invading his realm. My Degas gaffe proved heaven-sent, securing his throne in Dansby's eyes. But I learned a lesson: go slower and select my objectives with greater care. I didn't plan on carrying water for Jean-Henri, but the misstep marred my status with Dansby and I would make certain he didn't have buyer's remorse for taking me on.

"What if I misfire again?"

Dansby pressed a forefinger on my tux shirt. "Then the formerly illustrious Adam Barrow will fade into the night, and I'll dismiss or shoot you."

I managed a smile. "A lot depends on luck, Phillip."

"That's always the case, but I'm depending on your God-given talent."

"I don't think He gives guarantees."

"Delaudier's catalog is in my office," Dansby said. "Take a look and let's talk again before I leave. Remember, I want that da Vinci for my new museum. It's at the top of my list."

He spotted a fashionably dressed elderly woman studying an Edward Hopper night scene, one of the show's highlights. He squeezed my shoulder, winked and strode to her. Arranging his brightest smile, he extolled the potential of the painting's future appreciation as she stared up at him, enraptured as he thickened his accent.

I grabbed a fresh glass and wandered the crowd, executing my duty and smiling at people who ignored me. Not that it mattered. After Kat's death, I'd raised my defenses or at least my awareness that very few people matched the front they showed you. It was delayed maturity, but I'd begun accepting things as they were, not what I wanted them to be.

I slipped into the gallery office and closed the door. Switching on the desk lamp, I placed my glass next to a stack of catalogs on Dansby's desk. The glossy Delaudier catalog sat on top of the pile, the Leonardo da Vinci drawing gracing the sleek cover.

Attired in evening clothes, a studio photograph of Roland and Isabelle Delaudier filled the first inside page. Belgian by birth, he inherited his money from a string of shops across Europe that specialized in over-priced prints and antique frames for galleries and upscale collectors. Isabelle was angular and thirty years his junior and purported to be a charmer in certain circles. Known to be extremely bright, she was not the typical trophy wife, but then I wasn't married to her. Both had immigrated to the United States and founded an upstart auction house that rivaled Sotheby's and Christie's in the city in quality, if not in quantity. They had steered clear of scandals that rocked the other houses, moving up rapidly into the rarified world of Old Master offerings.

I thumbed the slick pages to a double-page fold-out. The sepia drawing depicted a young bearded man in a plain robe, his hand atop the head of a small child. Da Vinci's eye and skill were astounding, the grace and anatomy incomparable. The piece measured 12x16, two pages of notes accompanying the glossy illustration. After five centuries, da Vinci remained a source of wonder, a genius who flawlessly rendered the human form or a complex machine of war. Everything seemed guided by the hand of God.

The catalog included other impressive work that dated from the 1400s, many bearing the typical caveat emptor: '*May be from the school of...* or *attributed to...*' I retrieved my champagne and tossed the slick brochure on the stack. I clicked off the light and sat in darkness for a full minute. I would make certain Phillip got what he wanted, then pick which mountain I selected to die on. But for the moment, I became the kid in a candy shop with his checkbook in my coat pocket.

Chapter Three

A Week Later

The night of the Delaudier auction, I walked from my apartment up Sixth Avenue. There was a slight drizzle, and the evening had turned cooler despite the onset of summer. I sipped a cup of Starbucks and thought about Dansby's marching orders. They were simple enough, but had I known about Enzo Riva and his book, I would have turned around and found a friendly bar.

As I savored the night air and my six-buck latte, I inspected the shops and restaurants along the street. The winds of chance had blown me from California to Chicago to New York, and I wasn't certain I liked my current stop. I enjoyed the city's hustle and vibrancy, but chose not to indulge in its self-absorption and disdain for those outside its self-imposed barricades. It had the advertised marvels and beauty, but approaching darkness cloaked its underbelly. In the final analysis, New York reminded me of a two-year-old *New Yorker* magazine in a dentist's office, the glamor bent and torn around the edges.

Delaudier Gallery displayed a convergence of acute angles and smoked glass that occupied a half a block south of Rockefeller Plaza. Designed at outrageous expense by a trendy architect, the cube reveled in what passed for Avant Garde design in New York circles. A garish display of lights illuminated a lobby spacious enough for the Knicks to hold a full court practice.

A few dedicated smokers enjoyed a last cigarette at the bottom of marble entry steps, trying to ignore one another before the bloodletting commenced. A chime sounded and a security guard waved them inside. A street person huddled a few yards away, crumpled hat turned up on the sidewalk. The uniformed sentry yelled at him and kicked the hat, sending loose change rolling into the gutter.

"Hey, what the hell!"

The guard ignored me and walked inside. I picked up the dirty hat, collected scattered coins from the street and dropped a buck in the hat, mumbling an apology about the officious jerk. In the lobby, I traded my topcoat for a claim check and joined the crowd of bidders and gawkers, new money contesting old wealth, a range war brewing among the over-privileged.

No one looked twice at me as I picked up an auction catalog from a young woman in a black cocktail dress seated near the door to the salesroom. She checked my name off a spreadsheet and handed me a numbered paddle that reminded me of a country church fan.

Clearly out of my net worth universe, I headed for one of four cash bars. Nursing my drink, I watched the cavalcade slowly make its way into the auction. Jean-Henri would have made a sensible companion, but he avoided contact with strangers, preferring his cloistered library to reality.

I'd come a long way from the dingy cottage above southern California's coast, courtesy of Phillip Dansby. People labeled me his gofer, but I swallowed the half-truth, content my brother successfully ran our gallery in Chicago, Dansby's infusion of capital keeping the doors open.

I finished my drink and trailed the crowd, holding my cardboard paddle like an unbaptized penitent. The oversized auditorium reminded me of a movie theater. Padded chairs stretched to both walls, the center aisle ending at a raised stage where a vacant podium awaited the auctioneer. An empty easel sat several feet away. In contrast to the cutting-edge exterior, thick royal blue curtains created the impression of a nineteenth century stage. Six young employees sat at a long table manning a bank of landline telephones.

I found a seat halfway down the aisle with a clear sight line to the auctioneer. I opened the catalog and found two late Renaissance paintings near the rear of the catalog that had caught my attention. Both showed the potential of being overlooked in the excitement, but Jean-Henri had dismissed them as inconsequential. I accepted his brusque dismissal with little argument. My instructions were to acquire the work of one of history's geniuses.

A nervous man in glasses and bow tie took the seat on my right and gave me a tentative smile, clutching his paddle in both hands as he glanced around. Egg-bald and dressed in a dated three-piece suit, I took him for a bookkeeper or assistant retail manager.

"This is my first auction," he said, gripping the paddle as though someone might grab it from him. "I'm not certain how all this works. Do I raise my paddle or call out a bid?"

"Just hold the paddle high until a spotter sees it and marks your bid."

"That's all?"

"That's it. They'll do everything else required to take your money."

He grinned nervously. "Actually, it's not my money. I'm bidding for my brother-in-law who's in the hospital with a kidney stone."

I nodded.

"He set a maximum amount he's willing to pay."

"Right," I said, feeling like his adoptive father.

"How do I let them know when I've finished bidding?"

"If they go above your maximum, just sit on your hands."

"Okay."

An old man with egret-white hair settled in the other chair beside me. Accompanied by the smell of mothballs and garlic, I sensed a refugee like the beggar on the street and wondered how he'd slipped past the guards. He sported a ragged white goatee and appeared sunken inside a heavy overcoat buttoned to his chin despite the warmth. Downy white hair gave him a professorial air. Hunched forward, stale sweat intensified his pungent arrival. Rolling his catalog into a tight cylinder, he fixed his eyes on the stage, breathing through his mouth as though the room had been sucked dry of breathable air. Two security guards craned their heads for a better look at him. I sensed a problem and wished I'd chosen another seat, but something in the old man's manner provoked my curiosity.

"Should be an interesting evening," I said.

"What? Yes, yes, *molto*," he muttered.

The man in the bow tie looked at him and grimaced at the reek of mothballs. A tall man in a trim dark suit and burgundy tie strode on stage and adjusted the podium microphone. Conversation fell away, and I craned my neck for a glimpse of Roland and Isabelle Delaudier as the speakers crackled.

"Ladies and gentlemen, good evening," the auctioneer said as though prepared to announce Nobel Prize winners. "Delaudier welcomes you to Auction Number 138. We're offering an outstanding collection tonight, Leonardo da Vinci's drawing being the evening's highlight." He adjusted horn-rimmed half-glasses and smiled at the overflow audience.

"Items in the catalog are heavily footnoted where appropriate. The customary cautions apply and are self-explanatory regarding provenance and payment."

The old man leaned forward as though ready to leap to his feet. Instead, he folded and unfolded the catalog.

"Let's begin, shall we?" said the auctioneer. "Please turn to Catalog Item Number One." He glanced over half-moon glasses as an assistant placed a framed oil on the easel.

"We'll start the evening with a portrait titled *Dutch Burgomeister* by Gerard Donck, circa 1500. You will see from the extensive provenance notes that this work..."

The catalog showed the da Vinci as the last offering and I tuned him out, listening to the bids only when they heated up. Positioning of a premier piece was a subject of debate, some dealers preferring early placement to loosen wallets. Others liked to heighten anticipation. Neither approach seemed relevant tonight. Delaudier had gathered first-rate offerings. Bidding moved rapidly, painting after painting was hammered down at premier prices. Money was falling like leaves: $750,000. $225,000. $1,600,000, with the da Vinci yet to come. I did a quick calculation and figured the commissions guaranteed a successful night for the Delaudiers.

The stand-in brother-in-law failed to win his bid, tugged at his bow tie with relief, and left. My remaining seatmate tortured his catalog as the bidding continued, the aroma of mothballs overpowering as he sweated through his coat. Oblivious to disdainful glances from those seated around us, he stared at the easel as each work appeared on stage. I ignored him and studied the backs of heads, speculating on Dansby's competitors.

Conversation died to a murmur with the da Vinci up next. Phones pressed against their ears. The Delaudier employees behind the dais waited as the auctioneer straightened. I had $40 million in my pocket, a nonentity about to do battle with the big boys, an unnoticed wild card in their midst. It was a rush.

"Ladies and gentlemen," the auctioneer intoned, his voice expectant, "we now come to evening's premier offering. Catalog Item Number 86 is a Leonardo da Vinci drawing of a young man purported to be the Christ."

A white-gloved attendant walked through the curtains carrying a small sepia drawing under archival glass framed in gold. Meticulously adjusting the frame on the tripod, he stepped aside, ready to sacrifice his life should the drawing tumble from the easel. Most in the audience leaned forward, several raising opera glasses for a clearer look.

"Scholars believe the sketch may represent a study for da Vinci's *Christ's Entry into Jerusalem* that includes a very similar figure without the child," the auctioneer explained. "The rendering is well-preserved, with no tears and only minimal spotting. Delaudier is proud to…"

A sharp whistle pierced the room.

Heads turned toward the old man whose fingers were at his lips. The auctioneer frowned in our direction and leaned closer to the microphone.

"If I may have everyone's attention."

My seatmate glared at the stage.

"You can see from the notes and illustration in your catalog that the work is signed with the distinctive *DV* in the lower right corner. I'm certain many da Vinci admirers in the audience are aware that his signature varied greatly from work to work. While this form is somewhat unusual, the drawing has been verified as being a later work rendered by Leonardo da Vinci in the period between 1510 and 1512. May we begin with a minimal bid of…"

"It is not the work of Leonardo!"

The old man ripped the illustration from the catalog, wadded it up and tossed the ball into the aisle. He rose to his feet before I could grab him, heads swiveling in our direction.

"You cannot do this!" he shouted. "This is not da Vinci!"

Before I could move, one of the uniformed security men reached past me and grabbed the old man's coat sleeve. Another heavyset guard edged down the row and pulled him into the aisle.

"You are wrong, all of you!"

Chairs fell over as the auctioneer banged his gavel, and the guards hustled their captive up the aisle. On stage, two employees steadied the easel, guarding the da Vinci.

I don't know why I followed the trio out of the salesroom. If I missed the da Vinci, Dansby would demand my head, but I didn't like seeing the elderly roughly handled. Excusing myself, I bumped past people and caught up as the guards frog-marched him into the lobby. I reached them just as a staff member opened the exit door.

"Hey, hold on! He's with me."

The guards stopped and faced me. Their captive sagged against them, and I tried to ignore the automatics on their hips. I walked to the largest one who tightened his grip, his prey in visible pain.

I gently pulled away the guard's hand. "This is my uncle. He's on medication for Tourette Syndrome."

Both of them looked at me without an inkling of what I just said. "It's a disease. He can't help what he says." They reluctantly released him, and I smoothed his coat sleeves, managing a smile at their benevolence.

"I'll make sure he gets home and won't bother you again."

"The crazy old bastard needs to be locked away," said the scrawnier of the two.

"I'll get him home," I repeated, edging away.

"Just get him the hell out of here."

"Thank you, officer."

I gently placed my hand on the old man's back and ushered him toward the cloakroom, where I handed over my claim check without looking back at the crowd that had gathered.

"What is this Tourette Syndrome?" asked my newest uncle, no longer sounding like a Bellevue escapee.

"Something you don't have. It was all I could think of." I retrieved my coat and led him toward the exit, people staring at us. "What were you thinking in there?"

"I had to stop it, *Signor....*"

"Barrow."

He stopped and gave a stiff bow. "I am Enzo Riva. I am sorry you became involved."

"You were almost arrested," I said, eager to get back to my seat.

"Such a thing would have been acceptable."

"Because of the drawing?"

"You know Leonardo?"

"I'm an art appraiser," I said, assuming a dubious title.

"Then you must understand this is not a da Vinci."

"Why do you say that?"

Before he could reply, high heels clicked on the marble floor. An attractive blond woman adorned with a name badge hurried toward us. Even in her distraught state, her body and demeanor complemented a simple knee-length black dress. I held up my palm, herding my charge toward the door.

"All over," I called.

Half way to the door she stopped us with an outstretched arm.

"We were just leaving," I gently pushed Riva in front of me.

"Are you together?"

I stopped, taken with her looks and professional demeanor despite the circumstances. "In a way."

"You came with him?"

"He took the seat next to me."

She gave me a quizzical look. "I won't ask the reason for his outburst and we won't press charges if he agrees never to enter the building again."

"I'm not his keeper, but that sounds reasonable." I looked at him. "It's a good deal. Thank the lady."

When he didn't respond, she looked at me more closely. "And who're you?"

"Adam Barrow."

"Sometime you can tell me what this is all about."

"I'll do that when I figure it out," I said, grasping the old fellow's sleeve so he wouldn't bolt.

The doors to the auditorium opened, and people filled the lobby, glancing at our little group. The auction, it appeared, had ended.

My interrogator nodded at a few departing bidders and turned back to me, and offered her hand. "I'm Leslie Strickland." I took her hand, and we stood looking at one another until she frowned at Enzo Riva again. "We've cancelled the da Vinci offering for tonight. Too much disruption to do it justice."

"It is not a da Vinci," Riva blurted again.

I shot him a look until he stared at the floor.

Leslie saw the paddle in my hand.

"I was going to bid for Phillip Dansby," I explained. "He'll be disappointed."

"You work for Phillip Dansby?"

"You know him?"

"I know he owns Gallery Britannia and a lot of other things."

I looked at her name badge again. "And you work for Delaudier."

She nodded, and I appraised the deep green eyes set in a soft face with minimal makeup, short blond hair expertly styled. The scent of jasmine perfume drifted my way each time the air stirred, firming my decision to learn more about my interrogator, even though the circumstances were less than optimal. Nothing ventured, nothing gained would have been emblazoned on our family crest if we had one. Beside which, she intrigued me.

"We could have a drink one night," I said, "and you can tell me about Delaudier."

She frowned as though trying to decide if I was real. "I may be crazy, but I think I'd like that."

We shook hands again, and she disappeared into the crowd. I guided Enzo out the door, the paddle still in my hand. I dropped it in the nearest trash bin. My companion pulled out a scrap of paper from his coat pocket. He fumbled for a pen and printed his name and address. No email or telephone number.

"I will look forward to repaying your kindness."

"No need."

"It was an honorable thing you did."

"Just tell me why you think the da Vinci's a fake."

"My entire life I study him, his work. You must not buy this drawing."

Before I could reply, he shoved the piece of paper into my coat pocket and clutched my sleeve, knotty fingers biting into my forearm. I looked at him and resisted pulling away. All kinds filled New York's ranks.

"That is where I live," he said, patting my pocket. "We must talk again."

A street person's claims meant little. Jean-Henri and a battery of experts validated the drawing to everyone's satisfaction, and I didn't want another foul up. I didn't need Dansby's ambition to acquire the da Vinci annulled by the fiasco I'd just witnessed.

"Come, drink wine with me," Riva begged. "You will see my book does not lie."

A book?

"Yeah, sure. We'll drink some wine. Just don't get into more trouble."

He nodded and shambled into the crowds along Sixth Avenue.

I stared after him. He appeared harmless, but he'd screwed up my evening. I had Dansby's orders and money, but the eccentric old gatecrasher almost landed us both in jail.

Despite the glossy catalog and Jean-Henri's assurances, Enzo Riva's protests stayed with me as I walked back to my apartment. It would be a simple matter to check him out and verify he was nothing more than a crazy in a city that spawned them like pigeons. Dansby was paying for my instincts and no one would be the wiser if I had a quiet talk with Enzo.

Chapter Four

Minutes later, I let myself into my apartment. Emptying my pockets on the kitchen counter, I found the crumpled note with Riva's address. I balled it up and tossed it in the trash can on top of the morning's coffee grounds. Staring at the wad of paper, I wondered again what prompted his outburst. Another lonely old man vying for attention in a city that had forgotten him? The impulse to help him completed my quota of kind acts for the week, but I couldn't shake the memory of his anger. Was Delaudier offering a counterfeit drawing? I retrieved the crumpled paper and smoothed it on the counter. Was he another street loon, or was I an easy mark for underdogs?

Word of the evening's disaster would reach Dansby soon enough and I'd have to explain my role. I looked at my watch. Early morning in London. Plenty of time for *mea culpa* when he returned. I'd done rash things in my life, but rescuing Enzo Riva at the cost of Dansby's da Vinci ranked near the top. I undressed and crawled into bed, remembering the adage that sooner or later you must pay for every good deed.

• • •

Next afternoon, the weather cleared, and I took a taxi to Riva's apartment.

The four-story building in the South Bronx was easing downhill. The shabby structure had endured multiple renovations, including an attempt in the late 1930s, converting to *Streamline Moderne*. The sidewalks were swept clean, but the street showed cracks and sewer odors lingered from the grates, remnants of a more glamorous era. The shabby surroundings seemed an unlikely place to discuss a priceless da Vinci with a confused old man, but Riva had mentioned a book, and I hoped he could show me more than a coffee table decoration.

Inside the cramped entry, I found his name on a row of mailboxes. I pressed the button that emitted a burst of static and irritated voice.

"*Che cosa?* What do you want?"

"Mister Riva? It's Adam Barrow."

"I know no Barrow."

"From the auction."

Seconds passed in the grungy foyer. A sharp buzz and the door clicked open. No elevator in sight. I took the stairs to the third floor and knocked on a dark green door smudged by countless knuckles. Hesitant footsteps and two bolts snapped open. The heavily creased face appeared, alcoholic breath escaping through the six-inch opening.

"Ah, *Signor* Barrow! My deliverer. *Prego, prego.* Come in, please."

Stooped at the waist, Riva led me into the apartment. Shirttail hanging over baggy trousers, his short-sleeve white shirt hung open at the collar, skin sallower than I remembered, his breath corrupted by age and alcohol. The unkempt goatee seemed sparser. Loose mottled skin on his bare arms hung crepe-like as though losing its grip on his bones.

Weaving between a collection of pitiful furniture, he bumped against a coffee table and indicated a lumpy loveseat, gathering up newspapers from the cushions. He displayed a sloppy smile and whistled at a yellow canary in an antique birdcage near a tiny kitchen. Two kitchen windows reflected sunlight off the adjoining building's brick wall. A single door led to a bedroom where I saw an unmade bed. A ragged patterned carpet added to the cheerless setting, broken only by a montage of cheap da Vinci prints on the walls. Except for the bird and inexpensive reproductions, the place had the charm of a blacksmith shop.

The canary trilled, and Riva clicked his tongue.

"Mind your manners, Piccolo. You have a guest."

The bird sidled to the edge of its perch and cocked its head at me. Riva folded his emaciated body into a dingy wing chair with a deflated sigh. Two glasses, a half-empty bottle of grappa and an unlabeled jug of chianti sat on the small table beside him. He wasn't drunk, but he'd begun the journey.

He waved a hand at the birdcage. "The little one serves as my mistress," he said, "only he doesn't eat as much."

This was a different man from the angry protestor at Delaudier, his beaming face mirroring drinkers who passed the happy midway point. He flourished the grappa bottle.

"Would you care for brandy, *Signor* Barrow?"

"Maybe later."

Riva studied the label and raised his hand in benediction. "*Nonino*," he said. "From Percoto. Northern Italy produces the best grappa."

He poured two fingers, and I winced as he downed the stuff without blinking. I gave him points for an iron stomach. The clear liquid always reminded me of paint thinner in a fancy bottle. I doubted I could learn much of value from a dedicated drinker, but I had paid for a cab ride and earned the right to hear him out.

"I'd like to talk about the da Vinci."

"It is not a da Vinci."

"That's what you claimed."

"*Che affair è quello tuo?*"

"I'm sorry, I don't speak Italian."

He drained his glass. "I ask, what business is this of yours?"

"You invited me, Mr. Riva. My employer wants the drawing. Anything you can tell us will help."

He grunted and seemed close to a confession. Instead, he raised the back of his hand toward me. "I know da Vinci like my own fingernails. He is my passion since I am a small boy in Anchiano where he is born. People are making a mistake."

"Yes, but experts examined the drawing. They affirmed…"

He waved an arm, the old man from the auction reappearing. "They understand nothing!" He exchanged the grappa for chianti and started to fill his glass when he slammed the bottle on the table.

"Rich people, they want to possess Leonardo, flaunt him to their friends." He coughed and caught his breath. "Hang his drawings and paintings on their walls and say, 'Look at me! I am more wealthy than you!'" He refocused on me. "If your *padrone* is one of these creatures, you should be ashamed to work for him."

This was going nowhere. "The da Vinci is important to him. He…"

Riva grunted and topped his glass with more wine. "Will he get his name in the newspaper? Tell everyone he owns a da Vinci when he does not?"

I decided wasting my time arguing with a fanatic ended my good deed for the day. I owed Dansby every effort to authenticate the drawing, but my cab ride to the rundown apartment accomplished nothing. I started to rise when Riva motioned for me to remain seated.

"Prego, prego," he sighed. A wave of pain seemed to overtake him. His lips lost their color. I waited as he managed an apologetic smile.

"I am a bad host." he said, his voice weaker. "You rescue me from the police and I become *adirato*, angry with you. You must forgive an old fool, but so many are wrong."

I waved away his apology. "Mister Riva, you mentioned a book at the auction."

Riva gazed at the dark red liquid in his glass. I waited and said nothing. If I'd learned anything about selling, it was to shut up and allow silence to make the decision. He gulped the chianti and uttered a sound that signaled resignation.

"All right, I show you a secret."

He pushed his frail body from the chair and walked behind it, motioning for me to help him. "If you will assist me, *Signor* Barrow."

Fearing he would collapse from the effort, I joined him and we tilted the bulky chair backwards, his arms quivering from the effort. Together we eased the chair's cushioned back onto the floor. I looked down and saw only bare space. No book on the floor or bulge in the carpet, only dust balls and a forgotten *Time* magazine. If he believed he'd hidden a book beneath the chair, the two bottles on the table muddled his memory.

I started to point out the obvious when he walked around the upended chair and knelt, grasping one of the chair legs for support. He ran a finger beneath the rough burlap that covered the chair's springs, separating the material from the discolored wooden frame.

He reached inside and withdrew a thick volume. Darkened by age, the leather covers were brass bound at the corners and edged with broad gilded stripes, the inlays as luminous as the day the binder had applied them. Two tarnished bronze clasps secured what appeared to be six inches of yellowed vellum pages.

Groaning from the book's weight, Riva got to his feet, and I righted the chair. He caught his breath and collapsed onto the cushions, cradling the book to his chest like a newborn. I waited until he caught his breath. The massive volume obviously hadn't come off a Barnes & Noble remainder shelf.

He caressed the scrolled Italian title, a heraldic coat of arms in gold leaf beneath the words. He patted the leather as though soothing a living organism. Picking up the grappa bottle, he raised it toward me with a questioning look. I relented and let him fill a glass for me. No advantage in letting him drink alone. I took a swallow and choked down my gag reflex. Riva downed half his glass and wiped his lips with his fingers.

"You see, *Signor* Barrow, others worked with Leonardo, men who lived in his shadow. A few possessed abilities, but history forgot or ignored them." A smile softened his features. "But that was as God intended. None equaled the master. His portraits show us a handsome man, a virile man when he was young. Possibly his Vitruvian Man was a self-portrait. You see, he was not always the bearded ancient that people see in books."

"Scholars say he was most likely a homosexual," I ventured.

"No!" Riva burst out. "One has only to study the manliness of his work, the men and women and children in his paintings and drawings. All else is gossip that pleases today's fools."

I wondered how the iconic figure would be seen today, sans the flowing beard and stern expression one saw in books. How would he have appeared? His voice? Mannerisms? The few illustrations of Leonardo left him in the nether world of ancient renderings, an enigma. Almost everything, including his sexuality, remained a debate, second-guessed by scholars and people shouting today's agendas.

Riva glared at me as though I committed a sacrilege. Scholars and historians generally agreed on the issue of Leonardo's sexuality, but I personally stopped making assessments based on fashionable assumptions, disregarding the herd that trekked behind Freud. Leonardo's volume of work showed equally beautiful women and girls as well as men and boys, innocent children and babes, even freaks and the grotesque. The question of his sexual preference did not increase or lessen his greatness, and as far as I knew, Freud never met the man, which left it all conjecture.

Attempting to return to the subject, I gestured at the elaborate book. "And this book proves Delaudier's drawing is a fake?"

"Not a fake, *Signor* Barrow. The drawing was not done by da Vinci, but it is not a forgery."

Back on the hamster wheel again, I downed more grappa against my better judgement. What was he saying?

"Then who was the artist?"

"You are owed an explanation, *Signor* Barrow," Riva began, "but first, you must share wine with me. Then I tell you a story few others have heard."

He poured more grappa and handed the glass to me.

He sat back, the ornate book in his lap. Closing his eyes, he drifted away. I allowed him a moment. If he had a story, how did it connect to the book? Dansby paid the bills and I needed evidence the old man knew something Jean-Henri had overlooked. The young ruled today's society and tended to ignore the elderly, especially when they said or professed something out of touch with their techno world. I'd lived long enough to accept old people have their stories, and I had a suspicion Riva's actions were more than a bid to claim attention. I could spare him a few more minutes in spite of the fact he reminded me of my father, a fellow art lover and lonely boozer.

Riva's head jerked up. "Not da Vinci," he mumbled.

"Your story?" I gently prompted.

He started to speak when pain flickered in his eyes again. He waited and after a moment made the sign of the cross. "Leonardo. *Fantastico*. God produced a miracle when He breathed life into him." He glanced at the birdcage. "Isn't that right, my beauty? Even you understand that."

I glanced at my watch and started to rise when his voice took on a more somber tone. "Do you know Leonardo, *Signor* Barrow?"

"I studied his work in college and graduate school." I held back telling him about the questionable signature, deciding not to stoke the flames.

"Universities," he said dolefully. "The gathering place of all sacred knowledge." He spread his arms wide, spilling wine on the carpet. "The resting places of all *informazione*, yes?"

"I had good professors who made life studies of—"

He aimed his index finger at me. "There is more in this world than misinformed men who write books."

This was getting me nowhere. "Mister Riva, you mentioned a story."

He lifted a hand from the chair arm, started to speak and shook his head, his hesitation replaced by a look I interpreted as fear.

"*Signore* Barrow, it's true you helped me, but there is much you do not understand." He raised the trembling hand again as though taking an oath and eased it onto the book cover.

"This is very old," he said. "It is the only…" His lips moved but his eyes were closing again.

I raised my voice. "Have people inspected this book?"

He opened his eyes, his words slurred. "Only a few old friends I trusted," he mumbled. "All dead now. People who understood."

I sat forward. "Could I see it?"

He mumbled under his breath and his head fell back against the chair.

"Mister Riva?"

The empty glass fell to the carpet with a hollow thump. I waited to see if he revived, tempted to ease the book from his grasp. My fingers touched the spine, and I stopped. A dusty old book proved nothing, no matter its age.

Conspiracy and contrarian theories multiplied daily and were common even in the art world's upper echelons. I'd played out my gut feeling about Enzo Riva and lost. The book meant nothing or he would never reveal its secret. You either stumbled across a lucky break or you didn't. I felt sorry for the old guy, but I had wasted my day. I'd chased a ghost on Dansby's time and the last thing I needed was another mistake.

I sighed, looked at the leather cover and eased off the couch, the canary silently watching me as though fearful I might wake its owner. Jean-Henri and the experts were right. Modern-day knowledge outweighed lost secrets and conspiracies. The bare apartment contained nothing but a birdcage and a life approaching its expiration date. I tiptoed to the door and let myself out as Enzo Riva softly snored.

Chapter Five

Late Afternoon
Road from Dosevski
January 3, 1945

Weisser fought off sleep, imagining Russian partisans behind trees on either side of the road. Gaps in the forest looked like missing teeth as he clutched the steering wheel and tried to concentrate. The truck bounced and slithered across the frozen ridges, all that remained of the backcountry road. Sub-zero air invaded the cab, defeating his greatcoat and layers of clothing. Aware of meager heat that rose from the engine through the floorboards, he grudgingly thanked the cold and jarring truck that prevented him from drifting off. Sliding into a roadside ditch meant a death warrant

Late afternoon shadows covered the road, the forest receding into blackness, silent witnesses to his flight. He could just make out train tracks paralleling the road on his left, the rails and crossties visible beneath the mantle of snow. He leaned over to pull the submachine gun closer. The tires momentarily left the ruts and skidded toward the ditch. He gave an involuntary yelp and forced the GAZ to obey his will, cajoling the balky truck back onto the frozen track.

Swallowing his fear, he glanced through the cab's rear window into the dim interior as though the crate might grow legs and take its chances in the forest. Relieved the straps remained secure, he attempted to dismiss the cold, tugging the red woolen muffler over his chin. Its warmth reconfirmed his judgment. At the first sign of winter, he'd plucked the woman's scarf from a pile of discarded clothing beside an execution pit.

"Not regulation," he said to the dashboard, "but the bitch no longer needed it, did she?"

Weisser had begun talking to the truck during the last twenty kilometers, fighting fear and lack of sleep, consequences of his decision. The bodies beside the tracks were mounds of snow by now, nameless faces added to the thousands Russia devoured every day. Months ago, he reasoned he would become a dead man if he stayed to fight, and a dead man if caught fleeing the front. Either way, he'd be one more anonymous corpse, nothing more. Careful not to voice his thoughts aloud, he resigned himself to whatever fate held for him until the reeking boxcar transformed his options.

The crate!

Its contents justified the danger of an unmarked road and possibility he'd be shot as a deserter at a roadblock unless his story held up. Either that or be butchered by Russian guerillas if luck turned away her capricious face. He had no clue whether the Russian advance overlapped him, or if he'd lost his way inside Prussia's eastern border. He knew how Jack felt climbing down the beanstalk with the golden goose, fleeing the giant who vowed to grind his bones.

Weisser's eyelids fluttered, his mind wandering. Did Jack steal a goose or golden harp? Not that children's fairy tales mattered. As long as he stayed awake and remained on a northwest heading, he would not go insane or die in a ditch.

He rolled down the window, scooped snow from the window ledge and smeared a handful over his stiff beard. The shock jerked his eyes open. He shoved more snow in his mouth and started to roll up the glass when he heard a powerful engine. The roar grew louder. He involuntarily ducked as a single-engine fighter swept over the truck, raising a blizzard of snow along the road, the prop wash jarring snow from tree limbs.

Weisser slowed and craned his neck out the window. The aircraft banked beneath the low-hanging sky and he glimpsed red stars on blunt wings. The Russian Yak-9 pulled up into a climbing turn, careful to stay below the clouds as the fighter swung behind the truck again. Weisser lost sight of his attacker, the noise fading.

He shook off his panic. After all, he drove a Russian truck, and surely the pilot could tell the difference between Russian and German vehicles.

His relief evaporated when he remembered he was behind German lines where everything represented a target to the Red Air Force. The roar grew louder again and cannon fire splintered tree branches to the right of the truck. A shell ricocheted off the truck's hood, Geysers of snow blossomed on the road ahead. The shark-nosed fighter thundered overhead, banked sharply and came around for another pass. Crouched low behind the wheel, Weisser's heart fell when the road ahead rose in a steep incline, making him an easy target.

Get out!

He stomped the brakes, fumbling at the door handle when he saw a black opening cut into the hillside on his left.

A rail tunnel.

Sweating, he scanned his side mirror for his attacker. The dot behind the truck grew larger as the Yak lined up its target again. A shallow ditch appeared on Weisser's left. He held his breath, tromped the gas pedal and swerved toward it. The truck's front end plunged down the shallow slope. Snow cascaded over the front bumper and thudded against the windshield.

The roar behind the truck grew louder. The GAZ careened onto the tracks and juddered along the rails, careening across crossties that threatened to destroy the rusted chassis. Ahead, bullets struck the face of the tunnel and Weisser felt hits on the tailgate. Rock shards from the tunnel face spidered the left half of the windshield. Crouching lower, he steered blindly into the void, cringing as shells sparked off the darkened walls.

Twenty meters inside the tunnel, he braked and relinquished his death grip on the steering wheel. Unable to catch his breath, he rolled down the window and gulped dank air. The darkness reeked of coal smoke, the clammy stone walls conjuring up the vision of a mausoleum. He rolled up the window glass and clicked on the headlights. The weak yellow beams cast a luminous glow twenty meters down the rusted rails. He switched off the lights to save the battery and sat in the shadows, listening for the Yak. The silence grew until he imagined a train hurtling from the darkness toward him. He dismissed the outlandish notion and sat unmoving for another ten minutes before he backed out of the tunnel.

Oblivious to the cold, he braked and opened the door, dropping to the ground. The wooden rail ties were splintered and gouged beneath his boots. Chips of concrete from the pocked tunnel entrance littered the snow-covered ground. Making his way to the rear of the truck, he lowered the tailgate. Groping his way to the crate, he struck a match and inspected it, relieved to find the wood undamaged.

Back behind the wheel, he reversed a few meters and flicked on the headlights. Tire tracks of his desperate escape from the road were visible in the ditch. He bumped over the tracks and eased down the incline toward the road. The slick tires spun on the icy slope and lost traction. The truck slid sideways and Weisser ground his teeth, willing the truck back onto the road.

"Come on, you sow!"

The GAZ's rear end slithered along the incline and for a moment Weisser feared his escape would end in the ditch. He eased the gas pedal down another few centimeters, and the tires found purchase on fallen branches. The truck tottered on the brink of the ditch until it lurched forward and found the road's familiar ruts.

Weisser lifted his foot from the accelerator and lowered his head against the steering wheel, his terror dissipated by the engine's reassuring rumble. When he looked up, soft moonglow shone through the bare trees, the forest a fairyland as the clouds blew away and reflected off pristine snow. Adrenaline chased away the lure of sleep and his hands stopped quivering. The Yak had failed to kill him, an omen his luck remained intact.

The sea has to be close, just a few more kilometers.

His courage restored, he slammed the floor lever into gear and steered his cargo toward what he hoped was an unfrozen Baltic Sea.

Chapter Six

Gagging slightly at the brandy's residue in my mouth, I lowered the taxi window to let the night air revive me. My visit to Riva's apartment had been a bust, sharpening the awareness that Dansby would chop my tenure in New York short unless I found another way to prove my value. He had been patient with me, and I wondered if he also felt Kat's loss. But all that could change. Any sympathy or second chance could evaporate. The thought of Kat accelerated my downward thoughts, and I decided failure was best discussed with a glass in my hand.

I directed the cab driver away from the glitz. It hadn't taken long to tire of New York's club scene, turned off by thudding rap and desperate look-at-me young women. I liked female company as much as the next hungry male, but velvet rope venues wore thin as displays of female flesh began resembling harems of wannabe hookers. Armands, an understated jazz club, became my oasis identified only by a dim blue neon sign two steps below street level.

I pushed open the door and avoided looking at two Degas prints hanging just inside the entrance, reminders of my recent screw-up. A saxophone solo washed over me as I parted a red beaded curtain, the silky notes diluting murmurs from the crowd that packed small round tables. Half of the patrons chose to overlook No Smoking signs, the atmosphere reminiscent of a time when smoke-filled rooms set the mood. A miniature dance floor attracted several couples. No one glanced at me as I weaved my way toward the bar, nodding at the piano player who returned my smile.

I found a seat at the zinc bar and ordered a bourbon rocks, hoping it didn't declare war on Riva's grappa. I turned to the dance floor where a man deftly spun his partner. The woman's long black hair fanned outward in a graceful arc, and an unwanted memory returned. I ignored the Makers Mark the female bartender placed in front of me and kept my eyes on the dance floor, half-expecting a resurrected Kat to turn and smile at me. Much as I tried to move past her death, my thirst for her remained, a reminder that I'd lost what I'd sought my entire life.

I loosened my tie and sipped the bourbon, determined not to relive the past. I'd planned on enjoying the jazz, letting good bourbon wash away Kat and my failed gamble on an old man. Hell, that wasn't too much to ask. Looking at my reflection in the bar mirror, I took another swallow and let the whiskey slowly work its magic. A reprieve gradually washed over me and I had begun to unwind when an attractive woman interrupted my reverie.

"Not your best day?" she asked.

I looked at the speaker, who was an attractive blond. She slipped onto the stool beside me, dressed in designer jeans and ivory silk blouse. She gave me the look of a fellow traveler alone at the bar. Any other time I'd have displayed my winning smile, but misery craves solitude.

"Work," I said, bar conversation not part of my plans for the evening.

"Long day at the office?"

"No."

The trio eased into a subtle variation of *"Tangerine"* and I fingered the ice in my glass, surprised when the woman stared at me. I glanced at her and sighed.

"What?"

"You don't remember me, do you?"

"Should I?"

"You promised to call me."

For a moment I came close to telling the woman she'd picked the wrong companion before I realized it wasn't her fault. I was hunched over the bar like a distraught husband wallowing in self-pity. I got the impression she had been enjoying the music without an ulterior agenda when I plopped down next to her.

"I did what?"

She gave a delightful laugh and lightly touched my coat sleeve. "Look," she said, "I'm not trying to pick you up. We met at Delaudier. At the auction." She maintained the easy smile. "You look like you need someone to talk to."

Click. The employee from Delaudier.

"God, I apologize" I said meekly. "It's been a rough week."

"No problem. You deserve a drink for helping the old guy." She paused and looked closely at me, her smile showing perfect teeth. "You mentioned that you work for Phillip Dansby. Are you a butcher? Baker? Candlestick maker?"

"Art appraiser," I said, a respectable title for somebody who didn't have one.

"You don't look like an academic."

"What am I supposed to look like?"

"Oh, the usual. Ratty pony tail, rimless hexagonal glasses. Needing a bath and wondering how to pay for your next meal."

I relaxed and enjoyed the fact that an attractive woman had engaged me in conversation. "Actually, I cut off the ponytail and made up the job description."

"I remembered your name later that night. You're the Adam Barrow who discovered the van Gogh, right?"

"I had a lot of help."

"I don't imagine you worry about meals any longer," she said.

I forced a smile. "It didn't work out. Bunch of lawyers stole it back."

"You were all over the papers. Roland and Isabelle were green with envy. The painting must be worth several fortunes."

I shrugged.

She gave me a pitying smile and raised her hand at the bartender who brought her another vodka and soda.

"Attorneys," she said lightly. "The bane and vacuum cleaners of all good fortune."

Neither of us spoke, and I figured she'd grown bored listening to a foundling's story. I returned to my drink when she removed a pack of cigarettes and a gold lighter from her silver metallic purse. She shook out a Winston and held it to her lips. I flicked her lighter and she steadied my hand steady, meeting my gaze over the flame.

"I apologize for my mood," I said. "I went to the old man's apartment. The one who claimed the da Vinci is a fake."

"You saw him again?"

I nodded, embarrassed as she looked sideways at me.

"Did you learn anything?"

"He claims he has a book that proves the drawing isn't a da Vinci."

She sipped her drink and looked doubtful. "Really."

I waved my hand. "A waste of time, but I had to check him out."

She raised her glass. "Proverbial ships passing in the night, then. You and me and him."

We clinked. "Or ships sinking in the night."

"A distinct option."

"Can I buy you another drink?"

She held up her full glass.

"Sorry," I said. "I'm not at my best tonight."

She offered her hand. "In case you've forgotten, I'm Leslie. Leslie Strickland" She seemed on the verge of saying more but sipped her drink instead.

We shook hands as I covered my embarrassment with a slight nod.

"It was my first time at Delaudier."

"Really? You seemed to know your way around."

"I'm originally from California by way of Chicago. You?"

"Florida. A little town in the panhandle that prefers oranges to art."

"You like working at Delaudier?"

She nodded, and I studied the mosaic ranks of bottles behind the bar. We'd reached the inevitable impasse of strangers, and I was determined not to ask if she was married or came here often.

"I'm guessing you don't like having eardrums destroyed by a club disc jockey," I ventured.

She nodded. "I prefer contemporary jazz. Matheny. Fourplay. George Winston. I like the groups here."

"Me too. Most of my jazz collection is in Chicago."

"Is it interesting valuing works of art?"

I got the feeling she wanted to keep the conversation alive. "I have help," I said, thinking of Jean-Henri. "I take it you like paintings?"

"Very much."

"You enjoy the New York art scene?"

Before she could answer, a man about my age man touched her shoulder and leaned down to kiss her. Athletically built and flaunting an expensive haircut, he wore a black blazer over an open-neck white shirt, New York's version of casual elegance. He ignored me and downed her vodka before she could protest.

"At least you could have ordered a decent martini," he said with a grimace.

She bumped him with her shoulder and introduced me. "This is Adam. He's an art lover too."

"Marshall Hampton," he said.

We shook hands, his eyes bright with the assurance of someone who had already enjoyed several martinis. His Rolex Oyster glinted in the subdued lighting as he turned back to her, dismissing me. He whispered in her ear, lifted one arm at the bartender and slipped the other around her waist.

"We're late, darling," he said.

Leslie left several bills on the bar and leaned close to me. "Remember your promise to call me," she whispered.

Surprised, I watched them head for the exit. She didn't look back, but the scent of jasmine lingered, leaving me with the sensation she'd rather have continued our conversation than be steered out the door by Mister Rolex. Most likely my libido, I thought, and the bourbon, but she *had* reminded me to call her. I didn't read too much into it, content to bask in the pleasure of talking with a fellow traveler who commiserated with my self-imposed melancholy.

I ordered another bourbon and stared at the entrance door as though I'd lost a friend. I thought about her unexpected invitation and decided it was the alcohol, a harmless flirtation. Chance meetings in bars were like carnival rides. Fun when they whirled you around, forgotten the next day. She was a striking woman and the first real temptation since I arrived in New York. I didn't believe in karma and she didn't seem the type to approach strange men at the bar. I'd created a problem for her at the auction, and the arrival of her tipsy companion confirmed a relationship elsewhere. The whiskey aided my powers of reasoning, and I decided Leslie Strickland enjoyed rescuing strays.

I sipped my drink and wrote off the encounter, attributing my temptation to a recent drought of female company. My thoughts drifted back to the da Vinci and the next auction as strains of Johnny Mercer's *"Skylark"* washed away her face.

Chapter Seven

Dansby Tower
New York City

Dansby returned from London the next morning. I received a summons to his office. Aware I faced an interrogation, I reassembled my story about what occurred at the auction. Clarice, Dansby's long-time assistant and gatekeeper, glanced up from her desk with a look of rare sympathy. She nodded at his office. Black horn-rimmed designer glasses disguised the fact she was proficient and ruthless when crossed. Middle-aged coquettish, she merged efficiency with a sense of humor about everything that occurred in the building.

"He's not smiling this morning," she said without looking up. "Jean-Henri's been in there with him for the last hour."

"Something I should be aware of?"

She winked. "What? You think I'd eavesdrop?"

I pulled open pocket oak doors and flinched at the harsh sunlight that poured through ten-foot windows set into the far wall. A woven Fiereghan Sarouk carpet smothered my footfalls as my eyes adjusted and I imagined I had entered Queen Victoria's vanquished world. Oversized mahogany furnishings. Dark wainscoted walls. A carved Italian marble fireplace. Lady Butler's Waterloo painting of *Scotland Forever* dominated the wall behind Dansby's desk. The Scots Greys' charge at the battle completed the illusion of a retired colonel's quarters, the setting a jarring contrast to Delaudier's glass and chrome cube.

Seated on a burgundy leather couch to my right, Jean-Henri Bonnet looked up, a china cup in one hand. Well-preserved in his late forties, his most arresting feature was a mass of sleek black hair that appeared professionally dyed with no hint of grey. Meticulously parted on one side in the fashion of a past era, the effect was offset by white jeans and a starched white shirt, a casual counterpart to Dansby's chalk-stripe navy blue Bond Street suit. Both men abruptly paused in mid-conversation and I had the feeling I'd interrupted a discussion concerning me. Dansby waved me to a chair.

"Ah, the Good Samaritan," he said humorlessly.

Jean-Henri took a sip of tea and studied the pot of Earl Grey on the table in front of the couch with a satisfied look.

"I wanted that drawing," Dansby said without preamble. "I'm disappointed you allowed an old man to disrupt the auction."

"I didn't *allow* anything. I happened to sit next to him, that's all."

"From what I hear, you assumed the role of his benefactor." His tone must have been one he favored for bumbling recruits. "You work for me which means you represent my interests in public."

"I don't like to see old men abused."

Dansby slumped back with an audible sigh. "Rightly so, but God knows what the upshot will be."

"We're fortunate the da Vinci's still available," Jean-Henri interjected.

Dansby waved his hand. "But will Delaudier offer it again? That's the question."

"He was a confused old man, nothing more," I said.

"But did you raise an issue of legitimacy?" Dansby swung his eyes back to me. "You also made enemies of Roland and Isabelle. They can be a spiteful pair and may withdraw the drawing from next auction."

"They're in business to make money," I reminded him. "If they have proof of authenticity, the incident won't make any difference."

"Proof?" Jean-Henri exclaimed. "We have…"

Dansby held up his hand. "These are vindictive people, Adam. As I said, Roland Delaudier is not to be trifled with, and his wife is no basket of warm puppies. They may well get their arses on their shoulders and pull the drawing off the market."

"Worse still," Jean-Henri added, "it would be criminal to see it questioned because a shadow's been cast over it." He leaned forward and placed his cup on the delicate Dresden saucer. "God forbid it disappears into Saudi Arabia or the Far East."

Dansby dismissed the possibility. "I want it for my museum, so that can't happen."

Jean-Henri shrugged. "We may have lost our chance."

"No," I said.

"No?" Jean-Henri said. "You're a fortune teller, Mister Barrow?"

Mister Barrow now. Banished from the inner circle.

"Delaudier will sell it to the highest bidder," I reminded him, "no matter what concerns may have been raised."

Jean-Henri sat forward. "There's no question of legitimacy. A scientific inspection was performed by authorities whom I know and trust. Age analysis. Paper and ink testing. Molecular examination. You and I both inspected the piece, Phillip. We saw the results."

I was rolling a boulder uphill, but Riva's outburst refused to go away. He must have had a reason to disrupt the auction despite what a boatload of experts decreed as invincible proof. Something worth risking arrest and humiliation.

"What if the experts are wrong?" I ventured.

Jean-Henri exhaled. "I examined it myself. Your agitator sought a warm place to sleep, nothing more."

"You weren't there."

He sat back and crossed his legs with a shake of his head. "It takes more than a few art degrees to comprehend the truth."

"You're right." I said. "All my attempts at infallibility have failed."

"Enough," Dansby said.

He got up and went to the floor-to-ceiling window, observing the street thirty stories below. Slowly rising and falling on his toes, he stared down at the traffic. "You actually believed this old man of yours?".

"Not at first, but I can't shake his conviction."

"I'm about to put $40 million on the line, Adam. I require facts."

"I can't, only that he's Italian and…"

"Italian!" Jean-Henri burst out. "Impeccable credentials."

Feeling like a chastised schoolboy, I resisted the urge to dump the pot of tea over his bald dome.

"You may well have lost my da Vinci," Dansby said, turning to me from the window.

"He was… adamant." The assertion formed the only defense I could muster.

"But is there tangible *proof* at the moment?"

"No."

I started to tell them I'd visited Riva, but stopped short. I'd seen nothing but the covers of an old book. Dansby might be right. I'd possibly lost the da Vinci he craved. I knew I should apologize for my impulsive actions, but the nagging doubt held me back.

Vindicated, Jean-Henri poured more tea and waited for the axe to fall on my neck as Dansby locked his hands behind his back. If I looked at my situation from his vantage point, I'd screwed up and managed to shortcut my New York career.

He glanced at Jean-Henri with a slight frown. "Since we have breathing space while the Delaudiers decide what to do, I'd like another look. I don't think Roland will resist a second inspection since a doubt's been raised."

Exasperated, Jean-Henri shook his head. "An unknown da Vinci is a godsend, Phillip. Americans gorged on Old Masters and Impressionists in the 30s until nothing of consequence remained. We must not lose this da Vinci."

"It's my money, and it's quite a bit of money," Dansby reminded him. "Best to put the smallest doubt to rest." He picked up his desk phone and asked Clarice to schedule an appointment with Roland Delaudier.

"It won't hurt to take another look."

A few minutes later, Clarice stuck her head around the door and said Delaudier had agreed to a private showing later that morning.

．　．　．

The wind picked up as we walked the three blocks to the Delaudier building. Jean-Henri avoided looking at me and Dansby's hands were buried in his topcoat pockets. I'd seen the look before, but couldn't decide if he contemplated my dismissal or considered the possibility the drawing might be a fake. As we entered Delaudier's grandiose lobby, Riva's words echoed again as I remembered the confrontation with the two guards.

It is not a da Vinci.

A young woman rose from an antique desk and asked our business. Dressed in a conservative dress and blazer, she dialed a house phone before escorting us to a private elevator. No one spoke on the ride up. A smile glued in place, she escorted the three of us to a lavishly furnished conference room on the third floor and opened the door. Standing just inside the door, a burly man with a crushed nose made eye contact with each of us as we entered. Dressed in a blazer that matched our escort's attire, he wore a black tee shirt and looked as though he'd be more at home in the shipyards.

Nothing had been spared to impress clients who might be invited into Delaudier's inner sanctum, the value of the lavish furnishings exceeding the value of everything I owned. Across the room a slender middle-aged man rose from an Empire chair and smiled at Phillip. He wore a tailored light grey suit, the color complimenting his mane of silver hair that seemed at odds with intense eyes. Moving with the vitality of a younger man. Roland Delaudier nodded at Jean-Henri as he gripped Dansby's hand with a wry smile, the corners of his eyes crinkling with amusement.

"Phillip," he said, "I wish I were handing over the da Vinci and accepting your check this morning."

"That would be the best of both worlds," Dansby said. "I missed the excitement but my associate tells me it was quite a show."

Delaudier turned to me as though abruptly aware of my presence.

"I take it you're Adam Barrow," he said without offering his hand. "Leslie told me you assisted the trespasser who disrupted the auction."

My infamy had spread, and I wondered what else she'd told him.

"I was trying to keep the old fellow out of trouble."

Delaudier glanced at Dansby and nodded as though tolerating a child's excuse for breaking a valuable vase. "Commendable, but this person planted the suspicion we were offering a fraud."

"He was confused."

"Yes, well, confused or not, he caused a stir. I imagine that's why you want another look."

"I have no doubts," Jean-Henri interjected. "My analysis of the drawing was conclusive."

Delaudier bowed in appreciation and I couldn't help but notice his movements and speech reflected a privileged upbringing. Despite his genteel deference and restrained manner, I detected a harder undercurrent, a distant kinship with Dansby's pragmatic view of the world.

He turned back to Dansby with an air of polite resignation. "I suppose it's only natural to desire another look. Would anyone care for coffee or water?"

Dansby glanced at his watch. "Thank you, but I have a busy morning."

Delaudier gestured to the hulk beside the door. "Salvatore, please have the da Vinci brought in."

The man left the room and Delaudier turned to me.

"You've not inspected it, Mister Barrow?"

"I saw it at the auction."

"I think you'll agree it's really quite magnificent."

A few minutes later, the framed drawing arrived, accompanied by a stunning woman and a man I recognized as Leslie Strickland's date at Armands.

"This is my wife, Isabelle," Delaudier said to me. "And this is Marshall Hampton, our CFO."

The slender brunette walked to her husband and kissed his cheek, studiously ignoring me as she greeted Dansby and Jean-Henri. Thirty years her husband's junior, Isabelle Delaudier sported 1920s bobbed hair, Zelda reborn, the updated version of a Gatsby ingenue New York was home to high fashion models and two-thousand-a-night escorts, and Isabelle Delaudier combined the allure of both, a high-end fantasy. Dressed in what I guessed to be a Dolce and Gabanna black pants suit, she and Roland seemed the perfect salt and pepper couple, a wedding cake decoration waiting to be photographed by *Vanity Fair*.

Hampton gently arranged the da Vinci on the conference table and gave me a quizzical look. I followed him to the table and peered over Dansby's shoulder. I had studied da Vinci in college without ever inspecting an original this closely. Every detail seemed alive, the sheer artistry superior to anything I'd seen rendered by pen and ink. Laid down on sepia paper, the strokes and shading were as crisp and fresh as the day they'd been created. The drawing showed a young bearded man in his early thirties, the robed figure strong and well-proportioned. The boy at his side was a waif in dusty clothes and peasant sandals. What I was seeing was not a preliminary sketch but a complete work. The child's expression captured in a moment of reverence. When Dansby moved aside, I bent closer, resisting the urge to press my fingertips against the glass, wanting to touch the paper once handled by the master.

All of my doubts vanished as my eyes roamed the drawings. Whatever Enzo Riva's book purported to show, the old guy had to be mistaken. The two figures could only have been conceived by da Vinci. No one spoke as I bent closer to the drawing, taking in every line, my nose a few inches above the glass. Holding my breath as if it might blemish the drawing, I started to raise my head when I noticed the signature.

I stared at it, trying to recall variations of Leonardo's signature I'd seen in countless drawings and paintings. He wasn't a consistent signer, but his signatures had flair: an artistic script or elegant block letters, *Leonardo da Vinci* or *L da Vinci*, or a finely rendered *LDV* or interwoven *LDV*, but never the unembellished signature I saw at the bottom right corner.

Jean-Henri appeared beside me. "Satisfied?"

I stood, unable to take my eyes from the signature.

"impressive."

Marsh Hampton walked to the table, failing to coverup the aftermath of morning whiskey as he offered his hand. "I remember now," he said. "You were with Leslie at Armands. I remember her mentioning you worked for Dansby."

I started to reply when Isabelle Delaudier interrupted me.

"You're not from New York, Mister Barrow?" The velvet voice betrayed Scandinavian origins.

"Chicago. California before that."

"Chicago," she said languidly, as though Chicago existed in South Dakota. "Land of Alphonse Capone and other criminals. The Second City, as it were."

Dansby had been right. A model trophy wife with all the appeal of a snake charmer, only I saw the snake in the basket.

I smiled. "I never knew Chicago held the patent on criminals."

Dansby suppressed a smile, while Jean-Henri looked aggrieved that I hadn't willingly swallowed her slight.

Roland Delaudier seemed to reassess me and I got the sense he didn't see many people joust with his wife.

"Quite so," he said. "My wife forgets New York isn't the center of the universe, although the majority of our fellow citizens agree with the premise." He squinted at me. "You *are* the Adam Barrow who found the van Gogh, am I correct?"

The New York Times had proclaimed me a hero of the moment: *Gallery Owner Rescues Unknown Van Gogh Painting.*

"I saw it when I last visited the Getty," Delaudier added. "My congratulations." His smile lacked any semblance of sincerity. "Too bad the courts ruled against you. You came close to joining the ranks of disgusting wealth."

"I could have managed that," I smiled.

Hampton laughed as Isabelle watched the exchange without speaking. Dismissing me, she lifted a gold cigarette box from a side table and plucked out a French clove cigarette, looked around expectantly until Marsh flicked his lighter.

Roland reached over and snapped the lighter shut. "We discussed your smoking," he said, forcing a smile. "Not in the building."

She glared at him and returned the cigarette to the case. Turning back to me, she said, "The next auction may suffer because of your actions, Mr. Barrow. Bidders may feel constrained to reconsider the da Vinci."

"You mean helping an old man will depress the value of a da Vinci?"

"You know very well what I mean."

"He wasn't making much sense, Ms. Delaudier. He insisted he owned an old book that proved the drawing wasn't genuine." I didn't mention I'd seen a book. "He claims this book proves the drawing is not an actual da Vinci."

Everyone stared at me.

"An old book?" Isabelle scoffed. "You can't be serious."

To hell with her. Dansby trusted me with his money. He did not expect me to gamble it away, while she made a profit. Like Jean-Henri, I owed it to him to be certain how he spent his money, and the unadorned *DV* signature on the drawing raised danger signals.

"By helping this… person , you may have caused irreparable damage."

She seemed ready to accuse me of sinking the Titanic when Roland spoke up.

"Isabelle, please."

"On the contrary," I said. "The added publicity and trotting out your experts again should raise its appeal." I flashed her my best smile. "No need to thank me."

Roland, obviously enjoying our contest of insults, said, "Well, all things considered, I think the auction will do quite well." He indicated the frame on the table.

"This one, plus our other da Vincis."

Jean-Henri looked at him, then at Dansby.

"Others?"

"Yes. three more, in fact." Delaudier said, relishing our surprise. "We uncovered a cache of unusual proportions."

Recovering his aplomb, Dansby said, "Four other da Vincis would definitely be an unusual find."

Jean-Henri regarded him. "Would you care to divulge the provenance?".

"Not just yet," Roland said.

"I only ask because of concerns about art stolen during the Holocaust," Jean-Henri persisted.

"Ah, always an issue," he said. "I understand your concern, but I assure you there are no issues regarding provenance." He gave his wife a wink. "We know the seller quite well and I think it's safe to say we'll shake the art world to its core."

Dansby tried to conceal his hunger. "May I see them?"

"All in good time, Phillip. A talented businessman saves the best for last. Builds the anticipation." His smile broadened as though the scent of money was in the room. "I'll have our photographer make prints for you. You'll be the first to see them and decide for yourself if they're worth your time."

Dansby didn't press the issue. He picked up his topcoat. "Thank you for indulging us today. I'm most certainly still in the market for the drawing."

"Call me personally if you or Jean-Henri have questions," Delaudier said. "You also, Mister Barrow."

Isabelle strode from the room as the rest of us shook hands, almost friends again.

Chapter Eight

How do you deal with a thought that develops a power of its own, one that harasses you like a bill collector on commission? The drawing's unusual signature stayed with me and wove its way into Riva's claims. Unable to dismiss either, my curiosity grew. The drawing astounded me, but so did the forged Degas painting that blemished my credibility only a few weeks earlier. I didn't have Jean-Henri's encyclopedic wisdom, but two warning flags required answers, or at least an explanation. Convinced Riva deserved another hearing, I decided to make one final attempt to inspect the book.

The rain came down harder during my lunch hour. I skipped my usual sandwich and lucked out, hailing an empty cab outside Dansby Tower. Rain pounded the taxi, the downpour unable to blot out the driver's Bollywood music. Accompanied by the strains of Indian sitars and an enthusiastic cast of singers, I endured the musical crosstown ride to Riva's apartment.

Inside the musty vestibule, I brushed rainwater from my sleeves and shoulders, hoping Riva hadn't passed out as I pressed the intercom button.

Static and a click. *"Cosa vuoi?"*

"Mister Riva, it's Adam Barrow."

"What you want?" The voice sounded weak but sober.

"To talk again. About your book."

Another sharp click and I thought he had cut me off. I turned to leave when the inner door buzzed and snapped open. I took the stairs and knocked on his door. It inched open and Riva squinted at me, his mouth slack.

Less than a week had passed, but he seemed a husk of his former self, the sparse goatee dotted with breakfast crumbs, his sallow cheeks drawn and unshaven. He wore the same stained white shirt buttoned at the collar, his trousers loose on his hips.

The apartment seemed barer than I remembered. Unwashed dishes and the sour smell of a sick room greeted me as I stepped inside. What appeared to be the same two water glasses and bottles sat on the table beside his chair. The canary peeped its welcome, and I whistled back. Riva ignored the bird and shambled to his chair, indicating the couch I'd occupied during my last visit.

"*Prego, prego,*" he sighed

"Mister Riva…" I began.

"Enzo, please." He picked up the grappa bottle and unscrewed the cap.

Not a good beginning.

"You remember my last visit? You showed me your book."

He waved the bottle at me and smiled sadly. "I think so. My memory runs away with the years. I remember last time I am a poor *ospite.*" His hand shaking, he poured a hefty dollop of grappa in his glass and downed the shot. "A bad host."

Relieved when he didn't offer to share the bottle, I sat forward, deciding to press the issue before he drifted off again. To my dismay he picked up the second glass, poured it half full and handed it to me. With only coffee and a roll for breakfast, the prospect of Italian turpentine before lunch promised a high price for another conversation. I'd labeled myself an art investigator and told myself that dedicated investigators did whatever was required. I took a sip and fought to keep my face neutral. Riva grinned and refilled his glass to the brim.

"*Saluti.*"

He took a generous gulp and hunched forward in his chair. The effort produced a grunt of pain. Drawing a ragged breath, he refocused on me.

"I tell you a secret, *Signor* Barrow. I am a dying man."

He held up a hand to stop my questions.

"My doctors, they tell me I will not live through the winter. Then they tell me I cannot drink wine with the medicine they give me, that wine and grappa harms me." He laughed until the sound liquefied into a raspy cough. He took another swallow, wiped his goatee and held up his glass. "As if this could cause more pain."

Was he was telling the truth or had the alcohol created delusions? "I'm sorry," I finally managed. "I work for a very rich man whose doctors might…."

Riva waved away the offer. "No more doctors, no more," he grated. "When you have lived this long, you listen to your body. The doctors are good men, but they are guided only by their education."

What can you say when anyone tells you they are dying? When they know their body has betrayed them?

He read my pity. "You must not concern yourself, *Signor* Barrow. I have lived a long time with few regrets, the worst being the loss of my wife." He sipped more grappa, his rheumy eyes two thousand miles away. "You see, in Italy, I was a locksmith. It was a good living, but also a temptation for a poor man. Our son, Antonio, he also makes a mistake and Anna and I, we must leave. Anna, she is struck by a taxi outside this building the day after we arrive in America. She is looking up at the tall buildings, and the next second, she is gone. She makes a mistake, and God takes her. Since then, I am alone."

Inspecting the book seemed trivial as I absorbed his sorrow, but it signified the reason I found myself drinking cheap grappa for lunch. If getting hammered with a lonely old man before noon produced what I sought, I'd make the sacrifice.

"I'm very sorry," I said.

He nodded, and we raised our glasses to her memory.

"Can we talk about your book?"

"Ah, I remember. I showed Melzi's book to you." He motioned to my glass. "Drink and then we talk about the master's work." I held out my glass like an obedient soldier and he filled it. I held my breath, and swallowed more grappa, my throat already numbed by the first infusion. The brandy smoothed New York's edges for the first time since the auction.

"You are an educated man, yes?"

"I have several art degrees."

"Tell me why you come back," Riva said. "Why the book is important to you." In spite of his obvious pain, his eyes were clear, and I knew my next words would have to pass inspection if I expected to see the book's contents.

"I don't want my employer to make a mistake," I said. "He's not just a rich man, Mister Riva. He wants to build a museum where the public can admire the art he's collected." I hoped Dansby's intentions might overcome Riva's revulsion of those he deemed unworthy to possess a da Vinci. "That's why he wants to own a da Vinci."

"My protest concerns him?"

"Yes."

A small lie, but it contained an element of truth. Dansby had his own reasons to go slow, but I'd added a small doubt about the drawing's authenticity. Whether we both made a mistake might well depend on Riva's book.

He frowned. "Who will buy this drawing?"

"There'll be another auction."

"Whoever buys it will be cheated," he declared.

Now or never.

"Why are you so certain?"

"You have time to hear an old man's story?"

Did he have proof of his claim at the auction or had I befriended an old man who enjoyed rare company? Rain thumped against the kitchen window and I decided his story beat the hell out of trying to find a cab. More than anything, I wanted to inspect the book.

"Francesco Melzi." Riva said as though the name began a prayer. "You remember the name from your studies? He was Leonardo's pupil and constant companion for fifteen years. Melzi was a very capable painter born to a noble family. Leonardo was his mentor and loved him like a son. Others traveled and studied with the master, but Melzi, he was his favorite and the most talented."

"It's been a long time since I sat in a classroom," I said.

Riva waved his hand. "No matter. You can look him up as you say in America."

"Melzi wrote the book?"

He gave me an impish smile. "In a way."

I stared at him, tired of riddles. What the hell was he talking about?

"Melzi died in 1570," he continued. "Only a few of his paintings survive, but *questa è la vita.*"

I shifted on the couch, my patience fading. "You'll have to translate."

"That is life," Riva explained. "Few of us succeed in everything, you agree?"

I nodded and sipped the raw brandy. I didn't need an art lecture or philosophy lesson, but I had no choice except to hear him out.

"Melzi, he spends fifty years collecting Leonardo's work, what learned men call his *Codex Urbinus*. After the master dies, he gathers his sketches, his notes on painting, everything he can find. He remained devoted even after death."

He struggled from the chair. "Here, I show you."

I tilted the chair back as before, and he retrieved the book. I righted the heavy chair, and he sank into the cushions, grimacing from the effort. He opened the book and made a contented sound, as though he held the keys to the Treasury on his lap.

"As I told you before, our eyes rarely behold work that is... *diverso*... very special. Leonardo, he draws and paints beauty and what God has created." He frowned and swiped his hand over the book. "Not like Bosch who saw only man's ugliness and punishment for his sins."

He turned the yellowed plates slowly as if he had descended into them, lost in what he saw. I leaned forward and saw page after page of drawings and notes on every page; the notations entered by a precise hand. Impressive though the contents appeared, they were nothing more than an elaborate sketch book.

Disappointed, I said, "This is one of da Vinci's sketchbooks?"

The old man eased the dusty volume closed. "No. What you see is not da Vinci."

Out of patience with the words he insisted on repeating, I shook my head. "Claiming the Delaudier drawing is not a da Vinci accomplishes nothing, Mister Riva. We were almost arrested and I was nearly fired."

Riva's lips trembled. "I am sorry, but to understand Leonardo, you must also see what he is not."

I didn't need more riddles. "That's why Delaudier employs art authorities. To verify what they offer and to…"

He started to reply but a surge of coughing caused him to wince in pain.

"Please," he gasped. "Let me finish my story." He tugged a handkerchief from his trouser pocket and wiped his mouth. "Melzi, he inherits everything. Even the drawings and paintings from Leonardo's last studio. Melzi also gathers the work of his students, those who aspired to equal the master. He records what he sees but keeps his work secret. Few people saw his work before it disappears." He lightly tapped a page. "This book contains only truth, *Signor* Barrow."

"How did you come by it?"

"My father, he studied art as a young man until he must work to support his family. After the war, he helps clear a ruined abbey in Milan. In the cellar behind a collapsed wall, he finds the book wrapped in layers of sheep's skin. He doesn't tell the monks or anyone what he finds." Riva's voice turned wistful. "I do not know why. It was possible he feared others would think he steals the book, that he is a thief. After he dies, I find it along with his other books. He shows it to me once when I was a boy, but I understood nothing about its secrets."

The grappa tested my patience, and I didn't try to hide my frustration. "Even if it's a true record, what does it prove? It's only a history."

Riva closed the cover and used a corner of his handkerchief to wipe the gilt lettering. Straining, he leaned forward and laid the heavy volume on my lap. I felt the weight of centuries across my knees and lifted the front cover, amazed at the book's thickness, the mustiness of old leather and dry parchment wafting upward.

"Look at the title, *Signor* Barrow. *'Ombre di Leonardo'.*"

I looked at the gilt letters surrounding the heraldic crest; the words dimmed as rain clouds passed over the building. "What's it mean?"

"*Shadows of Leonardo,*" Riva said. "A clever title, as you will see." I ran my fingers over the letters.

"Francesco Melzi prepares this book to leave the world a record," he explained. "He used his talent to copy what he sees, copies everything to the last stroke. Hour after hour and day after day, he draws and copies. He knew others would one day claim the honors due Leonardo."

A single figure or multiple drawings covered every page. Many images crowded against one another, while other pages showed a head, anatomical detail, or mechanical device, the amazing drawings unaffected by age. According to Riva, every sketch in the volume had been expertly copied by Melzi's pen, his talent obvious. Each drawing had been laid down with loving care, and I recognized several da Vinci's works from books and museums. The images filling the pages overwhelmed me and I could only stare as I reverently turned the pages.

"These are exquisite, but I'm not sure what they prove."

Riva pointed to writing at the bottom of every page, each in the same hand.

"Read what Melzi writes," he said.

"My Italian's not very good."

"Then I translate for you."

Knowing them by heart, he read them upside-down, pointing to the first one.

"*The work of Alberto Ganza, 1479.*" He turned the page. "*Drawing of an old woman by Leonardo da Vinci, 1480.*" He turned another page and pointed at the notation. "*A sketch by Andrea del Verrocchio, 1472.*" Another page. "*Painting: The Magi by Leonardo da Vinci, 1481.*" Another. "*Saint Paul by Giorgio Volterno, 1471.*"

He sat back. "These are all Melzi's copies and notes," Riva said. "His final offering to Leonardo." He leaned forward and met my eyes. "The drawings are *magnifico*, the notes his gifts to us."

"Gifts." I tried to calculate the importance of what I held. "May I take a photograph of a few drawings?"

Riva appeared not to have heard me. "Melzi drew all the sketches you see here. Some are copies of the master's drawings and paintings, but not all. Melzi also copies the work of many talented students who studied with Leonardo. Melzi tells us which are the master's work and which were done by his followers."

"Just a few photographs?" I ventured again.

He looked at me, his eyes suddenly clear. "I do not think so, *Signor* Barrow. I do not want the book to tempt those who would use the book to their advantage."

Disappointed, I found a delicately rendered head of the Madonna. On the following page, the perfectly rendered hands of an elderly man. "And these?"

He craned his head and read the notation. "The work of Andrea Ricci, a talented student from Florence. Neither is the work of Leonardo."

I randomly turned several more pages until I found the Christ figure and young boy. Smaller than the offering at the auction, but the same image I'd inspected in Delaudier's conference room down to the most minute stroke. Riva smiled as I leaned closer to the drawing.

"It is the same drawing you saw, no? The work of Donato Volpe. He was a wonderful student, one who possessed part of Leonardo's genius. They even shared the same initials." He raised his palms to the ceiling. "The drawing at the auction is his work, not Leonardo's." Riva lightly ran his forefinger across the notation at the foot of the page. "Look what Melzi writes. There is Volpe's name."

Melzi had faithfully copied Volpe's drawing down to the last pen stroke, including the strange *DV* signature in the lower right corner. I had little doubt I was looking at a copy of the drawing offered by Delaudier. Only it wasn't a work by da Vinci.

"Copies of da Vinci's work," I muttered.

Riva flipped his hand back and forth, mischief in his eyes. "Some are, many not what you believe you see."

I lightly touched the page, aware I should be wearing protective gloves, but unable to resist the contact. I eased the book closed, aware of its inestimable value.

"Why have you hidden this?"

"The book is very dangerous. It separates sheep from goats. I believe there are those who would threaten museums and collectors who believe they own Leonardo's work. I am only a poor locksmith, but I study the pictures in books and museums. I compare them to this book, and I find many are the work of his students. The people who own them could be blackmailed or threatened, *Signor* Barrow. Worse, there are those who might tear the book apart, destroy Melzi's notes and sell the drawings as Leonardo's work."

I emptied my glass without flinching and understood what frightened him. It had become common knowledge that an astounding amount of works in museums were forgeries or mis-attributed, but few of them were removed when the truth leaked out. Dansby told the story of a major museum's wealthiest donor who contributed truckloads of money and eventually donated an Old Master painting later identified as a forgery. Rather than embarrass the donor and lose his patronage, the museum left the painting on its wall with his name on a plaque beside it. Add extortion to embarrassment and I understood how Melzi's book could be weaponized.

Riva held out his spotted hands, and I returned the weighty tome to him.

"I must find the person who will honor Melzi's work," he said, "who will not use my book to harm others."

No matter Dansby's past sins, he didn't need to add blackmail or fraud to his resume.

"I work for a man named Phillip Dansby," I said. "He's a very wealthy art patron. He can find a safe home for your book." Jean-Henri's face appeared, and I relished the thought of handing him the book.

Riva frowned and shook his head. "I do not know this Dansby."

"Let me arrange a meeting. You can then decide."

He shook his head again as though he hadn't heard me. "I must be certain it finds a safe place."

"Mister Riva, my employer has doubts about the drawing at Delaudier." A half-truth, but I needed to reassure him. "I'm certain he'd be willing to make sure the book doesn't fall into the wrong hands."

Riva laid the massive volume on the floor at his feet and eased himself up, grasping the chair arm for support. "Come see me tomorrow," he wheezed. "We will talk more about this man."

Disappointed, I stood and realized I was slightly drunk again. The book lay on the threadbare carpet at my feet and I stared down at it. In the wrong hands, the centuries old volume could fall on the art world like an anvil.

Chapter Nine

East Prussia Border
Unmarked Road
January 4, 1945

Weisser's mind strayed. His rancid clothing repelled him despite the freezing cab, but he ignored the stench, concentrating on the road. Late afternoon shadows stretched across the ruts but the storm had stopped, the featureless landscape on either side lulling him into a white dreamworld that could kill him. He glanced at the snow encroaching on the road, recalling skiing vacations with his brother in Austria before the war. Dieter had been younger and the better skier, but he was dead, killed in Normandy.

At least, Weisser thought, he'd been spared Russia.

Limbs heavy with snow overhung sections of the road, concealing the ditches which represented deathtraps for the truck. He'd been trapped behind the wheel of the GAZ for 24 hours, captured by the ruts that kept the truck centered. The rusted frame protested every jolt and pothole, and Weisser listened for a cracked piston or thumping rod that would spell an end to his journey. He cursed the truck in one breath and cajoled it in the next, forcing his eyes to defeat the lure of sleep.

What remained of two Waffen SS Divisions were dug in twenty kilometers to the west, but Weisser steered north for the coast, finished with the war. His orders had been clear in the beginning. Cleanse the Eastern Front of Jews and other *Untermenschen*. He'd done his duty, but nothing remained but the promise of a bullet or worse. Now, he had no intention of allowing the Bolsheviks to shoot him like a starving dog, not after his discovery in the boxcar.

His thoughts produced a bemused smile, remembering better times. He'd traveled a long way from the classrooms of Heidelberg and Berlin. Afternoons in the old university libraries studying medieval art. Heady nights pursuing the Erikas, Ingrids or Annalieses in local *hofbraus*. The good times came to an end when his professors conformed to Party lines. His studies lost their appeal and money from his skinflint father dried up due to faltering grades, stopping altogether until he found himself looking for a job.

He found work in the small restoration shop in Bremen. An apprentice restorer relegated to a backroom, disposable at the first sign of hard times.

"Low man in a nothing company," he mumbled to the streaked windshield.

Not that it mattered any longer. The entire street where Gross and Tegtmeier existed remained little more than rubble, his humble position ludicrously redundant.

He removed the ridiculous Russian fur cap and ran a glove through his uncut black hair, picturing himself in a tailored three-piece suit from Kochlers. Weisser doubted the exclusive men's store still stood. Most likely the shop joined other piles of bricks after three years of air raids by the British and Americans.

His untenable situation coincided with his subscription to *"Der Stürmer"*. Julius Streicher's newspaper printed the truth about the Jewish conspiracy. How the Jews had worked to defeat Germany in the last war, causing economic disaster. Any remaining interest in art shriveled to a minor extravagance as his eyes opened to the dangers facing the Fatherland.

He walked away from the drudgery and volunteered for the SS. A year later he transferred to the *Sicherheitsdienst*, Heydrich's security service. To his delight, promotions came quickly in the SD. His superiors selected him to head up a Jewish suppression battalion, first seeing action in Poland, then Russia. In the beginning, arrests meant growing numbers of detention camps, but the leaders soon devised more effective cleansing methods.

Sick of the endless road, Weisser's anger rose. A blind and unsympathetic world had ended the crusade, bringing down Germany for a second time, but there were no reasons why patriots like him must shoulder the consequences. The cargo at his back provided a reward for his valuable work. He'd trade his discovery for a fresh life, one he could only just imagine. Maybe display the crate's real gem to impress women or new friends until he needed more money. To display such a wonder would place him at the apex of wealthy collectors.

Craning his neck at the windshield, he sought a glimpse of the morning sun. If he headed north, the sun would be slightly on his right. Overcast skies confused his sense of direction and added to his uneasiness. How much farther to the coast, and would he find an ice-free port? Twice he heard artillery's rumble over the straining engine and resisted the urge to speed up. The gas gauge needle edged below the quarter mark and Weisser forced his eyes away. Soon he would use the fuel from the extra petrol cans. When that was gone, his dreams would die in the snow. He pushed away the thought.

Either I make it or I don't.

Everything had been against him from the start, but he preferred the odds over the Russian Army's desire to kill him. Agony crept into his left hand and the familiar plan flared as he jammed his glove beneath his armpit.

In 1942, his special action group followed the army's advance, eliminating pockets of human trash. Following a minor skirmish, Wehrmacht troops handed over a Russian political officer and a squad of wounded Red Army soldiers to his unit. About to order them shot, the crazed Commissar broke away and slashed Weisser's hand with a bayonet hidden beneath his clothing. He lost three fingers. The stumps healed slowly, the pain intolerable as winter deepened. The agony tormented him until he found the girl at the pit.

His unit had collected a mob of keening Jews outside some godforsaken village in Belarus. Ordering the civilians stripped naked, his men watched and laughed as Weisser shoved them a pit they dug. He raised his arm to give the order to fire and stopped.

A girl about ten huddled at the edge of the pit, golden hair shining among the mass of the shivering human targets. Weisser ordered the rifles lowered and walked to her. Bony arms wrapped around her body, the naked child stared up at him as he lifted the tresses of blond hair. Thick and luxurious, the locks cascaded below her waist. He fondled it, an answer presenting itself as he recalled U-boat crews wore socks woven from camp victims' hair. Weisser ordered a private to remove the hair with his trench knife. He raised his arm to give the order to fire when a bearded rabbi turned and yelled at him.

"*Vi isu derleb ikh im shoyn tsu bagrobn!*"

Weisser waved down the rifles.

"What is he saying?" he yelled.

A bespectacled woman, eyes brimming with judgement, faced him and answered in perfect German. "It is an ancient Hebrew curse. He says we will outlive you long enough to bury you."

For a surreal moment, Weisser saw himself fall into the pit. Tightening his grip on the blond mane, he gave the order, unaware of the ragged volley of shots.

Next day he found an old Russian babushka who wove the hair into thick liners for his gloves. Flexing the stumps against the steering wheel, he dismissed the memory. Curses frightened only children and the ignorant.

"What are you thinking?" he muttered. "Keep your eyes on the road."

He marveled at the hoarse sound of his voice in the refrigerated cab. Reduced to talking to himself to remain awake, he savored his last six years. His duty explicit, he required no justification. Not ever.

And the crate was proof!

So incredible to stumble on such a prize. He had exercised ultimate power for six years, but power without profit or a future meant little. Before the discovery, he had accepted death in the snow as inevitable. Now, he could clearly envision a fresh life. Find a ship, toss his uniform and slip into new skin, reborn. His wonderful fortune would grow with a lifestyle the likes of which few ever imagined. Lightheaded, he pounded the steering wheel.

"Anton Weisser!" he yelled. "Bon vivant!"

Chapter Ten

Dansby Tower
Early Morning

I sat in front of Dansby's desk and watched him fiddle with a cigar clipper. He seemed distracted, and I wondered if the axe would fall today. Raindrops raced down his windows, the grey skies matching the mood in the room. He tossed the clipper aside and folded his arms on the desktop.

"So," he began, "you're no longer enamored with the fellow at the auction?"

"He's a boozer." I felt guilty about the sobriquet, but unless Phillip inspected the book, it was senseless to defend Riva. Besides, if he'd decided to can me, nothing I said would change his mind.

He turned his chair to watch the rain. "From what I gather, this fellow would have made a scene no matter what you did."

A reprieve?

He gave a knowing smile. "I can understand the Delaudiers' anger. Both of them can be thousand horsepower bastards when it suits them."

I looked at the angry horses in the painting above his head and seconded his opinion. "You sent me to spend your money at the auction, Phillip. After misjudging the Degas, I don't need another mistake. Not with the money you allocated."

He nodded slowly. The rain against the window held his attention until he spoke. "It would have been my mistake, not yours. In any case, I'll go with you to next Wednesday's auction."

My guess was he'd convinced himself I needed a chaperone. Or his clout to get me past Delaudiers' security.

"What about Jean-Henri?"

Phillip made a derisive noise and sat back. "He doesn't *do* auctions, as you Americans say. Seems they offend his sense of propriety."

"Just as well. He's not my biggest fan."

"Of course he's not. I bring in a *wunderkind* and he's as jealous as a cuckolded husband."

"You put a lot of faith in him."

"Far more than you place in a drunken old man," he said pointedly. "Jean-Henri's never failed me. I admit there are occasions where I get the bit between my teeth. He's my reins and halter as it were. Never lets me take the jumps without looking."

"I'll try to do the same."

He studied the raindrops as though they confirmed his judgment.

"Jean-Henri has decades of knowledge, but you possess a rare sixth sense, dear boy. You proved that with the van Gogh, and I'm willing to abide your obsession with this stranger. Where Jean-Henri sees paint and technique, you see beyond the obvious. If the old man's claim was valid, you'd have saved me millions." I said nothing, and he changed direction.

"I think we should sit down with an authority Jean-Henri trusts. Manfred Morrison is an insufferable ass, but he's respected in New York art circles. He's a savvy sort and I see no harm in hearing his opinion. Do you agree?"

"Can't hurt."

For the moment, Dansby had returned to an even keel, and I decided against pushing my luck. Riva's book remained in the wind, but Dansby appeared to have partially regained confidence in my judgment. We discussed how to approach him and decided I'd arrange a meeting before the upcoming auction. In the meantime, I'd have the dubious honor of meeting Morrison.

• • •

Manfred Morrison lived the life of a tenured professor at Columbia University. A recognized authority for over three decades with several books on Renaissance art to his credit, he was an expert in his field, his sonorous voice adding verbal weight to his expansive paunch. An imposing figure with tonsured gray hair, he favored three-piece Italian suits tailored to conceal his bulk, flaunting the latest power ties. A regular at gallery openings and charity events, the media loved him, as did society wives and elderly doyennes. He looked the part of a successful board member, ingratiating himself with collectors and newspaper columnists alike. Nicknamed "M&M" by the media, I once heard Dansby claim it meant more and more publicity.

Morrison condescended to meet with us next morning, much to Jean-Henri's delight. Clarice brought in coffee and tea, and the four of us took chairs around Dansby's small conference table. Fingers interlaced across his vested abdomen, he tilted his head back and studied me as if dissecting a new species.

"You're the person who disrupted the da Vinci auction. Roland told me what happened."

"The old man claims he owns a book by Francesco Melzi," I said. Jean-Henri grunted, and I knew I'd stepped in it.

Morrison flapped a hand as though backhanding the air between us. "Ah, yes, the old Melzi fairytale." He gave Dansby a patronizing smile. "An urban legend of sorts, Phillip. Scholars dismissed its existence years ago."

"I saw the book," I said. "One illustration refutes the Delaudier drawing."

Morrison narrowed his eyes. "Did you take photos?"

"Riva doesn't want anyone to know he has the book. He's afraid it'll fall into the wrong hands."

"Rubbish!" Morrison exploded. "I don't doubt you saw a book, but did you verify its provenance? Are you qualified to judge its veracity? Will this person show it to experts who can vouch for it?"

I ignored his rational questions, grasping at straws. "Even the signature on the drawing is wrong."

Morrison reared back as though I'd poisoned his coffee, a Philistine wandering through his comfortable world.

"Preposterous."

"I certainly have no doubts," Jean-Henri interjected.

Fric and Frac, I thought. A matched pair.

Dismissing me as unworthy of further debate, Morrison turned to Jean-Henri. They reminisced about a past collaboration until Dansby interrupted them.

"Manfred, you inspected it. I want your personal assurance. Why do you believe Roland and Isabelle discovered a genuine da Vinci?"

"And rightfully so," Morrison placed his coffee cup on the table and looked at Dansby with an expression reserved for lesser breeds. "I fully understand your concerns, Phillip, but it's the find of the decade."

"Tell me why you're certain," Dansby said.

Morrison shifted into a self-deprecating mode. "Well, I had the assistance of several professionals, of course, but I made an exhaustive study of the drawing and my colleagues fully agreed with my analysis. Roland has scored a coup, a bevy of unbelievable proportions."

"What types of analysis?" Dansby asked.

In his element, Morrison reared back and contemplated the ceiling.

"Experience, for one thing," he said as though banishing other options. "Remember, I also assisted in verifying *Salvator Mundi*."

The undiscovered da Vinci painting had turned up in a Louisiana auction in 2005. Undergoing extensive examination in New York and London, it eventually found its way to Christies where it sold for more than $450 million, a record for paintings.

"I assisted in the early confirmation of its legitimacy," Morrison continued. "Paint analysis, infrared, x-rays, artistic technique, comparisons with verified da Vinci work. Every test imaginable. And," he added, "we exercised the same diligence on Roland's da Vinci."

Much to his chagrin, Morrison had not received credit for his part in the verification, letting the New York media know he'd been academically slighted.

He brushed his trouser leg, closing further discussion. "I have no doubts about the work."

Jean-Henri nodded agreement. "There, Phillip," he said. "There is your opportunity to own a da Vinci."

"I'm only saying we should go slower," I said. "Examine Riva's book before the next auction."

"And where is this book of yours?" Jean-Henri said.

I had no answer.

The three of them looked at me until Morrison pulled his bulk from the chair. "I have no reservations, Phillip. It's a da Vinci."

•   •   •

Slumped at my desk, I watched rain assault to my office window. The view from the thirtieth floor was normally spectacular, but it seemed New York conspired with the weather to encourage what was turning out to be a lousy week. The fact remained that Riva would never share the book with people he didn't know or trust, at least not at this point. The image and weight of the leather volume persisted, enjoying the reprieve when my iPhone chimed.

"Adam?"

It took me a second to recognize Leslie Strickland's voice.

"If you're free for lunch, I thought we might compare notes on local jazz clubs," she said.

I hadn't planned on venturing into the rain, but her call dispelled my reasoning that I represented a humane project for her. After my intervention at the auction, I imagined the Delaudiers were arranging my passage to Devil's Island.

"I'm free," I said, "but I don't want to get you fired."

"If you mean Isabelle and Roland, they'll get over your interference once the da Vinci brings top dollar. Do you like Chinese?"

"As long as it's not one of their favorite restaurants."

"We'll hide."

She'd gone out of her way to avoid escalating the scene with Riva. In a city of appealing women, only her face stayed with me after Kat's death. I blamed my isolation on the fact that I'd sidestepped serious relationships since moving to the city, committing to work and trying to move beyond the past. Perhaps I needed to raise my head and take a closer look at my caller.

"Where and what time?"

She named a restaurant in Chinatown, and we agreed to meet in an hour.

Zhou's China Gate was a respectable-looking storefront on 39th Street in the heart of the old Chinatown. Getting there took only a few minutes with a driver who considered yellow lights and stop signs challenges and inconveniences. Few of the unrenovated buildings topped eight stories. Built in the 30s and 40s, iron fire escapes fronted old brick facades. Red and yellow banners in Chinese lined the sidewalks, an overhead maze of power lines crisscrossing the street.

The air teemed with exotic cooking odors as I escaped the death taxi. The rain had stopped, and I collapsed my umbrella as I ducked inside Zhou's red door.

A life-sized brass Buddha confronted me inside the vestibule. I looked around but saw no sign of Leslie. A doll-like Chinese woman in a red silk sheath ushered me past a four-stool bar to a table in the rear. I told her I was waiting for a guest and gave her Leslie's name. A bowing waiter appeared, and I ordered a Tsingtao. Diners filled the remaining tables as savory aromas wafted from two open kitchen doors. Sizzling woks competed with the faint strains of oriental music. I watched the door, eager to see Leslie again. I adjusted my tie and finger-combed my hair, symptoms that I'd been too long without female company.

Leslie came through the red door five minutes later. The hostess took her umbrella and helped her out of a black raincoat as they chatted. Leslie wore a green turtleneck that complemented the eyes I recalled from Armands. Her comfortable outfit failed to disguise the physical charms I remembered as she followed the woman's pointing finger and spotted me. I stood, appreciating her grace as she maneuvered between the packed tables.

"You found it," she said with a smile.

"The cabbie did all the work."

I couldn't take my eyes from her. Gold hoop earrings seemed designed for stylishly cropped hair. Wisps of fine blond hair accentuated her long neck, I caught the familiar scent of jasmine perfume from Armands as a waiter pulled out her chair.

"I'm glad you could join me," she said.

"Light day in the Dansby salt mines."

My beer arrived with an unordered martini for her. Obviously a regular, she thanked the waiter in Chinese as he poured beer into my Pilsner glass. We declined the obligatory pot of tea and raised our drinks in a silent toast. She took a small package from her shoulder purse and handed me a gaily wrapped square.

"A Greek bearing gifts," she said. "Or is that a scrambled metaphor in a Chinese restaurant?"

I pulled the ribbon and found the new Pat Matheny CD.

"Thank you. I don't have this one."

"His guitar work is outstanding."

I tucked the CD into my jacket pocket, and she opened her purse. She took out a pack of cigarettes and lit up. She saw my surprised look. "Madame Zhou kindly told the New York smoking police to kiss her Oriental ass, that her patrons would be allowed to smoke, and that protestors could find another restaurant if smoking offended them. So far, they haven't sent the Nanny Police to arrest her."

"I guess she can ignore the rules until they arrive."

"I don't think that's a problem. The Chinese have a bevy of interesting contacts at City Hall."

She brushed a strand of hair off her forehead and sipped the martini. I drank my beer and felt like I belonged in a bowling alley. Isabelle Delaudier was an intriguing woman, but Leslie Strickland gave off waves of desirability.

She inhaled and blew smoke to one side. "I heard about your little scene with Isabelle and thought you might need consolation."

"A drink with you cures all ills," I said, feeling out of practice. "Is this the part where we tell each other our life stories?"

She gave me a tolerant look. "If you like."

"First, I owe you an explanation. What happened at the auction was a spur-of-the-moment thing."

"No explanation required. This is New York, national home of the crazies."

"A culture shock for you after Florida?"

She sipped her drink. "You remembered."

"Where in Florida?"

"Wadesville," she said. "A nothing intersection in the panhandle just off the Gulf. What Southerners call the Redneck Riviera. Both my parents died when I was ten and I lived with my grandmother in a double-wide. When she died, I couldn't wait to get out of there." She leaned across the table. "I'll tell you another secret. My name's not Leslie. It's Wanda Strickland. Wanda from Wadesville." She gave a bitter laugh. "Can you think of anything more redneck?"

"How'd you end up at Delaudier?"

She twirled the stem of her glass. "I guess you'd say Roland Delaudier rescued me. My first piece of luck after I escaped. For some godforsaken reason, my grandmother owned a small Frederick Friescke. It was her pride and the only thing of any value she left me. I went to Delaudier to sell it and Roland ended up giving me a job."

"And before that?"

"I worked as a cashier at a Dollar Store in Wadesville." She exhaled a plume of smoke and stared across the room. "Not what you'd call a cultural experience unless you count guys in pickup trucks hitting on me. I tried junior college in Tallahassee, but was bored out of my mind. One day, I quit my job, grabbed the Friescke and bought a bus ticket. Poor girl comes to bright lights, big city. A shopworn Hollywood ending, but I'm never going back, not ever." Her smile returned. "You?"

"My brother and I were raised in California," I said. "Our father lived his life as a clever drunk and con man. I left home as soon as I could, got the art bug and worked my way through college. Saved my money and opened a small gallery in Chicago. Nothing special until the van Gogh. The lawyers eventually won and Dansby hired me."

"And you came here to work for him."

"Temporarily." At least I hoped so.

"Actually, you were the hero when you found the van Gogh."

"Fame and fortune without the fortune."

"I read about that," she said. "You work for one of the wealthiest men in the world."

"I got lucky."

"How'd you meet Dansby?"

"He was a friend of my father. He calls me an appraiser, but I'm a glorified art hunter."

She smiled. "Hercule Poirot in New York."

"More like Inspector Clouseau."

The waiter appeared with an order pad. When our pork dumplings arrived, she waved off another proffered pot of tea and ordered the next round of drinks without asking me. Shoving aside the chopsticks, she picked up her fork.

"I hate those damn things," she said. "I feel pretentious trying to eat with them."

A trace of the trailer park orphan appeared as she forked dumplings from the straw steamer vessel. Bent over her plate, she ate as though the waiter might suddenly reappear to take away the food. My presence seemingly forgotten, I wondered what the Delaudiers thought about her table manners, or if she cleaned up her act in their company. We ate without a word, and I found myself enjoying her lack of pretense in a city of wannabe sophisticates.

When we finished, she sat back with a contented sigh. "My favorite restaurant," she said. "My little town wasn't too keen on Chinese restaurants, and Marsh thinks Asian noodles are starchy junk."

I'd resisted asking about him, but she'd opened the door. "What's his position at Delaudier?"

"Our CFO," she said, vacuuming a noodle between her lips. "He drinks too much, but he's a really smart guy."

"I think we're supposed to say 'liquid dependency' today."

"Whatever, but he's sweet when he's sober."

I smothered a flash of jealousy. "What's his story?"

"Harvard grad," she drawled in Bostonese. "Left Wall Street to invest the Delaudiers' money. Marsh is the black sheep of his family, but scary smart about money. He doesn't know shit about art or people, but Roland claims he's a financial guru."

She raised her hand at the waiter. My two beers had tasted good. I pushed my luck and ordered a third. A three-beer lunch tested my capacity for a productive day, but Leslie seemed immune to the martinis.

"I just wondered," I said, trying to sound casual. "You two seemed close at Armands."

She didn't flinch. "I'm not sleeping with him if that's what you're asking."

I raised a shoulder in self-defense. "None of my business."

Our drinks arrived and we fell silent again. I rubbed the condensation on my glass and wondered if I'd overstepped my boundaries. "How do you to keep the Delaudiers happy?"

"I'm in charge of catalog production, advertising, whatever's needed to make us look good. Roland found I have a knack for it, and if other problems appear, I fix things so he and Isabelle don't work too hard. Like the scene with you and the old man." She brushed away another wisp of hair. "There's not much I can't handle."

Her smile concealed a hard undercurrent, and I believed her.

"Marsh told Isabelle about meeting you at Armands and she assumed the worst. She sees conspiracies where money's concerned. She believes you and Dansby are trying to drive down the da Vinci's price." She drained her glass. "She can be a bitch without much effort."

"Who was the Neanderthal by the door?"

"I'm guessing you mean Sal."

"What does he do?"

"Salvatore Testano. It's his job to know what happens in the building. He's tied to Isabelle's apron strings, her personal bodyguard. Possibly a little more, who knows."

"He looked at me like I was a free steak dinner."

Leslie wiped the corner of her mouth with a finger and grinned. "Gee, I wonder why."

It seemed the incident with Riva wasn't going away.

"And Roland?"

"He pretty much does whatever Isabelle tells him to do."

"Dansby says he's originally from Brussels. What about her?"

She shrugged. "Isabelle came to the States with him and they spend money like they're printing it. Although I'm not complaining."

"The business does that well?"

"That's a question you'd have to ask Marsh."

"Is Sal a partner?"

"God, no. He's protection. You were lucky he didn't find you and Riva in the lobby." She tapped the top of my hand. "You should know he's not happy about missing the opportunity. Isabelle pays him more than he's worth but keeps him on a tight leash."

"Good to hear."

She savored the martini and sat back. "Having money makes everything more fun, doesn't it?"

I changed the subject. "The catalogs are well done. Were you a marketing major?"

"Adam, I had one year of college."

"Sorry."

Great job, I thought, wondering if I could find another stupid thing to say. She seemed content to talk; the martinis were catching up with her.

"There wasn't much money after I paid my grandmother's hospital bills," she said. "Selling the Friescke got me on my feet and the job at Delaudier pays the bills. I'm not doing badly for a country girl nobody gave a shit about."

She picked up her martini glass and wrinkled her brow, realizing it was empty. Shrugging, she allowed the light back in her eyes.

"What's with the old man? Did he ever say why he caused a scene?"

"He's a Leonardo aficionado. Grew up in the same town in Italy and made a life study of him. He's harmless."

"I hope he hasn't been running around the Louvre yelling the Mona Lisa's a fake."

"Actually, I met with him. At his apartment. He lives alone."

"You saw him again?"

I held up two fingers. "Twice." I needed to believe I wasn't out of step and Leslie seemed an interested listener.

"He showed me an old book he claims could change everything we know about da Vinci's work."

"Really?" Her tone echoed Jean-Henri, and I wondered if I'd just ruined a nice lunch.

"What it contains refutes all the experts."

"That's ridiculous, right?"

No matter what, I couldn't get past the unusual signature. I held back telling her about it, or Melzi's notes. If that's what they were. I had only Riva's assurance Melzi had written the notes. I could be chasing phantoms, but every time I tried to dismiss the book, Riva's anger pulled me back like an anchor snagged on a stump. I'd Googled variations of Leonardo's initials and signatures without finding a match to what I saw on the Delaudier drawing. I started to tell her about my misgivings but figured I'd already created problems for her. The waiter arrived with the check to rescue me.

"My treat this time," she said, picking up the bill. "Let's hope for a happy ending. It's a wonderful piece and you have to admit the old guy isn't a Rhodes scholar. Your boss wants the drawing and my employers will make a lot of money. There may even be a few extra bucks left over for me."

The beers kicked in and I found myself nodding in agreement. Riva's book might be a clever hoax, another Degas. I'm no academic drone, and just maybe I'd been blinded by a likeable old man and a book everyone else saw as a pipedream. I lived an enjoyable life in New York under Dansby's wing and he'd forgiven my earlier gaffe. Why not ignore the complete disaster? New York wasn't my style, but I'd gotten lucky after the van Gogh, and I didn't need to add stupidity to my list of missteps. My gallery was afloat in Chicago and I was having lunch with a bright woman who grew up with more hard knocks than I. If I could reach beyond her destructive childhood, I might finally let go of Kat. No matter what happened between us, I wanted to see more of her. I lifted my empty glass.

"To our da Vinci," I toasted.

I liked the sound of 'our' and she touched my glass with hers, amazed that I'd discovered a kindred soul in a Chinese restaurant. We were two sides of the same card, born into a world that deemed us inconsequential. Smiling, we clinked again, and I pushed Riva back in his box.

Chapter Eleven

Twenty Kilometers outside Königsberg
January 5, 1945

Weisser saw the fallen trees across the road and trod on the brakes. The truck skidded and he lunged for the weapon just as he recognized German helmets. Remembering he was driving a Russian truck, he fumbled at the window handle. He rolled down the smudged glass, waving his arm and ducking his head against the expected fusillade of bullets.

"*Kameraden!*" he yelled. "*Ich bin Deutsche!*"

Three soldiers warily approached the truck, Shoulders draped in camouflaged ponchos, their long greatcoats dragged in the snow. Weisser stepped from the cab and showed his empty hands. A Waffen SS sergeant, muffled to his ears in woolen scarves, inspected him while the other two lifted the truck's canvas with their rifle barrels. An officer emerged from a camouflaged position beside the road and Weisser saw colonel's leaves on his collar. Relief swept over him until he remembered the crate.

He sprang to attention. "*Herr Standartenführer.*"

Swathed in layers of clothes, the colonel regarded Weisser with skepticism. His emaciated features seemingly carved by razor blades, he wore a soft peaked cap and enlisted man's poncho, a Schmeisser strapped across his back. He stopped in front of Weisser and inspected his SD collar patches.

"A fellow zealot," he said.

"Sir."

Haggard bearded faces stared at him, and Weisser tried not to stare at a body in a frozen pool of blood beside the road.

"Nothing in the truck but an old wooden crate, sir," called one of the soldiers.

The colonel turned to the sergeant. "We're short of ammunition and reinforcements and we get him," he said, gesturing at Weisser. He kept his eyes on him and inclined his head toward the body in the ditch. "Rudi there tried to slip away. One less rifle but deserters and cowards aren't much use to us, are they, sergeant?" The non-com shifted his Mauser and spat in the snow without lifting his gaze from Weisser. The wire-thin colonel grinned humorlessly. "What are you running from, Major?"

Heat crawled up Weisser's neck Best not to cross swords with a Waffen SS colonel, particularly one who looked as though he hadn't slept in a week. Weisser cleared his mind, aware he'd need his wits and more than luck to escape the colonel's clutches.

"Not running, sir," he said. "Following orders."

A grunt. "Hear that, sergeant? He has permission to leave the front."

"I have written orders to deliver a shipment for *Reichsmarschall* Göring. My orders are unmistakably clear."

He looked over Weisser's shoulder. "And you have a single truck all to yourself, *Sturmbannführer?*"

"If you'll allow me, sir."

The colonel sighed and gestured toward the GAZ as artillery erupted in the distance. "By all means, major," he said, "but hurry if you will. Time is short as you can hear."

The sergeant followed Weisser, who retrieved the papers. The colonel scanned them and returned the sheaf of papers.

"Typical," he grunted. "We need ammunition and you're hauling junk for Fat Hermann."

Weisser straightened and pretended offense. "I only follow my orders, as I'm sure you do, colonel."

His interrogator peered over Weisser's shoulder at the empty road, no longer listening. "Our orders are to delay the Ruskies. Hold their asses here as long as we can." He glanced at the sergeant who handed Weisser a bolt-action Mauser and helmet.

"Rudi won't need these any longer," the colonel said. "You do remember how to use a weapon other than your pistol, Major?"

Weisser's illusions about skirting the roadblock evaporated. Conscripted for a delaying action against Russian tanks meant the end of his dreams. And most likely his life. He scanned the woods for anti-tank guns but saw only two soldiers cradling tank-killing Panzerfausts, measuring their new recruit.

"Ivan needs this road for his tanks," the colonel said. "No way to maneuver through this damned forest. The division needs time to dig in and we're to delay the bastards as long as we can. We were promised tank support but I think someone forgot about us." He swung the submachine gun under his arm and studied Weisser with a look bordering on contempt.

"Welcome to the war, Major, and the ass-end of the Totenkopf Division."

"My orders…"

The colonel turned and walked away. "Don't mean shit now," he called. "Sergeant, show him his position."

Weisser kept his face neutral, calculating an argument would place him alongside Rudi in the ditch. He watched the GAZ driven a hundred yards down the road and parked between two trees, hastily camouflaged with branches.

The sergeant stepped beside him. "Major? This way."

Weisser followed the bent back, noting how few foxholes were scattered on both sides of the road. Camouflaged with rotted logs and piles of snow, they represented a forlorn hope at best.

"Do your duty, Major," the colonel yelled in a mocking voice.

Weisser replaced his fur cap with the dented helmet. A few curious faces turned to look at him but lost interest, intent on watching the road. The sergeant handed him a bandolier of extra rifle clips and pointed to a shallow foxhole a few yards off the road, the most forward position in the roadblock.

"Rudi's," the non-com said. He jumped the ditch and inspected the shallow depression with a professional's disgust. "You'll need more protection than this. Dig it deeper and pile limbs in front." He shot Weisser a sympathetic look. "I'd get my ass in gear if I was you," he said, adding a belated, "sir."

Weisser slung the Mauser and dragged broken limbs to the position. Scooping handfuls of dirty snow from the bottom with numbed hands, he resisted the urge to weep. The root-filled hole looked like a freshly dug grave, and Weisser recalled the old Rabbi's curse.

"… *We will bury you…*"

He eased into the foxhole and crouched low, shivering. Cold seeped through his two pairs of trousers, the smell of raw earth all too familiar as he recalled the pits and trenches. He piled the extra ammunition clips along the lip of the hole and inspected the greasy stain on the Mauser stock. Most likely all that was left of

Rudi, he thought. He tried to recall his combat training, but the truck drew his eyes back down the road. Only a short stroll away, the GAZ represented all his hopes and dreams, but it might as well be a thousand kilometers away at the moment. He patted his coat pocket for a cigarette and remembered he'd smoked the last one at the train station.

Nothing to be done but wait for a chance to break away. And pray an uncaring God would intervene to save him. If he panicked and ran for it now, he'd wind up with Rudi, and if he stayed in the damned hole, the Russians would kill him. Close to tears, he pressed his helmet against the earth, a fortune abandoned less than a hundred meters away.

"To be so close," he sobbed.

A banshee shrieked overhead. The road exploded and showered him with clods of earth. He eased his head above the foxhole rim. Three Russian T-34 tanks crested a rise several hundred yards away, the white-washed beasts surrounded by hordes of Russian infantry. More explosions drove him deeper into the hole. Another wail and Weisser hugged the ground. His gloves pawed at the frozen mud. He peered over the rim again and saw two white-caped German soldiers dart through the trees, lugging bulbous tank-killing *Panzerfäuste*.

Weisser groaned. Three Russian tanks and two *Panzerfäuste*.

He glimpsed a dirty white cape crouched behind a tree, the anti-tank weapon aimed at the lead tank. A sharp crack and the lead tank burst into flames with a satisfying *whump*. Russian infantry swept the woods with automatic fire, and the two remaining tanks trundled forward.

Behind him he heard the familiar clank of treads.

Two massive German Tiger tanks halted on the road. They opened fire and the second T-34 exploded, its turret crashing down beside the burning chassis. One of the Tigers fired again, and the remaining Russian tank erupted in flames.

More Russian tanks loomed behind the three wrecks, firing as they raced forward. A Tigers burst into flames and the other slammed into the ditch, smoke pouring from its open turret hatch.

Weisser had seen enough.

He bolted from the hole and ran. The colonel straddled the road, the Schmeisser aimed at Weisser's midsection, but a storm of Russian bullets flung the officer aside. Weisser leaped over the body and ran past the burning Tigers, losing his helmet as acrid black smoke choked him. He could not bring himself to look back as more men leapt from their holes and sprinted for the rear, the roadblock disintegrating. The GAZ was less than a few meters away.

Weisser's ankle turned in an icy rut and he fell, flinging the rifle away as he regained his feet. He scrambled into the truck cab and fumbled at the ignition switch. The starter whirred and died. Bullets churned snow and trees around the truck. The engine caught on his third try. Two soldiers lunged for the running boards and missed, their cries lost in the explosions. The truck fishtailed onto the road, tracers crisscrossing in the rear mirror. Weisser flinched, but no bullets ripped into the tailgate. Head down, he kept the accelerator on the floor. After a few kilometers he let out his breath and switched on the headlights, allowing the truck to settle into a cautious pace again.

Twilight descended on the massacre behind him. The sounds faded and darkness swallowed the headlight beams, the only light in the forest. The unmarked road forked, and he blindly swerved right where he hoped the sea waited.

The engine stuttered and coughed twice. Weisser swallowed the lump in his throat, remembering the bearded Rabbi's curse. The noise settled back into its monotonous drone and he ran a hand over his face. *To hell with the old Jew. Reason and intellect triumphed over a dead religion.*

Refusing to accept the prospect the road might cut by partisans, he concentrated on the feeble headlight beams. The road twisted and turned, the forest closing around him like a collapsing tunnel. What if the desolate road was a dead end? He glanced at the petrol gauge approaching the Empty mark. He groaned and hunched forward, coiling his aching fingers around the steering wheel, willing the truck forward until his hands and shoulders throbbed.

He pushed away the pain and recalled the instant he saw the crate's contents. Not just a tourist in a museum this time - it was his! He was the treasure's last hope, its savior. Providence would not let him die beneath Russia's godforsaken snow.

Smiling through cracked lips, he rolled down the window and imagined he smelled the sea.

Chapter Twelve

New York
Late Afternoon

Ready to leave the office next day, Clarice peeped her head around my door and with a look of pity. "You're being summoned again,"

I entered the lion's den and found Dansby at the window peering down at the street, his back to me. This seemed his favorite perch to ponder decisions. He waved a hand in my direction without turning.

"Close the doors."

I pulled the pocket doors shut and sat on the couch Jean-Henri had occupied during our last meeting. Foregoing his throne behind the desk, Dansby took the armchair across from me.

"We need to talk again about what's happened," he said. "Morrison could be right."

I kept my mouth shut. I wanted to avoid another argument with the man paying my bills. I didn't press the issue that I was certain the da Vinci was not a da Vinci. My lunch with Leslie almost persuaded me otherwise, but not quite.

"You're sure about what you saw?" Dansby asked.

Before I could answer, a knock interrupted us. The doors slid open and Jean-Henri saw me. He started to leave when Dansby called to him.

"No, come in."

Jean-Henri selected a seat at the far end of the couch. Clarice followed him with a porcelain pot of tea. She placed the tray on the inlaid coffee table and poured a cup for the Frenchman, returning in a moment with two mugs for Dansby and me. The coffee arrived in white ceramic mugs bearing Dansby's former Guards regimental badge. Despite the British preference for tea, he'd converted to American coffee. I preferred a stronger option, but accepted the heavy cup with a sly look from Clarice.

"We were discussing the auction again," Dansby said. "And Adam's book."

Jean-Henri poised mid-sip and rose to the bait. "I thought Manfred made it clear this old book's a legend."

Despite my best intentions, I couldn't keep my mouth shut. "The book clearly shows Donato Volpe created the work."

Jean-Henri avoided my eyes and made a show of blowing on his Earl Grey. "Absurd."

"I accept you're the authority," I said, "but Melzi catalogued most of Leonardo's important work."

"You can't be certain Melzi even authored this book of yours."

"You can't be certain he didn't."

Jean-Henri exhaled, out of patience. "You're unable to produce this book of yours, yet you have no problem dismissing noted scholars who examined the drawing."

Dansby held up his hand. "Enough. I want to talk about Roland's hoard of da Vincis."

"Were you aware there were more?"

"No, and that concerns me."

"Do you trust the Delaudiers?"

"As much as any auction house."

"Until you examine the book, I think we should be wary of them," I said.

Jean Henri looked imploringly at Dansby. "The drawing we saw is priceless, Phillip. Why not these others?"

Dansby went to his desk and returned with a glossy white folder that bore the Delaudier logo. He removed three 8x10 photographs and spread them side by side on the table. Jean-Henri and I leaned over them.

A metal ruler lay beside each drawing. The style seemed unmistakable. Each drawing measured approximately 10x14, the ink impressions rendered on sepia-tone paper. The drawing we inspected. A woman with exquisite facial detail. A shy young child rendered from a three-quarter perspective, looking back over her shoulder. The troubling *DV* signature appeared in the lower right corners of all three.

"Beautiful," breathed Jean-Henri. "The same experts vetted them?"

Dansby nodded and returned the photos to the folder. "Including Morrison."

Still holding the folder, he went to the window. "These are appealing, but the first drawing tops them by a mile." He turned to me. "I want it."

The more he ignored my misgivings, the larger they loomed. He had to inspect the book.

"And I want to be certain you don't make a costly mistake."

"The Italian book again," Jean-Henri scoffed.

I slid the photos apart. "Delaudier said there were three other works. There's only two here. Where's the other one?"

He shrugged. "Possibly he counted my da Vinci as the third."

My da Vinci. In his mind, he already owned Donato Volpe's drawing.

"The three of us need to agree these are on the level," I said.

Jean-Henri joined Dansby at the window. "'On the level'? Now there's a new academic term."

Dansby stared out the glass and tapped the folder against his palm. I sensed his growing impatience.

He turned back to me. "Occasionally, I rather think you're carrying this Doubting Thomas thing too far, Adam."

"I thought that's one reason you brought me to New York."

"I didn't intend for you to raise havoc in the process."

To hell with both of them. I was doing my job. Dansby hired me to track down what others overlooked, but I found myself in a war with academics. Every self-preservation instinct told me to walk away. If he wanted to gamble millions on a mis-attributed da Vinci, I couldn't stop him. He had big financial shoulders and could survive a mistake, and I could catch the next flight to Chicago. His money kept me afloat, but being Jean-Henri's whipping boy wasn't in my job description.

"Then buy the damn thing. Phillip," I said. "You've got your watchdog's guarantee."

Jean-Henri rose and marched to the pocket doors. He pulled them open and walked out without looking back. Dansby's shoulders sagged, revealing the soft spot in his armor: a spoiled child with tunnel vision, disappointed his new Xbox failed to live up to expectations.

He regained his composure and closed the doors, resettling in his chair. "He's a touchy bird but he'll get over it. Remember, he has a reputation to uphold."

"And you should remember I didn't fall off a turnip truck."

He straightened, opened his mouth and shut it. We had a long history, and we both realized we had reached a point that put it at risk. Instead, he changed the subject.

"This woman who works for the Delaudiers," he said. "The striking blond. It's none of my business, you understand, but I take it you'd met her before?"

"Only casually."

"She's quite lovely." He looked straight at me. "Are you getting past Katia's ghost?"

A tinge of guilt. "Leslie Strickland is a woman I met in Armands."

"Lucky boy."

"I appreciate your interest, but I'm more concerned about the drawing." I didn't see any reason to tell him about my lunch with Leslie. I didn't need more complications at this point in the game.

"What does she know about the da Vincis?"

It was a fair question. "I have no idea."

"What do you know about *her*?"

"Phillip."

He tented his fingers at his lips to hide his smile.

"How did we get from the da Vinci to my love life?"

"Just remember all work and no play makes Adam a bore."

I let him enjoy his dissection of my personal life. "At least you appear to have an ally at Delaudier," he said. "You'll need one after making enemies of Roland and Isabelle."

"Are you sure I should go with you to the next auction?"

"Who'll stop me? They like my money too much."

He had a point, but it didn't make me feel better. I started to ask him to accompany me to Riva's apartment but decided I needed to have a talk with Jean-Henri first. He and I were working at cross-purposes. Bashing heads, to be more accurate. Worse, we'd crossed a line and become adversaries. The time had arrived to confront him, if for no other reason than to come to find a working relationship. I'd known Dansby since my boyhood, but my status, despite the van Gogh, couldn't match Jean-Henri's encyclopedic wisdom. He represented inestimable value to Dansby, while I remained the long-shot. Jean-Henri and I played the roles of loyal sons devoted to pleasing a father figure, but we'd allowed sibling rivalry to come between us. I needed a truce. Otherwise, we were all rushing into a very expensive disaster.

• • •

I trekked to the Jean-Henri's office at the end of the hall, planning what to say. I found him sitting at his glass top desk surrounded by books. His office was pin neat as though organized by Martha Stewart, mine as if a goat had wandered in and thrown up.

I closed the door. Laying his pen on a legal pad where he'd been making notes, he looked up as if expecting me. He sat back with a knowing smile.

"I imagine you've decided we must have an understanding of sorts."

I added clairvoyance to his considerable skills. Despite my good intentions, I felt as though I'd entered the headmaster's office to explain why I broke curfew.

I forced a smile. "You read my mind."

"Well, sit down." He went to a mahogany sideboard beside his desk where a set of delicate cups and saucers flanked a silver teapot. "Tea?"

"No, thanks."

Like Dansby's office, a vast window admitted a stream of sunlight. The late afternoon sun divided the room in two, leaving Jean-Henri in shadow. Surprisingly, the office contained no paintings; the walls decorated only with black-and-white photographs of Paris and New York. Two silver-framed 8x10 studio photographs of his partner Gerry stood on his desk.

He poured a cup of tea and resumed his chair. "I think people believe my drinking tea is an affectation to please Phillip," he said, "but actually, he prefers coffee, while I cannot abide American coffee."

These were the first words I'd heard him utter that did not pertain to art. Gathering his thoughts, he closed an open book beside the pad. "I assume you want to discuss this book of yours," he said.

"That and reach accommodation."

"Then let's get to the crux of the matter, shall we?"

"Riva's book, the da Vincis, or my working here?"

"Ah! *Un homme simple.* Right to the heart of the matter," he said. "Actually, all three, but let's talk about the first two."

No dancing or obtuse preliminaries. "I know you don't believe the book is authentic."

"*Non.* I do not. I don't know what you were shown, but it changes nothing."

"Then we've agreed to disagree on the first point. If I'm sure about anything, I'm sure Melzi's book is real. You have a right to your doubts, but what I saw should at least be examined. What I do mind is you putting me down in front of Phillip. You have your job and I have mine."

"I acknowledge that." He took a sip of tea and returned to the sideboard to add cream, leaning against the edge as he looked down at me. "Your job is to chase ghosts, while I prevent Phillip from making expensive mistakes. The forged Degas was a good example."

One point to him.

"And if I can produce the book, what then?"

He shrugged. "Then I will make a determination."

"The notation I saw attributed the drawing to Donato Volpe. Melzi's entire book is a record of what Leonardo created and what his students produced.

"So the legend claims."

Exasperated, I said, "You haven't seen it. The sheer volume left little doubt that I held proof in my hands."

"I don't doubt you saw an old book, but was Francesco Melzi the author, or did an unknown proclaim himself an authority on Leonardo? That person wouldn't have been the first to do so. You cannot be certain unless experts study the book."

"The signature on the drawing we examined is wrong," I persisted. "I never found where daVinci signed in that manner."

A patronizing smile. "You are an expert on how he signed every drawing and painting, *n'est pas?*"

All this was accomplishing nothing. I had nothing to offer other than what I saw at Delaudier was not da Vinci's work. Jean-Henri's arrogance and closed mind put everything at risk, including my relationship with Dansby. Rushing to defend myself, I blurted out my first angry thought.

"You and your gay friends believe the rest of us are simple-minded," I said, feeling heat fill my face. "That somehow the straight world lacks your sensitivity and intelligence." It was a baseless accusation, and I watched his eyes fill with hurt and resentment.

"I see you find my... lifestyle disagreeable. Does that give you the right to ignore academic objectivity?"

Embarrassed, I held up both hands, conceding my thoughtless accusation. I had no defense, and my temper only made things worse. "I apologize. I don't give a damn about your lifestyle or your sexual preferences. This is about Phillip not making a mistake."

Obviously struggling with his emotions, Jean-Henri stood. "We have nothing more to discuss."

I remained seated without moving. I had screwed up. His personal life was none of my business. He was one of the most recognizable experts in the country, and I had just blindsided him. He was welcome to whatever choices suited his genes, and my attack had widened the valley between us. I reluctantly got to my feet and walked back to my office, hearing him softly close his door behind me.

Clarice met me in the hall with a stack of Delaudier catalogs I'd requested.

"Is Phillip still around?"

She shook her head. "He left a few minutes ago."

My options fast evaporating, I needed to put Riva's book in Phillip's hands.

• • •

It was dark when I left the office. I tossed the catalogs into a drawer and found I was the last to leave. I started back to Jean-Henri's office to apologize again, but changed my mind. He was gone, and the damage was done.

I passed a new bookstore on my way home and stopped to look in the window. After a few moments, I realized I wasn't in the mood to browse, unable to stop replaying my confrontation with Jean-Henri.

The Franklin Place complex where I lived was a refurbished office building that included trendy shops and a pricey convenience store at street level. Most of the stores were open and shoppers packed the lobby, the mosaic brown and cream marble floor a survivor of pre-renovation days. Nodding at familiar faces, I took the elevator to the fifth floor.

I touched my key to the door lock, and the door swung open. Faint light from the street cast a murky glow across the living room, the rest of the interior in darkness.

Looking up and down the empty hall, I stood in the doorway, debating what I should do. This was New York, where I knew better than to boldly go, where a stranger had gone before. I should have taken the elevator back to the lobby to find security. Instead, I took a tentative step inside and found the light switch.

My bookshelves were empty, books scattered everywhere. Not a single volume remained on the shelves and my disfigured coffee table lay on its side, one leg broken off. Books were strewn from wall to wall, many ripped apart, broken picture frames flung against the walls. I picked up an enormous book of Impressionist reproductions. Pages were ripped out as though the intruder acted in a frenzy.

I walked through the carnage, wondering if the thief spared my bedroom. I flicked on the light. Half of my most prized art volumes were strewn across the bed and on the floor. My anger peaked, and I stepped inside without thinking.

Something heavy banged into the back of my skull. Suns exploded and my last conscious sensation was face-down on the floor, fuzzy carpet fibers in my mouth.

• • •

The overweight police sergeant exhaled cigarette breath and watched the EMT gently part my hair, searching for signs of bleeding. The young paramedic sported a bushy moustache and cropped blond beard. He gave the impression of teenager surfer masquerading as an adult, but his fingers were gentle as he dabbed antiseptic on the lump.

"How long was I out?" I muttered.

"Hard to say." The youthful guy wiped his hands. "More than a few minutes for sure."

The cop leaned closer and peered at the swelling on the back of my head, his blue uniform reeking of tobacco and dried sweat. "You're lucky, Mister… Barrow" he said, reading my name off the New York driver's license he had removed from my wallet. "A resident saw your open door and called downstairs."

"I don't feel lucky."

Slumped forward with my arms on my knees, I winced as the white-coat eased me back against the couch cushions. I looked around at my living room that begged for federal disaster relief. The sergeant straightened, wheezing as he adjusted his pistol belt and surveyed the ruins.

"You gotta lot of old books here," he said, inspecting the apartment. "Any antiques or other stuff that might attract a scumbag?"

I gingerly shook my head. "New sound system and a few of original watercolors. Nothing else worth stealing."

He shoved a book with his toe and looked at the remains of my little library. "Looks like a nut case or junkies who got their kicks trashing the place. You need to check all your belongings and see what's missing."

The EMT handed me a plastic ice pack. "Keep that on the swelling tonight," he said. "There's no blood, but you need to go to the hospital and let them check for a concussion." He patted my arm. "I think the NFL would bar you from the next couple of games."

When he left, the policeman picked up a shadeless brass lamp just inside the bedroom. Holding it up by its ferrule with a handkerchief, he dangled it in front of me. "I think your burglar used this when you interrupted him. The detectives will check for fingerprints." He gave a modest belch, an invisible fog of raw onions filling the air between us as he pointed to the square lamp base. "Ain't my job, but my guess is you got thumped with the flat side, not the edge. Otherwise, we'd be bagging you up."

"I guess this is my initiation to New York."

"You new here?"

"Yeah." The word made my head throb.

"Welcome to the Big Apple, rotten core and all."

He told me again to check everything and that a detective would talk with me tomorrow. After he and the EMT crew left, I sat back and held the ice pack in place, surveying my living room. Too bad the city didn't add clean-up assistance to police and medical services. A lot of my books were a total loss, but Dansby knew people who could repair the other damages.

I closed my eyes and levered my body off the couch, clutching the armrest until I was certain I could walk without sampling the carpet again. A quick inspection of the apartment showed nothing missing. My CD player, desktop computer and state-of-the-art turntable were untouched. Even my spare watch and two twenty-dollar bills remained on my dresser.

With the ice bag held against the back of my head, I experienced the customary aftermath of being violated. In the kitchen I took the vodka bottle from my freezer and poured a healthy shot, returning to the couch. It was obvious I'd disturbed the thief before he could grab anything of value, but why destroy my books and almost kill me? The cop's theory about a freaked-out meth freak made the only sense.

Chapter Thirteen

East Prussia
Outskirts of Königsberg
January 6, 1945

The truck swerved toward the ditch. Weisser jerked awake and swore. He wrestled the vehicle back into the cement-like ruts, the tires hard as stone as they spun for traction on the icy road.

"*Scheisse.*"

He rubbed his heavy eyelids with the thumb of his glove. He'd drifted off for a moment, back at the pit with the rabbi hurling senseless Yiddish at him. He took a rasping breath and swore at his lapse. He'd cheated death at the roadblock and escaped by sheer luck. By all odds he should be lying dead with the other fools, but mental lapses killed you as surely as a Russian bullet. Maybe the old Teutonic gods decided his cargo was too valuable to destroy. He always believed great art assumed a life of its own and he'd been appointed its guardian. Clinging to the thought, he rubbed his face again, the skin numb with cold. Every breath produced a translucent veil of fog. But he was alive and that was all that mattered.

He picked up the canteen to splash water over his face and found its contents frozen solid. He tossed it against passenger door and tried to ignore the trees pressing against the road. The forest slid by like an out-focus film strip as though resenting the truck's intrusion. Weisser saw no signs of human life. Only abandoned farms and outbuildings among the trees, as though he'd made a wrong turn into a universe without war. If such a thing still existed, he imagined an emerald city where he would sell his cargo to the highest bidder. With a new name he'd become a new man, a respected owner of fine art.

His eyelids fluttered. Adulation by his peers and formal parties where he'd be a guest of honor. Tables laden with delicacies. Fine wines and good beer. Dancing and willing women. He could almost touch the fantasies. Just a few more kilometers…

He jolted awake again. Swiping a half-frozen gloved hand across his eyes, he yelled at himself. He'd survived the attack at the barricade, but lack of sleep pursued him like a wolf that smelled a wounded rabbit. Another day on the road and he'd end up in a ditch, killing him as surely as a Russian peasant in uniform. He squinted through the smeared windshield, weary of frozen skies that smothered the sun.

Goddamn the cold!

Worst winter on record, the communiques claimed. Minus 25 degrees Celsius. The endless miles of snow were unable to mask a pungent odor, a sour smell one could almost taste. Leaves, earth and corpses as though the godless Russians rediscovered the Czar's God and enlisted Him to punish the fleeing German army.

Behind him, persistent artillery murmured above the clattering engine. He resisted the urge to look back, afraid of veering off the road again. If an advance Russian patrol found him, he would be an easy target. His only hope was to keep moving, willing Königsberg to be free of ice.

Despite his resolve, his fear of being captured by the Russians returned. The dregs of all Russia. Mongols and ignorant peasants from Siberia and God knows where. The Russians weren't taking SS prisoners, and worse rumors were circulating. Torture. Mutilation.

Unbuttoning his coat, he ripped off the SS skull and crossbones and stuffed his identification booklet between the seat cushions. Regaining control, he submerged his fear and settled into an agonizing 20 kilometers per hour, his legs cramped, his buttocks slabs of refrigerated flesh. He hadn't seen a German presence since the roadblock and he'd been lucky so far. His rank would get him past roaming field police, especially if they believed his tale about Göring's crate. After all, SS officers didn't desert in the face of the enemy, did they?

Ahead, clusters of figures materialized out of the mist. Weisser slid the PPS closer, slowing until he recognized trudging files of civilians pulling handcarts, German women and children fleeing the Russian onslaught. Spread across the road, there was no way around the rabble, possessions piled atop every conceivable conveyance,

He braked. A woman in a ragged shawl scrambled onto the running board, her breath fogging the window. She clutched the sill and he reluctantly rolled down the window. Plump and young, Weisser didn't find her attractive, but she would be prime fodder for Russian soldiers bent on revenge.

"Is there room in your truck for the children?"

Weisser waved her away. "*Nein, nein.* I have ammunition to deliver to Königsberg. You are blocking the road."

"Just a few?" she begged. "Inside the cab with you?"

Desperate faces crowded closer, more children appearing.

"The Russians…" she said, her voice wedged between fear and pleading. "We're hearing stories. They—"

Weisser almost weakened. He looked down at the grimy child gripping his mother's hand, but the moment passed. The crate meant too much. He pried the woman's fingers from the truck and yelled at the others crowded around the truck.

"Get off the road!"

Distant artillery sounded again. The woman's eyes widened, and she reached down for the child, holding the girl up to the window.

"Please, take my daughter."

The filthy child peered at him, dirty fingers grasping the sill. Revulsion swept over Weisser. If the Reich fell, no decent German deserved to live in the infamy that would follow. People such as these had squandered their place in history. Cowards and slackers deserved what they'd earned.

Weisser shoved the child away. Mother and daughter fell onto the road, the woman's hand stretching toward him in final supplication. He ignored her, jammed the gear lever into first and released the clutch. The truck bounded forward, scattering the exiles. Heedless of arms that grabbed at the canvas sides, Weisser looked away from the side mirror and kept his eyes on the road, tires thumping over dropped possessions.

Crowded together, the refugees watched their deliverance disappear in the fog.

Chapter Fourteen

Dansby, Haley, and I emerged from the stretch limo fifteen minutes before the Delaudier's second auction. It was only a brief walk from the office, but he'd invited Haley and that warranted a limo ride.

I approached the garishly lit building apprehensively, the exterior more sterile than my last disastrous visit. Maybe the lump on my head skewed my thinking, but I believed great works of art deserved settings that drew more attention than their owners.

The night sky threatened rain. Gusts of wind buffeted the front windows, the lobby chandeliers swaying as employees ushered us through the immense entrance doors. Haley's generous decolletage was on full display, a perfect setting for a glittering diamond necklace. A gift from Dansby? I trailed the glittering pair, feeling I'd returned to a crime scene.

A buzz followed us down the center aisle. With Haley clinging to his arm, Phillip appeared in his element, flashing his patented smile and stopping twice to shake hands, waving at others in the crowd.

Roland Delaudier had reserved three seats for us on the first row beneath the auctioneer's podium. Murmurs quieted as we took our chairs, Phillip next to me. On the other side of the aisle, Leslie Strickland sat beside the Delaudiers, Marsh Hampton by her side. She gave me a small frown and touched the back of her head with a questioning look. I nodded and shrugged as all four of them leaned forward to stare at me.

Hail, hail, I thought, the gang's all here. The Horsemen of the Apocalypse, plus Dansby's forty million dollars. Okay, Leslie wasn't Death or Famine, but I wondered about the others. Dansby leaned close to my ear.

"See anyone who looks like your assailant?"

"Here?" I said.

"Don't be fooled. A lot of the biggest thieves in New York are sitting here."

Forearms on my knees, I stared at the forest green carpet as Phillip chatted with Haley. Her charms on display for those around us, I sensed I'd become invisible despite my role in the last auction. I twisted in my chair and scanned the sea of faces, hoping Enzo Riva hadn't slipped past security. In reality, I guessed he occupied his lumpy chair cradling the grappa bottle. Part of me hoped he had sense to stay away, and another side wanted Dansby to experience his fervor. Whatever motivated him, the old guy wasn't a whacked-out activist.

Dansby caught me looking around. "Looking for the old man?"

"I guess."

"Let's hope he stays away. I want this piece."

"I'll say it again, Phillip. Don't bid on it."

His jaw muscles knotted and I went back to inspecting the carpet, the evening's events out of my hands. Dansby paid me to use my eyes and brain, but it was his money and if he wanted to throw away his money, I couldn't stop him. Being told to butt out, I vowed to keep my mouth shut, but it grated on me. I recalled the moment I first laid eyes on the hidden van Gogh, knowing what I saw was undoubtedly the real thing. Now, the sensation reversed itself. Riva's book was a reality, and I almost wished he'd run onto the stage, shouting his mantra: *'It is not da Vinci!'*

The stage curtain rustled, and the same auctioneer stepped to the lectern. He shuffled notes and looked up with an ingratiating smile.

"Good evening again. As I'm sure you're aware, this is a special Delaudier auction. We're offering only a single item tonight, hopefully without the theatrics."

An undertone rippled through the crowd and two assistants brought the drawing onto the stage and reverently centered it on the easel beside the podium. Dansby leaned forward and fixed his eyes on the gilded frame. Without a paddle, he knew the auctioneer would have eyes on him. It would require only a nod to bid.

The auctioneer smoothed his tuxedo lapels and pulled the microphone closer. "All right, ladies and gentlemen, let's begin by reviewing the unquestioned legitimacy of this exquisite da Vinci, shall we? As the catalog states, a panel of highly qualified experts vetted the drawing, led by Professor Alphonso Denardo of Rome, followed by…"

I tuned out the sales pitch. Roland and Isabelle Delaudier were taking no chances, reminding bidders that the old man's outburst meant less than nothing.

The auctioneer droned on, hyping the bona fides in detail, citing a laundry list of authorities in the United States and abroad, followed by five minutes of indecipherable scientific detail to lull potential bidders into a catatonic state of reassurance.

Eyes fixed on the drawing, I tried to dismiss Riva's outrage and Melzi's sketches. Da Vinci was both men's passion, but had I misread the frightened old man? Was Riva so scared he suppressed the truth?

The auctioneer leaned close to the mike. "Ladies and gentlemen, let's begin the bidding, shall we? May I have a starting bid of five million?"

A paddle went up in the back of the room.

"I have five million. Do I hear ten?"

Another paddle several rows behind us."

"Ten million is bid. May I have fifteen?"

Dansby raised a finger. The auctioneer nodded.

"I have fifteen million in the front row for this lovely da Vinci."

It is not da Vinci!

I touched Dansby's arm and shook my head, unable to contain the impulse. He shot me a look and jerked his arm away.

The auctioneer looked at Delaudier, then the bank of telephones. "I have fifteen million. Do I hear twenty?"

A young woman at one end of the phone desk raised a finger and nodded.

"Very good. I have twenty million from our phone bidder. May I have twenty-five million?"

Dansby nodded again.

"Ah! I now have twenty-five million down front. Do I hear thirty?"

The auctioneer glanced at the phone bank where the young woman nodded again. "Very good. I have thirty million."

Before I had time to think, I clutched Dansby's wrist, his ivory cufflink biting into my palm. "Don't do this, Phillip."

He glared at me with a look I'd never seen, the face his SAS enemies saw during their last seconds on earth. I tightened my grip. I'd stepped over a boundary. For reasons I couldn't put into words, Enzo Riva's warning overshadowed my future and Dansby's millions.

The auctioneer pointed his gavel at an older gentleman behind us.

"Thank you, sir. I have thirty-five million from the gentleman in the fourth row."

Dansby looked at my hand. He paused for a long moment and glanced at the bank of telephones. The young woman at one end caught the look and looked away.

"Thirty-five is the bid," the auctioneer repeated, looking down at Dansby. "Do I hear forty?"

Dansby eased his wrist from my grip. The room fell silent, unaware of the battle we'd just waged. I waited for his head nod, surprised when he sat back with a bare shake of his head. A murmur went through the audience. Roland Delaudier leaned forward and scrutinized Dansby.

The auctioneer stared down at Dansby again. "The bid is thirty-five million. I need forty."

Dansby didn't move. The auctioneer glanced at the Delaudiers. "Last chance," he said. "The bid now stands at thirty-five million."

Ten seconds passed in the hushed room before the gavel rapped the podium top. "Sold to Mister Howard Tenenbaum for thirty-five million dollars."

A burst of conversation and people stood, heads turned toward Dansby who remained in his chair. He whispered to Haley, who appeared more confused than usual. He didn't look at me, his gaze following the da Vinci as it disappeared behind the curtain.

I stared at the empty podium, uncertain what had just happened. It was as though Big Ben abruptly stopped, the gong muzzled, clock hands spinning in reverse. Haley mirrored my confusion and stared at Dansby. I watched Leslie follow Marsh Hampton up the aisle without looking back as animated conversation broke out in the crowded room. The Delaudiers walked to us, Isabelle glaring down at me.

"You missed it, Phillip," Roland said, his voice hovering between disappointment and resentment. He looked around to make certain the chairs behind us were empty. "You let the old Jew steal it from you. Tenenbaum got the bargain of the century."

Dansby stood and speared Delaudier with a stare he reserved for business adversaries. "Howard's a friend, Roland." His anger receded, and he replaced it with an affable grin. "I simply liked several others you showed me. Why buy one da Vinci when I might acquire two or three?"

Delaudier sighed, momentarily mollified. "Well, I'm glad you're still in the game. I'd hate to see you miss an opportunity"

"That's unlikely unless your telephone bidders become over-enthusiastic again."

Roland opened his mouth and shut it. Isabelle looked as though she regretted not having a pistol in her sleek silver purse.

"Next time, Roland," Dansby said, slapping him on the shoulder. "I'll look forward to the next auction."

They shook hands and the Delaudiers left us exiled beneath the podium. I found myself staring at the empty stage, wondering what role I'd played in Dansby's abrupt change of mind.

"Jean-Henri won't be a happy camper," I said.

Dansby slipped his arm around Haley's waist and gave me a rueful grin. "He'll get over it in a year or two."

"You didn't believe me, Phillip. What changed your mind?"

His eyes were fixed on Delaudier's staff and workmen who were busy disconnecting the telephones and stripping tablecloths. He started to reply, then kissed Haley's cheek and gently patted her rear.

"Darling," he said, "why don't you go find a glass of champagne in the foyer? I'll be along in a moment."

His eyes followed her up the aisle, the view a welcome respite from the past few minutes. I looked around to be certain we were out of earshot.

"Roland's not happy," I said.

"I know. The old charlatan expected the da Vinci to bring a lot more."

"I don't think you bowed out because of me. You wanted this piece and had no intention of letting me stop you. What changed your mind?"

"I'm not certain," Dansby said absently.

The workers were hauling away tables, and he seemed absorbed in the activity on the empty stage. "It occurred to me that Roland and Isabelle always employ the same bevy of experts when there's a debatable offering."

"I would think that's in their favor."

Dansby looked at me as though I'd failed my mid-terms. "It's a little too cozy."

When you can spend eight figures on a craving, temptation becomes an enemy if you want to remain a billionaire. I was a neophyte in Dansby's universe and knew he trusted only a few people. Stories had appeared about several individuals who tried to swindle him and were never found. Police investigations came to nothing. No one filed charges, but Dansby didn't reach his elevated status by allowing those who cheated him to saunter away.

"I think Roland smelled blood in the water," he said.

"You don't trust his research?"

"God, no! When there's significant money on the table, there are always a few in academia who see an escape from their dreary salaries. They're human, which translates into bribable. I trust Jean-Henri, but damn few others." Dansby looked back at the bare podium as though willing the da Vinci to reappear.

"Let's put it another way," he said. "I learned a long time ago that whatever you most desire doesn't simply fall in your lap, especially if you make your desires known. Having sufficient money is never a substitute for caution. I'll possibly hate you in the morning, but tonight I needed more certainty about what I was buying."

"I'm flattered you put forty million dollars of trust in me."

"You played a part, but don't get above yourself, dear boy."

"What did I miss?"

Dansby smiled in a way that made me glad I wasn't one of his enemies or competitors. "An old ruse, I think. One discreetly employed in the auction world in certain dire circumstances. I may be getting old, but I'm still aware of my flanks as it were. Like you, I must depend on my instincts and tonight didn't smell right."

"You lost me."

The smile disappeared. "The telephones. Telephone bidding is common enough, but I always imagined invisible buyers create a temptation, a clever way for the house to run up the bidding if it's willing to gamble. Or is desperate or unscrupulous. If so, they plant a phantom bidder on the phone or in the audience. Keep the bidding moving upward, but the auctioneer's got to judge the moment. If he ends up with the sham bid, the house goes home with the goat."

"Are the Delaudiers that desperate?"

Dansby shrugged. "The da Vinci represents an impressive amount of money, especially when one considers they appear to own it outright. It also concerns me there's scant provenance. For example, if it were to come to light that it's Nazi war loot, I'd find myself in a major lawsuit and most likely lose whatever I paid." He looked back at the stage again. "Where the deuce *did* they acquire it?"

I'd wondered the same thing.

"They've always been above reproach," he said, "but it's possible old Tanenbaum may have gotten us off the hook."

"But if the Delaudiers are making money hand over fist, why take a chance with a scheme that obvious?"

"I have no idea, none at all."

I realized Dansby had his own questions and possibly doubts about the da Vinci and the Delaudiers. Maybe, I decided, I played a part in his change of mind. Feeling partially vindicated, I followed him up the aisle as he headed toward Haley. It had been a long evening, and I was convinced more than ever that Enzo Riva needed to show Dansby his book.

Chapter Fifteen

Next morning, rain showers descended again with no sign of relenting. I pushed aside paperwork Clarice had left on my desk and flopped back in my chair. I wanted closure to the whole damn issue, and Riva held the answers. I pulled out my cell to call him and remembered he didn't have a phone.

Resigned to finding a cab in the metropolitan monsoon, I picked up my raincoat when the desk phone rang. I almost ignored it, but the thought of dodging downpour beneath a tired umbrella reordered my priorities.

I snatched up the receiver. "Adam Barrow."

"Well, you're in a delightful mood," Leslie Strickland said.

I tossed the raincoat and umbrella on my chair and sat on the corner of the desk, her voice taking the edge off my mood. "It's raining and my coffee's cold."

"Poor baby. All the more reason to talk to me."

"You made a quick getaway last night." My imagination formed unpleasant pictures about what happened after she disappeared with Marsh Hampton.

"Marsh and I were the designated hosts at a reception after the auction," she said. "Isabelle expected us to put a good face on what she considered a catastrophe. Given the original estimate, she thinks we left millions on the table."

"Auctions produce surprises." What was I supposed to say?

"She and Roland believed Dansby had a higher level of interest."

"What did you think?"

I could almost feel her shrug over the phone. "It's not my job to second guess bidders."

"Dansby's full of contradictions, but he's unbelievably savvy beneath all the bluster."

"Savvy is an understatement."

"I didn't want him to make a mistake, but it's ultimately his decision."

"Isabelle and Roland are worried the old man influenced his decision. I think they need him now, especially his money."

I didn't mention his suspicions about the phone bids or a panel of experts. "I thought the auction went well. Dansby may have set a lower price in his mind."

"Maybe, but Isabelle believes the first auction played a part. All that business with you and Enzo Riva."

"Dansby and Jean-Henri don't give Riva's claims much credence," I said, a polite way of admitting they thought I'd overstepped my boundaries with Dansby. "If Jean-Henri Bonnet tells Dansby white is black, Dansby rarely argues." That wasn't always the case, but it was near the mark. The Frenchman's sway over him trumped my influence by a mile.

"Well, what's done is done," she said. "I just wanted to make sure you're okay. I know you're busy."

She waited and I cursed myself. Say something, dammit!

"I meant to call you," I said. "Matheny's CD is great."

"I wasn't going to talk to you again if you hated it."

"Let me buy you dinner and I'll give you a review."

"When?"

"Pick a night. My social calendar's clear."

"Friday, then," she said. "You select the place this time."

"Any particular restaurants you avoid?"

"None. I'm in your hands."

A tempting image. "I'll surprise you."

Chapter Sixteen

On Friday, I called Leslie and told her I'd pick her up at eight.

Next, I buzzed Clarice. It was time to show Dansby the book and convince Riva to let him to safeguard it. If it helped Dansby's cause, I'd let Jean-Henri inspect it and render his opinion. It was a risk, but I was already in over my head, and the more I considered what Riva had said, the more I agreed with the dangers he envisioned. The opportunities for blackmail were limitless, especially with multiple fortunes at stake.

"I need to talk with Phillip," I told Clarice.

"He's got a full schedule. Let me see what I can do."

She reappeared at my door a few minutes later. "His only time today is lunch. He has a reservation at his club." She looked dolefully at me. "With Jean-Henri."

"Wonderful." I didn't need our resident critic ruining lunch.

She looked as though she relished the scene. "Three's a crowd, but you can handle it."

Dansby's driver picked us up just before noon. I had come close to asking him if Jean-Henri could buy his own lunch elsewhere, but no doubt my nemesis harbored the same thought about me.

Membership in The Saint Hastings Club required a family tree with deep roots in the city. Over a hundred years old, its hallowed premises screamed old money and privilege. The polished brass and massive oak door were opened to old leather and cigars, and I expected to see ghostly images of Carnegie and Vanderbilt haunting the foyer. In Dansby's case, the Hastings had made an exception, shunning other applicants who carried the plague of new money.

Shown to a corner table, I fortified myself with a Basil Hayden on the rocks, while Dansby and Jean-Henri ordered straight-up Scotch. The ride from the office had been quiet, Jean-Henri and I avoiding one another's eyes, while Dansby conducted business on the limo's built-in phone. When the drinks arrived, he took a sip, his expression indicating he anticipated that lunch would be interesting.

"The gang-of-three meets again," he said. He looked at each of us. "Who wants to open the ball?"

"What happened with the da Vinci?" Jean-Henri asked.

Dansby started to reply when the waiter arrived to take our order. When he left, Jean-Henri leaned forward. "Did the bidding get out of hand?"

Dansby flapped the napkin in his lap. "Actually, no,"

Confused, Jean-Henri said, "But it did sell, did it not?"

"Oh, yes, just not to me."

Jean-Henri gave him a quizzical look. "I thought we were in agreement. That you had no doubts about its value."

"Authenticity isn't the issue," Dansby said. "I felt like I was being played like a fat grayling chasing a plump, dry fly. That the Delaudiers were getting too greedy, feeding out float line for me to gobble up their cast."

I took a swallow of bourbon, enjoying the surprise on Jean-Henri's face.

"So, you passed on a fabulous da Vinci," he said.

"Just so," Dansby said, "but Roland claims he has more and I suspect he learned a lesson."

I couldn't resist the opening. "In fact, my objection was the reason Phillip saw the light."

Before Jean-Henri could protest, Dansby reached across the table and patted his arm. "Adam's red flag didn't put me off," he said. "I simply didn't care for Delaudier's tactics."

Jean-Henri shook his head as though I sat on Mars and not at the table. "Hopefully, Barrow's claim did not play a part."

"Both of you need to see the book," I said.

"I plan to," Dansby said.

Jean-Henri looked stunned.

"I want you to see it too," I said to him.

"I won't be dragged into this farce."

"How can you say it's a farce when you haven't seen it?"

Jean-Henri tossed his napkin on the table. "The book, the book!"

Heads swiveled in our direction and Dansby leaned forward. "This is not the place."

Jean-Henri ignored him and fixed his glare on me, his neck flushing. "If you knew your art history, you'd recall that tales about Melzi's book have been around for years. It's a myth. Rumors of its existence still bandy about like a shuttlecock. They have persisted for years. Centuries, in fact."

"I saw it," I said, looking at Dansby and spreading my fingers. "I held it in my hands."

"Enough!" Jeari Henri's hands collapsed on the white tablecloth, rattling the silverware.

Heads swiveled in our direction. I lowered my voice. "Look, if the book's a fake, you win all the chips. Besides, what does the old man stand to gain?"

"Attention? Fame? A television documentary with the starring role?"

"Enzo Riva's dying, goddamit."

More heads turned toward our table. "Gentlemen," Dansby said, his annoyance obvious.

Jean-Henri plunged ahead. "I regret his state of health, but the book's a hoax."

"So are you if you don't keep an open mind."

He colored more deeply. "Unlike you, I use my mind to protect Phillip's interests and reputation instead of chasing delusions."

"Then do your job," I said.

Our food arrived and Dansby brusquely waved away the two confused waiters. He tossed his napkin on the table and signaled for the bill.

"This is getting us nowhere," he said, signing the chit. "I'll leave the two of you to sort this out. Let me know when your argument produces anything worthwhile."

He marched out without another word, leaving Jean-Henri and me alone at the table.

I looked at my plate, then to Jean-Henri.

"Do you want to join me?"

"No." He followed Dansby and left me to enjoy my lunch alone.

.   .   .

I took a cab back to the office, realizing a piper waited to be paid for our little drama.

Clarice met me in the hall. "Well, I'm guessing the two of you ruined his appetite." she said. "He slammed his door when he came back and I ordered a sandwich for him from the deli."

"Is Jean-Henri back?"

"He didn't come back."

"I need to see Dansby," I said.

"Again?"

"Yeah, again. I'm a glutton for punishment."

"I'll see if he's finished his hideous pastrami and chopped liver."

She called me five minutes later. "He'll see you, but he doesn't sound happy."

I knocked on his door.

"If that's you, Adam," he called, "you've about used up your chips."

I entered and saw the wad of sandwich paper on his desk, a sweating bottle of Newcastle Brown Ale in his hand. His chair turned toward the window, tie loosened, he presented his back to me. I looked up at the Lady Butler painting and absently wondered what one of the charging horsemen would have given for a cold pint at Waterloo.

"This ongoing war with Jean-Henri," he said without taking his eyes from the window. "You present me with a quandary."

"That's not my intention."

"Nevertheless, you're forcing me decide. Should I continue to trust your instincts or send you packing?"

"I saw the truth," I persisted. "Just look at this book before you make a decision."

"Jean-Henri doesn't believe you."

"Okay, but before you send me back to Chicago, you need to decide for yourself. Be your own man this time."

Dansby swiveled his chair around. "You do have a set on you."

I was gambling, but he left me no choice. "I'll talk with Riva. Convince him to let you both examine the book. Jean-Henri can then dismiss it or authenticate it."

"The ultimate decision is mine," he said stubbornly.

"And if Roland sells you a fake. What then?"

"That's best left to me and Roland."

He straightened his tie. "Whatever happens, it's almost be worth my time to end all this."

"I'll talk with Riva," I said. "You owe me that much."

He turned the ale bottle in his hand and scratched at the wet label. "Do I now?"

My gallery in Chicago looked better by the moment. I was fed up with getting slammed around like a shuttlecock. The entire fiasco had become a contest I didn't want, and I wished I'd never met Enzo Riva or seen Melzi's book—if that's what it was.

I threw up my hands. "Do what you want, Phillip. It's your money."

He set the bottle on his desk. "Why are you so certain this book of Riva's holds the keys to the kingdom? You're not a trained authority, you know. Jean-Henri's near the top of his profession and deserves more respect than you're giving him."

"I don't doubt his credentials, just his open mind."

Dansby rose and strode to the window. Rocking on his heels, he squinted at the phalanx of buildings without speaking. After a full minute, he thumped the glass with a knuckle without taking his eyes from the panorama.

"All right, I rather think I should see at this book of yours," he said. "If it strikes me as worthwhile, I'll convince Jean-Henri to have a look. But if it turns out to be a canard, it may be time for us to part company while we're still friends."

"Fair enough."

"You're gambling a lot."

"The first van Gogh was a gamble."

"And you earned a gold star for your efforts," he reminded me. "I've known you since you were a tyke, but you're not a child any longer, Adam. Working for me, you're playing in a different league. Mistakes are for amateurs."

"Look at the book. Then decide."

"Oh, I *will* make a decision," he said. "I don't want to lose another da Vinci."

· · ·

That night I took a cab to Leslie's apartment on West 86th Street and thought about my meeting with Dansby.

I'd left his office feeling like I'd drawn a tie. I knew I should be grateful he took a chance on me. My own father spent my childhood focused on scamming his marks and anticipating his next drink. Providing parental advice was never his strong suit, but I ended up working for one of the wealthiest men in the country who treated me like the son he never had. If I failed him, I'd lose more than good advice.

When the taxi dropped me, Leslie buzzed me up to the twelfth floor. She greeted me at the door and gave me a kiss on the cheek that lingered a few seconds longer than I expected.

"You found me," she said.

"My Chicago hunting instincts," I said, "aided by my faithful Indian companion, a taxi driver from Calcutta."

The place was modest but well-furnished. Dressed in a simple knee-length burgundy dress and matching spike heels, the conservative outfit failed to conceal her enticing figure. As she collected her coat from the bedroom, I inspected the walls, surprised to see all the paintings were originals without a reproduction or lithograph in sight. Either Delaudier paid better than I thought, or Leslie had an admirer with deep pockets.

She caught me standing in front of a large beach scene by Burton Silverman.

"He's a New York artist. You like his work?"

"Very much. It doesn't require a lecture to explain what he was thinking when he painted it."

She laughed, and I remembered its earthiness. "It was a present from Roland," she said. "Part of my last bonus. He said Isabelle isn't a fan, so he found a way to dispose of it."

"Nice perk."

"It was very thoughtful. Roland can be a generous man."

"Money allows gracious gestures."

She looked at me. "Do I detect a note of envy?"

"Absolutely. The proletariat always envies the wealthy."

I studied the Silverman a moment longer, unable to resist calculating its value.

She pushed me out the door with a playful shove and locked her door. We headed to the elevator. "Okay, no more talk of money." She slipped her arm through mine. "Where are you taking me?"

"Nobu. We're doing Oriental again. The Japanese food's outstanding. No fish eyes or eel skin soup."

"I'll survive."

Nobu was one of my favorites. Subdued lighting and bare dark wood with unobtrusive servers. We sat at a window table Clarice had reserved for me, and I joined Leslie in a martini. We both ordered spicy Miso chips with tuna, followed by oysters with Maui onion salsa and seared scallops, sampling a flight of Sake along the way. When we finished, our second martini arrived. Fueled by the martinis and Sake, I felt the alcohol merry-go-round gradually start to revolve, Dansby and Riva fading away. Leslie sat back, her face in half-shadow.

"You ever think we're closet Asians?" she said. "Me taking you to Chinatown and you tempting me with Japanese food."

"We could do worse."

She returned my smile and leaned her elbows on the table, hands folded beneath her chin. Her blond hair caught the subtle overhead lighting and Kat's memory slipped a little farther away. Despite my resolve not to get caught up in another relationship, Leslie was a soulmate who pulled herself from the bog of a lousy childhood and shared my love of fine art. I caught myself and reeled my feelings back, realizing I was projecting my feelings onto her, a long-standing failing of mine. Leslie was the type who liked male company without next morning regrets. Or maybe there truly was an 'us' in our future. I applied the brakes and decided not to sprint, my experience teaching me to walk.

"We should try Italian next time," she said. "We're caught up in da Vinci, so why not pay him a little homage next time?"

"He seems determined not to go away."

"Is the good Major still in the hunt? For the other drawings?"

"Possibly. You remember I talked to Dansby about Riva's book? I think I've convinced him to take a look and make up his own mind."

She ran a finger around the delicate rim of her martini glass.

"Marsh said you mentioned the book when you inspected the drawing." She smiled and I guessed she was picturing the scene. "Isabelle wasn't thrilled. That when Dansby stopped bidding at the auction, she was livid."

"Because of me?"

"What'd you expect?"

"I can't let it go."

"Why?"

"It's my job to turn up artwork for Dansby." Much as I wanted an ally and confidant, I didn't want her to lose her job because of me.

"What does Dansby think?"

"He wants proof the book's real. Jean-Henri's not willing to concede anything."

She polished off her martini. "You can't blame either one. The Delaudiers verified the drawing and there're boatloads of money involved."

I grimaced, the alcohol loosening my resolve to keep her out of it. "I know, but I'm only trying to prevent Dansby from making a mistake."

"I thought that was Bonnet's job," she said.

"He didn't see Riva's book. I did." There. It was out.

"You need to be careful, Adam," she said. "Rumors could cost the Delaudiers money. You don't want a libel suit on your hands."

She was right. Roland, Marsh, Isabelle, Sal. They all heard me claim the drawing was a fake. Thirty-five million had passed hands, not including the Delaudiers' commission, but they believed the drawing was undersold and there were more drawings in the pipeline.

I settled the check, and we walked outside, met by the roar and horns of traffic.

"Want to see who's playing at Armands?"

Leslie shook her head. "Next time. Tomorrow's a busy day."

We took a cab to her apartment, and I walked her to the elevator. She pushed the button and turned, holding my forearms.

"I had a lovely evening, Adam."

Okay, Barrow, I thought, tonight isn't ending with an intimate aftermath.

"I want to do this again," she said, holding my eyes. "Soon."

"Bet on it," I said, swallowing my disappointment.

She kissed me chastely on the lips and joined two people in the elevator. She gave me a slight wave just as the doors closed.

I walked outside and took a deep breath. It was only eleven. I waved a taxi down and gave the driver directions to Armands. It had been a long day with a disappointing conclusion, and I needed a drink to restore my chipped ego.

Chapter Seventeen

Next morning, I returned to Riva's apartment and convinced him to meet with Dansby. He reluctantly agreed and I returned later in the day, disappointed when he hobbled down the front steps empty-handed. He'd managed to find an outdated garish tie, but his white shirt was clean. I got him into a taxi, relieved when I detected no trace of grappa.

"You didn't bring the book," I said.

"I do not know these men."

The wall remained firmly in place.

"Like you, they're admirers of da Vinci."

"Many people are admirers, but not all respect him," he said. "I talk with your friends but I can make no promises."

Disappointed, I said, "That's all I ask."

He stared out the window, and I could sense him rethinking his decision. The Melzi book was his life preserver in his sea of mistrust, and I wondered if parting with it might drown what remained of his life. Dansby and I decided to meet at Jean-Henri's apartment so as not to overwhelm Riva in a corporate setting. As we got out of the cab, his eyes darted up at the rows of gleaming windows where his inquisitors waited.

"Who is this other man? Is he also wealthy?"

"No," I assured him, "he's a scholar who respects fine art."

We didn't speak again until the elevator reached Jean-Henri's floor. I knocked and Jean-Henri opened the door.

I introduced Riva, whose eyes widened as he absorbed the tightly cuffed trousers, pink striped shirt, maroon bowtie and sports jacket of pale cream linen. Jean-Henri Bonnet, I realized, epitomized a modern version of what Victorian England labeled a fop, an example of New York's trendy sartorial splendor. The sides of his head clean-shaven and left only a faddish strip of gray hair along the top of his scalp. I looked at his younger partner who sat on a white couch, his ensemble more sedate.

Jean-Henri walked to him. "Gerry, why don't you run down to Ziggy's for a cappuccino while we talk business for a few minutes."

Gerry brushed past us with a shy smile and Riva gaped at two entire walls of art books arranged by size. Modern oak furniture dominated the spotless room, adding glittering touches to the white decor. The living room opened to the modern kitchen. A zinc countertop held a three-foot high tree mug and a stainless coffee urn, chrome barstools fronting the divider. Not what I had expected from a book-bound academic, but in sync with his eclectic tastes. Dansby strode to Riva, and offered his hand.

"Mister Riva," he said.

Schooled in putting those who mistrusted him at ease, Phillip beamed at Riva as though a celebrity had joined us. "It's a pleasure, sir."

Dansby assumed the role of host when Jean-Henri took a chair and folded his arms.

"Coffee?" Dansby asked, raising his eyebrows.

Riva and I shook our heads as Jean-Henri assessed his guest's shabby clothes. Foregoing further amenities, he sat forward, elbows on his knees. "Let me begin by saying I believe all Francesco Melzi's works have been catalogued."

Dansby was shaking his head at him, but Jean-Henri was off and running.

"I don't believe another exists, Mister Riva."

Riva gave me an anxious glance. "Then you would be wrong, *Signor* Bonnet."

The last thing I needed was another blow-up. For all of his intellectual curiosity and knowledge, Jean-Henri's ego could fill Radio City Music Hall.

"This book of yours," he said to Riva, "where is it?"

"It is safe," Riva said.

Jean-Henri sat back with a dismissive wave of his hand. "You're insisting the da Vinci drawing is not genuine?"

"Yes."

"I inspected the da Vinci, Mister Riva. Not only myself but a panel of specialists from Europe and the United States, all of whom verified the work."

"Then you and they are all wrong," Riva said with familiar firmness.

"Tell them about Melzi's book," I said.

Jean-Henri lightly clapped his hands. "Ah, yes. The mythical Melzi book. Please convince us, *Signor* Riva."

Riva ran his hands over the chair arms and looked at the door. "Myth?"

I looked at Phillip, who appeared content to let the conversation run its course.

My anger rose. "I've seen it, Jean-Henri."

"And did you know what you were seeing? Fairytales about this book have existed for centuries."

"It included the da Vinci," I replied. "The same drawing sold by Delaudier, but it was done by Donato Volpe. Even the signature was wrong."

Jean-Henri uttered a weary sound.

"There are enough examples out there to raise questions about this one."

Jean-Henri raised his eyebrows. "I don't deal in information scattered across the internet."

"Enough," Phillip said. "Tell us why you're so certain, Mr. Riva."

I waited for Riva to tell his story, but he was looking over Jean-Henri's shoulder as though he hadn't heard Dansby. Without replying, he laboriously rose from the couch and limped to the bookshelves, trailing one hand along the spines of Jean-Henri's collection as though greeting old friends. He stepped to a small framed oil of a child; a single spotlight accented the painting.

"Berthe Morisot," he breathed, leaning closer.

Surprised, Jean-Henri joined him. "You know her work?"

"Yes," Riva did not take his eyes from the painting. "Not many women joined the Impressionists."

Jean-Henri scrutinized his guest more closely. "You're familiar with the early French Impressionists?"

The watery eyes crinkled at the edges as he met Jean-Henri's gaze. "Being poor does not prevent me from learning, *Signor* Bonnet."

"You studied French Impressionist art?"

Riva shook his head. "Just an old man who appreciates locks and keys, but I learn much from pictures in books and museums. These artists, so different from Leonardo, almost a breath of spring air."

Dansby and I looked at one another and realized we were observing a one-act play as two characters unraveled one another's secrets, mutual wariness giving way to respect.

Jean-Henri looked at him warily. "Who are your favorites?"

Riva returned to the couch and looked back at the Morisot. "I was always drawn to lesser knowns," he said, "those the world forgot. Max Slevogt, the German artist, and of course, the Italians, Lega and Tivoli. So much talent many overlook today."

Jean-Henri looked at Enzo Riva, two strangers who discover they love the same woman.

Dansby walked to Riva. "Mr. Riva, I want a da Vinci for my new museum. To give him a place of honor."

Riva looked up at the imposing figure. "So many people want to touch Leonardo's work, to say they own him."

"Your book would turn the art world on its head," Dansby said.

Riva shrugged at the obvious. "It would also cause much disruption."

"It would enlighten the world," Dansby said. "Make it a more honest place."

Riva gave a small shrug as though we were selling him a promise he did not believe.

Dansby returned to his chair and removed a leather cigar holder from his blazer, preparing to light up despite a frown from Jean-Henri, who scrambled for an ashtray. He got the Montecristo going, squinting through the smoke.

"If Mister Riva will agree, we can have his book tested and vetted under his personal supervision." He looked pointedly at Jean-Henri. "Put aside any questions once and for all."

"It shouldn't be difficult to verify Melzi's handwriting. Compare the book's drawings to his other work," I said.

Jean-Henri crossed his legs. "I am in agreement if Mister Riva is amenable."

Enzo Riva stared at us as if considering to give up a child for adoption.

Dansby tapped an ash in the ebony ashtray and voiced Riva's fears. "Let's understand what can happen if the book is confirmed," he said. "If there's hard evidence the Delaudier's offering is fraudulent or mis-attributed, we'll do whatever's necessary to correct the situation. Many famous paintings are questionable. Adding da Vinci to the list would cause a worldwide stir. Nevertheless, I'm of the opinion the truth needs to be heard."

Riva collapsed into a fit of coughing. He squeezed his eyes shut in pain. I leaned toward him as Jean-Henri hurried to the kitchen and returned with a glass of water. Catching his breath, Riva gulped it down as Phillip and I exchanged looks. If Melzi's book was real, we needed to hurry.

Chapter Eighteen

"Doesn't Riva have a phone?"

Dansby's mood didn't match his bright red tie and designer grey suit as we waited at the curb outside our offices next morning. His limo pulled to the curb, and I settled into the rear seat facing him, waiting for the next jab. He clutched a folio containing photographs of the three new da Vincis and refused to meet my eyes. I wondered if he had second thoughts about the book and my value to him. Accustomed to his mood swings, I hoped I was wrong on both counts.

"What kind of person doesn't have a phone?" he grumbled.

"He can't afford one or he's too sick to care about telephones."

"He's not contagious, is he?"

"No." At least, I hoped not.

To be honest, I did not know how sick Riva was. I only knew he needed to safeguard the book and Dansby was his best bet. If he believed what he saw, he might avert a financial disaster and shoulder the role of a hero in the art world. And if I was honest with myself, I wanted to put a dent in Roland's and Isabelle's smugness.

Enjoying the car's posh leather seat, I found it difficult to fathom that a failing old man held the key to deception and misspent fortunes. If it fell into the wrong hands, Melzi's book would tempt them run an ugly little game—only extortion and blackmail weren't games.

"I am truly a gambler taking a chance on you," Dansby grumbled as the limo outmaneuvered around several busses. "I will be less than happy if you're wasting my time."

"It's a good gamble," I said, trying to convince myself I wasn't dragging him to Riva's apartment for an illusion on my part.

Dansby crossed his legs and pinched a flawless crease in his trouser leg. "As if we didn't have enough confronting us, Jean-Henri's apartment was broken into last night while he and Gerry were at dinner."

"What was stolen?"

"Oddly enough, nothing. Neither can find anything missing. Jean-Henri says his father's gold watch chain was in plain sight and that Gerry left over a hundred dollars on their dresser. They couldn't find a damn thing missing."

It sounded like a replay of my break-in.

We stopped in front of Riva's building and Dansby told the driver to wait. We trotted up the concrete steps and I rang the bell in the dank vestibule.

Nothing.

Annoyed by the claustrophobic entryway, Dansby shook his head as I pushed the button again. Sniffing the remnants of decay and stale cooking odors, he reached for the door handle.

"Waste of time."

Before Dansby could bolt back to the car, an elderly woman pulling a wheeled wire grocery cart opened the door and punched a code into a smudged keypad. I held the door open and we followed her into the building, ignoring her frightened look. We took the stairs and I stopped at Riva's door. I knocked and received another sigh from Dansby, who exhaled loudly. My time had run out. About to give up, I hit the door in frustration. It swung open and I almost fell into Riva's tiny living room, confronted by a familiar sight.

Books were scattered across the apartment's floor, sofa and chair cushions ripped apart and flung around the room. Cabinet doors in the kitchen gaped open. The familiar bottle of grappa lay on the floor where a circle of dried brandy stained the frayed carpet. The tiny canary chirped and danced on its perch as though glad to see me again,

Worse yet, Riva's chair had been tipped over on its back.

"Mister Riva?" No answer.

I walked to the small bedroom and found him face down in a circle of blood. A spray of dried blood and brain matter fanned across an old crocheted rug, a crusty red hole in his left eye socket indicated where the bullet exited.

Dansby brushed past me and knelt by the body, careful not to step in the blood. He started to touch the side of Riva's neck and pulled his hand back, knowing it was useless.

"One thing's certain," he said, rising. "An illness didn't kill him."

Sickened by the murder of an innocent old man, I stared down at his blood-soaked goatee, wondering if I'd played a part. Dansby rose and surveyed the apartment.

"As unfortunate as this is," he said, "we can't just walk away. I shouldn't think many limousines grace this neighborhood and the entire block most likely witnessed our arrival." He looked at me as though I planned to thrust him into a murder scene.

"Before we call the police, help me for a moment."

He followed me back to the living room, and I walked to Riva's chair. I tipped it backward.

"Hold this for me."

"What now?"

I ran my hand inside the frame. Melzi's book was gone as I suspected it would be.

We stepped around the strewn books, looking at three older volumes.

"I take it your book is not one of these," Dansby said.

"No. Riva hid it inside this chair and it's missing."

"So, our murderer found it."

"It appears that way."

"Then who has it?"

Two things were certain. Riva was dead and the book was gone. Was I a pariah, a carrier of bad luck as I had been for Kat? After the trail of bodies left in the van Gogh's wake, chasing lost masterpieces had become more dangerous than I imagined. I wandered around the apartment, trying not to disturb anything that might be useful to the police, wishing I'd never seen Riva or heard his tale about the book.

Dansby walked back to the bedroom and looked at the body again. "Wonderful. I'm in a murdered man's apartment with nothing to show for it."

He was right, but involving him in a murder hadn't been part of my plan.

"My fault, Phillip."

He ignored me and looked around the shabby room. "Damn! The newspapers will have a field day with this."

I dialed 911 on my cell and half an hour later a Detective Lomax and two uniformed cops arrived. Lomax was a middle-aged black man constructed like a former fullback. He removed a small notebook from his wrinkled jacket and planted himself in front of me, glancing at Dansby as though calculating the cost of the tailored suit. His shaven head glowed with perspiration and he looked like he'd rather be anywhere else than where he stood.

"You want to tell me about this?" he asked in a tired voice.

I explained finding Riva's body and what I knew about him. Lomax took our statements and shot questions at us for the next hour. Dansby answered with clipped responses and I supplied the rest. The two cops eyed us, Dansby trying to avoid quotes that might filter back to the media who would fall like rabid dogs on his presence in a dead man's apartment.

I took the lead answering most of Lomax's questions, explaining that Enzo Riva was a personal friend and that Dansby and I had planned to discuss an art matter with him. I watched the detective's face as he scribbled notes in the pocket-sized notebook, realizing he'd heard every tale imaginable. Phillip's high-profile visibility might buy us a temporary reprieve, but Lomax would be a fixture in our lives for the foreseeable future. I looked at Riva's body. A few nights ago, it could have been me lying in a pool of my own blood. Removing people was a murderer's solution to solving problems,, and I wondered why I'd been spared.

Lomax asked a few more questions and issued the usual warning about not leaving the city. When he closed his notebook, a uniformed cop knelt beside the body.

"Dead since last night by the look of him," he said. "Large caliber gunshot."

"You two have alibis for last night?" Lomax said.

"We're suspects?"

"You're the only two people I see in a dead man's apartment."

"Perhaps I should call my lawyers," Dansby said.

Lomax looked at him. "You need a lawyer?"

"No." I interjected. "We only found the body."

Lomax tapped the notebook. "This your cell phone number?"

I gave him my office number as well and pointed to the bird cage.

"I'll take the bird to a pet shop."

"You can't disturb the scene."

"You think the bird did it?"

He didn't laugh. He ran a hand over his slick dome and stared at me. I guess cops get used to smart asses.

"Take the damn bird."

Dansby and I walked from the building to the waiting limo. A crowd had gathered on the sidewalk and I wondered if any of them had ever known Enzo Riva or his dead wife. A gentle soul was gone, obliterated by a killer who placed money above a human life. On the drive back to our privileged world, an orphaned canary on my lap, I waited for Dansby to pronounce sentence on me. He remained quiet, one elbow on the armrest as he surveyed the sidewalks.

"This gives you a reprieve," he said, surprising me. "There appears to be others interested in this book of yours." The intelligence behind his eyes flashed in the car's tinted interior. "If I'd seen this book and found nothing, you'd be collecting your things and clearing your desk."

"And now?"

Dansby shook his head. Riva's death no longer seemed to concern him. He'd seen too many bodies on the battlefield to let another bloody corpse shake him.

"We need to go slower on the da Vincis," he said almost to himself as he turned back to inspect the crowds along Fifth Avenue. "I want one more than ever, but this morning raises a second red flag to say the least."

"All of Delaudier's drawings were credited to his students."

Dansby's face fell. "All three?"

"I'm afraid so."

"Well, that tears it."

"I'm sorry, Phillip."

I felt a stab of vindication, his disappointment thrown into the emotional mix. Facing me, he laid a paternal hand on my knee. "If I've learned anything in my advanced years, it's when to trust my gut as you Americans say. Examine the surrounding landscape for threats, if you will. It's a trait you and I seem to share. All this feels connected."

"I'm to blame. A lot of people including Riva might be alive if I'd left well enough alone at the first auction."

"That's rubbish, but his murder is one more fly in the soup." He glanced at the birdcage and made a face. "No matter what, do not think that bloody bird's going to end up in the office."

I stuck my finger in the cage. Piccolo pecked at the fingertip with a hopeful chirp, and the image of Riva's body returned. I was as clueless as the bird who found itself riding in a limo. If the killer stole the book, he had the means to make several lifetimes of money. The senseless death reconfirmed my fears. Dansby's street smarts and his willingness to tolerate me a little longer meant the Delaudiers windfall remained in limbo, but I was back at square one, holding a birdcage on my lap.

Chapter Nineteen

Königsberg
Morning
January 7, 1945

A kilometer from the center of Königsberg, Weisser slowed. Thick flakes of snow swirled across the road and he almost drove past it.

A bundled figure lifted his hand and Weisser counted five soldiers huddled over a barrel fire, stamping bundled feet.

An aging Wehrmacht sergeant limped to the truck. Wearing a whitewashed helmet and muffled to his ears in scarves, a threadbare greatcoat collar hid half his face. He eyed the truck and raised a Schmeisser machine pistol halfway to the window. Weisser rolled down the glass, a gust of wet snow striking his face as the sergeant held out a gloved hand.

"Papers."

Weisser composed an impatient scowl and unbuttoned his collar to reveal his rank. The sergeant lowered his weapon and came to slack attention.

"Sorry, *Herr Sturmbannführer*, but I must see your papers."

Weisser dug out his identification book and handed it to him.

"Is the port open?"

The man glanced at the booklet without looking up before he handed it back. "Frozen stiffer than a dead man's pecker."

"No ships in or out?"

The *Feldwebel* grunted. "Not unless they're on skates, sir."

"*Scheisse*," Weisser muttered. How far down the coast had the sea turned to ice? If the entire Baltic had iced over, all the risks had been for nothing.

"Any other ports open?"

The non-com appraised Weisser's drawn face. More and more of the army was slipping away, officers included. It was easier for those blessed with rank to bluff their way past checkpoints in their scramble to safety. But the SS was different.

He pointed down the road. "Last I heard, Pillau was still open. There's a chance it hadn't frozen over yet."

Several soldiers stood beside the sergeant with quizzical looks. One walked to rear of the truck and raised the canvas flap.

"Only a crate in here, sergeant," the man called.

"What're you hauling, sir?"

"Special consignment for *Reichsmarschall* Göring." Weisser handed him the letter.

The *Feldwebel* scratched his armpit and resisted shaking his head. "An officer hauling a single crate."

"I don't question orders, sergeant. I hope you're not foolish enough to do so."

"No, sir. It's just that…" The sergeant pretended to study the document a few moments longer, ignoring Weisser's frown. He climbed onto the running board and returned the documents.

"Well, I wish you luck, Major. Lot of men trying to desert. The SS hung about a dozen this week." He looked pointedly at Weisser. "I need to report this to *Hauptman* Fleischer."

"The SS doesn't explain its orders to army captains." Weisser examined the *Feldwebel's* lined face and frost-crusted eyebrows. The grizzled non-com was a survivor, an old stag who appeared savvy enough not to push his luck with the SS. Weisser locked eyes with him.

"You think I'm a deserter, sergeant?"

"No, sir."

Weisser noticed the sergeant's eyes on the Russian tommy gun on the floor. The PPS was a prized possession since few Russians were now dropping them and running away. The weapon was crude, but was more dependable in frigid temperatures, a prized possession at close quarters. The sergeant turned his head and spat over the front fender. He wiped his stubbled chin and looked at Weisser without speaking. The others drifted back to the fire, and Weisser saw questions in the man's eyes. Why was a single SS officer hauling a crate for Göring when the army was in full retreat?

Weisser hated prostrating himself before an enlisted man, but he needed to get to Pillau. He picked up the submachine gun with a conspiratorial grin.

"You need this more than me, sergeant." He handed the gun and spare drums through the window. "How about we trade? Your Schmeisser for the PPS and I forget you questioned my orders." Giving up the PPS was foolish, but he couldn't afford to explain himself to this Captain Fleischer or get caught up in the Wehrmacht's bureaucracy.

Wind rocked the truck on the unnamed road as the two men considered their options and consequences. Falling snow limited visibility to a few yards. The sergeant tugged up his coat collar and glanced over his shoulder at what was left of his squad. After a moment he nodded, and Weisser relaxed. No matter how small, the veteran needed any advantage that came his way, especially if he expected to see the Fatherland again.

The two men exchanged weapons . Weisser put the GAZ in reverse. The sergeant stepped off the running board and stuffed the spare drums inside his belted overcoat. Weisser drove around the huddled soldiers and the sergeant lifted the striped pole without saluting.

The windshield wipers fought an onslaught of driving snow. The GAZ plowed forward, the engine stuttering as though ready to abandon him. *Unless the truck could find a way to run on curses, he'd be fortunate to make another five kilometers.* The forest closed in again and he wiped his forehead with a stiffy sleeve, sweat prickling beneath his cap.

"A ship," he muttered aloud. "Just find Pillau and a damned ship."

Chapter Twenty

New York

Riva's murder had slammed another door in my face. In my favor was the fact Dansby's second sense kicked in, diminishing his hunger for Delaudier's offerings. The murder planted seeds of wariness, but with no proof to back up his suspicions. Without the book, Jean-Henri stood by his assurances that the drawings were authentic. I was the novice chasing my tail, my credibility in limbo.

No matter what anyone believed, I was convinced Delaudier had cheated the buyer at the auction, and that Dansby was next. The enormous question centered around the Delaudiers' complicity. Had Roland and Isabelle been led misled, or were they part of a murder and significant attempt to defraud clients?

Next day, another detective arrived at our offices to question Dansby and me. I related the old man's outburst at the first da Vinci auction. The cop seemed interested in the Delaudiers' reaction to the failed auction and I told him I hadn't spoken to them, omitting my conversation with Leslie. Unable to feel sympathy for the Delaudiers, I imagined the scene when the police intruded on their smug world. It was petty, but I still relished the prospect.

Two days later, Dansby called me into his office. Working in shirtsleeves at his desk when I entered, he wore a dove gray vest, his coat draped over the back of his chair. He motioned me to a chair in front of the desk and called Roland on the speaker phone, telling him he'd decided go slower on the remaining drawings. I heard protests and my name as he assured Dansby that a bevy of international academics had gone over the drawings, applying every test imaginable. Dansby uttered nice noises and assured Delaudier his honesty wasn't in question, that he and Jean-Henri wanted another look at the new drawings. That wasn't quite true. Jean-Henri remained a believer.

"The fellow's upset," Dansby said after he clicked off, "but that's understandable since he believed he was in the driver's seat. Now, he's seeing a windfall vanish like meat in a tiger's cage."

"I guess my stock isn't too high with him."

"You stepped on his cash flow."

"To hell with him."

"Yes, well, all this still leaves me without my da Vinci."

"So, what do we do?"

"Find this book of yours," Dansby said.

"It was never mine."

"But the damn thing's vanished, hasn't it?" he snapped. "No matter what I told Delaudier, I've no choice but to rely on Jean-Henri's judgment."

"I know you trust him, but he didn't inspect the book."

He frowned. "I'm afraid that's your problem. You created this entire issue."

My credibility shot to hell again, I trooped out of his office and instructed Clarice not to interrupt me for the remainder of the day. I closed my door and flopped into my chair, pondering what happened to Riva's book. Leaning back, I frowned at the pile of Delaudier catalogs on my desk. I closed my eyes against the immensity of the city outside my window, a labyrinth that had swallowed a single book. Either it had been stolen or Riva hid it again before he was killed. As much as I wanted a simpler alternative, both facts left me standing at a blank wall.

I opened my eyes when Clarice walked in without knocking. Using her finely honed extrasensory perception, she placed a glass of bourbon with two ice cubes on the corner of my desk, the libation from our client conference room.

"A gift for those in need," she said before closing my door.

I took a healthy swallow just as my desktop pinged. I ignored the incoming message, unwilling to interrupt the bourbon's glow and consoling sensation of feeling sorry for myself. Irritated by the monitor's insistence, I polished off the whiskey and buzzed Clarice.

"First, the drink definitely earned you serious points," I told her. "Second, how about holding my calls for the next hour?"

"I would, but you've got a female admirer on Line Two."

"There ain't no such thing, darling."

"She's calling from Delaudier."

Leslie.

I started to ask Clarice to tell her I was in a meeting, but the drink erased my self-pity. I needed diversion and Leslie qualified as far more.

"Put her through. And thanks again for the bourbon. You'll be receiving the vaunted Barrow lifesaving medal."

"And thank you for Piccolo," she said. "He's great company."

"Go ahead and put the caller through."

I propped my feet on the desk and picked up the phone.

"Hi, there."

"Mister Barrow, this is Isabelle Delaudier."

My feet thumped onto the floor. How was I supposed to conduct a conversation with a proven harridan?

"Mrs. Delaudier, how are you?" It was the best I could do.

"I would be much better if you agree to have dinner with me tonight." The invitation and voice were so intimate that it took me a moment to fashion a reply.

"Any particular reason you'd invite a reprobate from Second City to dinner?"

She uttered a girlish laugh. "Touché. Actually, Roland's out of the city and I have a proposition."

What the hell.

The laugh again, silky and promising. "That didn't sound appropriate, did it?"

I couldn't shake the sensation she was coming on to me. Was this the same woman who wanted me banned from her life?

"I'll ask again. Why me?"

"A business proposition," she said. "With a four-star meal thrown into the bargain."

"Will Phillip join us?"

She hesitated. "Just you and me. I'll reserve a table." The line stayed silent before she added, "You'll find I can be helpful, even persuasive in the right circumstances."

Bergman enticing Bogart at Rick's. Damn, the woman intrigued me despite the warning alarms.

"What time and where?" I heard myself reply.

"Nine o'clock. My driver will pick you up."

"You need an address?"

"I know where you live. I just want to know more about you."

She clicked off and I stared at the phone. Okay, I thought. That was interesting. I'd agreed to have dinner with a woman who would have gladly shoved me under a train last time we were in the same room. I decided against telling Dansby about the call, figuring Isabelle Delaudier would give me her reasons soon enough. How intimate a dinner I couldn't imagine, but spending time with an exotic creature like her wouldn't be all that arduous, so long as we didn't get near subway tracks.

I thought about Leslie, but my feelings appeared to be a one-way sentiment with little chance of reciprocation. I put aside my fantasies about Leslie and the Melzi book, curious about the coming evening. I left Clarice a note that I'd be out for the remainder of the day and walked several blocks to an exclusive men's shop. I sublimated my misgivings about Isabelle Delaudier and bought a new silk tie that the clerk assured me looked "fabulous." Armed with new sartorial splendor as I left the shop, pretty certain what the evening would bring my way.

• • •

My driver turned out to be Sal Testano, the outsized bodyguard from the auction house. Attired in a peaked chauffeur's cap and monogrammed blazer that failed to disguise his bulk, he glanced in the rearview mirror as I ducked in back of the oversized BMW.

"Hey. It's Mister Chicago," he said. "How's it hanging?"

I surmised this was chauffer chatter, Queens-style.

"You havin' dinner with Mrs. Delaudier, huh? You'll like her when you get to know her. She's a classy broad."

"You're Sal," I said. "From the auction house."

He reached over the front passenger seat and passed me a hinged walnut box. I put it on the seat and raised the carved wooden lid, finding a sweating sterling shaker and two crystal martini glasses nestled in red velvet padding.

"Vodka martinis," Sal said. "A little starter from Mrs. Delaudier." He cut his eyes to the mirror. "She's tough but generous, you know?"

The vodka was top notch, and I wondered if I'd misjudged her.

The black car shouldered its way across Manhattan's east side, running yellow lights and ignoring horns from taxis. Neon marquees and storefront lights flickered over the plush leather upholstery as I poured a martini, unable to shake the sense I was the main course on tonight's dinner menu.

"Drink up," Sal said over his shoulder as the car slowed. "Lotta traffic tonight. You might as well enjoy the ride."

The martini disappeared before the car halted in front of a four-story brownstone. Sal double-parked and told me to stay in the car. I poured a second martini and watched him ponderously take the steps two at a time. Before he could ring the bell, Isabelle Delaudier stepped outside. Dressed in a simple off-the-shoulder black cocktail dress and stiletto heels, her page boy black hair reflected the curbside streetlight as she glided down the stone steps, Sal in her wake. She wore no coat or jewelry, and my impression was she wore nothing beneath the dress. She opened the car door without waiting for Sal and slipped onto the seat beside me and a delicate fragrance filled the interior. She was not a traditional beauty, but embodied something female that exuded intelligence and a toughness she didn't bother to disguise.

Crossing her bare legs, she opened the wooden box and held up her empty glass. I poured a martini and she took a healthy sip before shifting on the seat to face me.

"Now then," she said, "let's get better acquainted, shall we?"

Sal grinned at me in the rearview mirror and I resigned myself to my fate.

. . .

La Fin proved to be a private dinner club that flaunted a black-tie doorman outside a smoked glass entrance. The man stepped into the street and opened the car door. When he held out his hand to assist Isabelle from the car, Sal jabbed two fingers on his chest and pushed him back. The startled doorman stepped away and Sal assisted Isabelle from the car.

Dimly lit, upholstered red banquettes bordered the interior walls. Deco sconces lighted the way and heads turned as I escorted Isabelle past the bar. The maitre d' showed us to a rear booth shielded by smoked glass panels decorated with hooved satyrs and naked nymphs. He ignored me and whispered to Isabelle in French as napkins were flapped into our laps, Pellegrino poured and drink orders taken. When he disappeared, Isabelle slid closer.

"Cozy," I said, aware only a layer of fine silk separated my hands from her bare skin.

"It's my favorite hideaway when I don't like the world," she said.

It sounded like a plea from someone who discovered their Rolls is out of date. "What's wrong with your world?"

She gave a small shrug, her scent inescapable inside the cubicle. "We all have our travails," she sighed as though reciting from a movie script. "Don't you have money problems, Adam?"

My god, the woman didn't know the meaning of subtle. "Nothing I can't handle."

She smiled, showing perfect teeth. "Then you're either a lucky man or naïve."

More vodka martinis arrived, and she touched her glass to mine. I resigned myself to go slow and took a small sip as the head waiter recited the chef's selections, surreptitiously dragging his eyes over Isabelle.

We ordered and she made her first stab at business. "I wish I felt sorry about the old man's death, but he cost us money."

Not very compassionate for a harmless old man who died with a bullet in his head. I said nothing and waited for the reason I sat in La Fin with such a warm-hearted creature.

"I realize you and Phillip are close, but don't you ever dream of having more? After all, your van Gogh's winging its way back to France."

"Dansby takes care of me."

"So that's all you want," she persisted. "To remain in his shadow?"

"I have an art gallery in Chicago."

"But it's not the same, is it? If you fail, you'll be back there, worrying about next month's light bill."

I hated the condescension that too much money generates. "If that happens, I'll use candles to light the place. Make it more intimate."

She laughed and ordered a bottle of Corton-Bressandes Grand Cru, removing a Cartier cigarette case from her purse. I lit her cigarette. This being a private club, I relaxed and enjoyed the tantalizing smoke, knowing the nanny police wouldn't burst in to arrest the usual suspects. A white-jacketed sommelier appeared and brandished the wine bottle. After the traditional uncorking and tasting ceremony, she sampled the wine, nodded. Inhaling the clove cigarette, she returning to her vodka. I switched to the exceptional white burgundy that came close to equaling Isabelle's performance. Curious when the other shoe would fall, I enjoyed the wine as Isabelle studied me.

"And if you didn't have to depend on Dansby's money? What would make you comfortable?" she asked.

We'd finally reached beyond rare wine and flirtation. She rested the tip of her index finger on the back of my hand and I resisted the urge to look down at the invitation. I had several decades' edge on Roland Delaudier, but married women, even those as tempting as his wife, were outside my pedestrian boundaries.

"Tell me why we're sitting here discussing my future, Mrs. Delaudier."

"Isabelle."

"Okay, we're on a first name basis now, but I still want the reason."

She didn't remove her finger, but her eyes lost a touch of their luster. "Roland believes you exert a certain influence over Phillip Dansby."

Ah, Roland had found himself back into the equation as the conversation inched toward money.

"Phillip and Jean-Henri don't need my advice to buy art."

"We need an ally," she said, dropping all pretense. "With this much money involved, we need someone to champion our cause."

I could kid myself that I didn't know what to expect next. Her touch was tantalizing, and I was always a pushover for a foreign accent, but I was more intrigued that she held the opinion they could buy me.

"And you believe that's me?"

"If you'll drop your insistence about this old book."

"You mean if I keep my mouth shut."

She pushed her plate aside, lighting another cigarette as though the answer should be obvious to a rube like me. Whatever she had in mind, I would never betray Phillip, but knowing how far she would go would be a revelation.

"I'd like to know more about the drawings," I said, hoping to come away with more than the excellent wine. "Where did you and Roland discover them?"

Her lips tightened. "They were legacies." She tapped the cigarette against the cut glass ashtray and watched the ash fall. "My mother's family owned them for years. I don't know how or when they were acquired."

"And your family is what? Danish?"

"Swedish."

"Sweden's an odd location for da Vincis to turn up. I thought Italians liked warmer climates."

She stiffened. "My mother never told me how the drawings came to be in the family."

"The Nazis stole trainloads of fine art," I reminded her. "A lot of it disappeared and then turned up in unusual locations."

She crushed out the cigarette and raised her chin. "Our drawings are heirlooms. My family had nothing to do with the Jewish question."

"Okay. I'm just trying to clarify the provenance."

"Then you're open to an offer?"

"How do you plan to tempt me?"

"Money, of course." Her finger floated up to my wrist. "Plus, I find you attractive."

"Like Sal?"

Her expression didn't change. "You're different."

"I'm flattered I made the cut."

"I can be very generous."

I remembered Sal's comment. "But I haven't heard your offer yet."

The finger fell away. "I'm not accustomed to negotiating, Mister Barrow."

I hadn't finished my wine, and we were back to surnames. "I thought that's what we're doing."

"Then you're willing to hear our proposal?"

"So long as it doesn't affect my loyalty to Phillip."

Betrayal of friends didn't make my list of faults. I didn't dance for pipers who offered to buy my loyalty. Whatever questionable genes my father had handed down, he skipped the disloyalty strand.

Isabelle sighed indulgently. "Money isn't about loyalty. Winners and losers are cut from different cloth."

"I guess that depends on how you define the losers."

Our food sat untouched and Isabelle drained her wine and punched a single key on her iPhone.

"Pick me up."

She signaled the maître d' and two waiters materialized to shift the table so she could rise without effort. No check appeared and she walked away as though I had made an indecent offer. We found ourselves on the sidewalk, the BMW idling at the curb. Sal opened the door for her and I joined her in the rear, no martinis in sight. Sal concentrated on traffic without turning his head, and I had the feeling I'd slipped a notch in his judgment. I formed a mental picture of him wielding a heavy lamp. The thought didn't frighten me, but it didn't make me feel warm and friendly either.

"I'm disappointed," Isabelle said without looking at me. "My sources said you were brighter."

"Sources can be deceiving."

"Obviously."

She lit her fourth cigarette in the past hour.

"Our offer's still open," she said. "Remember what I said about winners and losers."

Sal eyed me in the mirror and I decided the evening's festivities were definitely over. He stopped at her townhouse and ushered her from the car. The silent ride continued to my apartment, where my newly revised status didn't include him jumping out to open my door.

Watching the car roll away, I raised my hand to my face, finding the lost promise of Isabelle's perfume. I experienced a moment of what-could-have-been until I remembered her comment about Riva and definition of winners. She had confirmed that humans branched into two distinct species when the subject of money arose. Dansby stood to one side near the top of the mountain. The Englishman was a hard man, but his love of art came before wealth. He was one of the fortunates who indulged the obsession without forfeiting his humanity. Isabelle resided somewhere in the lower regions.

The opportunity to learn more about her arrived next morning.

Chapter Twenty-One

Dansby planted his elbows on his desk and frowned at an engraved card between his fingers. I sat across from him, wondering if I should inform him of the previous night's failed seduction. It had made for an interesting evening, but I suspected Dansby expected no less from Isabelle Delaudier.

He leaned back and tossed the invitation onto the leather blotter. "I guess I'm still on the Delaudier's A-list," he said. "It's short notice, but it seems there's a soiree at their home this Saturday night."

I smiled. "I got my summons this morning."

He looked mildly surprised I'd been included in the dinner party.

"I called Roland to Rsvp and learned Isabelle's mother and brother are scheduled to arrive from Sweden," he said. "Some sort of welcome, I suppose. Seems the mother hasn't seen her daughter in ages and the old girl's never been in the States." He exhaled a resigned sigh. "I've invited Haley to tag along. She can compete with Isabelle for best-dressed female. She'll be bored out of her mind, but she likes glitz and the Delaudiers will pop her eyes."

"Oh, I don't know," I said, enjoying his discomfort. "A purveyor of questionable art, his viper of a wife, and a Scandinavian crone who won't speak a word of English. Sounds like a fun night. You think Sal will dress up as a butler?"

Dansby ignored me.

"Why don't we arrive as a British peer accompanied by his courtesan and faithful retainer?"

"Shut up, Adam."

We sat looking at one another, most likely entertaining the same thought. Riva was dead, the book was missing, and neither of us knew how complicit the Delaudiers might be. I was the only person who'd seen hard evidence the da Vinci drawings were not authentic, but were the offerings an unintentional misstep or a major swindle? In Dansby's eyes, I'd crawled up a tall tree and sat on an exposed limb, sawing away, Melzi's book had become the bane of my life.

Dansby opened a humidor and selected a fat Cuban, examining its length and clipping the tip while I waited. I watched the wheels turning and had the feeling he was calculating my value again, considering whether I was indispensable or a burden. He removed an old army field lighter from a desk drawer and lit the blunt tip, drawing contentedly until a cloud of smoke partially obscured his face.

"If you'd checked your impulse to help strays, I'd have my drawing without wondering why I took you on."

"Right. You'd be the proud owner of a genuine Donato Volpe."

"So you say. I only have your opinion."

"Look, we've covered all that. Either you believe me or you don't. Remember, you held off buying the drawing at the auction."

"Maybe that was a mistake."

When I offered no further defense, he said, "I like you, but I'm afraid you may turn out to be more trouble than your father."

"I'd have to work hard to reach that pinnacle."

He grunted and pulled at the Cuban. "You're well on your way."

A room existed inside Dansby that he allowed no one to enter. Peel away the walls and he was a decent human marked by brains and pragmatism. For all his admirable traits, I believed he concealed a controlled ability to do whatever was necessary to get whatever he desired. I had no problem imagining his service in the SAS, that he'd dispatch a wounded enemy if the tactical situation called for a practical solution. He'd repeatedly shown kindness since I came to work for him, but I suspected a darker side existed alongside his humanity, a separate capability he took care to conceal.

I looked around at the trappings of his past. The guns, the flags. The immense painting of desperate men in battle. I'd allowed him latitude in second-guessing me, but enough was enough. I'd suffered a concussion and seen Riva dead on the floor. Odds were the book caused his death, and I didn't need Dansby's judgment when I had held the truth in Riva's apartment. I stood and leaned on the edge of his desk.

"I don't need this, Phillip. I told you what I saw. You and Jean-Henri are free to chase whatever the Delaudiers trot out."

A cloud of smoke hid his eyes. After a moment he nodded and tapped the cigar in an ashtray hammered from an artillery round. When he didn't speak, I gathered our conversation and my position had reached an end and turned to leave.

"Sit down," he said.

I didn't move or turn around, fed up with playing the role of a wayward child. When I reconsidered and faced him, he ran a square hand over his scalp.

"Please," he said with visible effort.

I sat.

Unable to restrain a frown, he blew out a veil of tobacco smog.

"Money can't do it all," he mumbled. The words seemed a confession, one he found difficult to admit. "I learned that lesson a long time ago. In my position, you require trustworthy people to guard your flanks. They make occasional mistakes, but it's with good intentions and if their poor judgment doesn't get you killed, they retain their worth."

"Why not hire a couple of cretins off the docks?" I said. "Pay them enough and they'll be loyal."

He waved smoke away. "That's not what I'm talking about and you know it. As the Bard said, I favor a band of brothers, not Judas creatures."

"I'm no soldier."

"No, but trust can be as valuable as men-at-arms, dear boy."

He balanced the cigar on the ashtray lip. I sensed he was remembering an incident in his past, a blunder or betrayal by someone he trusted. I thought about Kat and tried not to think of the mistakes I'd made.

"You may be foolhardy at times," he said, "but you won't betray me."

"Riva's book wasn't my imagination, and I believed his story."

"Well, if you can produce it, there'll certainly be an earthquake in the art world, I assure you."

"Then you want me to keep looking?"

"For the moment, let's hear what Roland and Isabelle have to say about this new hoard of da Vincis. Boring or not, the evening may prove enlightening."

. . .

I thought about calling Leslie and inviting her to join me, wondering if that would be good form if I invited one of the Delaudiers' employees. Showing up with her at a dinner party might not fit their social guidelines.

Saturday night I found myself in a tuxedo, riding in Dansby's limo and trying not to stare at the expanse of Haley's bare thigh as she accepted a drink from him. Thanks to the lavish use of electricity, the city looked like a Christmas tree no one ever turned off. Driving past the less fortunate in a chauffeured limo was now my revamped world, and I vowed never to accept the other side as the best I could do. I was still on probation, understanding people like Dansby didn't permanently subsidize waifs.

A somber doorman met us at the Delaudiers' townhouse. Two uniformed retainers escorted us through a marble lobby surrounded by scrolled mirrors and Deco light fixtures. We entered a paneled elevator and I wondered if the army of costumed extras came with the building, or if the Delaudiers employed them for special occasions. Either way, I entered the tasteful but contrived scene that seemed as though it had been lifted from a 1930s movie set.

The elevator doors opened and another cast member escorted the three of us through an expansive living area into the dining room where a twenty-foot dining table lacked only matching candelabras to complete the lavish setting. There were no children or pets, disorder of any kind being forbidden. Two massive crystal chandeliers shone down on gleaming sterling and crystal; rows of gold sconces lined wainscoted flocked walls. Each place setting meticulously arranged, tall vases of cut flowers positioned behind Louis XIV dining chairs. Liveried servants stood behind each chair.

Isabelle Delaudier stood beside the table next to a withered elderly woman, measuring me with an icy stare. I checked to be certain everything was zipped up and promised myself I'd keep my mouth shut and my ears open.

Isabelle shifted her eyes to Haley, while Roland engaged in conversation with a younger man, their heads almost touching. Dansby greeted our hostess, and we joined the two men, the four tuxedoes completing what might have passed as the evening's string quartet.

"Phillip," Roland Delaudier said. He ignored me and turned to the other man. "Nils, this is Major Dansby. Phillip, Nils König, Isabelle's brother. He's visiting us along with their mother. They only just arrived, our guests of honor tonight." He turned to me. "And this is Adam Barrow. He's…" He cocked his head at Dansby with manufactured confusion. "Tell me again, Phillip, what he does for you."

"My trusted confidant and associate," Phillip replied in a clipped tone. "He's also a lifelong friend, as was his father," he added, stretching the truth.

Isabelle joined us and Roland gave her a smile she did not return. Side by side in evening clothes, they looked like a formal set piece, planned additions to the formal room. But who knew about people? It was possible they had a trapeze installed in their bedroom.

Phillip and I shook hands with König who looked nothing like a poster boy for Sweden. In his fifties and immaculate in a tailored tux, his thick black hair brushed straight back. His dark eyes betrayed boredom with the evening and gave no hint of Scandinavian heritage. Hell, I looked more Nordic than Nils König.

"Nils's mother, Ebba, has never been in the States," Roland said.

I looked at his brother-in-law. "Then you've been here before?"

"Last year," he said, looking for the server with a drink tray. "I transported some artwork for Roland and Isabelle."

The champagne appeared and we each lifted a glass. I shot Dansby a glance, believing at least one mystery was resolved.

"So you're the anonymous da Vinci owners," Dansby said. "I assume the drawings cluttering Roland's vaults are your family's property?"

Nils König downed half his wine with a proud smile, displaying teeth so perfect they revealed an expensive dentist. "Isabelle talked Mama into allowing the firm to offer them at auction," he said. "Our family hated parting with them, but they deserve wider appreciation."

I had the feeling we'd just been served a large order of something you preferred not to step in, guessing the family would dry their tears when eight and nine figure checks arrived in their bank accounts.

"Everyone was amazed," Phillip said. "Quite the stir since it was believed most of his work is well catalogued."

A tiny vestige of color disappeared from König's eyes. "Family possessions, Major. We preferred to enjoy them ourselves."

"How fortunate."

I entered the fray. "But there's an solid trail of provenance, right?"

König turned to me. "If you find it necessary to trace the lineage, you'll find the family owned them for generations."

"Then there *is* bona fide trail of past ownership."

Exasperated, Roland waved his hand. "The da Vincis were never outside of their home."

Phillip looked at him. "You must admit that's unusual. A trove of priceless art with a clean bill of health." He grinned and rested a hand on my shoulder. "My assistant here has experience with hidden treasure, right, Adam?"

Relieved to steer the conversation in another direction, Roland turned to me. "Ah, yes, the van Gogh," he said. "A piece of luck."

"Blind hogs and all that," I said. "Like so much in the art business."

Roland looked offended and didn't reply. I looked around the lavish room as though I'd seen better. I might be the bastard at the family reunion, but Riva's murder took the edge off my presence, and the evening might provide answers.

Roland was still trying to figure me out when Leslie walked through the door on Marsh Hampton's arm. Dressed in a strapless white gown. I suppressed a groan and wondered how to arrange Hampton's early departure. I tried to make eye contact with her, but she looked past me. Was this a private business event or had she expected me to invite her? She went to Isabelle, and they laughed as though sharing a private joke. Poor Haley sidled closer to Phillip, a lamb surrounded by wolverines. I felt sorry for her, wagering she'd watch Dansby for which fork and spoon to use.

"Now that everyone's here, why don't we find our seats?" Isabelle said. Everyone located their name cards, and I eyed an impressive Matisse original mounted behind my allotted chair. Isabelle commanded one end of the table, Roland facing her at the far tip of the elaborate table. She gently pinged one of her wine glasses and lifted a hand toward the diminutive woman beside her.

"For those of you who haven't met her, I'd like to introduce Ebba König, my mother. Seated next to her is my handsome brother, Nils. They're our honored guests this evening."

The elderly woman seated next to her smiled demurely and took bird sips of her wine. Close to ninety, she styled her stark white hair in a flawless bun, her black dress fastened high on her neck with tiny pearl buttons and a diminutive silver brooch the only concessions to feminine adornment. Veined hands and sinewy neck failed to conceal she'd once been an appealing woman. I was reminded of a black and white 19th century daguerreotype as Ebba König sat upright in her high-backed chair Her eyes missed nothing, taking the measure of everyone and everything in the overstated room.

Isabelle looked around the table and announced how wonderful it was to see her again. I noticed Nils didn't look up, a half-smile on his face. He polished off his champagne and lifted the glass toward the server behind his chair.

Isabelle gestured to a fastidious gnome in a white tux who had slipped into the room, awaiting his cue. "George is this evening's sommelier," she informed us,

The unctuous little man bowed and announced the wine and menu pairings, asking each guest's wine preference. A fastidiously dressed man I assumed was the caterer floated to Isabelle and whispered to her. She nodded and he disappeared back into the kitchen. Wine was poured and everyone fabricated something to say to their seatmates. Everyone except Nils, who only glanced at his watch. Seated between his mother and Leslie, he sampled the first offering of wine and made a face. The server immediately filled a fresh glass and Nils downed it without sampling the new pour.

"The wine's not to your taste?" Isabelle asked him.

"No."

She gave a thin smile she resrved for intolerable chidren . "I'm sure we'll find something to your liking before you leave us."

Leslie, seated across from me, graced me with raised eyebrows at the exchange. I sat between Haley and Marsh and kicked myself for not calling her, wondering if the Delaudiers had commanded Marsh accompany her.

During dinner, Isabelle chatted with her mother and those around her without another glance at Nils. She performed her duties as the perfect hostess, a different woman from the schemer who attempted to buy my loyalty. As the bevy of servers cleared the small plates, I caught Ebba König's eye and jumped in, smiling at her.

"Sweden's an interesting country," I ventured.

"You are very kind," she replied in a reedy voice. "America is so different, although I've only seen New York." Her English was excellent with little accent.

"Where did you learn English?"

"I studied it as a girl. Learning it became my hobby."

"König isn't Swedish, is it?"

Isabelle laid a hand on her mother's sleeve. A warning?

Ebba König ignored her and pursed pale lips. "You are correct, Mister.... Barrow, is it? It is not Swedish."

"I didn't think so."

"How did you come to that conclusion?"

"It sounds more German."

"You're very perceptive, young man," she said, a defiant light in her eyes. "It's my married name. My husband was German. A refugee from the war."

Nils leaned across the table. "We were not concerned with blame when the hostilities ended. We are…"

Ebba König cut him short without taking her eyes from me. "Our name means *king* in German, you know."

Isabelle leaned close, patted her hand and whispered something to her. The older woman pulled her hand away.

"I was much younger than my husband. Isabelle and Nils came along later in our lives. Hans and I were resigned to never having children when they surprised us. My husband was a randy specimen," she said with a blush of pride.

"Mother…" Isabelle began.

"Oh, don't worry so much. These people are not naïve. They should know you and Nils come from hardy stock."

Isabelle looked relieved when silver serving carts appeared beside her chair and table conversation drifted back to the mundane after Ebba's revelations. Dinner proved a stiff affair, plates whisked away the moment each guest sat back. As expected, the food was excellent and vintage wines refilled empty glasses. Nils and Marsh showed the most appreciation for the selections and alcohol eventually lubricated conversation that drifted to art and ultimately, the da Vincis.

Roland dabbed his lips with his napkin and turned to Phillip. "So, Phillip," he said, "it might appear gauche to talk business at the table, but Ebba and Nils might like to hear your opinion about their da Vincis."

"Roland…" Isabelle began.

"No, that's quite all right," Phillip said. "After all, they're giving up family heirlooms."

Roland met his wife's stare. "Quite so."

Nils thrust his glass toward Phillip. "I for one would like to hear Major Dansby's explanation for passing on the drawing." His eyes retreated into the bottomless pits I'd seen earlier. "I think we are all owed his opinion why the first offering sold below estimates."

The chime of silverware and crystal halted and conversation died away. Dansby weighed his opponent in the hush, aware Nils had consumed more than a bottle of wine without touching his food.

"I don't try to guess what's in the minds of other bidders, Mister König," he said. "My vast and inestimable powers don't include mind reading."

Ebba König covered her mouth and tittered. She understood enough English to appreciate Phillip's jibe, apparently enjoying her son's discomfort.

"I don't see a soothsayer's turban, Nils," she quipped. "Mister Dansby doesn't appear clairvoyant."

Stung, Nils pointed a fork at me. "From what Roland tells me, you took an active part in deterring Major Dansby's interest. Roland also said you voiced personal doubts about the drawing. Possibly you had other reasons for driving down the bid."

I didn't wait for Phillip to rescue me. "I didn't know for certain if the drawing was authentic or not," I said. "In any case, I couldn't have afforded it unless Isabelle allowed me to pay a hundred dollars a week."

Ebba giggled, nodding appreciatively in my direction. Money, it appeared, hadn't overridden her sense of humor. Nils, however, found an adversary.

"From what I was told, you assisted in disrupting the auction," he said.

Nils had good command of the English language. I didn't need his accusations or benediction, and whatever his table manners, he lacked the grace to avert confrontation at a dinner party. Everyone looked at us, and I was about to elevate the fray when Leslie leaned forward.

"Mister Barrow came to the aid of an elderly confused person," she said. "I never visited Mister Riva's home and doubt he could have afforded anything in the auction."

Marsh, who was keeping up with Nils glass for glass, raised his voice. "We did all right despite the amusing little sideshow."

Leslie glared at him. "Marsh, eat and shut up."

He ignored her. "The piece actually came in at our lower estimate," he said, "but screw it. One never knows what to expect at an auction, does one?" He held up his glass for a refill and toasted his employers who glared at him. "Overall, however, my calculations indicate we had a very successful evening."

"Not for our family," Nils shot back.

Isabelle opened her mouth to speak and thought better of it. She turned to Phillip. "If there are questions about the da Vincis, the owners are here tonight. We can clear the air before the next auction."

"Any doubts raised by Enzo Riva are moot," Phillip said, "He was murdered several nights ago."

Leslie eased her fork onto her plate and looked at me. "I'm sorry."

No one spoke until Nils cleared his throat and raised his glass for another refill. "Well, that's one good turn of events."

I resisted the impulse to smash his face. Instead, I experienced a rare epiphany, one that should have occurred earlier. No matter what happened, Nils' relief verified my conviction the drawings were tainted. Watching his glass being refilled,

"Then the matter's closed," Roland said. "Phillip will have a crack at another da Vinci and everyone will come away satisfied."

I looked at Dansby who looked away and then at Isabelle who leaned past her mother to say something to Nils and I nodded at Leslie, grateful for rising to my defense. Considering my status with the Delaudiers, she'd taken a chance. It was the second time she'd rescued me, and her stock gained another hundred points in my eyes. If anyone deserved the truth about Riva's book, she was near the top.

After coffee, we made our way out. I felt a tug on my sleeve and Marsh Hampton steered me toward a guest bedroom, the wine glass still in his hand. Dansby frowned at me, but I followed Hampton. He closed the door and I started to speak when he propped his back against one wall and belched, his breath smelling like the bottom of a wine barrel.

"How's *that* for a set of in-laws?" he grinned.

"Not your favorite people, I take it."

"Nils is an asshole, Swedish variety. Roland can't seem to get enough of him, and the old lady's like a ghost enjoying the show."

"Why tell me?"

"And all that crap about heirlooms," he blurted, looking around for a bottle. "How bereaved are they if they're selling the damn things?"

When I didn't answer, he frowned at his empty glass. "Assholes, the bunch of them."

"Whatever. You work for them."

"There are things you and Dansby don't know."

"Like what?"

"Like the da Vincis' real history."

I was tempted to find Dansby and let him hear Hampton's doubts, but thought better of it. Opinions and accusations from a drunk did nothing to dispel doubts. My father had taught me that pandering to drunks was a waste of time.

Marsh pointed a finger at me. "Just tell Dansby to be careful. You too."

"Have you told Leslie any of this?"

"Leslie?" Marsh gave a crooked smile. "She's not interested in artsy details. She's earning more money than she's ever seen and that's more than enough for her."

There was an insistent knock on the door. Marsh opened it and Roland stood in the doorway looking inquisitively at us.

"We were discussing the pleasure of Leslie's company," Marsh said, reverting to his former wine voice. "Adam took offense, and we were about to settle the issue like men. Pistols or swords." A burp. "We haven't decided."

I shrugged as though Marsh was beyond reclamation. "He's just a little drunk."

Roland shook his head. "Go home, Marsh. We'll discuss this tomorrow."

I slipped past them and found the elevator. Dansby's limo idled at the curb. He and Haley ignored me and the ride to my apartment was quiet. I said nothing about Marsh's accusations. Dansby, plainly distracted, endured Haley's prattle about Isabelle's dress.

"Nils is a plonker," he said to me.

Haley screwed up her face. "What's a Plonker?"

I'd been around him long enough to gauge Dansby's moods and this wasn't his best. He was not someone to be played, and the Delaudiers and Königs hadn't quelled his uneasiness about the da Vincis.

He ignored Haley's puzzled look, leaned forward and gripped my knee.

"Find the goddamn book."

Chapter Twenty-Two

East Prussia
Coastal Road to Pillau
January 9, 1945

Weisser slipped from the truck cab and stretched, his knees and elbows stiff from the relentless cold. He'd taken a chance and slept for an hour by the roadside, hunched beneath four blankets until the agony in his finger stumps woke him. Sleep was a risk, but no worse than drifting off and crashing into a ditch or tree.

Rubbing a stiff glove over bloodshot eyes, he rotated his neck and fought off the temptation of sleep. The snow came down harder and covered the hood. He punched the starter, thankful when the engine rumbled to life. The wheels fought for traction and he sensed the truck was faltering, weaving from side to side like a punch-drunk boxer as it battled through the slush.

The chance of finding a neutral ship at Pillau seemed more distant than ever. Had he been delusional, believing he could escape with the crate? The godforsaken country had devoured the entire goddam German army, reducing duty and loyalty oaths to baubles of the past. He'd done his part. Any fool should have seen the end two years ago. The crusade was over. Defeat hurtled toward Germany from the east and west like mating locomotives. The SS had tried to shield the Fatherland and the world by removing the menace. The army and German people proved unworthy of their efforts and he wanted no part of what lay ahead. He'd done what was necessary. Why should he share in failure and disgrace?

The tires broke free of the ruts and skidded toward the ditch. Weisser swore at his lapse and hauled the tottering vehicle back into the furrows, gasping. For once he could not blame the rabbi's gibberish hurled at him from the edge of the grave. He cleared his mind and coerced his memory back to better times. Food, he thought. Think about your favorite foods. Hot strudel smothered in fresh cream. Pretzels and sweet mustard. Spätzle. The tastes burst in his dry mouth, then fled as the storm intensified.

Heavy flurries thumped at the slab-sided GAZ. His reserves near an end, he concentrated on the road to the sea and salvation. Frigid air inside the cab burned his lungs, and he bit his lip to stay alert. A gust of wind struck the tailgate and fishtailed the truck toward the ditch again. Suppressing a whimper, Weisser fought the ruts, pleading with the engine to hold together another hour.

A ship, Weisser thought, unable to banish the illusion from his brain. Big freighter, small freighter, fishing boat, scow. Any seaworthy vessel to steam away from the madness. Sail away and never look back... if Pillau remained open.

Despite the heavy gloves his fingers ached around the steering wheel, visibility less than twenty feet. His breath condensed into fog the moment it left his mouth, the vapor threatening to fall in his lap. He craned his neck forward. The rock-hard wipers smeared sludge and dirty snow over the windshield. He glanced at the Schmeisser on the seat. Bribing the sentry with the PPS had been foolish. If partisans penetrated this far south...

He slammed his fist against the steering wheel and yelled as pain shot to his shoulder. Grimacing, he leaned the submachine gun on the floor against the firewall, the only warm spot in the cab. The last thing he needed was a frozen weapon. If it failed him, partisans would butcher him, break up the crate and its contents or firewood, and scatter everything to the winds.

The wind abated and Weisser's hopes jumped as he glimpsed choppy open water through the trees on his left. Open water! The grizzled sentry had been right. No ice meant the port remained open. He added another five kilometers an hour and slowed only when he saw lines of civilians ahead. He held down the horn and the straggling column turned to stare, a few lifting a pleading arm as the truck sped past them. A line of telephone poles appeared. Their civilized presence lifted his spirits until he saw the naked corpses hanging from the cross-beams, many wearing only their boots. The SS liked decorating the poles with naked bodies as warnings to would-be deserters.

Ahead, a striped sentry pole blocked the road. A squad of soldiers clustered around a makeshift fire, stamping their feet, ignoring the refugees. Weisser braked to a halt. Relieved when he saw SS markings on the tunic collars, he tugged Göring's letter from between the seats and opened his coat to reveal his rank. Hands clasped behind his back, a buck-toothed *Untersturmführer* approached the truck. He scanned the photo in Weisser's *Soldbuch* and brought his heels together.

"You're free to pass, sir."

Relieved and disgusted, Weisser stared down at the youthful SS officer. "Your name, *Leutnant?*"

The chapped young face reddened "Reissler, sir."

"Don't you want to see my orders, Reissler?"

"Sir." Abashed, the officer sheepishly scanned Göring's letter.

"I need to deliver my cargo to the port master," Weisser told him. He pointed out Göring's signature. "You can see the urgency."

"Yes, sir. The place is a madhouse. It was once a U-boat training base, but most of the sailors are long gone. Just thousands of worthless civilians and the rump end of the army who don't want to be liberated by the Red Army." He looked closer at Weisser. "Sir, are you *the* Anton Weisser?"

"Unless someone has assigned me a new name."

"I was temporarily attached to *Einsatzkommando F*," the lieutenant said, He stamped his feet against the cold and flashed Weisser a toothy grin. "We followed your unit outside Kiev. You didn't leave us much to do."

"I trust you found work."

"Yes, sir. Always a stray Commissar or Jew."

"Then you did your duty."

"We didn't leave any garbage behind if that's what you mean," the boy said. Weisser hadn't heard the old fervor in years.

Weisser retrieved his papers. "As an officer, I'm sure you did your best. Now, tell me where can I find the port master if there is one."

The officer pointed down the road. "This road ends at the docks. Keep going until you reach a warehouse. You can't miss Major Baumann's office." Reissler made a disgusted noise. "He's old army brass who doesn't care for the SS."

"That's his problem. We have a way of getting what we want, don't we, *Leutnant?*"

Reissler grinned. "Yes, sir." He waved to his men "Raise the crossbar."

Weisser ground the truck in gear and looked at the petrol gauge. The needle touched the Empty peg, not that it mattered any longer. Half a kilometer later he saw whitecaps and the sea. Glutted with ships, the shoreline bristled with batteries of anti-aircraft guns. A vast wooden building loomed on a spit of land jutting into the harbor.

He slowed and halted at the harbor master sign above the building's entrance. He dismounted, his legs protesting the numbness. Slouched in the doorway a sentry cupped a cigarette and failed to notice his rank. Weisser yelled and waved the private to the truck. The man flicked away the cigarette, galvanized by the sound of authority.

"Watch the truck," Weisser ordered. "Shoot anyone who touches the cargo. Do you understand?"

"Yes, sir," the private mumbled.

"Do you understand me?" Weisser grated.

The sentry braced and stared at the truck over Weisser's shoulder.

"Jawohl, Herr Sturmbannführer!"

Weisser ran his eyes over the sagging GAZ with the sensation he was abandoning a dying subordinate who had done his duty. It was a stupid sentiment abut a piece of machinery, and he wondered what would happen to it now that it no longer served any purpose. Dismissing the thought, he pointed a warning finger at the sentry and walked into the warehouse, footsteps booming in the cavernous spce.

Orderly rows of desks and tables and uniforms occupied every square foot. A halo of narrow horizontal windows near the ceiling provided the only light, the temperature hovering near freezing. The exposed rafters were hazy with cigarette smoke as men and women auxiliaries wove between the acre of tables, clutching papers and documents. Behind a single massive desk on a raised platform in the center of the room, an elderly *Wehrmacht* major ruled the maelstrom. Weisser mounted three wooden steps and stepped before the desk. The corpulent harbor master did not look up, intent on stamping documents and issuing orders to anxious faces that crowded around him.

"Major Baumann?"

The officer rubber stamped a paper without looking up. *"Ja,* what do you want?"

In the midst of the chaos, Baumann appeared dressed for parade ground drill, his field grey uniform brushed and pressed, tailored to disguise the fact he was running to fat. North of fifty, with a monocle and moustache left over from the last century, he smelled of cheap cologne that fought damp wool and ripe sweat around him.

Aware of his own appearance, Weisser waited until the man looked up at him. "I have a critical shipment. It requires passage to a German port."

Baumann took in the SS insignia and squinted at Weisser as though the newcomer had requested a trip to the moon.

"A German seaport. Man, are you daft? British aircraft shoot up anything that floats toward the Fatherland. You wouldn't make it halfway to Stettin."

"Then what are those ships in the harbor?"

The harbor master tossed his ink pen on the desk. "Those are the lucky ones. They slipped past the Brit's Beaufighters and Mosquitos to bring in a few supplies, but no one wants to make the return trip. Not if they value their asses."

"What about neutral ships?" Weisser asked.

"Neutral?" Baumann tilted his head. "If your cargo's bound for Germany, why would you want a neutral ship?"

It was the question Weisser feared. Lugging a crate around the harbor, asking for a neutral vessel would only attract attention and the field police. He decided to push his luck with Baumann.

"My cargo is the property of *Reichsmarschall* Göring." Weisser handed Baumann the letters and lowered his voice. "I would imagine he'd be most appreciative if he can claim it after the war."

Baumann at first appeared not to hear the request. He shifted papers on the desk and drummed his fingers, looking around at his faceless charges, most of whom he knew would bolt at the first sign of a Russian tank.

Weisser saw a glint edge into the man's eyes as he looked up. Nothing awaited an overweight Major except a suicidal stand to defend the city. Years spent in the army with nothing to show for it, Weisser thought, except the uniform on his back and a dead or destitute wife waiting in Germany. Rare opportunities arose in everyone's life and the supply officer had recognized a solution. Yes, indeed, Weisser thought, the man appeared sufficiently intelligent to know a savior had arrived.

Baumann removed his ridiculous monocle and manufactured a crafty smile that confirmed Weisser's analysis.

"You think you can just sail away? You and your precious cargo?"

Weisser leaned forward and planted both fists on the desktop. "A cargo valuable enough to change two lives."

Baumann sniffed at the filthy SS uniform and slipped the monocle from his eye socket without taking his gaze from Weisser. He polished the oval with a clean handkerchief and screwed it back in place without hesitation.

"A neutral ship, eh? Let me check the manifests."

Chapter Twenty-Three

Marsh Hampton and Sal, dressed as black-clad ninjas, tiptoed through Jean-Henri's apartment, flashlights waving in the darkness. Sal plopped down on a white couch watching them and started to sing his version of Dean Martin's "That's Amore," while Marsh danced toward the rows of Jean-Henri's books, a martini glass in one hand...

I jerked awake and groaned into my pillow, paying the price for mixing champagne with red and white wine. Pushing aside unpleasant vestiges of the dinner party, I padded to the fridge, found orange juice, and drained the lifesaving liquid straight from the carton. In the bathroom I downed three Excedrin with a glass of water that tasted like toothpaste. I slouched back to the living room and squinted out my 12th floor window at the annoying sunshine, recalling Dansby's marching orders.

Find the book.

Simple enough—if I had any idea where to begin.

I started coffee and eased into a chair by the window, considering my options as I gazed across the cityscape in the direction of Riva's apartment building. He'd been my only link to Melzi's book. It had either been stolen or hidden by Riva. Still, the ruined apartment was a starting place since its occupant could no longer tell me anything.

Feeling the Excedrin work its magic, I went to the bedroom and searched my coat for the card the police detective had given me. I called the number and left a message. Pulling on a blue denim button-down shirt and jeans, I was lacing up my sneakers when the phone rang.

"This is Lomax," an impatient voice said. "You called me?"

"I need to get into Enzo Riva's apartment. He borrowed several books and I'd like them back." It was lame and I hated lying to a New York City detective.

I heard a sigh. "Okay, Tell the officer outside his door to call me. He'll let you in, but don't remove anything but your books."

I thanked him, then dialed Leslie's number, deciding I might as well blend pleasure with work. Had her appearance with Marsh at the dinner party been more than a business commitment? Did Hampton offer more, or had I misread the situation? A bruised ego overrode my jealousy, trusting that she'd given signals I might be more than a fellow art lover.

"Adam," she said when she answered. "I'm glad you survived last night. Wasn't that a delightful little event?"

"Oh, I don't know," I said. "Jousting with Swedish pricks like Nils sharpens my New York wit, if you'll pardon my French."

She laughed and I realized how much I wanted her in my life.

"I'm going to Riva's apartment," I said, "to try to find anything related to his book."

"You still believe in it?"

"More than ever after watching Nils's display."

"What about the mother?" she said. "She looks like a witch out of Grimm's Fairy Tales, but she seems like a nice enough old lady."

"You think she lures children to a little cabin and bakes them in her oven?"

"Or to an ice cave in the fjords?"

"Do they have fjords in Sweden?"

"Unless Norway has a patent on them."

She laughed again. "She's still sharp enough to jerk a knot in her son," she said. "Isabelle looked like she couldn't wait for her to shut up."

"I don't think either of us are on Isabelle's short list of favorites." I said, remembering why I'd called her. "Look, I'm going to Riva's to look around. Come with me and I'll buy you lunch."

The connection went silent and I wondered if she was considering whether I was worth a free meal.

"Can't do it," she said. "Roland's scheduled a photo shoot this morning for the next catalog. These things can last forever."

"Then call me when you finish up. We'll have a late lunch."

She paused, then said, "Okay."

Disappointed by her hesitation, I commandeered one of Phillip's cars and driver for later. He'd ordered me to find the book, so I took advantage of his resources, besides which I was sick of cabs that smelled like curry or pine odor eaters. I told the driver to wait and went up to the apartment. No cops in the hall this time, only a strip of yellow crime scene tape across the door frame.

I ducked under it and closed the door. Books and debris were still scattered around the room, a few marked with numbered evidence stickies. Black fingerprint powder covered almost every flat surface. In the bedroom I looked down at the dried bloodstain without speaking and turned away.

I went back to the living room. Tipped over, Riva's chair still rested on its back. Cushions and padding slashed open, the few other pieces of furniture destroyed by whomever had killed him. The kitchen cabinet doors gaped open and broken glassware littered the kitchen linoleum, the shelves swept clean either during the search or in a fit of anger. I stepped over the wreckage and looked around, examining the remnants of the room where I'd shared grappa with a lonely old man. I picked up a book, staring around at the fragments of his life. The police had found almost three hundred dollars hidden in a drawer on the bedroom floor, ruling out a robbery.

I walked to the overturned chair. The burlap covering ripped away. I ran my hand inside the opening.

Nothing.

I patted the chair. It had been a clever hiding place, but whoever killed him was smarter. Too many people knew about the book and I was partly to blame for that. A lot of collectors and museums would shell out big bucks to shield their da Vincis from the truth, and I imagined Leonardo and Melzi groaning in their graves with frustration. Whoever possessed the book would either conceal it, or rumors of fakes and fraudulent sales would turn the art world upside down.

I stood in the center of the room and looked around. For no discernible reason, it didn't feel right that the book had been stolen. Dansby put faith in my seventh sense and this time I felt he was right. Riva had been a cagey old guy, too cautious to leave Melzi's book hidden inside a chair, especially after admitting its existence to Phillip and Jean-Henri. I didn't believe in ghosts, but I sensed Riva looking over my shoulder as I tried to make sense of the turmoil he created.

I stepped over the chaos on the floor and walked into the kitchen where a clear glass vase of wilted flowers sat undisturbed on the sink. Someone other than me had liked him. I ran my fingers over dead petals that dropped onto the countertop. Peering closer, I reached beneath the wilted stems and plucked a small cardboard square from the vase. I shook water from the card and tried to read the sender's name.

Holding the dripping card between my thumb and index finger, I looked closer. The sender's name had dissolved, but the printed florist label was readable. Toliver-Banhill Floral Arrangements on East 70th Street. Located near the Frick museum, it seemed a ritzy neighborhood for someone to order flowers for a recluse.

I blotted the cardboard with a paper towel. Folding the card in the towel I slipped it in my pocket and walked through the apartment a final time with a small sense of satisfaction. Whoever sent the flowers knew Riva.

Phillip's car waited obediently at the curb. I picked up Leslie and we ended up in front of The Olde Boston Tavern. Settled in a sterile booth next to the front window, she looked around, appraising our fellow diners.

"Probably not many Yankee fans in here."

I laughed and hated Marsh Hampton a little more. We both ordered corned beef sandwiches on rye with extra horseradish sauce, creamy coleslaw and home fries. She ordered a Blue Moon draft with her sandwich and I opted for a Coke, not wanting to tempt the wine into doing war with my gut. The food surpassed our expectations. Neither spoke as we leaned over our plates, concentrating on avoiding the runoff of fiery sauce. I liked the way she felt at ease with the leaking sandwich, licking her fingertips in a manner that made it appear socially acceptable.

"I went to Riva's," I said between bites.

She didn't look up. "Find anything?"

I remembered the florist card and eased the towel from my coat pocket. She looked at the damp card and back at me.

"Only this."

"So?"

"I found it at his apartment."

She bent her head and read the label. "You think they'll tell us who sent flowers?"

"What else do we have?"

My spirits jumped at the fact she'd said "us." If I had to enlist an ally, she was my first choice for a number of reasons, the first being the fact I might be falling in love with her.

"Checking them out will only take a few minutes." I said as an idea took shape.

When we finished lunch, the waiter took pity on our greasy napkins and brought damp cloth napkins. We paid the check and rode to the upper eastside without saying much. I think we both silently agreed we were wasting our time, but her nearness and the perfume she wore made the trip worthwhile. Sitting across from me in the facing seat, she crossed her legs and I kept my politically correct eyes on the sidewalks, determined to keep my hormones under control.

Tolliver-Banhill looked more like an upscale women's boutique than a flower shop, with no tinkling little bell over the door to announce us when we entered. Like all florists the air was humid and syrupy with flower arrangements and greenery. A wall of temperature-controlled glass doors contained massive sprays of fresh-cut flowers. Anything as intrusive as a cash register or electronic billing devices had been vanquished in favor of an unobtrusive counter manned by an emaciated young man. Bent over an iPhone, his magenta shirt flared open at the neck, a gold hummingbird pendant dangling from a thin chain that complemented the two rings on both his thumbs.

We waited until he clicked off and gave us a tight smile. "Yes? May I help you?" he drawled.

I mimicked my best Bruce Willis and rested my arms atop the counter, inches away from his startled face.

"That depends on your willingness to cooperate."

He flushed and stepped back while I remained leaning on the counter. Pulling Lomax's card from my wallet I handed it to him.

"I'm Detective Frank Lomax," I said. "I need information about a customer."

He inspected the card and I gambled he wouldn't ask to see a badge. I could sense Leslie staring at me.

"This is Mrs. Arianna Turner," I said, gesturing at her without taking my eyes from the clerk. "She's the daughter of a man who was murdered last week. Your shop delivered flowers to him. I need the sender's name and address."

The clerk regained his composure and shook his head. "We don't divulge of clients' names. Our policy forbids—"

On rare occasions, the heavens beam down at you. Or at least show that the gods have a sense of humor. This time, their generosity arrived in the form of a police car that pulled to the curb outside the shop. The clerk froze in mid-sentence and I turned to see the black and white. I plucked the card from his fingers and brushed my elbows as though dust layered the countertop. "Okay, we'll do this at the station. What's your name?"

"Terrence Oliver."

"Look, Terrence. You can give me what I need or come with me. I don't care one way or the other. We can get a court order and you can explain to the owner why you closed up shop after refusing to cooperate with a police officer."

Terrence licked his lips and eyeballed the car. "Hold on a second."

He disappeared in the back and I smiled at Leslie. She shook her head. Terry returned with a copy of a receipt.

"A Miss Lucia Orellano," he said. "I wrote out the address for you."

Leslie glanced at me and started to speak before she changed her mind.

"You did the right thing, Terrence," I said.

He fingered the delicate hummingbird. "You won't tell her where you got her name, right?"

"Not to worry."

Leslie and I walked out and I looked sideways at her. "What were you going to say in there?"

"I think you're going to find out."

We walked to the police cruiser in case Terry was watching. I tapped on the window and asked the officer for directions to the Frick Museum. He pointed behind us and I thanked him while he scrutinized Leslie. I thanked him and we headed north along Central Park. I waved for Dansby's car to follow us.

"That was a ballsy performance," she said as we headed up Fifth Avenue.

"Saved a lot of time," I said, the adrenaline still pumping. "I'm sure Lomax would understand. The worst that happens is I get arrested for impersonating a police officer."

"Did you also arrange the police car?"

"Even impostors deserve an occasional break."

She took my arm. "Let's go meet this admirer."

. . .

Lucia Orellano lived on the park in a posh apartment building two blocks from the Frick. I hadn't expected Riva to have a friend this far uptown, but given the woman's last name, it seemed plausible. Whether she knew anything about the book was another matter.

The concierge in the chic lobby produced Orellano's apartment number when I flashed Lomax's card and told him we'd rather not be announced. We took the elevator to the fifteenth floor and an older woman answered the door.

"Miss Orellano, I'm Adam Barrow. I was a friend of Enzo Riva's," I said, mustering a look I hoped relayed sadness.

Statuesque in a blockish sort of way, she was broad-shouldered, somewhere in her late fifties or early sixties. Close to my height, Lucia Orellano wore a plain but expensive navy-blue dress. Dyed ebony hair failed to soften her square jaw or the expansive chin pointing in our direction. Dark eyes snapped to Leslie and back to me.

"How did you find me?"

"I was the one who discovered his body. Miss Orellano. Your name was with the flowers you sent."

Her chin came up, "You found Enzo?"

"A friend and I went to visit him. He was already dead when we arrived."

She stepped back and ushered us into an overly decorated room jammed with heavy furnishings of carved wood and dark upholstery. A gas log fire glowed in a miniscule fireplace, the marble mantle decorated with prancing cherubs. She gestured at a bulky settee, while she faced us in a claw-foot wingback chair. An overweight black cat perched on the back of the chair by her head, supremely ignoring us. Leslie and I sat side by side as though waiting for our hostess to scold us.

Removing a small black cigar from a worn leather box, she lit up and inspected us through the pungent smoke.

"How did you know Enzo?" she asked in a smoker's throaty voice.

"We shared an admiration of da Vinci and he..."

Lucia Orellano burst into laughter, exposing large even teeth and shaking her head. "Did he tell you he was from Anchiano, that he was born in the same town as Leonardo? That they shared a heritage?"

I sensed disaster.

"Enzo was not even born on the boot," she said. "He came from Sicily. the village of Savoca. His son had an affair with the wife of an important a man who was *cosa nostra*." Lucia looked as though the outcome had been predictable. "The boy was killed, of course. Enzo had some trouble of his own and emigrated with his wife."

I pictured bare rocky hills, ochre stone houses, men carrying short-barreled shotguns. I scrambled for something to say, aware Leslie was staring at me again.

"Was Enzo a friend?"

"He was my uncle."

"Your uncle." I looked around the luxurious room.

Lucia followed my gaze. "Despite his shortcomings, he was a proud man," she said, drawing at the cigarillo. "He would not accept my help or anything offered by his brother."

"He has a brother? In New York?"

"You know none of this?"

"No."

Her classical jaw tightened. She ground the cigarillo into an ashtray. "Then why are you here?"

"I hoped you might have information about a book he owned. A valuable book."

"I know nothing about a book."

"It's a very old book about Leonardo da Vinci," Leslie said.

The two women stared at one another. "We know a lot," Leslie said. "Like your uncle's name."

A glint of respect replaced Lucia's suspicions.

"You have courage," she said, "both of you, but some things are better avoided."

"Maybe I could talk with Enzo's brother," I said.

She uttered an abrupt sound. "You wish to talk with Joseph about a book?"

"Can you put me in touch with him?"

"You really don't know who he is?"

Leslie laid a hand on my arm.

Reeling from the succession of lies Riva had told me, Lucia Orellano pulled apart what I thought I knew. She drew on the small cigar and let smoke curl from her mouth.

"My uncle is Joseph Boscanni," she said. "Enzo was his half-brother."

Joey Boots.

Joseph Boscanni, the don who ran New York's mafia. His crews controlled most of the heroin trade and under-aged prostitution in the state and parts of New Jersey. A grandfatherly silver-haired don and bona fide monster, he successfully dodged indictments and grand juries. The newspapers and tabloids could not get enough of him, transforming him into a Tony Soprano anti-hero. His involvement made my day absolutely perfect.

"Joseph is taking an interest in who killed his brother," Lucia said. "He will be see justice is done."

Right, I thought, the kind of justice where a bloated body turns up in the East River or New Jersey junk yard. Sicilian family loyalty was more than a fictional device of movies and television. I might do a host of stupid things during my life, but involving Boscanni in the search for Melzi's book wasn't one of them.

Leslie cleared her throat. It was time to leave. I made appropriate noises about justice and the police. Lucia looked at me stonily and I surmised her hospitality had ended. Leslie picked up her purse as the cat watched without moving. I silently thanked Lucia who walked us to the door and opened it. No hand or words were offered and we heard the door close behind us.

Leslie faced the elevator door and giggled as we rode to the lobby.

"Joey Boots," she said as we exited the building. "You sure can pick 'em. Mister Art Investigator."

I reddened, unable to share her sense of humor.

"How did you know she was related?"

"I've been in New York longer than you."

"Why didn't you tell me before we went up?"

"More fun for you find out for yourself. The look on your face was worth the trip to the old gal's lair."

Enlivened by our visit with a mafia chieftain's niece, she said, "At least Roland will be glad to hear the book's gone forever."

"Sure. He can then sell more fakes and label them da Vinci."

"You know how this works, Adam," she said. "*Caveat emptor*. We offer art based on our best research. In this case, the König family."

I couldn't blame her for siding with the Delaudiers. We were on opposite buyer-seller sides of the fence. I started to remind her we had only the König's assurances, but I doubted such details interested her. If her employers made a boatload of money, a few dollars would trickle down to employees.

My thoughts drifted back to Riva, wondering why he'd lied to me. Maybe he'd been embarrassed, afraid his family's background would sully da Vinci's splendor. I'd never know his reasons and would have doubted the book's existence except I'd held it in my hands. Melzi's drawings had been real and I could still feel his book's weight in my lap.

"What will you do now?"

I lifted my shoulders and let them fall. "The book's real. Someone has it, but I know one thing. I value my body too much to attract Joey Boots' attention."

If the book was gone forever, I'd have to find other ways to research the remaining da Vincis. I had Jean-Henri as a tentative ally, but Dansby hadn't hired me to chase misattributed work. I believed what I'd held in my hands proved the Delaudiers were offering something other than da Vincis. I didn't know whether they were perpetrating fraud or making an innocent mistake, but I owed it to Dansby and Riva to find out.

Chapter Twenty-Four

Two nights later, I asked Leslie to join me for a drink, but she begged off. The Delaudiers had scheduled a staff meeting early next morning. Back at square one with no female company or idea what to do next, I considered my options. After a few minutes, I recalled our meeting with Lucia Orellano and the sand she'd thrown in the gears. I decided I wasn't in the mood to sit around my apartment, mulling over the consequences of what she told us. I pulled on a sport coat and headed out, giving the taxi driver Armands' address. Good jazz and good bourbon were poor substitutes for Leslie's company, but not the worst of companions.

As the cab weaved through traffic, I thought about the break-in at Jean-Henri's apartment. With nothing missing, a host of reasons pointed to an interrupted burglary. A noise in the hall or an amateur's loss of nerve would explain why nothing had been taken. No matter the reason, the timing seemed more than coincidental after our meeting with Riva.

The smokey lighting inside Armands cast a light blue patina over the empty stage. Valiant smokers defied the city ordinance, the walls hoarding decades of cigarette smoke from a time when people were allowed to make their own mistakes. The combo was on break but had drawn a small crowd along with a smattering of music-loving tourists. I was early, and empty seats remained at the bar. Settling myself onto a stool, I ordered a Basil Hayden from the blond bartender, outfitted in a sleeveless man's vest and black bow tie. One shoulder flaunted the tattoo of a prancing red unicorn. Appealing in a hard sort of way, she embodied a step up from college kids with a dirty bar rag.

"How's the new group?" I asked her.

She brushed lank blond hair to one side, removing a pair of stylish round glasses, her tired eyes reflecting she'd seen and heard almost everything from behind the bar.

"I liked the last one better," she said, cleaning the glasses, "but as long as they keep the doors open, positive, I can get used to anything."

"You work week nights?"

"I'm the owner," she said. "My bartender decided he needed some beach time and took off for the Keys."

"So, you're Armand."

She straightened the plastic condiments tray and gave me a crooked smile, revealing a set of braces. "Armand was my father's first name. Would you come in a place called Krabostawitz?"

"If the music was good."

She gave me a polite smile and headed to the other end of the bar. My upbeat mood wavered as I sipped my bourbon and watched the crowd. I missed Leslie, but thinking about her, I realized anything resembling a garden variety love life resided at the bottom of my tank. If I was honest, Leslie dulled the pain of Kat's death without requiring promises. She hadn't yet thrown me off the train, but it was always possible my fortunes would change. My amorous prospects aside, I needed to consider where we were headed.

I downed half my drink and was surveying the crowd when a thick-set man slipped onto the stool next to me. Just over five feet tall, he smiled, but the humor never reached his eyes.

"How you doin'?"

He was curly haired and clean-shaven and dressed in a suit perfectly tailored to his squat frame. A dark gray shirt flaunted gold cuff links that complemented a trendy yellow tie. A diamond ring caught the light, the stone large enough to strangle a chihuahua. He propped a foot on the bottom rung of my stool, leaning close enough for me to smell his aftershave, the unamused smile fading. A second presence loomed behind me as the bartender approached them.

"Hey, you're Adam Barrow, right?" Cuff Links said.

Before I could answer he looked over my shoulder and grinned at his companion. "See, I told you we'd find him here."

The bartender slid coasters in front of them and my new friend pushed them away without taking his eyes from me.

"Nothing for us. We're just talking, me and him."

She pushed the coasters back. "You sit at the bar, you have to order."

The man behind me cocked a thick forefinger and flicked his cardboard coaster at her. "We ain't thirsty."

"That's okay, Vincent," Cuff Links said. "She's just trying to make a buck. Two Buds, sugar."

I glanced at the bartender who walked away without looking back.

"Do I know you?" I knew it was a stupid question, but I had to hold up my end.

Capped teeth shone. "Not personally, but me and him had a bet where we'd find you. I bet on this dump, so I win."

I peered over my shoulder. The behemoth scrutinized me, scar tissue attesting to a life spent outside a monastery. Pushing three hundred pounds, he ignored his barstool and remained standing, his sizable gut pressed against my back.

"I'm happy for you," I said to his well-dressed colleague.

"Yeah, well, it's like this. Me and the guy standing behind you, we have mutual friends who were close to Enzo Riva." He gave a half-smile. "He was family, you know?"

Lucia Orellano hadn't wasted any time making a call after our visit.

I turned back to my drink. "I'm sorry for your loss."

The humorless smile returned. "Don't be a smart ass."

"Look, he was a colleague of mine."

The mountain behind me said, "Someone put a bullet in his head."

"Hey, Vincent, I'm talking to the man, okay?" French Cuffs took a pack of Marlboros from his jacket and held out the pack. "You want one?"

I shook my head, enduring the fleeting pang of an ex-smoker.

He returned the pack to his pocket. "The city's got all these pussy laws anyhow," he said. "I can smoke in here, but my wife says I need to quit. She says these things ain't good for you. I'm trying to make her happy, but I figure after thirty years, I figure it don't matter by now. There're worse things can happen to you, right?"

A single drop of sweat trickled between my shoulder blades, reinforcing the feeling now was not the time to debate medical advice. I nodded and finished my drink, desperate for another.

"But back to our problem here," he said, tapping my cardboard coaster with his forefinger. "You and your girlfriend were asking questions and—"

"She's got nothing to do with Riva's death."

"Whatever," he said. "All we know is you and some rich gonzo were the only ones there when the cops arrived. Nobody's seen or heard nothing since then."

The combo shuffled back on stage. The drummer hit a few warmup licks as my interrogator waited for some sort of confession.

"We called the police when we found him," I said.

"What, you want a gold star or something?" the man behind me said.

"Get off my case," I said without turning. "I didn't kill him."

"We didn't figure you killed him and called the cops," French Cuffs said. "We're looking for information about whoever killed a harmless old guy like him. He was the relative of a friend. Family, like I said. The cops ain't found jack shit and we thought you might tell us something useful."

"I'd tell you and the police if I knew anything else," I said half-truthfully.

"Yeah, it'd be a good thing if you did that," said his partner behind me.

"Shut up, Denny," his companion said irritably. "The man's trying to see things our way, aren't you, Adam?"

"With all my heart."

French Cuffs pressed a knuckle against my chest. "See? There you go being a smart ass again."

"I was talking to Riva about a painting, nothing more."

"Yeah, yeah, I heard he was nuts about art, but that don't get me closer to what I need."

The combo started a soft rendition of *The Last Time I Saw Paris* and I wondered if I'd ever see Paris again.

"Look, I lost a friend, so get off my case." I was tired of being intimidated. What would they do? Shoot me in front of a roomful of witnesses? It wasn't the mob's style, but maybe they would make an exception. "He was trying to help me and now he's dead." I forced myself to maintain eye contact. "I don't need this crap."

French Cuffs jerked his head back and looked amused. "Don't get your balls in an uproar. Nobody figures you for this. If they did, you'd already be gone. We just thought you might hear something." He dropped a twenty on the bar. "We'll be in touch in case you remember anything."

"Sure, okay."

"Enjoy your night, Adam."

His companion bumped my shoulder as they walked away. I watched as they crossed the dance floor, my heart slowing, aware I had added the mafia to my dance card. Tonight played out as one of those little dramas I'd tell my grandchildren after they watched *The Godfather*.

The bartender glanced at me and left a customer she was chatting up. She poured another Basil Hayden and set it in front of me. Fingering her blond mane over one shoulder, she leaned closer, and lowered her voice.

"This one's on the house," she said, "but it's your last drink in here."

"You're kicking me out?"

"I don't like your pals."

"If you mean those two guys. I don't even know their names."

"I do," she said, "and I don't want them in here again. You need to drink somewhere else."

"Thanks a lot."

I slipped off the stool, feeling as though someone had fired me for stealing company funds. She didn't break eye contact and I imagined her eyes following me as I pushed through the beaded curtain and found myself on the sidewalk. Just great, I thought. I looked up and down the street for my two playmates. They not only represented new wildcards, but their interest in Riva's murder got me kicked out of my favorite jazz joint.

Chapter Twenty-Five

East Prussia
Pillau Harbor
January 10, 1945

The swaying open boat weaved between two rusty flak ships that swept multiple 20mm batteries skyward. Weisser, dressed in civilian thick wool clothing and feeling slightly sick, clutched the launch's gunwales as cold North Sea spray doused him. Needles of sleet drummed his shoulders and bounced off the crate at his feet. He tugged at the oilskin tarpaulin and tested the ropes as Baumann watched.

Dirty grey waves smacked the launch's sides, increasing his uneasiness. He never liked the sea, its vastness foreign and uncaring. He would never admit it, but the ocean held a special fear for him, dropping off into ominous darkness, hiding creatures that lurked in its depths, not to mention that his breakfast was in his throat

Weisser saw Baumann grin as the bow slammed into a succession of foamy white caps. The harbor master found them a ship, but only at the cost of accompanying him and his cargo. The north wind picked up and Weisser jumped when small ice floes bumped against the boat's wooden sides. The helmsman held course toward a small coastal freighter anchored a quarter mile away, as though the ship wanted to distance itself from more tempting targets. Cargo booms and a soot-stained smokestack squatted near the vessel's squat stern. Weisser looked away and swallowed his anxiety at the thought of venturing onto the open sea.

The launch thumped against the front of the black hull emblazoned with the ship's name: *Kronan*. Baumann cupped his hands and yelled at a gaggle of deckhands who watched their approach. Gripping the rising and falling gunwales, Weisser watched as they lowered a narrow gangway onto the launch's bow. Two

German seamen secured the ladder and manhandled the crate up the sloped gangway. Weisser held his breath as they struggled to keep their balance. He followed Baumann up the narrow icy steps, lugging a suitcase and army knapsack, his eyes never leaving the crate.

On deck, Baumann shook hands with a bearded officer and turned to Weisser. "Meet Captain Magnusson, our host for the next few days. Captain, this is Major Kamhoven," he said, indicating Weisser.

Magnusson shook hands and measured Weisser as Baumann explained they were accompanying a crate containing hospital files and medical research papers. The captain shrugged and inclined his head with a wry grin. They followed him, stepping cautiously along the icy steel deck. Weisser ordered the two sailors to wait with the crate.

The captain's quarters stank of pipe tobacco and diesel fuel. Inside the warm paneled compartment, Weisser and Baumann shrugged out of their fur-lined parkas. The captain poured two shots of cognac and presented them to his passengers. Weisser quickly downed his and handed a small cloth sack to Magnusson. Grunting, the ship captain scratched his beard, removed his peaked cap and black pea jacket. Sitting at a collapsible chart table, he turned on a desk lamp. Untying the drawstring, he dumped the bag's contents over a harbor map. Gold and silver wedding bands spilled across the chart, sparkling under the light, several loose diamonds gleaming in the pile. Magnussen's thick forefinger pushed the plunder into a small pile.

"I was expecting more," he said in heavily accented German, "but these will do." He scooped the payment into the bag and looked up at Weisser with a grin. "After all, I would not want to interfere with your mission of mercy."

"How long until we reach Sweden?" Weisser asked.

"Magnusson lit his pipe. "Three days, maybe less if we don't get boarded or shot up. We'll sail up the west shoreline as much as possible. Crazy Russian pilots love to shoot up any ship they find. Even the British are sometimes too enthusiastic."

"But you can get us there," Baumann said.

Magnusson looked at him with a sly grin. "Of course, of course. I can see where Pillau will soon no longer need a German harbor master."

Baumann reddened and started to reply but caught himself. "We have our orders."

Magnusson relit his pipe, cherry-sweet smoke filling the cabin.

Weisser clamped his hand on the cloth sack. "You've been paid to get us to Göteborg," he said. "Your opinions of Germany's fortunes are not required."

"No offense. You will find Sweden most accommodating for gentlemen like yourselves."

"We're not to be disturbed during the voyage," Weisser added. "My meals are to be served in my cabin." No need to take the chance of some deckhand later remembering him to authorities.

"As you wish."

"And no one is to touch our cargo. We have very delicate instruments."

Magnusson studied the dead-eyed officer, aware of the holstered automatic on his belt. "It's unusual to have two German majors on board on my vessel, especially in times like these. I presume you have your reasons."

The man was too curious. "I wouldn't presume too much were I you."

"Never." Magnusson hefted Weisser's cloth bag. "You are paying passengers, nothing more to me."

He showed them to two cramped berths, piercing wind off the bow scouring the slippery deck. Baumann went inside his cabin and shut his door. Weisser followed Magnussen to his tiny berth and looked around as the captain dumped the duffel on the deck. A brawny sailor eased the crate next to the cot and Weisser shoved the suitcase of civilian clothes beneath the bunk. Both men left and Weisser sat next to the box, stroking the tarpaulin like an obedient dog.

He'd done it.

The ship represented neutral territory and with any luck he'd step onto Sweden's soil within the week. He patted the crate again. The contents ensured a life of indescribable luxuries. He would live like a prince, possibly a king once he converted the contents to hard cash. The captain seemed content with his payment, Weisser thought, but Baumann… the old fart had ogled the rings and stones too closely and his eyes rarely left the crate. The man most likely suspected him of hiding another fortune, waiting for an opportunity to cash in.

Weisser locked the door and removed the Walther from its holster. Placing it atop the crate within easy reach, he rechecked the cabin lock and stretched out on the bunk. Warm for the first time in weeks, he forgot about the demons swimming beneath the hull, pulled two heavy blankets over him and instantly fell asleep.

• • •

Two nights later, Baumann tilted his chair back in Weisser's cabin and cradled a glass of schnapps, his foot propped on the crate. Both men were dressed in civilian clothing. Baumann had brought a nearly empty bottle with him from his cabin. Weisser counted the drink in Baumann's hand as the officer's fourth, and his guest had obviously indulged before knocking on his door. Obblivious as Weisser nursed only a solitary drink, Baumann regaled Weisser with his exploits on the Western Front thirty years earlier.

"A *real* army in that one," Baumann freshened his drink and adjusted the ridiculous monocle. He sniffed wetly and wiped a finger across his generous moustache. "We kept our attention on winning the war, Weisser." The monocle slipped down his cheek, and he returned it over his left eye. "Objective back then was to beat the Tommies and French, not muck about with Jews. Would have succeeded if the odds had been more even." He tilted his glass in Weisser's direction. "All of you in black uniforms strutting around the streets. You would have been ordered into the trenches in 1914." He raised his glass in Weisser's direction again. "Waste of valuable manpower if anyone had asked me."

Weisser smiled. The old fool understood nothing about the greater struggle. Baumann's kind were still fighting the last war, content to sit in muddy trenches while Russian tanks rolled over them. In the thirties his army pals leapt at the chance to re-arm, readily swearing an oath to the *Fuhrer* to regain to their former glory and position in society, then plotting assassination when they no longer needed him. Lap dogs, Weisser thought, so long as Hitler gave them victories.

"What will you do in Sweden?" Baumann asked. "The damned Swedes pretend neutrality when it's convenient to save their asses. They sell their steel to the highest bidder, then claim they want no part in the war." His head bobbed. "You'll see when we get there. We'll be out of favor now the war's lost."

"Maybe everything's not lost," Weisser said. "What if the wonder weapons we hear about arrive in time?"

Baumann belched. "Wonder weapons! You don't really believe that nonsense, Weisser. Otherwise, you wouldn't be sailing away."

Weisser raised his glass. "What can I say?"

"See? You've already become a realist."

"Maybe I just wanted a change of scenery."

"*Scheisse.* You and this box of yours needed a way out."

It was in the open now, Weisser thought. Share the spoils would be next. Brothers-in-arms and all the camaraderie bullshit with the scent of money in the air. A fool like Baumann knew nothing of the risks he'd taken. He only wanted a meal ticket to ease the pangs of his desertion.

"I arranged to get you aboard this tub," Baumann declared, "and we'll walk down the gangplank together when we reach Göteborg, free men." He took a healthy swallow, coughed and waggled his boot on top of the crate. "Without me, you were just part of the rabble running from the Russians' pack of dogs." His heel tapped the crate. "I'm guessing whatever you found will provide both of us a new start." He gave a drunken grin. "I'll buy a nice little cottage and write a set of memoirs about my service in the glorious Third Reich. Find a nubile young flicka willing to put up with a relic like me, one of those naked blond girls the Swedes flaunt in their so-called health magazines."

Weisser arranged an indulgent expression. "You're a randy old bullshitter," he said with a fraternal smile. "And whatever I may be, I'm not the ungrateful type, Baumann."

Baumann let his boot fall to the deck and folded his hands over his stomach. "I always suspected you SS types were reasonable when it came to money." He pointed a stubby finger at Weisser. "We need to stick together when we make port. Like I said, the Swedes are traitorous bastards. They're interning our men in POW camps, ready to turn them over to the Russians. If we travel at night and keep our mouths shut, we ought to reach Stockholm in a week." He belched, the fumes reaching Weisser. "Easier to get lost in a big city."

Weisser nodded and kept his eyes down. "Same thing I was thinking. Safer if we travel together."

Baumann pocketed the monocle. Steadying one hand against the crate, he pushed himself up and gave Weisser a wink. "Used to hold my liquor better," he mumbled, sliding his hand along the bulkhead. He made his way to the cabin door. Weisser set his drink on the deck and slipped an arm around him.

"I'll help you to your cabin. No sense falling overboard this late in the game, eh?"

The night sky revealed blustery white caps as the ungainly ship wallowed in graceless movements. Weisser draped Baumann's arm over his shoulder and glanced at the bridge. A single seaman scanned ahead of the bow. He steered Baumann toward the stern, staying in the shadows, their boots slipping on the steel deck. If anyone spotted them, they were two drunks making their way back to their cabins.

"Cold…" Baumann muttered.

"Just a few more steps and we'll get you tucked in."

His breath sour, the older man pressed his mouth close to Weisser's ear. "I need another drink."

A gust of wind lashed their backs, and Baumann fell. Weisser went to one knee beside him, slipping the Hitler Youth knife from his boot. The blade was an old friend that performed its duty for nearly a decade. He held the knife tight beside his leg.

Baumann regained his feet and reeled to the railing. "Going to be sick..." He pulled away from Weisser and leaned over the side, vomiting into the wind and mumbling what sounded like apologies.

When he turned back Weisser pressed him against the rail and clamped a hand over his soiled mouth. Startled, Baumann pawed at the hand and tried to twist away. Weisser thrust the blade beneath Baumann's fleshy ribcage, twisting it into his heart. The monocle fell to the deck. Baumann grunted with pain, and Weisser felt his muscles relax. Holding him upright until he felt the last breath escape, the lolling mouth fell open and Weisser felt the dead man's bladder release. He checked the forward lookout again and lifted Baumann over the rail. He listened for a splash, but heard only the dull thump of the ship's engines.

He kicked the monocle overboard, wiped his hand on the rail and stepped back into the shadows, waiting for an alarm. Hugging the forecastle, he made his way back to his cabin, eager to wash the Baumann's stink from his hands. The man's disappearance would be simple enough to explain: Drunk and despondent over Germany's looming defeat and unable to face the consequences. Magnusson would never stop to search, not in these waters. Weisser undressed and cleaned up in a chipped basin. Running his hand over the crate beside the bunk, he slipped beneath the thin blanket and let the throbbing engines lull him into a dreamless sleep.

Chapter Twenty-Six

Two nights after my unexpected encounter at Armands, I phoned Leslie and told her about my two new playmates. Whoever killed Riva was in their sights and I didn't want her on the list. They didn't seem interested in her, but she needed to know the unforgiving Sicilian vow of *omerta* remained very much alive. In any event, the two bent noses gave me a reason to call her.

"Since I've been banished from Armands, I thought we might launch an expedition to find a new jazz club."

"Why not come over instead? I'll pick up some nosh and let you critique my CD collection."

We agreed on seven o'clock. I picked up a bottle of Syrah and called from the lobby. I took the elevator up and she opened her door. Her silk outfit hung loose on her body like lounging pajamas, a hint of jasmine perfume recalling the night at Armands. Barefoot, she wore no earrings or makeup, her short blond hair tucked behind her ears.

"Hi," I said, taken aback by her radiance.

"Come on in." She took the wine and I followed her into a kitchen that opened into the living room. "I made martinis and I have beer. Or we can pop the wine."

"A martini would be great."

She laid the bottle I'd brought in a wine rack and I watched as she poured two martinis from a tall crystal pitcher. I looked around the apartment. The modern kitchen was pin neat, her spacious living room arranged with comfortable contemporary furnishings in muted hues. Pat Matheny's guitar pulsed from her sound system. She returned with two glasses and she raised her glass.

"Cheers."

We sipped our martinis and she led me to a couch in front of a cold fireplace. I sat at one end and she curled up opposite me, bare feet tucked beneath her. I would have preferred her closer, but it was her place and she had her own menu in mind tonight.

"Tell me everything that happened at Armands," she said. "It sounds like something out of a movie."

"Two goons just appeared at the bar. Associates of Mister Boscanni. My guess is Lucia Orellano called him before we reached the street."

"Did they threaten you?"

"Not in so many words, but they knew Dansby and I found Riva's body."

"What about the book?"

"I don't think they care about books. Or even read them. They just want whoever killed Riva." I recounted the conversation at the bar and told her I swore to call them if I learned anything new. In that instant, I accepted that whoever killed a harmless old man deserved whatever happened.

"You'll never see them again," she said.

"Works for me, but they got me banned from my favorite jazz club."

"Every action has a reaction."

I lifted my glass toward her. "Not always a good one."

She finished her martini and thoughtfully tapped the delicate glass on her knee. "Was one of them short, dark complexioned with curly hair, a flashy dresser? The other like a heavyweight gone to seed?"

"You've seen them?"

"At Delaudier about a month ago."

"I didn't take them for art patrons."

"They met with Marsh several times."

Marsh handled the Delaudiers' money, and money was the only reason the mob existed. Toss in the Delaudiers, Riva's book, his murder, the Königs, and a questionable da Vincis, and I had a king-sized Gordian Knot. I'd stumbled into the middle of it because of the book, and I was no closer to finding it, much less knowing if the mob had anything to do with it.

"You told me he came from money but his family disowned him. Any skeletons in his closet?"

"Nothing that involved criminals."

She got up and went to the kitchen. I sat back and enjoyed Matheny's smooth guitar compositions.

"Where money's concerned, Marsh is a smart guy, but he takes chances," she said from the kitchen. She returned with the pitcher and placed it within easy reach on the coffee table. She sat closer to me, perfume sharpening my awareness of her as she poured refills. "He drinks too much and he tries to prove he's smarter than anyone in the room."

"It's possible he made some kind of deal with Curly and Moe without Roland knowing about it." I was groping for answers, digging at every possibility.

"I guess," Leslie said. "I think I saw them once, but he never told me what they were discussing."

"Could he and Roland have hired them to get rid of Riva? To make certain the book disappeared?"

"Roland wouldn't stoop to that."

"Could Marsh be involved in something else? Drugs?"

Leslie shook her head. "He drinks, but I've never seen him use drugs."

The answers were in the wind and I couldn't see them. I smiled, determined to make our evening about more than Marsh's coziness with the mob.

"And you, lady? No secret deals with the Boscanni family?"

She held up three fingers. "Scout's honor. What about you? How'd you connect with Phillip Dansby?"

Did she want the long and sordid version? She confessed to coming from Florida with nothing but a suitcase and that she wanted more. Was I any different?

"He and my father were old friends," I began. "Back before Dansby started minting money and my father rode off into an alcoholic sunset. I guess you'd call my father a gentle drunk, but he drifted away from us and everyone that mattered in his life. After our mother died, he aged in front of our eyes and seemed to give up. My brother and I pretty much grew up on our own until I walked out and put myself through college. That's pretty much my life story, except Phillip saved my life when I found the van Gogh. It's a long story, but if he hadn't come along, I'd be dead."

Even now, the whole thing sounded like something I dreamed up to gain her sympathy.

"That's the short version," I said, "my take on how I ended up here."

She topped her glass from the pitcher and stared at city's lights beyond her window before she turned to me.

"You think that earns you pity points? I'll bet you never collected empty soda bottles to afford bologna, or let boys cop a feel in the backseat just so they'd buy you a Big Mac." She held her glass up to the light as though contemplating an old friend. "This was my closest friend before I turned sixteen, a half pint of Smirnoff when I could afford to buy it. I was one step from crossing the line to selling my favors for more than a burger, but I got lucky. I saw what booze did to my friends and I promised myself I'd get out of there after my grandmother died." Her voice cracked. "I'll never go back."

I waited a beat and raised my glass. "Here's to more in life."

"Damn right."

She sipped the vodka and ran her tongue over her lips as she savored the hundred proof bite. Unlike Marsh, her problems hadn't impaired her ability to handle alcohol.

"We're too much alike," she said. "We're still running. You from California, me from Florida. You from an alcoholic father, and me from becoming a boozy slut. So far, we've made good decisions, both of us."

"We need to create new biographies."

She shook her head. "You're already a hero, finding the van Gogh and all."

"I doubt it. When someone writes the van Gogh's history, the lawyers will most likely forbid any mention of me."

I watched her slip back into her memories and said, "If you had a crystal ball, what would you see in your future?"

A bitter laugh. "What I don't see is Wadesville or any dump like it. I may not have your education but I like New York. I can make it here." She slid closer and grinned. "How you gonna keep 'em down in the orange groves when they've experienced the big city, right?"

She kissed me lightly on my cheek and pushed a wayward strand of hair off her forehead, a habit that left me wanting to touch her face. The lonely strains of Matheny's "Last Train Home" filled the room and she set her glass on the table and walked to the floor-length window, hugging herself as she studied the panorama of lights stretching beyond the East River. I put my glass beside hers and went to her. I wrapped my arms around her waist. My hands glided over the loose silk. She leaned back into me and molded her body against mine. I kissed the side of her neck and she tilted her head back to face me. We kissed and I couldn't resist running my hands beneath her top, discovering she wore nothing beneath the blouse. I cupped a bare breast and she groaned, breaking away and pulling me toward her bedroom.

Standing beside the bed she pulled the blouse over her head and pulled off the silken pants, naked in the dim light. I caught my breath and stripped off my clothes as she pulled back the duvet and sprawled atop the sheets.

Thirty minutes later, we rolled apart, breathing heavily. She lay on her back and made no move to cover her nakedness. Her leg thrown over mine, we gazed at one another in the half-light and I dredged up an exhausted laugh.

"Damn."

"I know," she said. "It's been a while for me too."

She slipped out of bed and returned with our drinks and a lighted cigarette. "The proverbial after-sex cigarette," she said, still nude as she handed me my glass and climbed back into bed.

"Was it only the great sex?' I teased, raising myself on one elbow to enjoy the view.

She looked away and pulled a bedside ashtray closer. "What else did you want it to be?"

A sliver of contentment seeped away. To be honest, I might be little more than a fresh notch on her bedpost. At least that's what I told myself. I reined in my disappointment, reminding myself she had not just tutored a virgin.

"I don't want it to be the last time," I said.

"You mean there could be more than maneuvering me into bed?"

"I remember having help in finding the bedroom."

Her bare thigh pressed down on mine. "You mean I forced you into bed?"

"Oh, hell no," I laughed. "I just want to see more of you."

She stretched her arms above the headboard, extending her long legs full-length with a contented smile, comfortable with her nudity. Her skin glistened in the dim light that reflected off the walls, the cigarette illuminating her face and damp hair as she took a drag.

She turned toward me and ran a hand down her body. "More than this?"

"You know what I mean," I managed, unable to take my eyes from her.

She pulled the sheet over us. "I don't make commitments, Adam," she said, then punched me on the arm. "Wait a minute. I'm supposed to ask for a commitment."

She was right. We'd made love, but Kat's death taught me a lesson. No futures were guaranteed. Relationships either ended or they went forward, hopefully changed for the better. Leslie was turning out to be an enigma, but in the space of a few hours, I didn't want to lose her, no matter what happened.

"I'm not the smothering type," I said. "I need someone close until the smoke clears."

"Let it go, Adam. The book, I mean." She turned toward me. "Riva's dead and his book's gone. I don't care if you like Nils or his family, but Roland's proven the da Vincis are real. Dansby's hot to buy a drawing and you're the only thing standing in his way." She touched my cheek. "Can't you see Riva was nothing more than an eccentric?"

Despite my doubts, she made sense. I'd done my due diligence. It made sense for Dansby and Jean-Henri to take their chances and buy one of the da Vincis. I'd seen too many people die chasing the van Gogh and I didn't need to watch that happen all over again. Only I didn't like loose ends when my job was to keep a friend from making a major mistake. If he didn't take my advice and the da Vincis proved to be something else, I could walk away with a clear conscience. Riva's book appeared to prove the experts wrong and I owed Dansby to find the truth.

"What about you?" I asked. "Is the da Vinci so important that you'd overlook whether the Delaudiers are on the level?"

She stubbed out the cigarette in a bedside ashtray, the sheet falling to her waist as she sat up against the headboard.

"Not my job."

"I'd hate to see you get burned if it's not."

"Like I said, that's their worry. If they closed up shop tomorrow, I'd find something else."

"But not in Wadesville," I teased.

She found my eyes in the half light. "I'm not going back to a trailer beside a strip of asphalt, if that's what you mean."

"That's not what I meant."

She suddenly kissed me and rolled on top me, trapping me between her thighs. "I'm in glorious New York with you, and I'll be here if you need to talk. Or for anything else."

The music in the living room recycled and we found a greater urgency than a dead artist and his ancient book.

Chapter Twenty-Seven

Stockholm
Hornsgatan Street
July 8, 1968

Hans König whistled a popular Swedish tune and clenched his fist around the plastic handle, oblivious to the oversized folio's weight. His son Nils sauntered beside him, a light wind carrying a tang of the Baltic Sea as it lapped against Stockholm's eastern shore. The sun eked out meager warmth after weeks of overcast skies, reminding König of idle days on the grass beside Berlin's Wannsee Lake. Acclimated to the provincial Scandinavian city of canals and lakes, he'd learned to accept the watery environment, the stately old buildings and church spires reminding him of pre-war Berlin.

König quickened his pace, the ten-year-old boy hurrying to keep up. He glanced down at his son who eyed movie marquees along the street. Hands buried in his pockets, lank black hair in his face, the boy frowned up at him. König had objected to the boy tagging along, but Ebba insisted, anxious to get him out of her hair while she repainted the pantry. Brooding to the point of insolence, the boy mirrored his sister's temperament, both exceptionally bright but thwarting Ebba's attempts to civilize them.

König's hair showed only threads of gray, bristly black eyebrows free of age as a beam of sunlight found him. He smiled at passersby who returned his silent greeting, a fellow Swede enjoying a respite from the weather. Each would have been shocked by the worn leather scabbard and Hitler Youth blade snugged against his spine.

The oversized leather folio brushed against his leg like a faithful dog as he checked street numbers. Forsberg Gallery enjoyed an international reputation and the patronage of Stockholm's wealthy collectors. König had waited over twenty years to bring them something unimaginable.

The boy kicked a crushed soda can into the gutter and pointed at the portfolio. "How much longer before you sell that stuff?"

"A few blocks." He would not allow the boy's whining to spoil the day.

"Can we go to a picture show when you finish?"

"No."

"Why?"

König resisted swinging the folio at the pouting mouth. The thought of his son's surprised face tempted him, but he controlled the urge. Another block and he'd begin making himself wealthier than he'd ever imagined in the cramped little shop in Bremen. He regretted selling the smallest of the five drawings, but he'd run out of rings and jewelry to sell or pawn, and his growing family needed money. It brought a good price on the black market, but nothing close to what it would have fetched at auction.

His excitement swelled as he stepped into Forsberg's understated showroom trailed by Nils. Rows of sumptuous oils lined both walls, none bearing tedious price tags. König inhaled the scent of refinishing varnish and smelled money.

Two staff members ignored him as he leaned the leather folio against his leg and eyed the works on the walls. Nils slumped in an empty chair by the door, biting his nails with a bored expression. One of the dapperly dressed employees approached König, presuming the portfolio contained an amateur's art, another desperate artist trolling the city's galleries seeking representation. The man considered himself adept at assessing those who passed through the door. He appraised the arrival's scuffed shoes and forced a bland smile.

"May I help you?"

König drew himself erect. "You sell art, do you not?"

"If the work meets our standards." The employee placed a hand on his hip and confirmed König's off-the-rack suit with distaste. "We represent *very* few living artists."

Thirty years ago, König thought, I dealt very differently with such people.

"I think what I have meets your criteria."

He unzipped the folio and started to remove its contents when the other employee touched the man's arm and whispered to him. The man flapped a hand and sighed in König's direction.

"If you'll excuse me."

The two approached a stooped old man holding hands with an elderly woman leaning on a cane. The elderly couple stood before a large oil of a Madonna and child, and König sensed a problem. He could wait another few minutes although too many years had passed to be shunted aside by a degenerate. He motioned to Nils to stay seated and strolled closer, pretending to inspect a small landscape.

König couldn't make out the words but the man pointed at the painting, his voice rising. Both employees shook their heads, obviously uncomfortable with what they heard. The protests became louder until the second clerk walked to a telephone and dialed. König edged closer.

"Sir, I assure you we do not deal in stolen art of any kind," the prim clerk said.

"This is *our* painting," the old man said, his voice quavering. The woman tightened her grip on her husband's hand, eyes locked on the oil.

"The Nazis stole it off the wall of our sitting room wall in Vienna," she said. "In 1940."

"I'm afraid that's unlikely," the clerk stammered. "We purchased it from a very reputable dealer in Salzburg."

König looked closely at the couple and confirmed his suspicions although the evidence was obvious in this case. He'd long ago developed the ability to detect Jews no matter their denials. It was a talent on which he'd once built his reputation.

"There is no mistake," the old man insisted.

"I told you, sir. We…"

"I must talk with the owner."

The wife squeezed her husband's hand, an old fear in her eyes. "It's time we leave, Benjamin."

"No, Rachel. This is our painting."

The other assistant hung up the phone and returned. A rictus smile in place, he said, "I'm told special organizations in Great Britain and the United States investigate works stolen during the war. If they discover questions about ownership, the art is not sold until the issue is resolved. I assure you we will double-check the provenance of his piece, Mister…?"

"Epstein. Benjamin Epstein."

"Mister Forsberg will make absolutely certain we have undeniable title."

"I don't care about titles," Epstein said. "This belongs to my family."

"We will make every effort to verify provenance, Mister Epstein." He handed Epstein a business card. "Call in a week and you can discuss the matter personally with Mister Forsberg."

"Tomorrow," the husband said. "I will call you tomorrow."

König watched the couple leave. His heart pounding, he zipped up the folio and pulled Nils from the chair.

"Come," he said.

Engaged in an anxious exchange, neither employee noticed the man and boy leave. König slowed his pace after several blocks, the folio a deadweight in his hand. If people were investigating art that disappeared during the war, its contents might be on someone's list. He didn't care who owned the crate's contents before he liberated it from the boxcar. Göring's orders naturally omitted previous ownership. But then, the overweight looter wouldn't have been concerned with such details, would he?

König knew he had been lucky. Offering the work at auction might have raised questions—or it may have not have raised an eyebrow. He needed time to consider what he just witnessed. He cursed his loss of nerve but he could wait a bit longer. He'd secured his position at the firm as head of the restoration department. No need to put everything at risk this late in the game. He would bide his time and…

"Major!"

In a moment of carelessness, König broke his rule and looked in the direction of the voice. An overweight man in a cheap checkered suit hurried across the street, grinning at him, one hand raised in greeting. König looked away and increased his pace, surprising Nils who skipped to keep up. The stranger trotted to them and blocked the sidewalk, his grin widening. König detected the sour odor of schnapps as the heavyset man breathed heavily through his open mouth.

"Anton Weisser!" He huffed, displaying bad teeth. "I thought that was you."

An icy finger ran down Weisser's back. "I'm sorry. My name is Hans König."

The man winked, his watery eyes crinkling at the corners. "Whatever you say." He grabbed König's unoffered hand and pumped it with a crooked grin. "Just don't bullshit an old comrade."

König pulled away and bumped into Nils. The boy looked back and forth between the two men; his interest piqued.

König stepped around one of the last faces he wanted to see, "I don't know you." He attempted to maneuver past around the bulky intruder.

The man planted himself in front of him again, came to attention and threw up a sloppy salute. "*Hauptsturmführer* Ludwig Ziegesser. We served together in the Ukraine in forty-one. We got drunk the night before we cleaned out Bila Tservka, remember?"

The memory of the dirty Ukrainian village brought Ziegesser's younger face out of the past. He glanced down at Nils who took his hand with a confused expression. The boy possessed weaknesses, but had the memory of archivist. They would need to have a father-to-son talk about the war and the "battle" in the Ukrainian village.

König raised a hand in surrender with a weak smile. He didn't need an argument in the middle of the sidewalk. "Ah, Ziegesser. Of course. I didn't recognize you. You've added a few pounds."

"Not you, Major," Ziegesser grinned and shook his head. "You look just the same."

"A new life and better rations."

"Me too," The ex-SS captain grinned. "Come have a drink with me. I haven't talked with anyone from the old days in years."

König gestured at Nils and shook his head. "I have to get him home."

"Tomorrow night, then. We'll relive the good days, eh?"

"All right."

Ziegesser wiped his mouth with the back of his hand. "Good days back then. We got them all, didn't we? Jews, Gypsies, Communist lowlifes. The whole rotten bunch."

Pedestrians brushed past them. König needed to rid himself of the danger that had suddenly appeared. Did Ziegesser not realize the world resented their work? That they and their comrades were hunted even though their mission was cut short? Many fled to South America, but König had had no longing for the tropics with its incessant heat and ignorant peasants.

Now this fool.

He gripped Ziegesser by his shoulder and forced a grin. "Two Gold Crowns tavern at nine tomorrow night, then. It's not far and we'll have time to catch up."

The ex-SS executioner saluted again and lurched away. König cursed the day's second round of surprises. *First, the old Jews, then this ghost appears from my past.*

Then again, the two feeble old Jews may have saved him from disaster, one leading to exposure if his windfall was being tracked. The knowledge that his luck held lifted his spirits as the sun touched the street, then rejoined the day's conspiracy by slipping behind descending clouds that threatened to smother the city's church spires.

"Who was that, papa?" Nils asked.

"An old army friend."

"What did he mean about Gypsies?"

"He was drunk," Weisser said.

He watched Ziegesser disappear around the corner. Arranging his face, Weisser conjured up a smile for his son who stared up at him.

"Let's you and I have a soda and find out if you can keep a secret from Mama."

• • •

Finger stumps aching from the persistent drizzle, König rubbed his new gloves together and paused beneath the striped awning. Brushing raindrops from his coat, he checked the street a final time and entered the Two Gold Crowns.

A brimmed rain hat and topcoat collar obscuring his face, he kept his eyes on the floor he selected a rear booth away from the bar. The dim tavern hoarded stale beer and burnt coal, planked tables and booths guaranteeing privacy in the gloom.

The pub was empty except for a dozing barkeep and a bored waitress who ambled from a rear storeroom with a pronounced limp. Rain and cold weather, it appeared, persuaded regulars to remain by the home fires, drinking their Carnegie porter in comfort. In his favor, the overcast skies and leaded windows left the isolated booth in shadow. He'd passed the bar on occasion but never ventured inside. No one knew him and if queried by the police, the barkeep and waitress might vaguely describe a customer they'd never seen. He ordered a stein from the waitress who didn't give him a second glance as she hobbled away.

He checked his watch and swore. Ziegesser was late. The way his luck ran lately, he'd forgotten about their meeting and was drunk in some other bar. Stumbling into him after 23 years—what were the odds? The lout's careless mouth could get them arrested or worse. The Kikes were as vindictive as ever, murdering his old comrades. The Mossad made headlines the world over. One never knew who remained on their list, and König was well aware he might still be in their sights. Sweden was never the Zionists' favorite hunting ground, but he'd kept his head down just the same.

Until the fat fool appeared like a messenger from the past.

Disappearing into his adopted country, he chose König as his new name because it carried a vague connotation of royalty. Ebba, his wife, had been only eighteen when he married her and taken Swedish citizenship. The May-December union produced two unwanted children, but added to his cloak of anonymity. Content to wait for the moment to claim his fortune, no incidents had marred his new life, none whatsoever until Ziegesser appeared. Worse than the careless drunk, Jews were reclaiming their art and dredging up the past. In a single hideous day, his plans fell apart like wet newspaper.

His shoulder blades bit into the wooden bench, the beer gone tasteless. All his plans could evaporate unless he took action.

As though complying with the solution he'd decided upon, an obese figure appeared in the doorway and scanned the interior before lumbering to König.

"There you are!"

König smelled the stale clothes before Ziegesser's collapsed onto the opposite bench. Stuffed in a tan raincoat like a spoiled bratwurst, his sodden pants cuffs dripped rainwater on the floor. Sparse hair plastered to his forehead, his former comrade flashed a gap-toothed smile and raised a meaty hand toward the waitress.

"Two more, *liebling*," he called. "And bring a small brandy with mine."

He placed his palms flat on the table and beamed at König. "Damn, it's good to see a familiar face again." His looked around. "The Swedes are a sour bunch, aren't they? And the damn Jews who own the plant where I work." He waved a fat hand. "For some reason, they don't much like Germans either." He leered at his former commander. "Guess what's left of them hold grudges, eh?"

König reached across the table and gripped Ziegesser's sleeve.

"You should watch your mouth."

Ziegesser pulled his arm away. "Why? Because of a few Jews? You know what's it's been like for people like us."

"All the more reason to keep your head down."

"I'm not stupid," Ziegesser mumbled. "I came here to work after the war. Germany was shit after the capitulation, but I've kept out of sight and made a living." He looked around for the waitress when the drinks failed to appear.

"Now it doesn't matter," he said. "The Jews let me go. Pushed me out the door with a half-week's pay."

The waitress returned without glancing at either customer. König pushed aside the fresh stein. Ziegesser washed down the brandy shot with half his stein and wiped his mouth on his sleeve. His eyes watery, König saw what was coming.

"Can you help an old *Kamerad*? Just until I find work," Ziegesser said. "I hate to ask, Major, but they'll kick me out of my boarding house unless I come up with the rent." He attempted a reassuring grin. "When I find work, I'll pay you back and buy the next round. Hell, all of them will be on me! We can relive the good times whenever we like."

König smiled and rapped the table with his knuckles. "Capital idea." He looked at the hopeful face. "Finish your beer and we'll go to my bank. I'll withdraw enough to tide you over."

Outside, the rain fell harder. The street was deserted as the two men ducked from awning to awning. Hat pulled low, Weisser averted his face from the few restaurant windows and passersby. Bareheaded and tipsy from the brandy, Ziegesser ignored the rainwater running down his slack face.

"I knew I could depend on an old friend," he blubbered as they locked arms.

König said nothing and steered his former subordinate into an alley. Empty boxes and garbage cans formed a narrow passage between the two darkened buildings. Rain drummed on the tin containers as deeper shadows consumed the streetlights. Ziegesser stumbled and wiped his face, glancing back at his savior.

"A shortcut?"

König caught him and shoved him against the brick wall. Holding him upright with one hand, he reached beneath his coat and pulled the knife from its scabbard.

"A shortcut to end your troubles."

Bewildered when the blade sliced across his neck, Ziegesser's mouth fell open. He stared into his former comrade's eyes and Weisser pushed the blade deeper.

"I'm sorry, Ludwig. I'm too close to let you ruin things."

Warmth coursed over Ziegesser's chest. His legs gave way and he slid down the brick wall onto the cobblestones. Sitting upright, he jerked once and was still.

König did not move, the downpour diluting the growing pool of blood. He stepped away and observed the sitting figure at his feet for a full minute. He'd seen how hard it was to dispose of humans, astonished when they clung to life. Squatting down, he stared into lifeless eyes. Satisfied, he wiped the blade on the cheap raincoat and returned it to its scabbard.

"Too careless, old friend," he muttered.

He straightened and checked both ends of the alley. The immediate problem no longer existed, but the old Jews at Forsberg meant Leonardo would remain out of sight a while longer.

Chapter Twenty-Eight

New York

A week after my delightful romp with Leslie, I sat in Dansby's office with him and Jean-Henri, contemplating my good fortune in meeting her and observing our cozy little group. I cradled my Starbucks cup and refused to allow the Frenchman's stare to distract me as he sipped his tea. He eventually returned the favor by ignoring me and pretending to study the room.

Dansby clasped his hands atop the desk and looked back and forth between us. My attention wandered to the fierce expressions of the Scots Greys riders behind his desk. Lady Butler had captured the ferocity of their famous charge minutes before they were virtually annihilated. Searching the young cavalrymen's excited faces, I tried to recall if I'd ever experienced such a moment. My first sight of the van Gogh qualified, but nothing else measured up. Light from the double windows highlighted a vivid red scar that snaked from Dansby's hairline onto his forehead. Knowing his violent background and love of all things beautiful, I considered my theory about violence and art. Had an education bred fierceness out of him, one of the rare fortunates who eschewed violence to live a better life? Observing Dansby, I realized again he possessed both sides of the coin.

Gentleman," he said. "Put aside your personal war for the moment." His tone confirmed his less than buoyant mood as he directed his gaze me.

"What about Riva's book?"

"Nothing, although a couple of Italian gentlemen seem unduly upset over his death. They picked Armands to express their displeasure to me."

"Did you recognize them?"

"Leslie Strickland and I visited a woman who turned out to be Riva's niece. I think she passed my name along to Joe Boscanni."

"Joey Boots," Dansby mused. "You're moving up in New York circles."

"Or down where no one will ever see me again."

"Not if you behave. If Riva was family, they'll only be interested in who killed him."

"Now we have gangsters to contend with," Jean-Henri said. "This non-existent book…"

"… might hold the answer to whatever the Delaudiers are peddling," Dansby interrupted. "Whether they're offering genuine da Vincis or running a game needs to be determined."

I turned toward Jean-Henri and spread three fingers. "All three drawings were studio work. None by his own hand."

Jean-Henri returned his teacup to its saucer, intransigent as ever. "This is an exercise in futility, Phillip. We cannot allow this opportunity to slip away."

Dansby's freshly-shaved face reddened. "We're chasing a fox and you two are the lead hounds. Only you've lost the scent and we're running after our own arses. I'm not accustomed to playing the fool."

"Phillip, I…"

"Do shut up, will you, Adam? I need to think."

Jean-Henri's teacup covered his smile. Dansby's tone had assumed a parade ground quality, one I imagined he employed with a raw recruit. Jean-Henri and I resumed our study of objects in the room, looking everywhere except at one another. Dansby picked up his pen and jabbed the desk blotter with a metronome cadence, staring at the small dents for nearly a full minute. When he looked up, he focused on me again.

"I realize you're sure about whatever you saw, but we need to go back to square one. While I trust your instincts, you have to be spot on with your conclusions."

I resisted a sigh and assumed what I hoped was a repentant look. Having produced no evidence of the book's existence, I'd run out of arguments and was on a short leash.

"So, here's what we'll do," he said. "Go to the Delaudiers and tell them I sent you to take another look at the new drawings. Be contrite. If they believe I'm back in the game, they'll smell money."

"And what am I supposed to look for?"

"Signatures."

Exasperated, Jean-Henri sat forward. "Phillip, a lot of famous artists varied their signatures. Some didn't bother to sign at all. Every aspect of these works tells us they are da Vincis. Who's to say he didn't change how he signed them?"

"Perhaps, but I want more research to verify the signatures," he said. "I'll depend on you to look for anything that indicates a discrepancy."

He turned to me. "Take one of our cameras and photograph the remaining drawings. Jean-Henri will conduct his own research."

Another tilt at the Delaudier's egos didn't brighten my day, but what choice did I have? Dansby wasn't ready to lunge at the tempting bait they dangled and I owed him whatever he needed to make the right decision. Clarice placed the call to Roland and I was granted admission at two o'clock that afternoon.

● ● ●

Shown to the same room where we'd inspected the first da Vinci, Roland and Nils stood in front of a floor-to-ceiling medieval tapestry, trying to conceal their impatience Sal Testano eyed me from one corner in his chauffer's uniform, hands crossed in a fig leaf pose. Roland greeted me with a smile that reflected his irritation.

"The pariah returns."

"This won't take but a minute."

"Is this your idea?"

"Phillip's. He wants a few photos before he makes a decision."

I removed the Nikon from its case and a white-gloved employee arrived. He meticulously arranged the ochre sheets on the conference table. I removed the lens cap, selected the macro setting, and leaned over the first drawing, bracing my elbows on the polished tabletop.

"No flash," Roland warned.

He opened the draperies and admitted sunlight. Images of the signatures filled the camera screen and I took several shots of each drawing, more strongly convinced than ever that I was not looking at the signature of Leonardo da Vinci. I straightened and returned the camera to its case. The Delaudier employee reappeared and whisked away the drawings. Roland followed him from the room. Sal closed the door behind him and Nils stepped to me.

"What do you think all this is accomplishing? Dansby's other man, Jean-Henri Bonnet, has no doubts."

"Dansby's a careful man. Doesn't like to spend millions on mistakes he can avoid."

"You're the one making a mistake. You have no idea what we are about to unveil."

The three other drawings had been verified. Why the hell was he angry? I decided to press him a little more.

"I doubt we'd be interested in more misattributed work."

He stepped closer. In Sweden they might not understand the rule about invading private space, but it was one of my favorites.

"You're saying my family is trying to cheat you?"

I started toward the door and turned back. "Let me give you some free advice. If you're running a scam, I wouldn't pick Phillip Dansby as a mark. You might want to read up on him. He doesn't forgive or forget."

Sal grunted and Nils straightened. "He does not frighten me."

The pundits were right. Stupid cannot be repaired.

"I understand my sister tried to enlist your help," he said.

"I've never been good at playing games."

"Excuse me?"

"It means I don't work with crooks."

He flushed. "You and your employer may well find yourselves in court."

"I wouldn't recommend going up against Dansby."

He looked at Sal and grinned. "You're right. My father taught me there are simpler remedies for your kind."

I was sick of being threatened. Enzo Riva had died a lonely violent death because he wanted to protect Leonardo's legacy. I started to walk away from the taunt when the image of Enzo Riva's body returned.

I grabbed Nils' jacket lapels and shoved him against the wall. I jammed my fists beneath his chin and tightened my grip.

"Don't ever threaten me again."

Sal jerked me away. "Hey! Hey! Hey!" he roared. "You ain't supposed to touch him."

"Then tell this bastard to watch his manners."

Sal released me and I gave the white-faced Nils a final shove against the wall, splintering a frame containing a small Felix Cals landscape. Roland opened the door and Leslie followed him into the room.

"What in god's name is going on?"

Sal shot his cuffs, everyone transfixed as though frozen in a movie still. Nils, his tie askew, gasped as I stepped back and braced myself. Without another word he brushed his lapels and walked from the room. Leslie stared at me and I started to explain until I realized this wasn't the time or place. I grabbed my camera and walked past her and Roland, finding myself on the sidewalk again. I stood there for a full minute, ignoring people who rushed past me. Nils has said something about an unveiling, but I had enough to ponder without another surprise. I owed it to Riva and Dansby to prove the book was real. No matter what Jean-Henri and Manfred Morrison deduced from their examinations, I was convinced da Vinci's hand never touched Delaudier's drawings.

With nothing to prove my contentions, I felt like I was pounding concrete with a rubber pickaxe. The realization ruined the rare spring day and I ignored empty cabs as I trekked to my office.

Chapter Twenty-Nine

Leslie invited me to her place next day for what she promised would be a Southern-style dinner. When I asked her to define what I feared might be chitterlings and collard greens, she promised a surprise. Much as I needed relief from the impasse I'd reached, I tried to beg off but she insisted, my culinary fears amusing her.

The night surprised me in more ways than one. She served me a rich shrimp casserole complemented by sweet stewed tomatoes, fresh baked cornbread with real butter, ending with pecan pie. Downing two servings of everything except the pie, I toasted her culinary skills with a glass of the Rombauer Chardonnay I'd brought and helped clear away the dishes.

After we cleaned up, we carried the wine and our glasses into her living room and settled on the couch, our bare feet on her coffee table, my shoulder touching hers.

"A woman of many talents," I said, running a contented hand over my stomach.

"You're actually acknowledging I possess talent outside the bedroom?"

"Definitely."

"Don't think my cooking will be a regular occurrence. I only learned a few recipes from my grandmother."

"I wish I'd met her. She must have been some lady to raise you."

Leslie pulled back with a crooked smile. "A lady? That's the first time I ever heard anyone call her that. She always carried a gun in her purse and had a sailor's mouth when someone crossed her. We didn't have much, but she made sure I knew what mattered in this world."

"And what is your definition of what matters?"

"Whatever keeps me out of places like Wadesville."

I poured more wine for us. "Was it really that bad?"

"Try growing up in a trailer on concrete blocks. I scrounged every dime so I could afford tampons. From the time I was five, I remember people looking down on us because we lived in a twenty-year old piece of crap and drove a Plymouth held together with spit."

She was downing wine almost between sentences. Looking at the empty glass as though it had cheated her, she walked to the kitchen and pulled another bottle of Chardonnay from her cabinet. She popped the cork and resumed her seat beside me, topping our glasses.

"I want everything I missed growing up," she said. "That defines 'real' for me. I don't want to be Isabelle, but I want to live like her. I don't care if that sounds shallow. It's what I want."

"It's a long way from Florida to Delaudier. I'd say you made progress."

She leaned forward, placed her wine glass on the table and slipped her arms around my neck. "No more talk about poor little Leslie," she said, kissing me. "We're sitting here while my king-sized bed is going to waste. As they say in movies, I think we should retire to the bedroom."

I couldn't think of a viable counter-argument and let her pull me to my feet.

An hour later, I fell back and wiped my sweaty face with a corner of the sheet. Leslie got up and headed for the bathroom, glancing back over her shoulder at me with an I-told-you-so look. Something more enticing than her nudity struck me when she returned with two glasses and the bottle, comfortable with her body as though it was simply a beautiful fact of nature. It struck me I could spend the rest of my life with such a woman.

She poured the wine and settled back. Neither of us spoke for several minutes until I tested the waters again.

"This could be a regular thing," I said, "you and me."

"Are you asking for commitment again?"

"What more could I ask in a woman? You can cook and you like art. You've also got an edge I like and you're a great lover."

She raised an eyebrow. "Only great?"

"Okay, superior to anyone in the known universe."

She propped up on one elbow and lit another cigarette off the first. Settling back on her pillow, she stared at the ceiling. "I told you, Adam. I'm not ready for promises. Why can't we just keep what we have? I'm enjoying life. I don't want to complicate it with long-term commitments." She waved a hand through the cigarette smoke. "You've heard all this before."

I let it go. The argument broached no middle ground with her. Not yet, anyway. I didn't want to push her away, but my feelings for her were growing. It was becoming easier to relegate Kat to the past as Leslie and I spent more time together. I'd learned that the harder you pushed someone, the farther away you pushed them. Time would provide the answer in Leslie's case.

"Do you like New York?"

I heard her desire to change the subject. "Yeah, it's okay."

"I love it."

"Sounds like Wadesville's long gone."

"I'll never go back. Never."

"Not even to visit your grandmother's grave?"

She tasted her wine. "She always talked about going to New York, but she never made it. I didn't want to leave her there when I left, so I had her cremated. I brought her ashes with me and scattered them in the East River so she could see the city every day."

I raised my glass. "Good idea."

"Is your father buried in California?"

"Right next to my mom. I go to their graves when I'm out there. My mom died early and I never kept in touch with my father after I left home. It's the only thing I can do now."

She got out bed suddenly and walked into the living room, arms wrapped around her bare breasts, looking around the room as though it belonged to someone else. Not bothering to slip into her robe, she opened the sliding glass doors and, glass in hand, stepped onto her balcony in all her glory.

I pulled on my boxers and followed her with the bottle. If residents in the high rise across from her building peered out their windows, they were getting a free peepshow. Leslie spread her arms wide and basked in New York's ocean of lights, the electrical glow illuminating her body.

"You asked what I wanted!" she yelled, pirouetting on one foot, providing neighboring voyeurs with a splendid view of her assets. "This with no limitations!"

I heard the wine take her somewhere else. She refilled her glass and she held it toward me, her eyes reflecting the city lights.

"Your neighbors are getting something more," I said. "Especially the perverts."

I took her hand and pulled her inside, closing the doors behind us.

"We could do it on the balcony," she giggled.

The wine made it a tempting offer, but I pushed her toward the bedroom. "I might get too excited and fall off."

"I thought people from California did things like that," she pouted.

"I've no doubt some do, but the police might not like it." I pulled her into bed. "Anyway, your mattress is much softer than a concrete balcony."

Chapter Thirty

I sat at my desk next morning, drumming a pencil on the blotter, fantasizing about Leslie and avoiding the murky waters where I found myself. I'd left the photos in Jean-Henri's office and passed Phillip in the hall. He graced me with a curt nod without speaking and I sensed a widening crack between us. Frowning at the cup of cold coffee on my desk, I looked up when Clarice placed a sealed envelope on my desk. The front was blank.

"What's this?"

"The delivery boy said it was for you. Possibly another female admirer?"

"Fat chance."

I broke the seal and removed a white note card that bore a precise hand, the small cursive letters learned in a strict classroom many decades earlier.

Mister Barrow,

If convenient to your schedule, please join me at 2:00 today at Alexandra's Tea Room. I understand it is located just off

Broadway. From what I've read in guidebooks, it seems very nice.

Please come alone.

Ebba König.

A dozen people could have sent me invitation that morning, but Ebba König was at the bottom of the list. Pleasant as she'd been, we hadn't exchanged more than a few dozen words at the Delaudiers' dinner party. I informed Clarice I'd be out for the day, went home and changed into my best suit and tasseled loafers, presuming the imposing little woman and a tea room deserved a modicum of formality.

The front of Alexandra's evidenced only a peeled wooden door and painted window depicting a delicate teacup. Past the lilac door, the interior worked at cheerful despite the black tinned ceiling and the long corridor of a room flanked by round tables the size of large pizzas. A single display shelf at the register offered flowered cups and saucers for sale. Whatever the tea room lacked in ambiance it made up with warm bakery aromas. Cozy wasn't a word associated with New York, but Alexandra's Tea Room came nearest the mark.

Ebba König sat in the back, slender hands demurely folded in her lap. She wore a stylish knee-length black dress, a tan lightweight coat draped over her shoulders to fend off the air conditioning. Despite her age, she presented the appearance of a more modern woman than I'd seen at the dinner party. She waved and I joined her, pulling out a wire-backed chair, careful not to bump the dainty table as I sat down.

The delicate hand she offered appeared almost translucent. "Mister Barrow, I appreciate you accepting my hasty invitation. I plan to return home later this week and felt we should talk before I leave."

"I'm sorry you're not staying longer, Mrs. König."

"Ebba, please."

"All right."

"Your country is charming in its own fashion, but I miss simpler things."

"Some days I feel the same."

She smiled indulgently and motioned the waitress over. Tea wasn't my favorite, but I let her order for both of us. When a white porcelain pitcher arrived, I filled both cups and she took a sip, closing her eyes in pleasure until she returned the cup to her saucer.

"To business,' she said crisply, "as my son-in-law likes to say. No one knows I'm here."

She gave a girlish titter, a schoolgirl who'd sneaked off to a secret rendezvous. Her eyes serious again, I watched her search for words to begin. She started to speak, then stopped. I recognized she was close to walking out and placed my hand atop hers.

"Anything you tell me stays with the teacups," I assured her.

Her head bobbed once as if confirming her decision. She held up one hand, the faint scent of dusting powder mixing with chamomile steam.

"A moment, please. This is difficult for me."

I waited and rubbed my thumb over my cup's painted purple iris. In the subdued lighting, Ebba König looked two decades younger, her hair firmly gathered in a tight knot. She studied her cup as though it contained the words she sought, her spiny fingers tapping the porcelain before she looked up.

"Hans, my husband, was a war hero," she began. "He was wounded in Russia. His left hand was badly injured, and he was invalided out of the army. Shortly before the war ended, he emigrated to Sweden."

Emigrated or deserted, I thought as two women occupied the table across from us. Ebba lowered her voice.

"Hans never talked about his war service. He was, how shall I describe him? Private is the best word, I imagine. We didn't socialize much and the war was never discussed, a subject that only made him angry." Intelligence danced behind her blue eyes.

"I'm not a naïve old woman, Mister Barrow. Despite what my son said, I'm aware the Nazis looted conquered countries. I can read and I've seen the films of the horrible camps. Innocent people were robbed and murdered." She straightened. "I don't want such things associated with my family."

I assumed a sympathetic air. Nils and Isabelle obviously hadn't known everything about their father or the things she had hidden from them for years.

"What are you telling me?"

"Hans was… harsh with the children," she said. "Possibly that's why they grew up to be who they are. Like all boys, Nils worshiped his father, but Isabelle went her own way. She cared only for material things we could never give her." She frowned at her cup of cold tea. "Isabelle said you had words with Nils and that creature Sal."

She drew a breath and I began to feel like a father confessor. "I don't think I ever truly loved Nils, not like a mother should love a son," she said. "He was too much like his father, an apple dropped too close beside the tree as the English say. Isabelle…" she sighed, "Isabelle is Isabelle, and I do not trust that husband of hers, Roland. He is too much like her." She lifted her eyes to me. "You must think me a terrible mother."

"I don't think that at all. I'm enjoying the tea and your company." What else was I supposed to say? I started to add more, but she held up her hand again with a sad smile.

"I'm boring you with family talk, but there's another reason I wanted you to join me today."

Her eyes took on a deeper hue, showing vestiges of Vikings and ancient sea raiders. Ebba König, I saw, was forged in harder metal than her son and daughter.

"My husband was a good provider, but I loved him less and less as the years passed. It's possible I'm simply a woman incapable of love, Mister Barrow." Her reedy voice mirrored tears at the corners of her eyes. "I never understood why that happened, but I had the feeling there was something terrible buried in his past."

"The war damaged a lot of men. Some…"

She cut me off. "No. It was something more."

"I'm sorry," I said, wondering how to comfort her.

Ebba pushed aside a wayward wisp of white hair. "When we married, Hans promised me a better life one day. He swore we would live like royalty, just as his name indicated. He never explained why he believed this, and his job barely kept bill collectors from the door. But one day, our little bank account suddenly overflowed with money. He claimed it was an inheritance from an uncle in Germany and I didn't question our good fortune."

"I have to ask again. Why tell me all this?"

She held up one bony finger and met my eyes. "First, my maiden name was Norberg. It is a respected name in Sweden, even if Nils and Isabelle have forgotten their roots. I do not want it connected to the sale of the drawings."

I started to reply when she held up a second finger.

"Also, Nils lied to you."

I had the feeling she was about to confirm my worst suspicions.

"The da Vincis are not family heirlooms, Mister Barrow. Hans brought them with him from Germany."

The first fracture in the Delaudiers' story. "There's a book."

"Yes, I heard about your book. Isabelle and Roland were discussing it as though I wasn't in the room. I don't understand what it all means. However, it concerns them a great deal."

"The book proves the da Vincis were done by other artists."

She shrugged. "I know so little about art. Isabelle and Roland are greedy people and believe your book represents danger to them. There is a lot of money involved." She held my eyes. "At my age, you begin to think of things other than money, Mister Barrow."

The answer to the puzzle might be revealed as she divulged her secrets.

"One final question if I may. How did your husband die?"

She stared into her cup and I waited, tension suspended in the air between us. Engrossed in her teacup, Ebba König appeared to return to another time, one she obviously didn't wish to relive. I respected her privacy and waited and knew it was useless to press the issue, that I'd blundered into a forbidden part of her life. When she finally looked up, I strained to hear her whisper.

"That is best left in the past."

I reached across the table and impulsively laid my hand on hers. I resisted patting the frail flesh, fearing a display of sympathy was not something she wanted or required.

"When are you leaving us?"

Her head came up, her eyes dry. "Saturday."

I removed my hand. "I'll be sorry to see you leave. Thank you for telling me all this. I have an obligation to be certain that Major Dansby does not make a costly mistake. He pays me well, but he's also my friend."

"I sensed that at the dinner party." A single tear reappeared and she looked at me as though seeing another person. "You should have been the son I bore," she softly whispered.

I forced down the knot in my throat with the inescapable feeling my long-dead mother had sent this woman to somehow protect me. I covered my embarrassment with a swallow of cold tea, unable to find words. Ebba König was a vein of gold in a played-out mine.

She rescued me with a wry smile. "I am only doing a stranger a kindness," she said. "At Isabelle's party, you appeared a lamb at a table of jackals, you and the young blond woman with Major Dansby." The smile softened. "I have no wish to see you devoured."

"I'm not a lamb. There's enough jackal in me to disappoint you."

"Be that as it may, Mister Barrow, you should remain on your guard. Nils and Isabelle do not care if the art is tainted. They see only a great deal of money."

We chatted a few more minutes about her return to Sweden. I insisted on paying the bill over her protests, and we walked outside. I found her a taxi and watched exhaust smoke obscure the white blur in the rear window, feeling the loss of someone I should have known my entire life. Lost in my feelings, I failed to see Sal cross the street a block away.

Chapter Thirty-One

Stockholm - Rastengarden Hotel
Early Morning
January 10, 1979

The leader held the encrypted message beneath the single floor lamp.

Dear Son:
Your Uncle Harold requires your presence in Stockholm.
Aunt Esther appreciates your visit to make certain he knows we still think about him. He remains too sick to travel and our fondest hopes of returning him to Israel cannot be realized. Please be certain he fully understands our disappointment that he must remain in Sweden.
End of message.

He kept his back to the others and hid his smile, ignoring the sweat and stale cigarette smoke that permeated the cheap hotel room. Three air mattresses on the floor further attested to the Department's tightfisted bean counters.

In his mid-fifties, the tall figure exuded fitness uncommon for a man his age. Sinewy-thin with melancholy eyes, he placed his cardboard coffee cup on the floor and reversed the wooden chair. Straddling it, he crossed his arms over the back and faced his three companions. His features took on new life as morning light wedged between the cheap curtains. He thought about what he should say, wondering if they could comprehend what the moment meant to him. Not that such things mattered any longer. He'd waited thirty-five interminable years for the words that appeared on the paper.

Yanni, his second-in-command, bent forward in a frayed overstuffed chair and waited for him to speak, thinning blond hair barely covering his pink scalp.

Yanni had conducted surveillance for the past two weeks, melding into crowds, taken for a nondescript Swedish office worker despite being born in Kraków. A meticulous observer, his cheap spiral notebook was filled with detailed observations about their target and his habits.

Two younger men sprawled on the couch wearing short-sleeved white shirts despite the chill in the room. Side-by-side, they could have passed for brothers or weight-lifting instructors. Ex-IDF soldiers with heavily muscled forearms, both were products of a Kibbutz many miles from the nondescript government building in Tel Aviv.

"We have approval," the leader said.

The three men looked at one another without speaking.

"One more time. Five minutes maximum at the quarry, then straight to the airport. We leave both cars in the parking garage. The rental agency will be called and told where they are."

The one called Yanni screwed up his face. "I have to drive his car?"

"Like we planned. A deserted car on the road attracts attention."

"Why not push it into the quarry?"

"If it burns, it'll attract the police."

"I don't like driving the bastard's car."

"Just to the airport."

One of the new operatives sat forward. "And if a car comes along?"

The leader kept his voice even. "We covered that."

The two younger men were on their first mission. Mistakes meant prison in a foreign country. Both were combat veterans, but he knew every pitfall and weakness of covert assignments. All missions depended on timing and adherence to the plan. Missteps or last-minute disagreements created errors no matter how many times an agent went into the field. First missions were worse. They manufactured amateur mistakes.

"When we stop, leave the boot open," the leader reminded them for the tenth time. "If another car happens by, look busy and don't make eye contact. You've seen photographs of the road. It's in bad shape, so traffic will be light."

"It's a shortcut to the motorway," Yanni added. "Nothing but an abandoned quarry about a kilometer from the main road. No businesses and only a few abandoned houses. The target uses it to save a few minutes on his commute."

No one spoke and the leader waited until the younger men made eye contact with him. "We're clear?"

Nods.

The tall man picked up a duffel bag. "We need to be in place by eight o'clock. Check the bedroom, closets, everything." He pointed at the coffee cups and paper plates on the floor. "Those too. I want nothing left behind."

• • •

König laid the leather folio on a blanket in the car trunk. Braced against the suitcase he'd concealed the previous night, the folio would be safe enough until his flight. He slammed the lid and dropped into the driver's seat, warding off the cold numbing his seven fingers. He'd worn the old hair-lined gloves, recognizing today would be special.

Brittle morning sun reflected little warmth from the snow on the ground, but he ignored the Volvo's frigid interior. Hands atop the steering wheel, he stared out the windshield and did not move for half a minute, recalling the old Russian truck and relishing what lay ahead. After disembarking from the ratty Swedish steamer so many years ago, the true Anton Weisser would assume his rightful place in the world. He'd need another name, of course, but that was unimportant. Names were labels, like greeting stickers at business events, anonymous and disposable.

I've wasted so many years, he thought, but today made it all worthwhile!

His former life as an art restorer had proved useful, a necessity required to blend in. Scraping out a living to support a wife and two children, he was careful not to become careless or too comfortable. Old enemies had long memories.

He regretted the necessity of disposing of Ziegesser, and he lamented selling the one da Vinci drawing, but living close to the financial edge left him little choice. The quiet sale to a collector raised no questions and allowed him to live unobtrusively among the Swedes without embarrassing complications. As for Ziegesser, there'd been no inconvenient investigation into his death, nothing to connect him to the body in the alley. Unlike his former subordinate, he remained a benign presence in a land of its indifferent foreigners. Newspapers occasionally reported the violent death of old comrades, proof the vindictiveness would never abate. Knowing his enemy, König vowed to tread beneath the Jews' radar. The Mossad was efficient if nothing else, and Weisser understood the value of efficiency.

He started the car and saw Ebba part the kitchen curtains. He waved at her and felt a trace of loss. She was a dutiful wife, soft and compliant, even though she bore him two contentious children he'd never wanted.

He waited until the curtains closed and put the car in reverse. No doubt there would be days when he'd miss her, but there were always other women, younger women attracted to his new lifestyle that money guaranteed. Weisser looked at the plain cheerless house, unable to restrain a smile as he drove away for the last time. His spirits rose as he increased the distance between his old and new life. His luncheon appointment at noon was the last rung after thirty-five years buried in Stockholm.

He went over the details again. A final cash payment and forged passport from the Saudi in exchange for the rest of the drawings. He'd then board a private plane to Cannes with the forged papers he had assembled during the past five years. Carrying only the suitcase, he'd wipe Sweden's boredom from his shoes, accompanied by more money than he could spend in two lifetimes. Bollintell Art and Painting Restoration had no idea today would be his last day. The firm had unknowingly provided his means of escape when a minor official from the Saudi embassy sought restoration of a horrid little oil painting. Conversations and a lunch invitation from the man revealed the resident ambassador was related to the Saudi royal house. Several more lunches and an expensive dinner revealed one of the Saudi princes was an avid art collector. More dinners secured an appointment with the ambassador, then a meeting with the prince who readily agreed to König's asking price for the da Vinci drawings. The prince, it seemed, cared nothing about money or dead Jews, seeing only the opportunity to own a collection of da Vincis, a coup unrivalled in the art world.

Traffic proved heavy due to a road scraper and banked snow along the roadside. Twenty minutes later König turned onto a secondary street. A familiar road appeared on his right and he swung the Volvo onto the isolated cutoff, wincing as his tires endured a succession of potholes. The deteriorating road was a deterrent to most drivers, but it lopped five minutes off his drive to the motorway.

König considered the cracked leather gloves atop the steering wheel. He'd found the relics in the bottom of an attic trunk. So long ago, he thought. A time when I exercised the absolute power of life and death, the supremacy of ancient kings. A time when I...

Ahead, a stalled car blocked the center of the road, the trunk lid open. A jack was propped under a front bumper and three men in business jackets stood at the fender looking down at the tire. König swore and slowed.

Stupid Swedes. Just push the damn car to the side of the road.

A fourth man with sparse blond hair, shirt sleeves rolled to his elbows despite the cold, stepped toward his car, waving his arms, a helpless smile on his face. König glanced at his watch and rolled down his window as he braked behind the stranded car.

"Thanks for stopping," the man said. He pointed at the car. "Some idiot at the rental agency forgot to include a tire iron with the jack."

"And you need to borrow mine," König said.

König checked his watch. The meeting with the Saudi wasn't scheduled for another three hours.

"All right," he said. "But hurry. I have an appointment."

The man motioned his two younger companions to the Volvo. Weisser sighed and absently noted the fully inflated tire beneath the jack.

The morning was off to a poor start, but he could afford to be magnanimous on this of all days. He released the trunk lock and stepped out. He turned toward the rear when an arm looped around his neck and one of the shorter men kicked his feet from beneath him. Someone caught him before he hit the ground. Strong hands wrestled him into the rear of his car. A rough black hood slipped over his head and two sets of legs pinned him to the car floor. He felt the engine start and the sound of the second car. He reached for the rough hood, but a gritty shoe pinned his face to the freezing floorboards.

"Don't move," a young voice ordered.

König recognized the accent and cursed his stupidity. One mistake in three decades. So close, he thought. A shudder convulsed his body and he cursed himself again, calming himself as he considered the possibilities of escape. Someone might happen along the lonely road, or his captors might become careless. No matter what happened, he would show them German steel, unlike the naked dregs who soiled themselves at the trenches.

A few minutes passed and the Volvo braked. Hands dragged him from the car and snatched the hood from head. The blond man stripped him of his coat and tossed it aside. Shivering, vapor escaping his mouth, König blinked at the surrounding arena of pointed firs laden with the last snow. A sharp stone lip split the earth a few meters away and he recognized the abandoned quarry.

The oldest of the four shoved him in the back. "Walk to the edge."

König looked back at him. "My name is Hans König. I am a Swedish citizen."

"You are Anton Weiser. It's taken us a long time to find you, *Sturmbannführer*."

Weisser swallowed bile at the back of his throat and glanced at the other three who looked on dispassionately. "Whoever you are, you've made a mistake. I can prove who I am."

"We saved you the trouble." The angular man spun Weisser around and held a yellowed SD *Sicherheitdienst* identity card a few inches from his face. The photograph showed a younger Weisser with more hair but the face left no doubt.

The faded card was a death warrant. There would be no repeat of Eichmann's abduction, no midnight flight on El Al, no show trial in Jerusalem. His life and plans were over. Arranging his features as the cold knifed through his thin dress shirt, Weisser scrutinized his executioner's worn shoes and cheap polyester shirt.

"How did we miss you?"

"You didn't." The tall man pushed up his coat sleeve and exposed a faded blue tattoo on his left forearm, a 9mm pistol in his other hand.

Managing a smirk, Weisser pulled himself upright as another shiver overtook him. He raised his chin with a defiance he didn't feel. "Only Auschwitz employed tattoos. They were overworked in the final days and stopped using them."

The blond one walked to his companion and inclined his head toward the pit, his voice impatient.

"Do it," he grated.

The tall man jammed the pistol muzzle against Weisser's chest. "Turn around and walk to the edge."

Weisser straightened and marched to the brink with all the dignity he could muster. At the edge he looked down at the jumble of huge stone slabs a hundred feet below. His ruined hand throbbed in the cold, but he ignored the old wound. Ashamed when wetness soaked his trouser legs, he started to speak when a spectral voice echoed off the sheer rock walls.

We will outlive you long enough to bury you.

Weisser opened his mouth to scream and never heard the shot.

The leader walked to the edge and peered down at the red smear on the jagged rocks before he turned to the others.

"Anyone want to look?"

No one moved.

"Why here?' the blond man asked. "You could have shot him in the car."

"I wanted him to look into the pit."

No one spoke and the man with the tattoo walked past them to the cars.

Chapter Thirty-Two

New York
Franklin Place Apartments
June 2018

Temperatures in the city spiked during the day, bringing heat and humidity. Shoes off, I thanked the air conditioning gods as I sat in front of my television. I turned off the volume, shunning the breathless revelations about the latest crisis in Washington. Ignoring the succession of anxious faces, I closed my eyes and replayed my meeting with Ebba König. She hadn't revealed anything I hadn't suspected, confirming the drawings were not family heirlooms. Worse, she seemed troubled how her husband had acquired them.

My thoughts were interrupted by a knock on my door. I opened it, shocked by the disheveled figure who leaned against the doorframe.

"Can I come in?"

"Sure," I said, stepping aside in my sock feet.

Marsh Hampton looked as though he'd been dressed by a blind man and mugged on his way to my apartment. His Hermes tie was undone, a dribble of grease down the front of his shirt. Wrinkled black trousers completed the disheveled appearance, his eyes indicating he'd managed little sleep in the past few days. He looked up and down the hall and slipped inside, closing the door.

He headed to the nearest chair and collapsed, further loosening his tie until the knot hung halfway to his belt.

"You want a drink?" I said.

"I do, but I'm afraid if I start, I won't be able to stop."

I pulled out a barstool and sat facing him. From what Leslie had told me, refusing a drink was new for him. He gazed at my carpet until he looked up and met my inquisitive stare, his smile despondent, almost apologetic.

"Something's happened you need to know," he said.

"I think I need a drink."

"Go ahead," he sighed. "I can't afford one just now."

He'd never been in my apartment and he looked around listlessly, one hand rubbing the chair arm. I took his advice and went to my counter to fix a drink.

When he remained silent, I slipped on my shoes and walked back to him. I expected for him to renounce his abstinence as he watched me take a swallow without speaking. I flipped off the TV and resumed my perch on the barstool, waiting.

"You own a gun?" he asked.

"No."

"Might be a good idea to get one."

I tried to think who would try to kill me and drew up a list. Nils made the inventory. Even Roland if that was his style. Sal, if someone paid him. Add the mob if they were convinced I had anything to do with Riva's death. Even Isabelle seemed a longshot on a very bad day.

I assembled a smile. "That's a great conversation opener."

"I hate the damn things myself," he mumbled. "Except for my dad's fancy shotguns. When I was a boy, he and I hunted. I always liked …"

"Marsh, why are you here?"

He lingered in the past for a long moment and said, "They were planning on the da Vincis getting us out of the hole. The drawings were Santa Claus and an unlimited line of credit wrapped up in a package with a bow. Only the jolly old elf isn't coming down the chimney to rescue us."

"They being the Delaudiers?"

"The whole damn family with me tossed into the soup for seasoning."

I felt I was back in Riva's gerbil cage, asking questions that led to more questions. "Rescue them from what?"

"You really don't know, do you?"

"If it's about the drawings, I have my own theories."

"There's more."

"More than what?"

"Everything." He rubbed his palms over his knees. "The drawings, Roland, Isabelle, the Königs, the whole damn charade. It's all going to shit."

I slipped off the stool and poured myself another drink, feeling I would need it. I sat back down.

"So, you came to tell me I needed a gun."

He nodded and let his head fall back against the chair. "The auction house," he began. "Impressive, right? Famous architect. Tons of glass and stainless steel. An instant New York landmark and nine-figure debt without the interest." He circled a listless hand in the air. "Pile all that on top of Roland's and Isabelle's lavish tastes. You saw their townhouse. They spent like it was Christmas and no one listened to me. Said they had a failsafe."

"A failsafe," I said, trying to keep him on track.

"Then you and your book came along and screwed up everything. You and Riva set off a firestorm. Scared the hell out of them."

"Marsh, what are you telling me?"

He looked up at me "The old man was right. The da Vincis aren't da Vincis."

"Roland's experts verified them," I reminded him. "No one believes me."

"Roland had your so-called experts in his pocket. He bought them."

Dansby had been right. Money could buy a select few academics if you applied enough of it.

"And the Königs?"

"Nils told Roland he found a folio in the trunk of their family car after his father was murdered. The German bastard had robbed some poor Jew during the war. Nils smuggled them into this country hidden behind cheap prints. Claimed the prints were gifts. Must have been a busy day at Customs because no one looked twice." He patted the chair arm and looked ready to bolt. "It was a lock until the old man claimed they were fakes."

I felt vindicated, but something else worried Roland and Isabelle other than Riva's book and the threat of a bad financial year. Something that scared Marsh Hampton as well.

"The book's gone," I reminded him, "and you have the other three drawings. We're talking millions." Leslie had said Marsh was a financial wizard and I didn't think I was telling him something he didn't already know. "You and Roland can get past this."

He closed his eyes. "Not this time."

His collar was limp with sweat although the air conditioning was pouring out a frigid blast. He eyed the drink in my hand and licked his lips. I reached behind me and set my glass on the counter.

"If the auctions don't bring what's expected, it isn't the end of the world."

"Not in your world," he laughed, "but mine sure as hell is about to end."

"Tell me why."

Forearms on his knees, his voice desperate, he purged himself. "Frankly, our cash flow stinks. Always has. When Roland couldn't raise the money for the new building and he had a pile of other debts." He shook his head at the memory. "We made a deal with the wrong people. He left it to me to work out what he called the details. I convinced our benefactors that the da Vincis were a lock, that they'd get their money back with their usual truckload of interest."

"You're talking about the mob?"

His head snapped up. "Hell, yeah, I mean the mob or organized crime or whatever they're calling it now. Our financial savior was an uptown firm that turned out to be a front for laundering Boscanni's dirty money, lending it to desperate or stupid people like us. The weekly interest alone..." His grim smile failed. "Default penalties involve substantially more than a black mark on your credit rating."

"So now you're going to run."

"As fast and far as I can. If I don't, they'll try me on for size before they get to Roland. Remember, I put the deal together. My name's all over everything."

I wondered how someone supposedly as smart as Hampton allowed himself to get involved with Boscanni. Some people, I guessed, didn't pair their brains and reputations with common sense. "Why not move up the auction and sell the da Vincis? Get these people off your back?"

"Roland and Isabelle are afraid it'll look like a fire sale. They're scared out of their wits. They're afraid even the painting will fall through."

"A painting," I said, my suspicions growing. "A da Vinci painting?" Was this Nils' and Roland's surprise?

Marsh nodded. "I've never seen it, but Roland claims it's astounding. Nils found it with the drawings."

I stared at him, my brain switching off. "An oil painting by Leonardo da Vinci."

"Yes, dammit!" Marsh shouted. He shook his head apologetically and held up a hand. "Sorry. I don't know one painting from another. I can't even tell you if the damn thing's real. Roland claims it depicts David and Goliath. Told me he keeps it locked in his vault and swore me to secrecy. Not even Isabelle has the combination to the hidey-hole in his office."

A new da Vinci painting. Calculating its value on today's market would be close to impossible. I bent closer and tried to get Marsh to look at me. The chances it was something than another Volpe seemed infinitesimally small.

"You're sure it's a painting by Leonardo da Vinci."

"Roland claimed he almost peed himself when Nils showed it to him."

I couldn't remember seeing a reference to a David and Goliath painting, but I hadn't scrutinized every page of Melzi's book.

"Marsh, what's its condition? Is it framed or rolled?"

"I didn't see it. I told you he keeps it locked away."

"Does Leslie know all this? The loans and the painting?"

Marsh shrugged. "She was never part of the deal. She likes art, but she's more interested in what it's worth. She and I…" A laugh died in his throat. "For a while I thought we might be something more, but there's someone else." He sagged against the cushions and I felt a tug of guilt for having bested him in the end.

I brushed away Leslie and tried to comprehend the existence of a da Vinci painting, one of the art world's greatest rarities. More Delaudier misdirection like the Volpe drawing, or had Nils fooled him again? If Riva's book included the painting, did Melzi confirm it was Leonardo's work, or rendered by one of the master's students? The book, wherever it might be, raised the stakes

Marsh thrust himself from the chair and offered his hand. "I wish you luck. You and Leslie both."

"What will you do now?"

"Disappear." He dredged up a wan smile. "New York's lost its charm for me."

We shook hands. I started to close the door behind him when he stopped and turned back.

"Don't forget the gun."

Chapter Thirty-Three

After Marsh left, I called Leslie despite the late hour. She picked up on the second ring and I heard strains of George Benson's "On Broadway" in the background.

"Is it too late?"

A moment of silence. "No, that's okay. I'm reading up on da Vinci, filling in some blanks."

"Marsh just left my place."

She didn't sound surprised. "He's a night owl. What did he want?"

"He thinks he's in danger."

"Why?"

"Loans to Delaudier from the wrong people. He said the auction house was over its ass in debt."

"That's news, but why come to you?"

"He believes I'm in danger."

"Well, he might be right. Someone did attack you. Did he give you any reasons?"

"He believes Riva's book poses a threat."

I heard Leslie draw a long breath. "But it's gone."

"Disappeared, but someone may think I still have it."

"Do you?"

"No."

"Then you're not in danger."

My uneasiness didn't match her confidence. Marsh had been petrified. I decided to go all in and tell her about the painting. "Marsh also told me Roland has a da Vinci painting in his vault."

She gave a small laugh. "Was he drunk?"

"Cold sober."

"Come on, Adam. There's no da Vinci *painting*."

"You didn't see how scared he was."

I waited as she turned off the music. "Get some sleep," she said. "We'll talk about all this tomorrow."

After I hung up, I thought about her. I got up from my couch and turned on television, finding a British show on archaeology. As I absently watched three academics discussing Roman ruins, I recalled Marsh's comment about artwork stolen during the war. The Art Loss Register in London tracked and identified art looted by the Nazis during World War Two. They had helped me during the search for the van Gogh. I got up and went to my desk. I found a manila folder and located Neville Durrant's name and phone number. Next morning, I accounted for the time difference and telephoned London at nine o'clock. The other end chirped with the peculiar British ring tone and a cheerful female receptionist answered.

"Good afternoon. Art Loss Register. May I help you?"

I gave her Durrant's name and she transferred me.

"Neville Durrant here," said the public-school drawl.

"Mister Durrant, this is Adam Barrow in the United States. We spoke last year."

I'd been less than open with Durrant during our last conversation, pretending I needed information on a Cassatt during my search for information on the van Gogh.

"Ah, yes, Mister Barrow. I recall our previous conversation." Typical British composure with only a slight hint of annoyance. "The Mary Cassatt that miraculously transformed itself into a van Gogh."

"I apologize for misleading you. It was a... sensitive situation."

"Well, all's well that ends well, I suppose. What can I do for you?"

"No subterfuge this time," I promised. "I believe a collection of da Vincis stolen by the Nazis were smuggled into Sweden at the war's end."

I must have sounded like a broken record if he'd followed my story about the van Gogh.

"Da Vincis, you say. Well, we certainly don't see many of them. He only produced approximately twenty paintings in his lifetime that we know of, plus a virtual cornucopia of drawings." Durrant paused. "If I may ask, what was the country of origin of these drawings?"

"Most likely Russia."

"That's unusual," he mused. "It's rare we receive claims from anyone about Russian losses. The Russian army stole hundreds of European pieces when they conquered Germany, but you're saying these da Vincis might have been looted property of Russians during the war. That the Nazis stole them."

"I believe a German officer who served in Russia brought them to Sweden. Beyond that I've got no information about their former ownership." I decided not to raise the question of authenticity.

"Yes, well, anything's possible, I suppose," Durrant mused. "It's conceivable your da Vincis were owned by a Russian or Jewish family that no longer exists. If you know your history, Mister Barrow, you'll remember the fate of Russian Jews and civilians during the war."

"Anything in your files would be a great help."

"Yes, well, we'll have a look."

"When should I call you back?"

"There's not much regarding Russian requests, so it shouldn't take long."

. . .

Durrant called back two hours later.

"I had two interns go through the Russian and Polish files," he said. "I'm sorry to disappoint you, but we've not been contacted regarding claims of looted da Vinci art from the former USSR. Frankly, the authorities there have been less than helpful during our limited contacts. They're more concerned with holding onto foreign art that Soviet troops looted from Germany. You might call it their *re-looting* program."

"Damn," I muttered. König had served in Russia, but how and where did he acquire the pieces? And were they the works of Leonardo?

"If it's any help to you, we did find a copy of a directive from the Luftwaffe Air Ministry," Durrant said. "It's dated December 12, 1944. The document ordered that a crate of—and I quote here— "valuable artwork" be shipped from Mogilev to Berlin. Göring signed the order himself, but there's no indication of the crate's contents."

I thought about the order for a few moments, but could make no connection to Hans König or whatever his actual name might have been. Göring remained the consummate looter until his final days, living in a dying fantasy world. All I knew for certain was that Ebba König claimed the da Vincis hadn't arrived in Sweden until the war's end.

I thanked Durrant for his help and hung up, contemplating that a lost da Vinci painting had possibly been added to the mix. No matter what I thought of Jean-Henri, he was Dansby's long-time associate and I owed him the courtesy of revealing the painting's possible existence. I walked down the hall to his office and stuck my head around his door.

"Got a minute?"

Bonnet's eyes were fixed on his window, contemplating something on the skyline. His head jerked around and he swiveled toward me, waving at a chair.

"Just thinking about Riva," he said.

"His book was real." He waved his hand as though the thought was a fruit fly. I was tired of hearing myself say the words, but the drawings weren't Leonardo's work, and I wasn't backing off until someone proved me wrong.

"Ebba König told me we have a problem. That she believes her husband looted the drawings during the war."

"That might be easy enough to prove."

"I checked with the art registry in London. No one's claimed ownership of looted da Vincis."

Jean-Henri acted as though he hadn't heard me. "Crazy as he appears, I can't get Riva out of my head," he said glumly. "He was too passionate to attempt some kind of swindle. Besides, he must have known he was near the end. Where was the gain for him? His murder just hastened the conclusion of his life."

"So, am I forgiven for defending him?"

"Almost. You're still the new boy on the block."

"Okay, but I want to apologize again for offending you. I'm not a homophobe, but I'm not always politically correct either. My mouth occasionally outraces my brain."

Bonnet waved his hand. "You didn't say anything that Gerry and I haven't heard before."

I walked to his desk and held out my hand. "Friends?"

Surprised, he grasped my hand with a wary smile. "Friendly opponents, I suppose," he said.

He released my hand and I reclaimed my chair. He turned back to face the window, his body language more relaxed.

"I only wish I'd seen this book," he said.

"We're both lucky Phillip didn't bite on the first drawing."

"Possibly, but Delaudier has three more. I think we should steer him away from the others until we get more verification."

Jean-Henri bit his lip as though reassessing his role. I visualized him wrestling with the fact he'd reassured Phillip about the first da Vinci.

"I'll take another look," he said, "if that will make everyone happy."

The moment arrived to roll another stone in his path. I didn't relish bringing up a painting I'd never seen, having only Marsh Hampton's word that it existed. He'd been frightened and ready to bolt, but he had no reason to lie.

"There's something else."

Jean-Henri groaned. "How I've come to dread those words."

"Marsh Hampton came to see me late last night. He claims Roland Delaudier has a painting by Leonardo."

Jean-Henri sat up.

"He said the subject is David and Goliath. I looked through my references and couldn't find any mention of the subject."

Jean-Henri picked up a pen, a glimmer in his eye. "That doesn't mean it couldn't exist." He drummed the pen against the blotter. "A new da Vinci." He gave a tight smile and gazed out the window. "That would turn everything on its ear. If it's real, of course."

I sat forward. "Look, even I don't believe his tale. This is da Vinci overload. Roland and Isabelle and the Königs were reaching too far. Expecting such a painting to be real is a little much."

"But it *could* exist, Adam," Jean-Henri said, his excitement rising. "Remember, we uncovered da Vinci's *Salvator Mundi* only a few years ago and it sold for close to a half-billion dollars." His drifted off again. "Another da Vinci is almost unthinkable but not entirely unfeasible."

I noted we were back on a first name basis. "Ebba König said her husband brought everything from Russia. They weren't family heirlooms, as Isabelle and Roland claimed."

Jean-Henri grimaced and steepled his fingertips. "That's not welcome news."

"Marsh also told me the Delaudiers are in serious debt. They borrowed heavily from a Boscanni front and they're being pressured. Marsh is afraid the loan sharks will come after him too. I don't think Phillip knows any of this."

"I've heard nothing about financial troubles."

"You need to tell Phillip. If it's true, the Delaudiers might be more desperate than we thought and that casts the da Vincis in a new light."

"Have you checked with the Registry in London?"

"I called. No one's come forward to reclaim looted da Vincis."

"Did Hampton say anything else?"

"Only that someone might try to kill me because of Riva's book."

Jean-Henri laughed. It was the first time I'd seen anything approaching humor. "I was once tempted to join your list of assassins. But after listening to the old man…"

"I hope I can take you off the list now."

He gave a wry smile and I wondered if he was joking.

Chapter Thirty-Four

Daylight was fading when I decided I'd given Dansby a full day's work. After my reconciliation with Jean-Henri I wanted a drink and remembered the Esquire Lounge in the old Lambreth Hotel a few blocks away. No live music, but the hotel was nearby. I sat at my desk a few more minutes and decided instead to go back to Riva's apartment for a last look. I needed some kind of lifeboat, an assurance I hadn't overlooked some hiding place. Lomax had probably pulled the guard off the door, and with any luck I could talk the landlord into letting me look around since little was left to steal.

Exiting the building elevator, I nodded at the lobby guard and pushed through the revolving doors, the humidity and tsunami of car fumes encasing me like a wool army blanket. Office workers and tourists filled the sidewalks and competed for taxis. I walked two blocks south to the venerable old Lambreth where cabs jockeyed for hotel guests, a proven tactic that allowed me to skirt the competition.

My driver dropped me at Riva's building and I paused on the sidewalk, looking up at the edifice of faded red bricks. The drab setting seemed a fitting place for an old man to die—only not with a bullet in his head.

I stood on the first step and pretended to scroll through my iPhone, trying not to appear out of place. No one paid any attention to me and I lucked out when two young men jogged up the steps past me, holding hands. I followed them inside. Enamored with one another, they ignored me and punched in their entry code. I followed them inside and waited until they bounded up the stairs.

Looking up, I saw the lightbulb on the second-floor landing had burned out or missing. I resigned myself to two flights of stairs in the dark and was halfway up the first flight when the entrance door clicked open. Two kids, a boy and a girl about six, ran past me up the stairs and disappeared. I heard the door open and close again and looked down the stairs. A muffled figure dressed in a brimmed hat and raincoat stood just inside the foyer, and I later remembered wondering why anyone wore a coat on muggy summer night.

A flash lit the stairwell. Pain ripped through my left arm.

I fell backward, my hand losing its grip on the bannister until I landed face up on my back, pain shooting through my left side. I never knew how long I lay on the gritty stairs, staring at the water-stained ceiling. I heard the door open and close, vaguely thinking how foolish I looked sprawled upside-down. I rolled over and grabbed the railing, pain racing to my brain. I pulled myself to my feet, surprised when blood dripped from my hand onto the stairs.

An elderly woman opened the entrance door, saw the blood, screamed and dropped her bag of groceries. Dimly aware I was going to pass out, I staggered outside and stumbled down the steps. Streetlights and headlights wavered, and I made out a Yellow Cab stopped at the traffic light. I weaved to the driver's window and leaned against the car.

"Would you please call an ambulance for me?" I said, amazed at how calm my voice sounded.

The driver, a heavy-set Hispanic woman, took me for a drunk and started to wave me off when she saw the blood.

"Damn, you need to sit down, amigo. Get in back and I'll call my dispatcher."

The driver behind us started to honk, and she flipped him off. *"Vete al infierno con tu madre!"*

"I don't want to mess up the seat," I slurred, the lights going out as though a prankster manipulated a rheostat.

"Just get in. I drive you."

I opened the car door and collapsed across a blanket-covered seat. The woman driver got out and slammed the rear door. More horns and the car started moving, the driver yelling something in Spanish. Sprawled across the seat, my last memory was Consuela Contada's permit on the rear of the front seat. I smiled at her photograph and passed out.

Chapter Thirty-Five

I awoke in a narrow bed, chrome metal retainers on either side of me. Beside the bed, a beeping monitor displayed my vital signs. Clear plastic tubing from an IV bag snaked beneath the sheet covering me, the room reflecting the ambiance of all hospitals this side of the moon with its digital equipment, bare walls and pungent medicinal odors.

It took a few seconds to remember how I ended up a patient: Riva's, apartment. The stairwell. The figure in the doorway. Who found me and how I got to the hospital were gone.

A square of heavy gauze covered my upper left arm, held in place by clear tape. The enjoyable effect of whatever they filled me with was fading, replaced by an intense throbbing in my arm. Cotton-mouthed, I swallowed what felt like gravel dust, lifted my head and saw a blue plastic pitcher on the bedside table. At the same moment, I spotted Dansby in a chair near the door.

"Water," I croaked.

He rose and walked to the bed, filled a Styrofoam cup, and bent the accordion straw toward me. I sucked at icy water as he watched, his face neutral except for a smile beginning at one corner of his mouth.

"It's not Makers Mark, but it probably tastes better right now," he said.

The pain in my arm grew intense, but the ice water was nectar. "How long have I been here?"

"About four hours."

"Somebody shot me, Phillip." A stupid declaration that produced a toothy grin.

"Yes, I know. I've seen the symptoms before."

"I was at Riva's apartment building."

"The book?"

"One last look."

"Any idea who shot you?"

"Too dark."

"You were fortunate, you know."

"My arm?"

Dansby looked amused. "I'm afraid it has a minor hole in it."

"Hurts like a mother."

The pain cranked up and he saw my face twist.

"Hold steady and I'll get the nurse."

He walked outside and a nurse appeared almost immediately. She slid a syringe into the IV port and took my pulse. "A little gift," she said. "You'll feel better in a minute."

Leslie brushed past Dansby and tossed her purse on the chair. She leaned down and kissed me lightly on the lips. I grinned stupidly at her, the drugs softening her image.

"I leave you on your own and you end up in the hospital," she said, keeping one hand on my good arm. "This is the second time someone tried to kill you."

"Third time might be a charm," Dansby said.

"I went back to Riva's in case I'd overlooked something," I said, the words strangely hollow in my ears as the nurse left.

"And got yourself shot in the process."

I wanted to shrug but realized it would hurt too much.

Whoever shot me had followed me. I tried to remember the list of possibilities I had compiled that morning, but the morphine began its symphony and I dissolved into Disney World.

"Wasn't my plan," I said, my mind slipping into fellowship with all mankind.

The door swung open again, and a harried doctor walked to my bedside, managing a reassuring look they taught in med school. He inspected my wound, took my pulse again and listened to my heart with a cold stethoscope.

"So, how are you feeling?"

"Great. The nurse just sold me some morphine," I said, enjoying my glibness.

"Your injury won't warrant much of that, but we'll keep you comfortable."

Hell, at that moment I was enjoying the euphoria, overlooking the fact I had a bullet hole in my once sacred body.

"What's the damage?" I grinned.

"You were lucky, Mister Barrow."

"This is your definition of lucky?".

"The wound's in your upper left bicep." He placed a cold hand on my forehead. "A soft tissue wound with only minor muscle damage. Missed the bone, but you lost some blood. Another six inches to the right and it's a different story." He looked at my chart in his hand. "We irrigated the wound and closed up the entry and exit sites. Gave you a tetanus shot and loaded you with antibiotics. You should be out of here tomorrow. After that, I'll check you again in about a week unless complications pop up." He turned to Dansby and Leslie.

"Best he gets some sleep now."

"I'll pick you up tomorrow," Leslie said. "Call me when they give you a release time."

She kissed me again and the doctor followed her out the door. Dansby walked to the bed and lifted one corner of the dressing, inspecting the discolored flesh. I twisted my neck, unable to see the wound.

"A trifle," he proclaimed.

"My butt hurts worse than my arm. I think I landed on it when I fell."

"You'll have one of those orange and purple lovelies."

I tried to smile, but my face seemed incapable of moving, the morphine finding a home.

I squinted up at him. "Did Jean-Henri tell you the Delaudiers owe a lot of money to the wrong people?"

"He told me."

"Marsh warned me," I said, fighting the urge to drift off. "Said I should buy a gun. Lots of money involved."

"Rather hard to buy a weapon in New York unless your Sicilian friends are willing to supply one."

"Phillip, do something for me," I said groggily. "Find out where she lives and get some money to a Miss Consuela Contada. She's the driver of Yellow Cab who brought me here." I was slipping away. "Just take it out of my next check."

"Right you are. I'll take care of it."

I drifted deeper into the endorphin cloud. "Do I have medical coverage, Phillip?"

My words came through a hollow tube from far away. They were slurred but I liked the sound. Peace to the world. Understanding for everyone.

"Oh, no," he grinned maliciously, peering closer at the two holes in my arm. "You're paying for all this. I'll tell Clarice to dock your salary."

I was wondering if he was serious when the nurse walked in and saw Dansby bent over the exposed wound. She let out an audible gasp and pushed him away, re-taping the bandage.

"Sir, you'll have to leave or I'll call the floor nurse."

He ignored her and winked at me. "Make certain they fit you with a proper sling. I want you back at work."

I started to remind him I'd just been shot when my eyelids closed.

When I woke up again, a figure in a rumpled suit stood by my bed. Another man with cropped red hair sat in the visitor's chair, perusing *Sports Illustrated's* swimsuit issue. I blinked away the drugs and saw Lomax's coffee-colored face inspecting me.

"We need to quit meeting like this," I managed.

He didn't laugh, and I presumed all detectives had stunted senses of humor.

"The murder's an ongoing investigation," he said. "I heard you were shot at Riva's place and decided we needed to talk again."

I blinked and wondered if I was a suspect or victim.

"Can't stay away from Riva's, can you?"

I tugged the oxygen line away from my nostrils and tried to smile at him. "I think I will from now on."

Lomax bent closer. "I think I should have talked with you a little longer."

"Maybe you should talk to whoever shot me."

Lomax leaned an inch closer. "What a brilliant idea. Killer returns to the scene like in the movies."

"I didn't kill him." I knew I sounded so sincere he'd have to believe me.

"Suspects always say that."

From a gunshot victim to a murder suspect in a single leap. But what did it matter? We'd become friends when I explained everything.

"You find anyone who saw what happened?" Phillip asked.

Lomax showed exhaustion. "As our civic-minded citizens say, 'we ain't seen nothing or no one.'. No one suspicious entering or leaving the building. We talked to the two kids who heard the shot, but they don't remember seeing anyone except you on the stairs. Building's not upscale enough to warrant surveillance cameras. Our best guess is a fucking phantom shot you."

"Phantom of the South Bronx," I mumbled.

Lomax's humor must have expired during the day because his expression didn't change. "We found the slug in the wall. Too mangled to do ballistics much good. You were lucky it was only a .22 and the light in the stairwell was out. Either the shooter was a poor shot or he missed his target in the dark."

Had Boscanni changed his mind and sent Cuff Links to correct the oversight? But why hadn't he finished the job? Maybe he liked me too much.

Lomax placed another of his cards on my table next to my water pitcher. "Call me if you remember anything."

He walked out trailed by his partner and I drifted into wonderland again.

Chapter Thirty-Six

After the usual paperwork delays, the hospital released me next afternoon. I managed to dress myself and lost the argument about being wheeled out in the mandatory wheelchair. The effects of the painkillers lingered, and I would have agreed to almost anything to get away from the enforced confinement and loss of privacy. I knew the doctors and nurses had my best interest in mind, but I felt like a malingerer, the perception enhanced by the Vicodin.

Leslie picked me up at the exit in a new Lexus. My arm in a blue hospital sling, blazer draped over my shoulders, I hated feeling like an invalid. I levered myself out of the wheelchair with my right arm with as much composure as I could manage and eased into the contoured passenger seat, my bruised posterior protesting.

"Nice car," I grunted, trying to make myself comfortable.

"Roland has issues, but he's not cheap."

She leaned over and kissed me with a poor-baby look of pity. I shifted to a comfortable position and looked around, inhaling the heady aroma of pristine leather. Leslie reached over and helped me pull the seatbelt over my right shoulder, the Vicodin keeping the pain at bay.

"How's the arm?"

"The sling helps as long as I keep popping pills."

"Let's find a pharmacy and get your refill."

A few blocks away she stopped at Walgreens. I ran my hand over the seats when she went inside, admiring the car's luxurious appointments, glad I didn't have to drive in a city that long ago outgrew cars. She returned and said the prescription earned me a dozen opioid wonders, tucking the plastic bottle into my coat pocket. I watched her concentrate on the traffic, confident in her driving skills as she occasionally gave me an inquisitive glance.

"I never saw the reward in going back to Riva's place," she said. "The ratty little apartment is too small to hide anything large. And you got yourself shot in the process."

"I had to keep looking." It was as close to the truth as anything I'd rationalized lately. Whoever used me as target practice believed I knew something and didn't hesitate to make sure I kept it to myself.

"You couldn't describe the shooter to the police?"

"No."

I told her everything I'd told Lomax, replaying the scene on the stairs again. I recalled the entrance door opening and turning to see who it was. A dark shape at the bottom of the stairs, then the muzzle flash. Consuela Contada told the hospital I'd staggered out the door to her cab, but I'd lost that part.

"Another robbery attempt?" Leslie said.

She had a point, but it didn't feel right. Getting attacked in my apartment by a sneak thief was bad luck, but getting shot by another thief was too much of a coincidence. The chain of unlikely events began when I started talking about Riva's book.

"I think the painting upped the stakes," I said slowly, replaying events. "Everything's changed if there's a painting by Leonardo. If Marsh was right, someone other than Roland might know about it. A lot of people understand what it would bring in a private sale. The money would set up the seller for several lifetimes. Let him disappear onto some island. Even buy the damn island."

Leslie bit her lower lip and didn't take her eyes from the street. "I think falling down the stairs did more damage than getting shot," she said. "No one's laid eyes on this painting and you're seeing conspiracies."

I slumped back, careful not to bump my arm on the console, and knew she might be right. I was building castles without stones, constructing a case for a painting no one had seen. All that aside, I owed it to Riva and Dansby to play it to the end.

"Have you heard from Marsh?"

"Nothing. He's disappeared."

I stared out the car window. "If he was right, the painting's a wild card. No one mentioned a painting until he came to my apartment. Without Riva's book, I can't even prove the drawings are misattributed. I checked with the London Registry and they have nothing on them or a missing painting."

"There you go," she said, nodding. "The important thing now is to keep you alive."

We drove without speaking. I closed my eyes and leaned my head against the window. Marsh was close to Roland and overheard things. Why would he invent a story about a painting? Leslie, thinking I'd dozed off, jumped when I said, "You never heard Roland mention it?"

She sighed and glanced across at me. "Adam…"

"I know, but it won't go away. Remember, I'm supposed to find art for Dansby. If there's even the slightest chance the painting exists, I have to pursue it."

"Okay. What happens next?"

"I want to check Roland's office. Marsh claimed he kept the painting in a private safe." I assembled a smile, half-puppy dog, half-gunshot victim. "Any way you and I might take a quiet look?"

"You're serious?"

"Sure, we won't steal anything," I said, keeping the grin in place. "Just take a quick look around."

Leslie braked hard at a traffic light without looking at me. I could imagine her thoughts spinning like slot machine wheels, calculating jailtime and the potential loss of her job.

"You're fun in bed," she said, "but that's asking a lot."

I grinned at her. "My brother Wes calls me the Raider of the Lost Art."

"That's terrible."

"C'mon, we'll pretend I'm Indiana Jones and you're my squeeze." It was the best I could come up with, thanks to the Vicodin.

She shot me a look. "Squeeze?"

"Feminine associate, girlfriend, whatever you like."

The light changed, and she floored the Lexus, leaving a teenage trail of black rubber. Dodging a delivery truck, she swerved into a No-Parking zone and stopped, twisting in her seat to look at me.

"All right," she said. "If it exists, I'd like to see it too, but you're wasting your time. We'll take a quick look around and get out of there. If we get arrested, it's going to cost you dinner at Le Bernardin with a bottle of Krug Brut. 1988, when we get out."

"You've got expensive taste in wines."

"You know the vintage?"

"Only when Phillip orders it."

"You're buying this time, big boy."

She unclicked her seat belt, leaned over and kissed me without knowing she'd assumed the role of my last remaining ally.

• • •

She called the next day and said Roland and Isabelle were hosting a client dinner party that night. She had begged off, claiming she had a date, so we agreed to meet outside Delaudier at 10 o'clock after the cleaning staff finished up. I took a cab and got out across the street from the building. She was waiting half a block from Delaudier's entrance.

"Go to the back entrance and wait," she said as we approached the building. "I can finesse Harry, the night security guy. He makes his rounds every hour, but we'll be gone before he gets to Roland's office."

"Cameras and alarm system?"

She held up a small receiver, dropped it to her purse and headed to the front entrance. I walked to the rear loading dock. A few minutes later she unlocked the reinforced metal door, and we took the back stairs to the third floor without speaking. My arm reminded me I had a bullet hole in it. I felt lightheaded at the top of the staircase and held up one hand, pretending to adjust the sling as I caught my breath.

"Remember," she whispered, "this was your idea."

I nodded and waved her on, the overhead lights dimmed. The carpet muffled our footsteps as we passed her office and headed toward Roland's enclave. Two massive mahogany doors with hand-carved Oriental scenes guarded the hall.

"His and her offices," Leslie said, staring deadpan at Isabelle's door on the left.

We stepped to Roland's door and she produced the clicker. She a punched a red button twice. The keypad beside the doors glowed green. She pressed five numbers. A soft click and we slipped inside his office, easing the door closed.

"Don't turn on the lights," she said.

The drapes were drawn but Manhattan's lights and marquees illuminated the room with a soft radiance. A huge arrangement of lilies sat on a table beside the door, the odor permeating the spacious office. Two carpeted steps led down into an enormous sunken room reflecting Roland's tastes. An elaborate partner's desk.

Built-in mahogany bookcases on three walls fronted by a library ladder on rollers. A massive solid slab of white Calacatta marble the size of a refrigerator crate dominated the center of the office, surrounded by dark green leather wing chairs and a matching couch. Coordinated rugs were compatible with the color of money.

Leslie skirted the room slowly, running her fingertips over the furniture, while I went to the desk and pulled open drawers, thumbing paper and hanging folders. I doubted I would find photographs of the painting, but possibly he'd left a trace in a careless moment. Giving up, I stood back and scanned the oversized desktop.

Nothing.

I started to walk away when I saw an ugly knife atop a stack of paper. It seemed out of place among other antique accoutrements and I picked it up. The blade showed signs of repeated sharpening. I gently ran my thumb along the edge. Razor sharp. The black handle was decorated with a red and white inlay, a black swastika in the center. The scrolled inscription on the steel blade read *Blut Und Ehre!*

Leslie saw me examining it.

"A gift from Nils," she said. "He said it's a Hitler Youth Knife that belonged to his father. He claimed he was sick of it and thought Roland might get a kick out of it."

I turned it over in my hand and reread the inscription. 'Blood and Honor.' A touching sentiment.

"Roland said Nils and his father weren't all that close," she added. "I guess he wanted to get rid of the thing."

I replaced the knife and looked around. "Where's the safe?"

She walked to the nearest bookcase, stood on tiptoes and pulled out a single book. She reached into the space and stepped back. The section shelves pivoted with a low hum and revealed a massive stainless-steel door, rivaling anything at Chase.

She swept her hand at the entrance. "Voila. He once told me Isabelle would have left him if she knew what this thing cost."

"Who has the combination?"

"Only him. He doesn't trust anyone with it."

"What if something happens to him?"

"Then I guess we're all SOL."

If he stashed the painting in the vault, there was a strong possibility Roland intended to dispose of it in a private sale and pay off Boscanni. If it turned out the painting *was* looted Nazi art, no one would ever see it again.

The pain in my arm flared again, and I leaned against his desk, looking around the room so different from Enzo Riva's pathetic apartment. My quest for his book had taken a twisted trail and I wondered if I would ever hold it in my hands again. I'd had help in the search for the van Gogh. Kat. Dansby. Even my father had played his part from the grave. I had only Leslie this time, and I needed her to tell me Marsh had been wrong, that there was no painting.

"You believe Marsh knew what he was talking about?"

"He never said anything to me and we were close."

I must have looked hurt because she came around the desk and nuzzled my cheek, careful not to bump my arm.

"I'm sorry," she said. "That was a long time ago."

Her hair smelled like lilacs and I kissed her until she broke away and whispered in my ear.

"There's more to life than a painting."

She pulled me around the desk and walked to the couch. Unbuttoning her blouse, she let it fall to the floor and looked back at me.

"How's your arm?"

"Serviceable in the right circumstances."

Her bra and thong followed her skirt.

"The boss's couch looks comfortable if you're up to it."

Her body pale in the shadowy light, she laid back against the sleek leather and patted the cushions.

"We've got an hour before Harry makes his rounds."

Chapter Thirty-Seven

Still basking in Leslie's inventiveness, I slowly dressed next morning. My arm ached after last night's exertions on Roland's couch, and her comment about my standing in his way resurfaced as I grabbed a cab to the office. Still savoring the previous night, I took the elevator and slipped past Clarice, whose hobby was dissecting my love life.

Stacks of Delaudier's evaluations of the da Vincis sat in a neat pile on the center of my desk. Dansby had marked each one, requesting me to take another look to either confirm or deny their legitimacy. Roland had delivered the assessments by courier, making every effort to assure that Phillip didn't pull out of the next auction. Verification was Jean-Henri's job, but he'd most likely reviewed the evaluations before they found their way to my desk. It seemed redundant, but I owed it to Dansby to take one more look.

Two hours later I repackaged the folders and stood, stretching and testing my arm. I sat down again and studied the envelopes. The most striking anomaly was conformity. Every authority confirmed the Delaudiers had unearthed a gold mine. No one hedged, no dissenting opinions, which was odd. The list of scholars was impressive, but so far as I knew, only this group had assessed the drawings. Technical analysis was detailed and conclusive. They had all wanted a first look at the da Vincis and each fell in line, dismissing the questionable signature. It appeared Dansby had been right: Roland and Isabelle had hand-picked the experts and possibly paid off any dissenters. Even if it cost a tidy sum, the payoff would far exceed the expense.

Were the Delaudiers running a serious scam or were we implying too much? In a court of law, there would be no evidence without Riva's book.

Far more interesting to me, no one questioned provenance. Who had owned the drawings for 500 years? Where had they been before König acquired them?

According to Ebba, her husband brought them out of Russia with him, but no record existed of missing da Vincis. Not in Russia or anywhere else. No claims had been registered by surviving Jews or Russians who were conducting crusades to recover stolen property. Durrant had also raised the question of Göring's order. How did the fat bastard know about the drawings, and why had he ordered the shipment of a single crate? You could make the argument he was delusional at the end, and that left only Hans König who brought the drawings to Sweden. He had held the answers, but what had happened to him?

I gazed at the appraisals and thought about Ebba König's unwillingness to talk about her husband, an undercurrent she couldn't bring herself to discuss. An alarm bell rang like a railway crossing warning, the same sensation I'd experienced when the van Gogh revealed its hiding place. One obvious answer remained in front of me, but I had looked away after talking with the Art Registry that had no record of stolen da Vincis. I replayed my conversation with Ebba and Durrant, then Googled the Israeli consulate in New York on my iPhone.

An information page led me to a Contact Us icon with instructions to email all inquiries. Instead, I dialed the general number. I listened to a recorded message in Hebrew, then recorded options in English until I was finally connected to a pleasant young woman manning a help line.

"Israeli consulate. How may I help you?"

I gave a false name and served up my fake story. "Yes, I'm seeking information about a man named Hans König who died forty years ago. He may have been an Israeli citizen."

I was transferred to another woman who politely listened to my request. I explained König was my great uncle and that I was a compiling a genealogy chart.

"We don't keep those records," the polite voice said. "You'd have to contact your embassy in Israel. They may be able to connect you with someone who can help."

I thanked her and hung up. My remaining options were circling the drain and I was about to leave for lunch when my cell phone rang.

"You inquired about Hans König," a male voice said. No pleasantries or introduction.

I sat up. "Can you help me?"

"The New Bean coffee shop near the consulate. Five o'clock. We can talk there."

The voice clicked off and I thought about the call as the day dragged on. I had called the consulate on my cell, but the caller knew my office number, and I'd been contacted within 30 minutes.

I left at four-thirty and headed toward the consulate on 2nd Avenue. The eleven-story nondescript structure sat between Park Avenue and the East River. It was a functional 50's building with regimented rows of darkened windows reflecting the taste of an unimaginative architect. The small coffee shop was a block away, updated with colorful posters of mugs and coffee beans decorating the walls. I ordered a black coffee, loaded it with Equal and dairy dust and waited. The place was empty and I took a seat near the front window, watching the street.

A stocky nondescript man detached himself from a doorway across 2nd Avenue. He crossed the street, inspecting the crowds. His open-necked shirt and baggy suit marked him as someone other than a financial whiz from one of the surrounding towers. He opened the door, walked directly to my table and stood over me.

"Mister Barrow, my name is Ephraim."

No verification or request for identity. Someone had done a fast check on me.

He pulled out a chair without offering his hand and sat facing me.

"You know my name?" I asked.

He waved away a bearded youth who approached the table. My host's humorless smile wavered with strained tolerance, his teeth very even and white, complementing blue eyes the color of the Mediterranean. I placed him in his mid-forties, his tanned face lined with creases beyond his years.

"The consulate has very good resources."

It didn't strain my intelligence to realize I wasn't talking to an office drone.

"If we're going to talk, I need your full name."

"Ephraim. If you require more, I'll leave you to enjoy your coffee."

I didn't like being on the downside of serious conversations. "I'd like your first and last name," I repeated.

He got up to leave.

"Okay, wait," I said.

He sat back down and rested his arms on the table. His scarred hands looked capable of breaking off a piece of the wooden top.

"You're in the art business, Mister Barrow, and you work for Phillip Dansby as an art researcher. You discovered a lost van Gogh last year and you're now engaged in verifying da Vinci art work. I'm sure all this is all very exciting for you, but why did you contact the consulate about Hans König?"

My call had obviously been recorded, my name quickly researched.

"My inquiry concerns valuable artwork he once owned."

The smile turned contemptuous. "König, art lover."

"That wasn't his profession?"

"He wore that uniform when it suited him."

"He performed other duties during the war?"

Ephraim studied the backs of his hands. "Oh, yes."

"And after the war?"

"He worked for Bollintell Art and Painting Restoration in Stockholm. He died in Stockholm in 1979."

I threw a dart in the dark. "If he lived in Stockholm, you know his real name."

He appeared not to hear me. He raised a hand toward the counter and ordered an espresso.

"This will not be approved on my expense sheet," he said, a half-smile returning when the coffee arrived. "Espresso is off the approved list."

"My treat," I said.

"Thank you."

"Look," I said. "My job is to trace lost art for Phillip Dansby. I need to know if I'm chasing art looted during the Holocaust. This Hans König is my only link."

The espresso arrived, and Ephraim sipped the scalding black brew, watching me

"You know better than me, the Nazis stole everything they could find," I said. "König, or whatever his name was, may have been one of the looters. I'm talking about extremely valuable art no one has claimed."

"If that's the case, your artwork was most likely owned by a family that no longer exists." The trenches around his eyes deepened. "I don't have to tell you that art wasn't the only loss during the war."

"Tell me what happened to König."

"It's no secret, Mister Barrow. If you'd followed the story in 1979, you'd have learned his actual name. After his death, the press received an anonymous tip that König's real name was Anton Weisser, a former SS Major who commanded one of the special action groups that attempted to eliminate every Jew in Europe." He paused, retelling a story he knew only too well.

"You want to know about Anton Weisser? His work began in Poland in March of 1941. Later that year he participated in the massacre of 34,000 Jews at Babi Yar near Kiev. His unit and other *einsatzgruppen* units then slaughtered 55,000 Jews in Latvia. He then transferred to the region around Bialystok where 170,000 more Jews were killed. Ordered into the Ukraine in 1942, Weisser took part in the annihilation of the Mizoez Ghetto."

I thought I knew the history of the Holocaust, but the sheer enormity conveyed by the numbers stunned me. It was as though small cities had been wiped away without a trace. How could anyone dispose of humans like cattle? As I sat in the dreary coffee shop, a pall of guilt descended on me. Did a few works of art mean anything in the face of such depravity?

Ephraim studied his espresso. "In 1943 Weisser and his murderers took part in the liquidation of the Krakow Ghetto, followed by the total elimination of the Riga Ghetto. In 1944 they travelled by train to Hungary in search of more victims. From there, he returned to Russia, exterminating pockets of surviving Jews even though there were few left. After the Russians conquered East Prussia, we thought Weisser had died in the fighting until he surfaced in Stockholm."

He pushed his cup aside. "What else can I tell you, Mister Barrow? Only God saw how many others were murdered in forgotten towns and villages. Few records survived. Personal testimony after the war revealed Weisser was responsible for more than 100 deaths by his own hand."

Ebba König had ample reason to bury her husband's past.

"How did he die?"

He shrugged. "You can read about it if you like. The Swedish papers say he was shot. His body was found at the bottom of a rock quarry outside Stockholm. Of course, the papers blamed Israel for his death."

"And his murderer was never found?"

He noticed I was grimacing, rubbing my upper arm. "You're in pain, Mister Barrow?"

"An accident," the wound frivolous in light of what I just heard. "Tell me what happened to him."

"I can only say his death entailed no loss. I know nothing about the circumstances."

Ephraim was a good liar. My inquiry had sent up flares. I little doubted my table mate was most likely Mossad, dispatched by the agency to ascertain what I knew, and if I might be privy to how Weisser actually died. Israel's reprisals had tailed off as old Nazis died, the agency turning its attention to its terrorist neighbors. Israel was less popular than ever with the world media and resurrecting a forty-year-old assassination would only supply more reasons to side with her enemies. Still, I needed to know the circumstances of Weisser's connection to the da Vincis.

"No matter how Weisser died," Ephraim said, "it was a long overdue death."

He did not appear to relish Weisser's demise or how it occurred, but there was no lamentation that a mass murderer no longer breathed the same air as the rest of us, nor had been brought before a court of law.

"Can we agree there's a line between justice and revenge?" I asked him.

He crossed his arms on the table. "Justice is a very clean word, Mister Barrow. Vengeance, I grant you, has ugly connotations." He lightly tapped the scarred tabletop with a forefinger and leaned closer. "If they could speak, six million men, women and children would tell you one is as good as the other. When the courts rule against a tiny nation like Israel, justice becomes twisted and the dead demand a reckoning."

He gave a scornful smile. "Otherwise, we would become sheep again, Mister Barrow, waiting for the wolves' return. Marking time until another Holocaust."

Legal versus moral were arguments above my head. "And there's nothing you can tell me about Weisser."

"If you mean his business dealings after the war, no. You must uncover Major Dansby's truth on your own."

The da Vincis now seemed a wealthy man's pastime. Lost art deserved to see the light, but my pursuit now appeared a mockery after the horrific events that occurred 80 years ago. Whatever his real name, Weisser's death surpassed any statutes of limitation or public opinion. In far too many instances, governments imposed legal technicalities condoned by individuals complicit in the worst war crimes.

"Whatever the truth, he got what he deserved," I said. "He was…"

Ephraim drained his espresso and stood. "I will only say again there was no mourning in Israel."

He thanked me for the coffee and I watched him leave. He melted into the crowds and I sipped my lukewarm coffee as streetlights popped on. I had no doubt he knew every detail of Weisser's death. I wasn't an ardent Zionist, but I'd sleep better knowing justice had persevered over a world of hypocrisy and historical ignorance. I'd come to another dead end, my despair partially offset by the fact Anton Weisser never lived to profit from his crimes.

A monster who successfully eluded justice for three decades had transformed himself into Hans König, while concealing the da Vincis' existence. There was no way to prove it, but my guess was the real owners were lost to history and that Weisser planned to sell the work once he believed he was safe. Ebba's children discovered them and set the Delaudiers' plan in motion.

Contacting the consulate had been a long shot. I'd found part of the story, but I still had no proof where the da Vincis had come from, or if they were even authentic. Without Riva's book, I was back where I started, having only succeeded in stirring millions of ghosts in their mass graves.

Chapter Thirty-Eight

I sat at my kitchen counter the next morning clad in running shorts and a t-shirt from Chris Botti's last concert. I'd piled open books beside my coffee mug, trying to push aside my conversation with Ephraim and the images he had unwittingly inserted into my comfortable life. I opened one volume and summoned the effort to conduct more research into the drawings, looking for a clue about the David and Goliath painting. I could not locate even a footnote that Leonardo contemplated such a work. No mention that a patron ever commissioned the scene.

As always happened when confronted by Leonardo's work, I was diverted from my search by the scope of his talent. Talent was a weak word to describe what transpired between his brain and his hands. Leafing through the larger reproductions, I paused to admire the double-spread photo of the Ponte Vecchio bridge spanning the Arno River. Another modern photo depicted the lush hills of his native Tuscany where he'd painted the spellbinding portrait of Lisa di Antonmaria Gheradini, known to the world as Mona Lisa. Page after page of detailed sketches drew my eyes. Dissections of human anatomy, disfigured faces and an array of futuristic machines still stunned today's art lovers and scientists. If a new painting came to light, its impact could not be measured in terms of money alone.

My reverie abruptly ended when my iPhone buzzed and Dansby changed everything.

"Roland Delaudier was murdered in his office last night," he said without preamble. "The security guard found his body this morning."

Taken aback, I said nothing.

"Our friend, Detective Lomax, is there now. He seems to cover the entire city, or else he's a rabid art aficionado," Dansby said.

I thought about my midnight foray with Leslie on the couch and wondered how much forensic evidence I'd left in Roland's office. My fingerprints and DNA were all over his desk—and the couch.

"Does Leslie Strickland know?"

"Lomax has already talked with her." Dansby paused. "You and Roland weren't what I'd call bosom friends. I hope you have an alibi for last night."

I didn't. Light-headed from stupidly mixing Tramadol with a bourbon, I'd stretched out on my couch and passed out.

"Actually, you may not be at the top of his list," Dansby said. "It seems the entire family has disappeared along with the drawings. The police can't locate Sal Testano either and no one's been able to reach Isabelle or Nils or the mother."

I tried to absorb what he was saying. The Delaudiers had begun the drama with their da Vincis. Now the drawings ceased to exist, at least within the confines of New York. My guess was they'd panicked, grabbed the drawings, and fled, knowing Boscanni would show up at their door for his money. Worse, if the painting existed, odds were it was gone too.

"I don't have anything to hide. I'll talk with Lomax."

"There's a good chance you'll be with him for a while," he said. "I'll tell Clarice not to look for you today. Just be careful what you say. Lomax will need all the suspects he can get."

"You're not cheering me up, Phillip."

"Just preparing you. Call me if you require the services of a good attorney."

He clicked off. I called Leslie but got no answer, wondering whether I should admit to Lomax that Leslie and I had been in Roland's office. I discarded the idea, thinking an unbelievably valuable painting was an excellent motive to kill him. I tried calling her again without luck. That left me without a clue what she had told Lomax. Our midnight visit didn't match the timing of the murder, but that would be academic if Lomax already decided I was involved. I got dressed and eased my arm into the sling, still debating what I'd tell him.

I cabbed to Delaudier and saw a cluster of reporters outside the building. I asked a uniformed officer at the front door to let Lomax know I was outside. Several reporters gave me inquisitive looks as the cop clicked on his pager, said something and waved me inside.

The now familiar yellow tape was strung across Roland's office door. Inside, Lomax was directing a group of police photographers and forensic people. A man

I took to be the medical examiner closed his black bag and said something to him. Behind them, the concealed bookcase door was open revealing the vault door.

Lomax was waiting outside the crime scene tape. He spotted me and nodded to the cop at the door.

"I heard what happened," I said.

Without replying, Lomax led me to Roland's desk where a dark burgundy stain had soaked into the carpet. "He was sitting at his desk. In case you didn't already know."

"Shot?"

"Back of the head. Like Riva." He looked me up and down as though expecting to discover blood-spatters on my shirt. "Small caliber revolver since we didn't find any shell casings. The mob favors them since they do the job without attracting attention. We found an empty cash box on the desk which gives us motive. No prints."

Lomax looked more beat than usual, bruised bags beneath his eyes. He ran a hand over his clean-shaven skull and pointed at the vault. "Miss Strickland said there may be more pictures in there, but we can't open the damn thing." He looked around the office. "From what the staff tells us, nothing else appears to be missing, but we'll find out for sure when they inventory the place." His tired eyes settled back on me. "You always seem to be around when there's a shooter."

"Or when I get shot," I reminded him.

I looked around. The office seemed more ostentatious in daylight and I tried hard not to stare at the couch. How much forensic evidence had we provided the good lieutenant?

"How'd you know he was dead?" Lomax asked.

"Dansby called me this morning."

"And how did *he* find out?"

I could tell Lomax was frustrated that other people seemed to know as much as he did.

"I imagine he has contacts even among the police," I said.

"You didn't know?"

I met his eyes. "About Delaudier being killed? How would I?"

"You got an alibi for last night?"

"Nope. I was at home. Alone."

"Bad luck for you."

We were starting to sound like Robert Mitchum and Richard Widmark from a *film noir* movie.

He nodded at the sling. "How's the arm?"

I flexed it with only a low hum of pain. "It's okay. I was feeling the after effects and went to bed early."

Lomax took out a small spiral notebook and made a note. "I understand you and Delaudier had words more than once. In front of witnesses."

"It was professional. We disagreed over some work he was offering. Not enough reason to kill him."

"Right. First Riva, then Delaudier and you getting shot. Why would I think you might be involved?"

"You can think whatever you want."

Lomax made another note. The room was cool, but a moist film of sweat glistened on his shaved scalp. I knew it had nothing to do with a bullet hole in Roland's head; he'd seen worse in his line of work.

"Could be someone cleaned out the vault," he said. "Can't tell yet since we can't open the bastard. The thing's computer coded. We thought we found the combination in the desk, but it didn't work. Either Delaudier changed the combination or the numbers don't mean shit. We'll take a look inside when a specialist gets here."

Riva could have helped them if someone allowed to live. "You can ask Isabelle Delaudier for the combination when you find her."

"Great idea except that's going to be a problem. We found airline confirmations on her computer for the whole family. They flew off to Sweden early this morning. They're gone, all three of them."

"A plethora of suspects."

"A what?"

"A lot of possibilities."

"Yeah, but it'll be hell getting to them. DA's office says Sweden's extradition laws are tough. Their government makes all the decisions. Red tape out the wazoo. From what Miss Strickland tells me, Isabelle Delaudier is a smart broad, smart enough to tie us up in the courts for years."

"There was a guy who worked for them. Sal Testano. Sort of a gofer and bodyguard. You might want to talk to him."

"Actually, we found Testano," Lomax said. "Someone at a Walmart parking lot reported a bad smell coming from a car. We found Mister Testano with half his head blown off. Someone had worked on him before they killed him. The coroner said they used an acetylene torch."

I blinked and thought about my two companions at Armands.

"Have you talked with Leslie Strickland? She worked here and knew the family pretty well."

"Miss Strickland claims she was just an employee and wasn't aware about Delaudier's business dealings."

I didn't say anything, wondering what else she told him.

Lomax looked at his notes and back at me. "There's also this financial guy. Marsh Hampton. We can't find him either. You know anything about his whereabouts?"

Marsh. I'd forgotten about him. He'd suggested I get a gun, but it was possible he already had one. He said they argued about the dealings with Boscanni. I figured he was long gone, but I dismissed the idea of him killing Roland. He wasn't the type to pull a trigger out of revenge. At least I didn't think so.

"Hampton came to my apartment a couple of nights ago scared out of his mind. Said he and Roland did business with one of Boscanni's fronts, a lending company that loan sharks to the upper business echelons. The auction house is in trouble and Hampton thought they might become targets."

Lomax grunted. "We know about the loans with East Coast Investments. We found the agreements in the desk. Lots of layers between ECI and Boscanni, but there's no doubt it's the scumbag's operation. He makes more off the interest than the budget of my whole division."

"Hampton said Delaudier was being pushed hard for repayment. You might want to start with Boscanni."

"Yeah, right," Lomax said with a tired smile. "He's got motive, but the bastard's slathered in Teflon. Even the RICO boys haven't been able to connect him to loan sharking."

"Can't you bring him in for questioning?"

"Sure, but he's lawyered up to his pinky ring. Without solid evidence he's connected to East Coast's operation, we'd be stopped cold."

"So that leaves me your number one."

"One of them, but I don't think you're this stupid."

Forensics would identify me as being in Roland's office, my fingerprints all over his desk and private papers. I might get lucky, but I didn't want Lomax to think I lied to him. Leslie was an employee, so her presence in the office would be seen as normal. Just the same, I'd leave her out of it and take my chances with part of the truth.

"Look, sooner or later you'll find out I was in here several days ago looking for a painting."

Lomax looked at me and I knew he was deciding whether to arrest me and work out the details later, but I guessed few suspects sauntered into his crime scenes to admit they'd done something that might implicate them in a murder. He glanced at the cop by the door as if making a decision before he looked back at me.

"When were you here?"

"Wednesday night. I hung around in the men's room until closing time. The security guy never checked." Hopefully, Lomax wouldn't talk with the guard.

"There's a keypad by the door. How'd you get in here?"

"The door wasn't locked."

"So, you're telling me you just walked in." He pocketed the notebook and sighed. "Like I said, I don't take you for being this kind of stupid, but you need to stick around the city and return my calls. Otherwise, you'll be back on my list."

My insides stopped quavering. I'd dodged another bullet for the time being, a cliché I didn't want to think about. Or possibly Lomax wanted time to look at everyone else before falling on me.

"All I know is there's a dog in the manger somewhere," he said. "I've got a shitload of suspects. Boscanni's crew. The Königs. Your boss, Dansby, and God knows who else. We can eliminate Testano, although that's not the best word to describe his situation." Lomax blew out his breath and looked around. "Why couldn't there just be a jealous wife or idiot who just wanted to rob the place?"

"Then we wouldn't need smart detectives like you, lieutenant."

He knuckled a bloodshot eye. "Very funny, Barrow, but you're still on my hit parade."

Chapter Thirty-Nine

Late next afternoon I went back to the office to return several books I had borrowed from Jean-Henri's library. Dansby caught me as I was leaving and invited me for a drink at his house. In all the time I'd known him, I never once set foot inside his home. His private life remained just that: Very private. Located on East 65th Street, the six-story Gilded Age edifice was 120 years-old. I sat in a spacious paneled den enjoying a thirty-year-old bourbon. He preferred to live without the Delaudiers' splashy lifestyle. Only the six stories and his artwork displayed his elevated status among the city's elite. His collection of paintings and art objects shamed many small museums.

Dansby mixed himself a drink. "Did you talk with your friend, Lomax?"

"We had the usual post-felony chat. We keep bumping against oner another and he's not willing to erase my name yet. He's like the husband who keeps coming home and finding the same man entertaining his wife."

"Does he have any other suspects?"

"None he's willing to discuss."

"That's why you're on his list."

"I figured that out. He said I was in the pool, but not the deep end."

Dansby retrieved my glass, walked to a mirrored bar and refreshed my drink without asking. Settled in his wingback chair, a look of distress clouded his face. "For someone who professes to be my art investigator, you have a special knack of involving yourself with firearms and dead people."

"Wrong places, wrong time, I guess."

"Whatever the reason, it's not healthy."

He rose again and went to a rolltop desk. Taking a small key chain from his pocket, he unlocked the top and removed an ugly black automatic pistol. Blockish and ungainly, the Glock appeared to be the same model Kat had given me before she was killed. Dansby ejected the magazine, checked that it was fully loaded and shoved it back into the grip.

"Do you know how to use this?"

I shrugged. "I know how it works, but I've never fired one."

He picked up the Glock and pointed to the safety. "All you need do is move this to the 'off' position, point and keep firing until you determine you're no longer in danger."

I took the pistol. "Sounds simple enough."

"It's not when someone is pointing a gun at you."

He made certain the safety was on and placed the pistol on the table beside me. I hadn't bargained for this. Just like the search for the van Gogh, what seemed an academic task was leading down darker roads again. I was learning that fine art was no different from cash or bearer bonds. If the payoff was tempting, people were willing to kill you. Dansby was a realist with years of military training and no hesitation to do whatever was necessary to stay alive. Whether I could do the same remained to be seen— something I had no desire to find out.

He gestured at my arm. "I see you removed your sling. How's the arm feel?"

"Sore, but I'm basically okay."

"I can always ask Jean-Henri to take over."

Where was this going?

He rolled his glass between his palms. "What do you want from all this, Adam?"

I raised my own glass with a half-smile. "To make you happy, boss."

"I'm serious."

It was a fair question. What did I want? The lure of the hunt remained strong, only now I had a host of complications. I'd started looking into a single drawing, but then people started dying around me. Ghosts of the van Gogh were raising their heads again.

"I guess getting shot just pissed me off," I finally said. "I want Riva's book and I want to find out who killed him."

"And I hope you harbor an aspiration to locate an actual da Vinci for me."

"That goes without saying."

"That may now prove more difficult since they've disappeared. Besides which, this is not your father's van Gogh. I don't want you getting killed because a piece of artwork may or may not be authentic."

"Finding the damn book would clear up a lot of questions for both of us."

I dropped the automatic in my briefcase and thanked him for the drink. I hadn't yet told him about the painting. It might be a ruby among Delaudiers' other rhinestones or just another *fugazi*. If it turned out to be real, chances were Roland's murderer stole it, or the Königs carted it off to Sweden. Either was a depressing thought, but it was possible the painting sat inside Roland's safe.

Outside, I headed back to Delaudier. Chances were Lomax might still be there and I needed to see if he'd had any luck getting the vault open.

• • •

Lomax was gone when I arrived outside Roland's office. The open door emitted the same alien odor as Riva's apartment after his shooting. A single cop stood guard at the yellow crime scene tape. He recognized me and held up his hand.

"Lomax'll be back in about an hour," he said.

I looked past him. A diminutive figure in a loose Hawaiian shirt stood by the open vault door. His sleek black hair shone in a bank of spotlights set up inside the open vault. The small man wore flesh-colored vinyl gloves, an open case of tools and electrical equipment at his feet. Two laptops and a bank of digital monitors occupied a collapsible table beside the massive door, snakes of extension cords crisscrossing the carpet. The waifish figure heard the cop and turned around, peered at me for a moment and broke into a grin.

"Adam, my man!"

It took a moment to recognize the face. Bennie Wong hadn't grown an inch or gained a pound since our college days when we haunted beer joints around UCLA. Other than his intelligence, I remembered Bennie drank enough beer for both of us. He had been a fellow art major and smartest guy in my classes, but I lost track of him after grad school. I waved and pointed at the blue uniform.

"He's okay," Bennie called to the cop. "Lomax said he was finished in here."

The policeman hesitated and stepped back. Conscious of the pistol in my briefcase, I nodded my thanks and ducked under the tape. Bennie met me halfway. Laughing, we bear-hugged, stepped back and bumped fists.

"Damn, it's been a long time," I said.

"Too long since The Cracked Mug."

"You still remember that place? We spilled some serious suds in there."

"All in a good cause," he laughed. "Getting wasted and arguing about the best artist who ever lived."

"There was never any doubt."

He crossed his arms. "Monet."

"Velázquez," I countered. "No blurry haystacks or endless water lilies."

"You haven't changed," he grinned. "Old school all the way." He looked around the room. "I'd invite you to sit down, but I'm not supposed to touch the furniture."

We stood there smiling at another until he said, "Last I heard, you were in Chicago. Found an unknown van Gogh, then lost it in a legal hassle."

"Long story," I said, weary of recounting what happened. "I have a gallery in Chicago, but I'm now working for Phillip Dansby here in New York."

"Dansby?" Bennie lifted his eyebrows. "I hear he's richer than Warren Buffet."

"No one knows, but he's in love with fine art."

"Whadda you do for him?"

"Scout around for work that may have been overlooked." It was the simplest explanation.

"Maybe you can save his wealthy soul in the process."

Bennie was always a closet Socialist, but I was happy to see a familiar face from better days. Since Kat's death, parts of my past had slipped away and I found myself filling the gap with work.

He was still grinning at me. "Never shook the art bug, huh?"

"Nope."

He gestured around the room. "Dansby get you involved in this mess?"

"He's interested in acquiring a da Vinci and Roland Delaudier was offering a drawing."

"Well, he's not offering anything now."

I set my briefcase on a tarp beside the desk that hid the carpet's blood stains. "I got here after they removed the body."

"Bad scene," Bennie said. "You meet Detective Lomax?"

"He's an old friend."

I gestured at the laptops and blinking equipment, trying not to stare into the lighted vault. "You with the police now?"

"Work," he said. "I couldn't find a way for a handsome Chinese lad to make a living in the art world, so I went back to school and picked up a couple of engineering degrees in computer science. A California insurance company offered me a job in their fraud section. I investigate stolen art, bogus claims, that sort of thing. I don't get to handle many Monets, but it pays the bills."

He took a business card from his wallet and wrote his hotel on the back. "Call me before I leave town and we'll have a drink."

I slipped the card in my jacket pocket. "And all this brought you to New York?"

"Roland Delaudier's been on our list for some time after he filed several claims for artwork stolen from this monster," he said, indicating the vault. "Anyway, I came here to investigate, but he's dead and the wife's disappeared." He waved his hand at the vault.

"The claims were bullshit. Declaring someone broke into that thing is a joke. It took me all night until I got lucky and worked out the ten-digit entry. The police found part of the entry code taped beneath his desk, but it seems Delaudier was a smart cookie. He wrote down six numbers, 523543, but not all ten digits. He must have kept the last four in his head. I ran the diagnostics and found the other four numbers." Bennie patted one of his laptops with obvious fondness. "Took me a while and cost me dinner last night, but you can't fool Captain Computer."

"You were always the smartest guy in the bar."

"Right, but there's more. I found three da Vinci drawings."

So, the Königs hadn't absconded with them.

Eyes shining, he looked at the vault door and motioned me closer. "I found something else. Something that freaks me out. Man, I might be seeing things, but there's a painting in there you need to see. Either it's real or one of the best fakes I've ever seen."

I kept my excitement in check. Marsh, it seemed, hadn't been crazy.

"A painting? Can I see it?"

He shrugged. "Why not? To the cops it's just another painting."

We stepped over the raised steel frame into the vault. The glare of floodlights reflected off stainless walls, the soft murmur of a humidity control system whirring as I looked around. The interior was small. Ten feet square at the most. It was empty except for the three framed drawings stacked in a metal bin marked with police tags. A wrapped rectangle rested on a table against one of the other walls. Measuring roughly 4x4 feet, it bore a similar identification tag.

Bennie picked up the bundle by its edges.

"All my life I've only seen work like this in museums and books," he said. "Holding this in my hands might be a once in a life experience if it's what I think it is."

A shudder ran through me as he removed a cloth covering from an ornate frame.

The image breathed life despite the harsh lights, the colors brilliant in spite of being laid down centuries ago.

A boy with flowing curly hair stood proudly erect, an empty sling dangling from one hand. I could sense his sinewy structure even beneath the rough tunic he wore, the triumphant figure dominating the scene. The short white tunic exposed sun-bronzed arms, the plain garment cinched by a simple cloth belt. His right sandal rested atop an enormous warrior's armored body. A severed head rested a few feet away in the sand. Shafts of sunlight from billowing clouds lit the scene. The boy looked upward, giving thanks to Jehovah for delivering an army.

The frame was cracked, old, and the signature in the lower right corner all too familiar: 'L Da Vinci 1502' in the familiar flowing scroll.

A new painting by Leonardo da Vinci.

Excitement coursed through me, unequaled since first laying eyes on the van Gogh. The signature could be a forgery, but Melzi had confirmed signatures by da Vinci's students. Had he recorded this painting in his book and, more importantly, did he attribute it to Leonardo? I thought back, but could not be certain I saw a drawing of the painting in his book. What seemed like minutes passed before I heard Bennie's voice.

"You still here?"

I blinked, my thoughts racing in a dozen directions. "Yeah, yeah."

The boy's triumphant face shifted a piece of the puzzle. I stared at the image, something struggling upward through the muck in my brain as I reverently re-wrapped the painting.

"These others are not da Vincis." I said, replacing the painting on the table.

"Damn, they look like the real deal."

"I wish they were."

"You found proof?"

I nodded. "Irrefutable."

"In a way, I sort of guessed that," Bennie said. "Too many da Vincis in one place." He studied the drawings with a crooked smile. "We found several questionable sales. If buyers had bought these and discovered they were fakes, we'd have been on the hook as Delaudier's liability insurer. Even with disclaimers, juries tend to side with the victims when they see deep pockets."

"What happens now?"

"Not up to me," he said. "The Delaudiers had a mountain of debt, both business and personal. Most likely, the estate will sell off what's left to pay creditors. From what we're hearing, there're also suspicions about the experts who verified these drawings and other work. Looks like money greased some palms." He lifted his shoulders. "The painting might be a top-notch fake too. If forgers like Landis and Sykes scammed the world for years, what would stop someone from painting a da Vinci? You remember even Meegeren fooled the experts with his Vermeer forgeries."

"But if it's an actual Leonardo…"

Another shrug. "In my opinion, buyers are going to be scared off by the scandal. My company will be lucky to recoup a small percentage of our losses." He pointed at the wrapped bundle. "Whatever happens, that's going to create a ton of controversy. A lot of important people are going to question its authenticity for sure. It'll fall under a shadow like everything else the Delaudiers touched."

In Bennie's eyes, odds were against the painting. The canvas could be priceless— or a clever copy by one of Leonardo's apprentices.

"Maybe there's another way to find the truth," I said.

"You find a way to channel Leonardo?"

"Maybe."

Chapter Forty

Roland Delaudier's murder hit the front pages of *Times* and the *Post* along with hints of questionable sales and other improprieties. Local morning TV shows led off every segment with the story. The *Post* hinted an art scandal might be tied to his death, while Sotheby's and Christie's cried crocodile tears that a competitor had been removed from the auction scene.

I called Leslie for lunch and headed over to her apartment. A light rain fell, clouds concealing the tops of high-rises and office buildings. She met me at the door of her apartment with a kiss. Bundled in a black Saint Laurent raincoat, she hooked her arm through mine and we took the elevator down in silence. Neither spoke until we reached the sidewalk and she popped her umbrella.

"Sorry about Roland," I said, ducking under it with her.

"Roland could have paid it all back if they'd given him time."

"The police don't have any clues except he owed money to Boscanni."

"You think Boscanni had him killed?"

"He's the only person we know about with enough reason."

She huddled closer and I thought about the magnificent painting Bennie Wong had shown me in the vault. Despite what I'd just said, its existence provided motive to a lot of people.

"I saw the da Vinci painting," I said.

She looked at me. "The police found it?"

"Yeah, but they don't know what it is."

"You think it's real?"

I was shaking my head before she finished. "I don't know."

"Roland told me he had a painting," she said, "but I never saw it." She gave the barest shrug. "Poor Roland. The simplest answers don't always work, do they?"

Her cheeks were wet. I couldn't tell if it was the rain or tears. "What are you going to do now?"

"From what the papers said, the business will be closed for good. I made a lot of contacts working for him. Something will pop up."

The rain slowed and I pulled her close. "I can always talk with Dansby."

We walked another block without speaking when a familiar voice broke into our unspoken thoughts.

"Hey, Adam Barrow. What a coincidence."

Beside me, Cuff Links' curly black hair gleamed in the misting rain. He lightly touched my elbow, smiling as though anticipating a long-awaited meal. His thickset companion loomed beside Leslie.

"You remember Vincent, right?" he said.

"How could I forget? You two got me kicked out of Armands."

"Hey, we're sorry about that. You got a few minutes?"

"We're headed to lunch." I said, trying to banish the memory of the stain on Roland's carpet.

"Hey, no problem. We'll drop you."

A metallic silver Town Car pulled to the curb, and Vincent opened the rear door. Leslie looked at me. I wanted to tell her to run, but she closed her umbrella and ducked inside. Cuff Links pushed me onto the cream-colored leather seat beside her and took the seat next to an older man who faced us.

Except for wraparound dark glasses, Joseph Boscanni gave every appearance of success and respectability, looking as though he slipped away from a board meeting to enjoy lunch with us. His expertly tailored suit jacket disguised his flabby frame, a red rose in his lapel. The smell of new leather and Boscanni's cologne was almost overpowering as he removed the sunglasses, his onyx eyes lingering on Leslie. He tugged at the soft woolen crease in his trousers as Vincent dropped into the front seat beside the driver and the Lincoln pulled into traffic.

"They were on their way to lunch," Cuff Links said to Boscanni.

Joey Boots' smile broadened as he appraised Leslie more closely "Let me take you to Nunzios," he said. "Both of you. Best Northern Italian in the city."

"We've got reservations, but we appreciate the invitation."

Both men laughed. "I'm sure you do," Boscanni said.

The Lincoln traversed the streets like a luxury tank, its powerful engine a subdued rumble, the car most likely armored.

"Sorry if Jimmy and Vincent frightened you," Boscanni said to Leslie. "I wanted a little privacy to discuss the recent events."

"I'm not that easily scared," Leslie said.

"Good for you," he said. "Lucia told me you were tough *and* attractive." He dragged his eyes over her again. "She got both right."

He turned to me. "I heard you got shot."

"Occupational hazard in the art business." Out of my league in the present company, it was all the macho I could muster.

"Told you he was a smart ass," Cuff Links said.

I kept my mouth shut and waited for the reason for our complimentary ride.

"I want to clear up a few things," Boscanni said. "Avoid a hassle with the cops."

"Okay," I said, trying to appear relaxed.

"Word got back to me that one of my companies lent money to this Delaudier." As if he wasn't aware of a multimillion-dollar loan.

"The cops think I killed him because he was welching."

"A nickname like Joey Boots tends to get you noticed."

Cuff Links backhanded my knee. "Watch your mouth."

Boscanni waved him off. "It's okay, Jimmy. The man's just trying to make a point." Cuff Links, it seemed, had a name.

Boscanni pulled up his trouser leg up and waggled a gleaming wingtip.

"Ferragamo," he said with an innocent grin. "No boots."

The grin evaporated. "Just so you understand, my companies don't collect loans by killing people who can pay. It's hard to collect from dead people. It was a lot of money, but Delaudier was good for it. Big time art generates a ton of cash flow."

Boscanni might be a thug, but he understood things like cash flow, no matter what generated it.

"And Salvatore Testano?" I asked.

Jimmy jerked forward. Boscanni held up a hand and Jimmy froze as though restrained by a choke leash.

"Testano." Boscanni grimaced as though worrying at a piece of gristle. "That's another story I heard about. Seems he ran his mouth when he got a few drinks in him. Partying is okay, but it's a mistake to believe you're always among friends, you know? Certain people heard him brag about popping Enzo." His eyes never left my face. "To be frank, it pissed them off."

"You know Testano worked for the Delaudiers?"

"Sure," Boscanni grinned, "I knew that, but sometimes in my line of work, it's pleasure before business," he said, enjoying the inverted maxim and look on our faces.

"Anyway, that had nothing to do with Delaudier getting himself shot. He must've pissed someone else off, who I don't know, but Testano was a separate thing. You can tell the cops not to waste their time trying to tie me to either one. Anyway, there are more pleasant things to talk about. Like where we're having lunch today."

He leaned over and squeezed Leslie's knee. She didn't flinch or pull away.

"Not to worry about any of this, hon," he said, sitting back. "I know you weren't involved in the money side of the business."

The dead eyes shifted to me, eliminating any lingering illusion he was a captain of industry. "And Jimmy here won't bother you again. This Sal Testano told my friends you had nothing to do with Enzo's death."

Welding torches had a subtle way of getting at the truth.

"Can we go to lunch now?" I said. "Just me and her?"

Boscanni turned to his capo. "Whaddya think, Jimmy? We all on the same page now?"

"Yeah, I think so."

Our host gazed out the window and seemed to lose interest in us. "Tell Gino to let them out at the next corner."

Jimmy rapped his ring on the glass partition and told the driver to stop at the light. He opened the door and Leslie followed me from the car. Standing on the sidewalk, we watched the rain-slick behemoth slide away, tires hissing on the wet street. Leslie gave me a quick glance with the barest hint of amusement, apparently unruffled by our ride. Lucia Orellano had been right in her assessment.

She popped her umbrella without looking at me and we walked to the restaurant without speaking.

Chapter Forty-One

I sat in my office and replayed our impromptu ride that produced more questions than answers. A tremor ran through me. We'd been lucky. No one on the street would have noticed two people getting into Boscanni's car. If he wanted Leslie and me dead, it would have been tough to connect him to our murders. Replaying our conversation, he seemed more interested in protesting his innocence and recruiting allies to shield him from the police. Neither made sense.

Leslie and I had no connection to Delaudier's assets or what the police might decide. Joey Boots had exacted revenge on Sal for Riva's murder, but that was a family matter unrelated to money. Boscanni didn't seem concerned the police would add Testano's killing to his thick dossier, but Roland's death was different. The high-profile murder meant the investigation wouldn't go away, and Boscanni didn't need the added heat.

Funny thing was that I believed him. It made no sense to rule out the one individual with the most motive, but he had a point about Roland repaying the loan. Rare art generated the kind of money that attracted a thug like Boscanni. If proceeds from the first drawing's sale were used to make a payment, it followed that subsequent sales would guarantee payback of the loan. The mob liked to make examples of deadbeats, but Delaudier's loan involved millions, according to Marsh. Why kill off a cash cow?

I swiveled my office chair to the window and considered the alternatives. If I ruled out Boscanni, who and what remained? The Delaudier scandal was assuming a life of its own and an enterprising reporter uncovered rumors of bribes in the academic community. The story went worldwide on the net as did all catastrophes involving the rich and famous. In the end, Riva had been vindicated, me along with him in a minor way.

In the midst of congratulating myself, Clarice looked in and said Dansby wanted to see me. Her voice dropped as she warned that he'd had another bad day, and that Jean-Henri was with him.

"Should I gird my loins?"

"Better you should bring a gun."

I hoped she was wrong. Much as I admired Dansby and respected Jean-Henri, it was time for them to sample crow. I'd been right since the beginning, thanks to Enzo Riva's love of his father's book and Francesca Melzi's foresight. The whole sorry affair cast a shadow over academic reputations, and given the outrage consuming the academic world, all art connected to Roland and Isabelle Delaudier was now highly suspect.

Anxious to separate themselves from aspersions cast on their credentials, experts immediately questioned the da Vinci painting, calling its legitimacy into question. Most labeled it a clever forgery along with the drawings. They claimed no records had been found that Leonardo ever painted David and Goliath, a fact they were quick to point out to the masses and art lovers who avidly followed the story. The orphaned painting was sequestered at an undisclosed location, and no one was given access to it beyond a bevy of hand-picked technicians whose interest was waning by the day. Questions involving where and when the König family acquired the incredible cache of da Vincis provided more suspicions of a massive swindle. Lomax kept my name out of his investigation and my role in the murder slipped under the media's radar.

None of this untangled the mysteries of the painting in Roland's vault, his and Riva's murder, and who tried to kill me—and what happened to Melzi's book?

Clarice didn't look up as I opened the heavy pocket doors to Dansby's office. He was on the phone, a whiskey and soda clenched in one fist. Jean-Henri, disconsolate, sat on the couch, hands in his lap. He looked up with an uncomfortable smile as Dansby stared at the papers on his desk, his ruddy complexion flushed.

"You mean they just sold the rights without notifying me?" he yelled into the receiver. "What kind of operation are you running over there?"

Someone at the other end didn't get far as Dansby vented his outrage. "I think they'll find the telecommunications business is not immune to cash flow problems. Tell them not to bother me again when they run out of money."

He slammed the phone down. "Wankers."

"You wanted to see me?" I said.

He jammed the documents in a drawer and stood.

"This painting," he said brusquely, looking between Jean-Henri and me. "I want a goddam realistic opinion based on facts. And don't bother telling me again that Riva's book is missing."

It appeared my opinion mattered little now. Without the Melzi book, I was a very small fish in an ocean of experts, a wounded baitfish circled by sharks. So far as I knew, I was the only living person who saw the book, but modern analysis overrode anything I claimed to have seen. I had only skimmed Riva's book without time to examine every image. My memory was anything but photographic, and if the painting had been included, I'd missed it.

"I don't have other opinions," I said. "I saw the painting for five minutes. It's a thing of beauty, but I can't give you a professional opinion."

"Too bad Riva's not around any longer," Dansby grumbled. "I'm certain he would have an opinion." His eyes narrowed. "If the drawing *wasn't* a fake, I missed my da Vinci."

"No, you dodged getting cheated."

We stared at one another. My credibility was in tatters, my tenure in New York was slipping away. I was most likely on my way back to Chicago, but the possibility didn't change the facts.

"They'll offer the remaining drawings at the creditors' auction," I said, "if you want a genuine Donato Volpe."

He let the jibe pass and said, "Bloody hell, Adam, your job was to find opportunities, not stir up a nest of snakes."

I looked at Jean-Henri who looked more abashed then triumphant by the heated exchange.

"Money changed hands among some of your colleagues," I said to him. "Do you still believe the drawings are real? That we missed an opportunity?"

Chagrined, Jean-Henri glanced at Dansby. "Given the circumstances, I can no longer be certain."

"Wonderful!" Dansby exploded. "No one out there is certain of a damn thing, not even the two of you."

"Well, I do know," I said. "I saw proof the drawings weren't created by Leonardo. They were done by one of his best students. They were not da Vincis, Phillip."

"That lessens hope for this painting," Jean-Henri mumbled.

"You've seen it?"

"*Non.* I am not included in the inspection, but their first conclusions suggest it's highly questionable. No one believes a da Vinci oil found its way among mis-attributed drawings." His head dipped lower without meeting my eyes. "I think the painting will receive affirmation that it's from the school of Leonardo, but nothing more. Someone may purchase it with the hope new information may surface one day." A shrug. "Who knows."

He was right. Too many questions remained after the scandal. In the end, the Delaudiers were defeated by their own cleverness.

"What's more," Jean-Henri continued, "there's not the vaguest evidence about such a painting in the entire lexicon of his work. There's no mention of a work depicting David and Goliath. It's remotely conceivable he painted it for a wealthy patron, and that it resided in a private collection for centuries. We've all heard such stories."

He was only saying what we all knew. Legitimacy would be left blowing in the wind, the odor of a clever fake hovering over the painting. All that was left was a work that scholars would debate for decades.

I started to reply when Dansby slammed his palms on the desktop. "So, after weeks of chasing whatever Roland dangled in front of us, I'm left without a da Vinci." He glared at me. "I employed you to find what others overlooked."

It was in the open now. Trying to stop him from making a costly error had somehow turned into a mistake on my part. I should have waited for him to calm down, but my anger surged until I no longer cared where it led.

"Your memory's gone selective," I said. "I remember you didn't trust Roland at the auction. You thought he was setting you up with phony telephone bids. Now I'm to blame for your decision to back away."

"That's very good of you to remind me."

Jean-Henri held a tentative hand. "You both need to—"

"I don't need your opinions just now!" Dansby erupted. "If you'd maintained your convictions, I would most likely own the drawing."

"You wouldn't own a da Vinci," I said doggedly.

His face grew redder. "And if you'd ignored a drunken old fool, we wouldn't be in this situation."

"I did my job." I swept my arm around the room of military accoutrements. "You're no longer in the British army, Phillip, and I'm not here to salute your financial genius. Jean-Henri and I aren't sergeants you order to polish your buttons. Our job is to make certain your appetite doesn't exceed your brain."

He stared at me without blinking, and I saw what his enemies feared.

"It's very good of you to point out my shortcomings."

"That's not my intention and you know it."

He appeared not to hear me. "You have a great deal of cheek for someone in your position. My mistake was believing you could assist me. It appears your talents are better suited to running a small gallery."

"That's not the worst thing that could happen to me."

No matter his anger, I owed him, convinced he'd saved my life in California and done all he could to help me retain ownership of the van Gogh. In many ways he reminded me of my father, his passion to possess art mirroring my father's need for alcohol.

He turned his back and went to the window to survey the skyline. I glanced at Jean-Henri who shook his head as though further argument was useless. No one said anything, as though we were strangers in a waiting room.

Without turning, Dansby said, "I appreciate your dedication, but I believe you're over your head here. I think it's best you to take leave and see to your gallery."

He didn't move. Jean-Henri looked away, realizing I'd saved him from a major mistake. In his place I was the one in front of a firing squad. If I walked out of the building, chances were I'd never return. Dansby's verdict seemed fair in the sense that I'd produced nothing of value for him. I remained the only one who'd seen Riva's book, and without it, nothing I said would rebuild his trust.

Chapter Forty-Two

I took the elevator down to the lobby with the sensation of an outsider who had ignored Members Only and No Trespassing signs. Faceless pedestrians brushed past me as I crossed the street, ticking off the high points of my short sojourn in the big city: Enzo Riva. His astounding book. Leslie. The König family. Getting up close and personal with New York's premier crime family. Worst of all, my involvement in two murders. I'd been battered and shot, and right or wrong, I'd prevented Dansby from acquiring what he most wanted.

Back in my patched-up apartment, I resisted the urge to mix a drink and feel sorry for myself. I changed into casual clothes with no plans for the rest of the day, unaccustomed to the unexpected freedom of being unemployed. An evening inside my apartment to rethink my mistakes didn't appeal, and I discarded the option. Against my better judgment, I decided I needed a drink or two or three and a compassionate ear to listen to my tale of woe. Guessing Leslie would be home while the cops pulled apart the auction house, I called, and she answered on the second ring.

"I think I just got fired," I said as a greeting.

Quiet on the other end. "Okay," she finally said, "you can join me in the unemployment line. You want to meet at the welfare office or a friendly bar?"

"Guess."

"How about I buy and you tell me what happened."

"You read my mind."

"There a cute bar a block from my place. The Coachman's Pub."

"See you in fifteen minutes."

I thought about taking the subway, wondering if I was still on Dansby's expense account. Walking seemed the smarter option to give me time to digest what had just occurred in Dansby's office. If he cut off my funds, my bank account would die a slow death. Whatever happened, I was going to need every dime when I got back to Chicago.

Leslie's choice of a meeting place wasn't the classic New York bar or what I might label as 'cute.' It had the appearance of an upscale franchise struggling to match old world ambiance with dark wainscoting and faux English signs. The mini-forest of ferns looked out of place among serious drinkers hunched at the bar.

I spotted her in a booth at the rear, trademark martini in hand, an Old Fashioned glass across from her. I weaved past the after-work crowd and sat down, her smile restoring what remained of my day.

"I ordered you a double Makers Mark on the rocks," she said. "You can always change it to a triple if you like."

I leaned down and kissed her cheek. "Easier to order another double."

"Dansby really fired you?"

I slid onto the bench across from her. "Not in so many words. He was more refined, a true English gentleman to the end. He suggested I take a vacation and left it open whether I'd be invited back."

"This all started with Riva's book."

I savored my drink, wishing I'd picked another seat at the auction that now seemed months ago. "I know."

She finished her martini and waved at the waitress, pointing to her glass. "Things would have been different if you'd never met him. I don't see how you could believe anyone who lived in that dirty little apartment."

"It was all he could afford."

She shook her head in disgust. "What are you going to do?"

"Hell, sue Dansby for workplace discrimination, I guess."

"A bias against Californians?"

"Something like that."

I contemplated the tabletop, our levity withering in light of the reality we faced; her employment had abruptly ended, while mine was no longer deemed necessary. Neither of us admitted it, but we were sitting in a kitschy bar pondering our unemployment. I wondered if what happened changed things between us. A Beatles tune on the sound system drowned out conversations around us as I leaned closer

"I shouldn't be crying the blues," I said. "You've got your own problems with Delaudier boarded up."

She started to say something and stopped when her martini arrived. Forcing a smile, she placed her hand on top of mine. "What about our little ride with Boscanni?"

"I'm glad it turned out to be friendly."

"Is that what you call it?" she said.

"Friendly? At first, I thought it might be our last one, but I think he's playing both ends against the middle. He knows we're talking with Lomax and thinks we might take some heat off him."

"You think he killed Roland?"

"Not personally. People like Jimmy take care of the details like that, but yeah, Boscanni's the only one who makes sense. Those in his line of work can't be seen as weak. If it got out that Roland welched without consequences, Boscanni's rivals would sense an opportunity. So, yeah, I think he cut his losses to make a point. Unless someone did him a favor and got to Delaudier first."

"Did Lomax say how the killer got past security?"

"That puzzles him. The guard says he didn't see anyone, but he may be lying or scared. People like Boscanni don't leave loose ends to testify in court."

I tasted my drink. Isabelle and her family were possible murderers, but I couldn't see any advantage in killing Roland; he was the only one who could get into the vault. And if he was cutting his losses and getting out, why leave the painting behind? He had planned on fleeing the country until a bullet stopped him. Or had it all came down to bad timing and his luck ran out.

"Lomax said Roland was killed with a small caliber gun," I said, "like the one used to shoot me. He told me the mob likes .22's because they're quiet."

Leslie lowered her glass. She dug a tissue out of her purse and I waited while she wiped her eyes, the first crack I'd seen in her defenses.

"I'm sorry," I said. "You didn't need details."

She wiped the corners of her eyes without blurring the mascara and took a deep breath before she gulped half her drink, conjuring up a slight smile. "That's okay, I don't know where I'll go from here."

"We can always move in together until something shows up."

There. I'd said it. Made the commitment. Given the circumstances, I hoped it was an offer she couldn't refuse, especially since she couldn't afford her upscale apartment any longer.

She touched my hand again.

"You're being kind," she said, "but I'm not ready for that."

'Kind' wasn't what I wanted to hear. She was the first woman I'd ever invited to move in with me. Since Kat's death, the prospect of adding someone to my life hadn't appealed to me. I'd taken the leap and realized I misjudged her feelings.

"I hoped we might be more than good sex," I said, hiding my disappointment behind a shrug.

She stuffed the tissue in her purse. "I told you. I want my own life. You're a wonderful person, but I don't want commitments. There's so much more I want to do. Moving in with you would… I don't know. Slam a lot of doors in my face."

I couldn't come up with a clever retort for her rejection. It was the first time I'd ever offered a serious relationship, something the women's magazines claimed was a deadly flaw in men, but how was I supposed to deal with what she envisioned as her future? Falling back on my limited experience, I knew pressure wasn't the answer.

I was fumbling for another line of reasoning when she pulled two twenties from her purse and laid them on the table. I picked them up and held them out to her. She ignored them with a small smile.

"Be grateful. It's the last treat I can afford."

She wasn't just saying no thanks; she was running. I'd fallen in love with her at the wrong time in her life.

She stood and glanced at her watch. "I have an appointment about a position at MOMA in half an hour. I don't think I'm qualified, but I have to start somewhere. I doubt Delaudier will be seen as the highlight of my resume."

I stood next to her, the bar's noise defeating the urge to renew my offer. "Call me if you need a reference at MOMA," I said. "Phillip wields some clout with art mavens in the city."

She gave me a chaste kiss, and I watched her weave between drinkers stacked three-deep against the bar, both of us apparently on our own now.

• • •

After she left, I sat down and pushed aside my Makers, deaf to the laughter in the booth behind me. The packed bar wasn't the best place to consider my situation, but I didn't want to go home alone.

I moved my glass in slow circles, painting condensation designs on the table. As I contemplated her refusal, something tried to swim to the surface, something I'd heard that was out of place. A burst of laughter erupted from the bar and the thought slipped back into the depths. When it failed to materialize again, I relegated it to confusion and went back to contemplating my artistic designs on the tabletop.

I was sick of thinking about everything, but the thought of Melzi's book refused to go away. A lot of things might have happened differently if I'd found it. I shoved aside the what-ifs, not allowing pipedreams to lead me into the pit of self-pity. The book was gone and without Riva's ghost to enlighten me. I was a voice crying in the wind and my bourbon.

I pulled several napkins from the container on the table and wiped away the condensation trails as though a clean pallet would slide the pieces into place. The polished surface gleamed as I smoothed away the last of the water, the heavy top so new that time and drunk patrons hadn't yet marred the polished wood. I ran my hand over the surface, recalling the oak wet bar in Jean-Henri's apartment.

The memory of their sudden bonding that day returned. Unlikely as it seemed, Riva had forged an unlikely connection to Jean-Henri during our visit. Riva, the former Sicilian locksmith and Jean-Henri, the New York art scholar. Alpha and omega, their only bond the abiding love of art. Recalling the scene, an improbable solution to the book's whereabouts raised its head. It was ridiculous, but the only possibility I could cobble together.

I didn't want it to happen, but slowly and painfully, the memory of Riva and the book moved the pieces around until I saw an ugly picture. I resisted the inclination to order another drink and ignore the obvious, but the laughter and music around me faded as though someone had turned down the volume. Whoever put my surroundings on hold peered over my shoulder as an unseen hand shoved the pieces into place. The thought that had escaped me moments earlier returned, and I saw what a fool I'd been. I stared at the tabletop. The book, the Delaudiers' scam, Roland's murder, the attempt on my life. Maybe I had seen the truth all along and thrust it aside, unwilling to consider what sat in front of me.

A burst of laughter startled me. I drew a deep breath and looked around. I caught the waitress's attention and ordered another double. As I waited, I tried to make the nightmare disappear, but reality sent out more tendrils like a tenacious weed.

Chapter Forty-Three

I left Leslie's money on the table and splurged on a cab that I could no longer afford. It was a ten-minute ride to Jean-Henri's apartment, and I needed time to formulate what I'd say.

Gerry opened the door before I could knock and stepped back. It took a moment before he recognized me.

"If you've come to see Jean-Henri, he's not here, but I expect him any minute."

Dressed in jeans, a pink oxford and navy blazer, he carried a green cloth shopping bag in one hand. "I was just going out to shop for dinner. Jean-Henri's due back anytime."

"Actually, I need to talk with him. I can wait if that's okay."

Gerry hesitated a second and shrugged. "Since you work with him, I guess he wouldn't mind."

"I appreciate it."

He moved aside, and I stepped inside the apartment.

"I'm only going to the market a few blocks away," he said. "Won't take me long."

"Take your time."

After he left, I eased into a low-slung chrome-and-leather chair and observed the obsessively neat room. I rethought my plan and decided hopelessness provided a strong motivator.

Everything around me had been decorated to impart an atmosphere of harmony and tranquility. The scent of furniture wax and Far Eastern incense lulled visitors into a tranquil state of well-being. I tried to imagine what would say if Jean-Henri came through the door, but my choices were limited. Coming to his apartment was beyond a gamble—it bordered on something a sane person would describe as desperation.

I stared at the floor-to-ceiling bookcases and gave free rein to the irrational thought that occurred to me at the bar. Spaces between the maze of colorful dust jackets displayed artifacts, photograph frames, everything in place just as they'd been during my visit with Riva. I tuned out traffic noise from the street below and tried to put myself in Riva's place, assembling a picture of what might have happened.

Alone in his dingy apartment, Riva knew his life was near the end. Dying alone meant Melzi's book would eventually be discovered by strangers with no guarantees where it would end up. He never thought a gunshot would end his life, but he must have feared the book's fate, making certain it ended in the hands of someone who understood its importance.

But who?

I had watched Riva's unexpected kinship with Jean-Henri, aware the connection brought a spark of hope into the old man's life. Melzi's book had become the center of his being and making certain it found its way to safety would have been his final act. Remembering Riva had been a locksmith in Sicily, the improbable thought had occurred to me how simple it would have been for him to wait until Jean-Henri and Gerry left for work, enter the apartment and hide Melzi's treasure in plain sight.

I scanned the hundreds of books on the shelves but saw nothing resembling Riva's book, my hypothesis evaporating. It seemed farfetched he'd been desperate enough to leave his book with someone he'd met only once, but I was out of possibilities, even the most unlikely ones.

I concentrated on the rows of colorful book spines. In keeping with the room's symmetry, the books were regimented according to size, heavier volumes at floor-level. Many were oversized coffee table hardbacks and thick reference books, some with well-worn dust jackets. Smaller books above them were interspersed with small memories collected by Jean-Henri and Gerry during their travels, but the rows of massive books on the lower shelves presented a solid front.

Pushing myself from the chair, I walked to the bookcase and knelt on the white carpet, wondering how I'd explain my presence on the floor if Jean-Henri or Gerry returned. They were due at any minute and I began pulling out large volumes, stacking them beside me and peering into the shelves' empty spaces.

Nothing.

I removed two rows of dust covered thick volumes, sweating from the weight of old books manufactured when paper quality was more important than a fast buck. My hopes fell as I found nothing but the blank wall behind them. I frowned at the pile of books beside me.

This was crazy.

All I needed to confirm my madness was for Jean-Henri to walk in and find me on my knees, sweating like a ditch digger, rummaging through his personal library. I doggedly pulled out another row of books and found… nothing. I rested on my heels and wiped my damp palms on the carpet, listening for the sound of a key in the door. I looked at the books around me and accepted I'd constructed an improbable scenario out of frustration.

Less than a dozen large books remained on the bottom shelves. Thick volumes, their tops layered with dust, the academic titles mocked my growing despair. I picked up several books I'd removed and started to replace them when I stopped. I'd come this far, so why not indulge my madness to the fullest?

Straining forward, I pulled out Volume One: *Major Discoveries and Dissertations on the Italian Renaissance*. Grunting at its weight, I laid the book on the carpet and reached for its companion when I saw a reflection of gold. I held my breath and removed Volume Two.

The leather cover rested against the wall, brassbound edges and familiar gilt engraving radiant in the shadows. I fell forward on my hands and knees, my face inches above the carpet as I stared at my discovery.

Riva had selected the perfect hiding place, realizing Melzi's book would be safe until Jean-Henri stumbled on it. I'd discovered it through sheer luck and… what? Legally, it didn't belong to me. Since no one knew of its existence, the book became the Frenchman's property. I eased it from its hiding place, experiencing a sadness that Riva had been the last person to touch it. I couldn't imagine Jean-Henri finding it without respecting its value. I crossed my legs and lifted the book into my lap, running my fingertips over the crest. It was a forlorn hope, but I had no other choice

I said a silent prayer, hoping my good fortune held for a few moments longer. The book's contents were as overwhelming as I remembered them, but I needed to find what I sought in the few minutes left to me.

A quarter way into the drawings, I stopped turning pages.

The full-page illustration was unmistakable. My heartbeat increased as I stumbled over Melzi's Italian notation. They were concise and even my rudimentary Italian left no doubt. I lightly ran my fingertips over the page where Melzi's pen had faithfully copied Leonardo's David and Goliath painting 500 years ago.

I took three photos of the image with my iPhone and replaced the book against the wall. I returned the other volumes, careful to keep them in the order I had found them. Checking to be certain Melzi's volume was hidden from sight, I stood and brushed the carpet nape from my hands and trousers, my eyes lingering on the bottom shelf. Riva had gambled his beloved book would be in good hands. Melzi's work was safe, but I now had a new agony, one that tore apart everything.

Chapter Forty-Four

The promise of summer was a tonic to New Yorkers. Tantalizing warm breezes mingled with the pungency of sidewalk garbage as I headed west from Jean-Henri's apartment. I lifted my hands to my face and inhaled the musty leather binding, resenting the wind that blew it away. Part of me remained uneasy about leaving the book, but it was safe for the moment.

The leading edge of summer had lured throngs of tourists into the streets like ants anticipating the return of picnic weather. The sidewalk was a game of pedestrian dodgeball, oncoming faces a blur as more answers fell into place. More than anything I wanted to join the celebration, but my thoughts drove me past them, rethinking what remained to be done, hoping I misread the key piece of the puzzle.

Ahead, the sidewalk abruptly ended at an oasis of greenery. Central Park's eight hundred acres rerouted cars and buses around the woodland sanctuary that filtered and repelled the exhaust fumes. Surrounding high rises sedately surrendered to the haven of broad, shady walks that meandered through a priceless forest of green space.

I crossed the street and entered the refuge that kept the frantic madness at bay. Bicyclers weaved past me along the broad walk, joggers and mothers with baby strollers enjoying the season's first hint of warmth. I found an empty bench and sat facing the lake, working through my dilemma, watching row boats crisscross the flat water, avoiding bored swans that tolerated their presence. I stretched my arms across the back of the bench and lifted my face toward branches that were beginning to flaunt green buds, a pastoral world encased in steel and concrete. A carriage drawn by white horses clopped past, the driver sporting a black top hat heightened the illusion of normality. Across the water, regiments of gray glass towers resisted the bucolic setting, their starkness grim reminders that my reprieve was temporary.

A wire-mesh trash bin beside the bench, today's edition of the *Times* deftly folded over the lip in case a visitor preferred reality to peace. I picked it up and glanced at the headlines, hoping to distract my thoughts. Turning the front page, I saw a small photograph in the bottom corner. The article announced unknown assailants had slain James Francis Falcone outside a popular Westside restaurant. Why, I wondered, did mobsters have a propensity to kill one another inside or outside restaurants? A second paragraph said Falcone was a known member of organized crime in the city and surmised he was the victim of the continuing violence over control of New York's illegal drug distribution. I stared at the blurred photo that had been snapped on what appeared to be courthouse steps. Cuff Links stared back at me with the smug smile I'd seen inside Armands and Boscanni's limo.

Dragged back into the present, I tossed the paper into the receptacle and stared at a group of children tossing crumbs to the ducks and swans. Trees and swans and horse-drawn carriages failed to keep my dilemma at bay, not with my previous number one suspect reclining in the city morgue. Caught amid Riva and his book, the obvious had left me with tunnel vision. Was that what I'd been doing since Riva's death, trading blindness for stupidity? Had the loss of Kat dropped a veil over my eyes? I wasn't built for the seamy world of Lomax and Boscanni, and I wasn't hired by Dansby to solve murders.

The Königs had ample reason to make certain the book never surfaced, and Nils hadn't been my greatest admirer. It was reasonable Roland put Marsh Hampton in the mob's path, and the ex-CFO wanted payback before he ran. But then everyone bolted, and that left only Boscanni, who decided to eliminate a bad debt as an example. Sal had been a wild card with no motive unless someone paid him. He'd become redundant, and with Boscanni's right-hand man in the city morgue, Lomax was left with a bird's nest of kinks and knots to untangle. I felt for him, especially since he couldn't see what had become sadly transparent to me.

I took the cell from my pocket and hesitated. Cupping the phone in my hand, I stared at the screen. The epiphany that had eluded me in the bar was clear now. It was the last scenario I wanted. If I was wrong, I'd destroy more than a friendship. Unable to tear my eyes from the keys, I decided to let the cards fall where they may.

I looked up at the children tumbling over the grass. I enjoyed the tranquility a few seconds longer, trying to convince myself I had not misread all the signs. It was getting dark as I got to my feet and headed to my apartment, hoping I was wrong.

• • •

I called Leslie when I returned home. She was the pragmatic type who saw the world without blinders. If I had missed something, she would see it. I hoped I was wrong and she would tell me I'd misread the obvious.

Remembering Dansby's pistol, I went to the bedroom and retrieved it from my closet. If I was right, chances were I might need it sooner than later. Laying it on the kitchen counter, I pulled out a breakfast bar stool and waited. Like one of those childhood puzzles where you maneuvered a BB around concentric circles and dead ends, I needed a solution tonight.

Leslie arrived an hour later, gave me a quick kiss and tossed her leather purse on my couch.

"This was definitely not a fun day," she announced. "You have anything for a thirsty lady?"

"I might have some wine in the fridge," I said. "The cheap stuff that comes in a cardboard box. They sell a lot of it in Florida trailer parks."

She gave me a puzzled look. "What are you talking about?"

"Wait, I forgot. You've moved up in the world. You prefer expensive vodka now, right?"

"Perfect," she said with a nervous laugh. "Be a life saver and pour me a straight up."

Wearing a severe black pants suit and demure white blouse, Leslie had dressed the part of a consummate New York executive, although her five-inch heels didn't fit the corporate image. I had changed into jeans and a stained white golf shirt, looking like hired help.

She dropped into a chair with an exaggerated groan, her hair freshly styled, offset by delicate pearl earrings. Even with Delaudier on her resume, I had little doubt someone would leap at the chance to hire her.

"You're always irresistible," I said. "You'll find something that suits your special talents."

She cocked her head with a dazzling smile. "I'll keep looking when I get back from vacation."

"I thought you were job hunting."

"Not yet. After all that's happened. I figured I deserve a break."

"Not as much as Roland. He won't be taking any more vacations."

"Now you're being ugly," she said with a slight pout, "because I won't move in with you."

"When are you leaving?"

"Tonight."

It sounded as though she'd made plans weeks ago. I was already in her past, but that was obvious now. I went to the fridge and removed a bottle of Ukrainian vodka. I hoarded it for exceptional occasions and this one was special, although not what I envisioned. It wasn't every day I watched a piece of my life go down the tubes. I took a martini glass from my cabinet and I filled it. Dansby's Glock sat a few feet on the other end of the counter. I thought about grabbing it, but was captivated by her lovely face as usual. Greeting her with a gun in my hand seemed a tad more than ludicrous. Just shows you how wrong you can be.

"I spent the morning buying new things," she said as I handed the drink to her. "It's funny being from Florida and not owning a single bathing suit."

"Hilarious."

"Oh, Adam, don't ruin everything. Nothing good lasts. I'll be back and we'll see each other again."

"I doubt it. Not after I tell Lomax what I know."

She placed her untouched drink on the coffee table and lit a cigarette, squinting at me through the smoke. I took the cigarette from her fingers and ground it out in the ashtray.

"What are you talking about?"

"I need some help with a few details."

She remained still, her fingers tapping the edge of the ashtray.

"You were good, clever, really," I said, "but a lot of little things began stacking up. I'd still be in the dark if you hadn't mentioned Riva's apartment at the dinner party and later in the bar. You told me you'd never been there, but then complained it was small and dirty. Twice."

"So, what are you saying?"

I was standing over her now, but she didn't seem to notice. "You also knew the combination to Roland's office. That's not something you share with an employee unless you're screwing them."

She dug another cigarette out of her pack and lit it. "I worked there, remember? And you must have mentioned Riva's apartment to me."

"No, I think you found out Roland was in trouble and about to leave you. I think that you confronted him and shot him. What was he going to do? Take the drawings and painting to Sweden? Board up shop in the middle of the night and leave you?"

She stubbed out the cigarette and didn't move.

"When Bennie Wong gave me the first six digits of Roland's combination it took me a while to figure it out that 527543 spells LESLIE on a keypad."

She looked up at me without blinking.

"I also kept thinking about that day in Riva's stairwell," I said. "It was dark, but I kept remembering the shooter was small. At first, I thought it was Jimmy Falcone, but the silhouette didn't fit. You were just the right size, Leslie."

When I walked to the bar and turned, Leslie stood by the door, holding her purse as though ready to leave. I walked to her and handed her the martini.

"Don't you want to finish your drink and hear the rest?"

"Why are you doing this, Adam?"

"What I don't understand is why you killed Riva? No one believed either of us."

She lifted her drink as though I hadn't spoken, admiring the contents. "You're not joining me?"

"Not today."

She swallowed half the contents. "Good stuff."

"Riva?" I prompted.

"I didn't kill him," she said. "Sal and I talked our way into his apartment. Using your name helped. Sal tore the place apart and got angry when he couldn't find the book. Riva got excited, yelling at us to leave. Sal took him in the bedroom and shot him."

She could have been describing a scene from a movie. No regret as though none of this was attached to her.

"How'd you convince Sal to help you?"

"Money, plus he hated Isabelle," she said. "He really liked her, but she treated him like he was invisible. All I had to do was be… nice to him and promise him money when the drawings sold."

How long had she planned this? Had she been clever enough to play us all since that first night in the lobby with Riva? Or had she and Roland seen a potential problem and decided to cut their losses by disposing of us?

She set her glass on the table by the door. "You really never figured it out, did you?"

"Not until today."

"Roland was good to me."

Marsh had said someone else was in the picture, but I never figured it was Roland until this afternoon in the park. She said his name as though it should have been obvious even to a dullard like me. I stared at her and pushed aside the mental pictures of them together, trying not to imagine their conversations about me, in bed and out. I kept talking, trying to salvage what remained of my pride.

"There were other things. Like your apartment. And Roland's gift of the Silverman painting. I Googled his prices. At least $40,000 for a canvas that size. And the new Lexus. All above your pay grade."

"Among other things." She smiled and I saw the other person beneath the expensive clothes. "Isabelle would have left him long ago if she knew what he spent on me."

"And if I'd found the book?"

She faked a grimace. "You'd have left us no choice. Roland had to get Boscanni off his back. He couldn't take the chance the auctions would fail or that the painting was a phony. Nothing was complicated until you and Riva showed up. When I broke into your apartment to look for the book, you walked in and I whacked you." She smiled again. "Not too hard, I hope. We just needed to get rid of the book."

Given that she had knocked me unconscious and shot me, I wondered what she knew about the drawings and painting.

"Did the Königs know about the drawings?

"They were worried, but it didn't matter so long as they walked away with full pockets. The old lady only cared about her precious family name."

"How was it supposed to work?" I thought I had it figured out, but I wanted to hear her say it.

"You are persistent, aren't you?"

"Tell me."

"All right. Roland would sell the drawings and painting, then divorce Isabelle. He'd give her half of everything as a settlement, then sell the painting and we'd be set for life. Then Sal got himself killed and Roland panicked. In fact, the whole family was scared shitless."

"So, you would be the new Isabelle. What did you plan, some tropical island where the two of you would sip rum and enjoy sunsets?"

"I think you'll agree Roland deserved better than her."

"And that was supposed to be you."

"It *deserved* to be me."

"You're wrong," I said, remembering Riva's bloody head and the bloodstains in Roland's office. "It just took you longer to shed your skin. Revert to that redneck from Wadesville."

She stepped back and pulled a small revolver from her purse, aiming it at my chest.

I nodded at the pistol. "Lomax said the mob likes to use a .22 sometimes, but it's also a lady's gun."

"It was my grandmother's."

"She would be proud of you now."

"Too bad you can't see how all this wasn't supposed to happen." She sounded more irritated than remorseful, almost bored. "Everything finally come together in my life. Roland said he trusted me. He even gave me the combination to his office and the vault, but the one to the safe didn't work. I'm guessing he lied or changed it. I would have taken the painting and disappeared, but I couldn't open the damn thing."

"The night you killed Roland. How'd you get back into the building?"

"I never left. I hid in a utility room until everyone left." Her words slowed at the memory. "It was bad luck, really. Roland wasn't supposed to be there."

"Best laid plans and all that," I said, intent on the small revolver in her hand. "Tell me, were your tears for Roland real, or were you crying because you lost the painting?"

She didn't appear to hear me. "He was going to Sweden with Isabelle. They'd be a happy little family again with millions from the da Vincis."

"Leaving you in the cold world again."

She lifted her chin. "Not entirely. He kept a small strongbox in his desk and counted out some money for me. Twenty-five thousand fucking dollars. I told him men like him usually left the money on the bed for their whores. He thought it was all some kind of joke, and when he bent down to replace the box, I shot him. The box contained over a hundred thousand dollars. I wiped it clean and left by the delivery door in the alley."

"Why'd you shoot me at Riva's apartment?"

"I only wanted to destroy the book so we'd get full value for the painting and drawings. I hated the thought of killing you." She manufactured a smile, but the revolver never wavered. "I really like you, Adam. You were more than a distraction, and if things had been different, I would have made you forget about Kat."

"Don't kid yourself." At least she wouldn't have that satisfaction.

Her smile faded as she caught me glancing at the Glock on the counter.

"You'll never make it, Adam."

She was right, and I didn't think she'd miss at this range.

"You brought your old life with you from Florida, "I said. "You caught a virus in that double-wide. You left it all behind, but it wasn't enough, was it, Wanda?"

Her expression didn't change, a cast metal statue, the revolver steady in her hand. The room grew quiet as though the traffic below had paused, waiting for the shot. The pistol never wavered and she seemed very at ease pointing it at me. I wondered if I'd live long enough to hear the ambulance as she inspected the apartment.

"I don't guess Lomax is in the next room," she said.

"You know the old saying. Never around when you need them."

She backed away another step and raised the pistol at my head. "Turn around."

I turned my back to her, my eyes drawn to the Glock again.

"There's no profit in this for you, Leslie," I said. "You'll be front and center on Lomax's list if you're not already there."

"You're forgetting Roland's little cash box. Lomax will never find me."

Sweat ran under my shirt collar. A siren wailed between the buildings and I heard her cock the pistol hammer. I'd lived long enough in New York and Chicago to know the siren was a firetruck, and that Lomax wasn't coming to my rescue. My back to her, I tensed my shoulders against the bullet. I looked at the bottle on the counter and closed my eyes. No one wants their last vision to be a vodka bottle. The air in the room stirred and footsteps whispered on my carpet. I guessed she'd stepped closer to make certain of her aim. A few seconds later, the door opened and closed. I waited a few seconds and turned,

She was gone.

I ran to the counter and grabbed the Glock, pausing before I eased open the door. The hall was empty. The elevator light glowed and stopped at the lobby level. I lowered the pistol, breathing hard as I imagined her heels tapping across the marble lobby, a figure in black vanishing into New York's crowds.

Wanda Strickland was in the wind.

I knew I'd never see her again, but why she'd let me live would remain a mystery as long as I lived. With her survival skills and Roland's seed money, she'd start over and search for her perfect life somewhere else. If the police found her, there wouldn't be enough solid evidence to convict her. She'd dump the gun and it would be my word against hers.

Amazed to find myself alive, I walked back into my apartment, poured a vodka and downed it. My hands shaking, I poured another. After a third, my hands stopped trembling and I fell into the chair Leslie had occupied. A broken cigarette retained her lipstick. I pushed the butt around in the ashtray and wondered why it took me so long to put everything together. Staring at red lipstick on the filter, I knew I'd never make a living as a detective. I'd connected pieces that led me to the book and painting, but I'd been no competition for a beautiful woman who saw an easy mark.

"Idiot," I said aloud.

I got up and dumped the butts in the trash. I found my phone, called Lomax and left him a message to call me. Not that it would do either of us any good.

Chapter Forty-Five

Sleep was impossible after Leslie decided not to kill me. No matter how I replayed every day since meeting her in Delaudier's lobby, I never saw a crack in his shell. She was good, and I'd only seen what she wanted me to see. I'd been too enamored or myopic to see what stood in front of me all along.

I got out of bed and pulled on a zip-up jacket. It was after midnight when I left the building, but I needed to walk, to mingle with other humans, most of whom considered themselves above shooting people. The night air felt leaden, the pavement gleaming like wet iron in the aftermath of the rain, the closed storefronts reminding me of deserted dollhouses. I scanned the strange faces passing me, seeking hers, but she was long gone. After a few blocks, I lost the fear of bumping into her and the possibility she'd changed her mind about killing me.

Night was not the smartest time to roam New York's side streets, so I headed toward Broadway and the people who rarely slept. I lost track of how many blocks I walked, unable to let go of the sound of the revolver being cocked. The click would be part of my life for a long time and I wondered for the hundredth time how I had been so naïve. The woman I'd begun to love had aimed a pistol at the back of my head. Another quarter-inch pressure on the trigger....

The memory sent my thoughts farther downhill. I was star-crossed when it came to women. Either that or I was the carrier of aberrant karma. I considered the likelihood of being a pariah of my own making, eventually dismissing the thought as a maudlin product of almost ending up dead on my apartment floor like Riva and Roland.

The farther I walked, the more I realized she never needed me or Roland. We'd been stepping stones across whatever rage flowed within her. Possibly, she's been born with flawed DNA, incapable of escaping her childhood, anger mutating into a need to pull even with the rest of the world. I didn't buy courtroom arguments that growing up poor justified a trail of dead bodies, and beautiful Leslie was no exception.

My dissection of her motives was more than self-righteous disdain. I hoped I had crawled away from my childhood and learned to be a better person, but I didn't kid myself that I was anywhere near complete. I discovered beauty in art before it was too late, turning it into something resembling a normal life, while my brother Wes fought our history with alcohol. We both carried scars, but I learned to let wounds heal without picking at the scabs or ripping off bandages. People who allowed old wounds to rule their lives invariably created their own unhappiness or self-destruction. I didn't claim total immunity, but I learned to recognize the symptoms. Leslie and Kat before her selected darker gods in their battles with old demons.

Weary of trying to fathom life's flaws, I approached a row of late-night kiosks lining the sidewalk selling souvenirs and junk. A newsstand anchored one end, and I bought a *Post*. The sleepy owner took my two dollars without offering change. I waited for a moment and let it go, the compulsory tip my good deed in a bad day.

A late-night Starbucks beckoned in the next block. Next to good bourbon, I could depend on coffee to blunt old memories and defeat new monsters.

The place was empty for except two teenagers behind the counter listening to Taylor Swift whine about a lost love. What the hell did she know? She wasn't old enough to be hurt by love or know what lay ahead. I tuned her out and ordered a double espresso from a kid with a stringy pony tail.

Waiting while my coffee brewed, I took a table and opened the page to an article about Delaudier's closing. In a cruel twist of fortune, the courts ordered all business and personal belongings to be offered to the highest bidder within the week. No mention about the drawings or painting. Disparaged and shunted aside in the stampede to tally up assets for hungry creditors, the painting remained under a cloud of suspicion. The academic community closed ranks to bandage up their soiled integrity, labeling the painting as highly suspect. Someone might take a flyer on it, but owning an almost-da Vinci amounted to little more than possessing a faint.

Only it wasn't a conversation piece or a fake.

The kid called out my espresso and went to the counter. From his expression, I guessed he saw someone lost or strung out from a day-long hangover or worse. He eyed me over the steaming expresso machine and I imagined he saw more than his share of late-night wrecks.

"Long night?" he asked as I paid him.

"Oh, yeah,"

He slipped my cup into a cardboard protector and snapped on the lid.

"Stay cool and be careful out there," he said.

I gave him a thumbs up and headed for the door, a few ounces of depression lifting from my shoulders. You never know where you'll find kind words when you need them most.

Heading up Broadway, I remembered Leslie's soft features and wondered again why she'd let me live. Would she ever think of me, or would I remain one of those blurred memories that surfaced after a couple of drinks? As I neared my apartment, I thought about the kid's words: *'... be careful out there.'*

It was good advice, but late in arriving.

Chapter Forty-Six

I sat around my apartment next day, feet propped on the coffee table, a trusty Old Fashioned in hand as an improbable idea gained a foothold. I laughed out loud, tempted to discard the outlandish notion, but I couldn't let go. The more I considered my plan, the deeper the truth carved a place my mind. Boosted by more two drinks, I remembered the boy's words. Careful didn't always work either, but I'd run dry of other solution. All I needed was confirmation before I risked everything I owned—or would ever own.

If I'd taken away anything from my close call with Leslie, it verified that the word "assume" was the most dangerous verb in the English language. My assumptions and mistakes along the way led to three violent deaths. I never pulled the trigger, but I needed to make certain something worthwhile came out of the mayhem.

I found Bennie Wong's card, hoping he was still in town. I called his hotel with no luck. I tried his cell next and found him working in Roland's office, still going through Delaudier's records after the police cleared out. He left word with the policeman stationed at the front entrance who let me in the building thirty minutes later. First thing I noticed were blank lobby walls and empty plinths along the staircase. The liquidation process had started early, every creditor waiting to dip their hands into the pot. I opted for the stairs to the third-floor, recalling my midnight foray with Leslie.

Manilla folder in hand, I saw. Roland's office door was open. Bennie wore a suit today, his coat draped over the back of Roland's burgundy chair, his fragile frame hunched over the desk. The impressive collection of bronzes I'd seen earlier was gone, along with most of the furniture and the couch Leslie and I had enjoyed. The vault door was closed and a canvas tarp covered the bloody carpet beside

Bennie. He leaned back in the chair and straightened a stack of papers and account books.

"You look like hell."

"Thanks. The art world gets ugly sometime."

"You're just finding that out?"

I collapsed in a chair, hoping I hadn't wasted my time. Bennie laid his hand atop the ledgers.

"You have any idea how much money the Delaudiers owed when they skipped?"

"Hard to believe there was any debt. They were making money hand over fist from sales and commissions."

"And spending it faster than it came in," he said. "The FBI and a slew of financial investigators let me look through these after they photocopied everything." He patted the ledger books. "We are first in line for restitution, but the leavings may not cover what we're owed. I found three instances where I think Roland and Isabelle scammed us. So far as I can figure, they departed our shores owing my company over five million dollars. And I ain't even started yet, old friend."

"Your firm join the extradition process in Sweden?"

"Hell, I don't know. I'm just a company mushroom."

I slid my folder across the desk. "I need you to look at this and keep a secret, Bennie," I said. "For old times' sake."

He stared at the envelope without picking it up and raised his eyes. "Lots of secrets in this glass mausoleum. Remember, I get paid to shine a light on them."

"This is something special, Bennie. If I'm right, I think I can help your firm recapture some of its losses."

He pulled the envelope closer. "I'm going to make a wild ass guess and say this has something to do with the painting in the vault."

"Is it still here?"

"The specialists returned it after they put away their magnifying glasses and magic potions." He grinned. "No one could think of a safer place. I'm the only guy with the combination."

"The researchers and self-appointed experts tore it apart," I told him. "They're trying to recover their reputations and cover their collective asses. No one's going to spend big money on anything connected to Delaudier."

"You've got to admit the damn thing's impressive, though," Bennie said wistfully. "Someone with more money than sense may be crazy enough to spend big bucks on it."

When I didn't reply, he picked up a wooden ruler and began tapping his teeth with the edge, inspecting me.

"You want to see it again, don't you?"

I hadn't laid eyes on Bennie in years. We'd been close in college, my confidant and soul mate in all things art, but did I still know him? Time does things to people, but he was the only person who could show me whether I was right. I didn't want to involve him if it might get him fired, I had no other choice.

"First, I want you to see what's in this folder. Then I want you to tell me you'll keep it confidential."

He paused, but I knew I had him hooked. He grinned and I watched the old Bennie resurface as curiosity overwhelmed his defenses and judgment. "Okay. I can always bunk at your place if I get canned."

He tossed the ruler aside and opened the folder. He removed the single sheet I'd copied from my camera. Donning half-moon spectacles, he leaned closer to the Xerox and didn't move for half a minute. Another ten seconds passed before he spoke, his expression suspended between awe and disbelief,

"Seriously, Francesco Melzi drew this?"

"That, and wrote the note at the bottom."

"Where'd you get it?"

"Long story that I'll tell you one day over all the beer you can drink."

Bent over the paper, he didn't move for another minute as he reread Melzi's notes, his eyes flicking back and forth over the drawing. I let him bask in the image until he laid aside the paper as though it was a sacred relic. He came around the desk without a word and went to the vault keypad. I picked up the paper and followed him inside as the vault door swung open. The wrapped bundle still rested on the table.

With Bennie's help we uncovered the painting. I propped it upright against one wall and bent closer. The overhead lights rendered the shepherd boy in all his simple glory. This was no preliminary study or an acolyte's attempt to emulate da Vinci. Every brushstroke had been laid down with exquisite care, the anatomy familiar to anyone who admired the master's works down through the centuries.

I held the drawing next to painting, comparing the two, Bennie head beside mine. The details in Melzi's copy were a perfect match. The tunic's drapery folds. Cracked leather sandals. The boy's beatific expression of adulation. Even the duplication of Leonardo's signature.

The painting was real.

I stood and handed the paper to Bennie who adjusted his glasses who knelt down and pulled the frame closer. His gaze shifted between my copy and the painting until he stood, gazing down at the 500-year old painting.

"I should report this," he said.

"If what I have in mind works, your company will get its money back."

He looked back at the painting. "No matter what happens, I can say I once held it in my hands."

I took the painting from him and rewrapped it. "You swore to keep quiet. At least until I resolve things."

He removed his glasses and broke into a smile. "You've got something planned, you sneaky son of a bitch."

"I think so, but only if this stays between us for the time being."

"Whatever you do, just make certain it finds the right home. And that I don't get my ass in a sling."

"Deal."

We shook hands and I returned the copy of Melzi's drawing to the folder. "Any rumors when the painting and Delaudier's other assets will be auctioned?"

"Before the weekend," he said. "Creditors are lining up and screaming, but there's not much left. He mortgaged or borrowed against almost everything. Everyone's grabbing what they can, trying to sweep the whole mess under the rug."

"I was serious when I said I can help your company recoup its losses."

"At this point, we'll take any help we can get."

We bumped fists and I headed back to my apartment. The voice inside my head yelled at me to rethink my plan. I could reveal the book to Dansby and Jean-Henri and let nature take its course. But then what? Jean-Henri would trumpet the painting's authenticity to the world, and even with his mega-wealth, Dansby would never pay what the painting demanded. Consortiums and museums would engage in bidding wars, the selling price soaring above half a billion dollars, ruling out even the wealthiest private collectors. He would not risk his empire for a single painting and one of the greatest discoveries of the century would grace some other wall.

• • •

They held the last auction at noon in the bare Delaudier sales room. The Delaudiers' few remaining personal items and leftover inventory had attracted a small crowd, mainly bottom feeders. I suspected the rest were curiosity seekers with shallow pockets. No tuxes or extravagant cocktail dresses this time around. The atmosphere in the lobby was morose, the familiar faces absent.

A few employees stayed around to collect their last paycheck and help with the final burial. A young woman at a single table recognized me. I gave her a business card and she handed me a paddle and four black-and white stapled pages. No glossy catalog.

"You're Major Dansby's stand-in, right?"

"That's me."

I walked away before she could ask more questions. The salesroom was a third full. I selected a seat in the center, avoiding eye contact with those around me. The sparse crowd appeared bored and I didn't see the usual faces that followed serious art. Several reporters stood in the rear, seeking a human-interest story in the aftermath of the Delaudiers' downfall.

A man with a bored expression walked onto the stage and tapped the podium microphone, adjusting horn-rimmed glasses. No white-gloved attendants or velvet curtains graced the stage behind him. Dressed in khakis and a sport coat, the balding liquidator was a downward leap from Delaudier's professional auctioneer.

A middle-aged business-type several chairs away leaned toward me and brandished the stapled pages.

"Not much in here," he said. "I'm playing bottom-feeder today. There's an antique table my wife wants, but the art is mainly a few old prints and third-rate artists."

"What about the da Vinci painting?"

He gave me a tolerant look. "Nice example of Renaissance art, but the experts agree it's not authentic. Good chance it's from his school which make it worth a few bucks, but I doubt he ever touched it." He tapped the papers in his lap. "Hell, they didn't even put an estimated value on it." He lowered his voice and glanced around, grinning. "Old Roland turned out to be some kind of crook, didn't he?"

When I didn't reply, he flourished the makeshift catalog again. "This whole thing's filled with more than the usual legal warnings about authenticity and lack of provenance. You'd have to be nuts to risk serious money."

The sound system emitted a piercing shriek. The man at the podium frowned and adjusted the microphone, fiddling with a wooden gavel. "All right," he droned, "we're ready to begin if everyone will sit down."

A worker walked on stage and placed the painting on an easel, creating a few murmurs in the audience. I doubted there had been much discussion where to include it in the makeshift auction. It was as though the liquidators wanted it out of the way as though disposing of it somehow closed the books on Delaudier. Even without a spotlight on its surface, the rich colors beamed out at the gloomy room.

I gripped my paddle and drew a breath.

The auctioneer gestured at the easel and read the catalog notes excluding the usual sales hype. He picked up the gavel.

"Do I have a starting bid?" he intoned.

A paddle went up. "Twenty-five thousand," said a dapper older man in the front row. I didn't recognize him and hoped he was bargain hunting for a conversation piece.

Another paddle behind me. "Thirty thousand."

A slender woman on the aisle behind me languidly raised her paddle. "Two hundred fifty thousand."

The room went silent. I twisted in my seat and recognized the woman as a representative from Christie's. Accompanied by an equally well-dressed man, they whispered to one another, heads close together, eying the painting. My plan was rapidly unraveling. How much was Christies willing to gamble?

The first bidder reentered the fray. "Two hundred sixty thousand."

"One million," the woman countered, holding the paddle above her head.

Flustered by the amounts, the auctioneer cleared his throat and darted his eyes around the room.

"The bid is one million dollars."

Now or never, I thought.

"Five million," I called.

Several people in the front row half rose from their chairs for a better glimpse of me. The auctioneer pointed his gavel at me, momentarily caught up in the excitement traversing the room.

"I have five million dollars from that gentleman."

The woman and her companion whispered to one another.

"Six million," she called.

The auctioneer started to repeat her bid when I waved my paddle.

"Ten million."

A rumble traversed the room. What a rush to bid money I didn't have!

For a few moments the air rang with silence. The auctioneer pointed toward the woman who said something to the man beside her and shook her head.

"The bid is ten million dollars," he said, looking relieved. "Anyone else?"

My Christies' competition stood and walked up the aisle without looking back. The auctioneer waited a few seconds longer and banged his gavel.

"Sold to the gentleman for ten million dollars."

I'd done it. Now if I only didn't get thrown in prison.

My seatmate leaned over the empty chairs separating us. "Good luck," he said, undoubtedly wondering if I required sympathy or a therapist.

I ignored him and headed toward the exit, disregarding the stares. When I got to the lobby, I signed a written copy of my bid, tore off a receipt and strode as casually as possible to the exit, waiting for someone to call for me to stop. Dansby's name worked wonders, but when it came time to collect ten million dollars, the lights would come on.

Outside, bright sunshine returned me to reality, my euphoria draining away as I headed for the office. The farther I walked, the more I second-guessed my decision. I possibly had just made myself a pariah in every corner of the art world. I was ten million dollars in the hole, hanging onto a broken limb by my fingertips, trying to avoid picturing my cellmates.

No one ran after me and I kept walking, experiencing an exhilaration I'd never known, recalling the euphoria on the cavalrymen's faces in the painting in Dansby's office. My fears abated with each step as I tried to console myself. Okay, so I'd just committed ten million dollars with only a tottering gallery and paltry checking account in my favor. What was the worst that could happen? I'd already been fired and legal action for making a false auction bid didn't carry the death penalty. With a good lawyer and the minimum wage going up, I'd never starve.

I took the elevator to my old office. Clarice was away from her desk and I slipped inside my office, collected a few personal belongings and dumped them in a box - nothing like planning ahead. I turned off the light and headed to Dansby's office, passing Clarice in the hall who looked up, surprised when I smiled at her.

"Is he here?"

"He's here. I'm sorry about all this, Adam," she said. "Sometimes, he's…"

I winked. "Not to worry. This won't take but a minute."

"You sure you want more abuse?"

I bent down and kissed her cheek. "The surprise is all his today."

Dansby was on the phone, his face mirroring Clarice's surprise when he saw me.

"I'll call you back," he said to whomever was on the other end.

"You need to call Jean-Henri and ask him to join us," I said. "He's a wealthy man, but he doesn't know it yet."

His hand resting on the phone, he said, "What are you talking about?"

"Just call him."

He glowered at me. I walked to his credenza and poured a cup of coffee from the insulated carafe. Walking to the bar I fortified it with a shot of his best Irish whiskey as he stared at me like I'd flown in from the window. He made no move to pick up the phone. I took a seat on the couch and crossed my legs, enjoying his perplexed look.

"Call him," I said again. "This concerns him too."

He frowned and buzzed Jean-Henri, who showed up a minute later. He glanced at my unexpected arrival, his face mirroring Dansby's surprise as I sipped my Irish coffee. Whatever I'd done was done. I refused to consider the consequences, enjoying the moment no matter how it turned out. Despite the possibility of losing everything, I lightly clapped my hands with a euphoria I'd never felt and set my cup on the table.

"Okay," I said. "Let's change everyone's life, shall we?"

Dansby bristled. "What in blazes are you talking about?"

"I just spent ten million dollars of your money."

It was one of the few times I'd seen him confused. Jean-Henri shook his head, looking back and forth between us.

"Ten million dollars of my money," Dansby intoned. "I believe that calls for an explanation unless you've lost your mind."

"I bought the da Vinci painting thirty minutes ago." Dansby stared at me. "With your money."

He blinked and glanced at Jean-Henri who hadn't taken his eyes off me.

"I also found Riva's book, Phillip," I said. "Jean-Henri had it. The book proves the painting is by da Vinci's hand."

"You *are* mad!" Jean-Henri burst out. "I've never seen this book."

"Nevertheless, you own it."

"What—"

"Riva broke into your apartment before he died. He hid it behind your other books."

"And you know this how?"

"Gerry let me in." I said, unable to restrain a grin. "I found it when he went grocery shopping. Riva left his most prized possession to you."

Comprehension slowly lit Dansby's eyes. "The painting. You found it in Melzi's book?"

My smile broadened as I handed him the auction invoice.

"It's a da Vinci, Phillip. I bought it for you. God knows what it's worth, but it's worth a helluva lot more than ten million." I looked at Jean-Henri. "Melzi's book alone is worth that."

Dansby stared at the piece of paper in his hand, absorbing that he owned a painting worth more than fifty times what I'd spent.

"An honest to God painting by Leonardo," he breathed.

"Melzi's drawing and notes confirm it," I said, watching a succession of emotions race across his face.

"If what you claim is true…"

"It's true."

His look justified every risk I'd taken.

"Congratulations, Phillip. You own a superb da Vinci."

• • •

It was nearing twilight, fading pink and gray clouds giving way to what would be a moon-bright sky as I stared out the window of the Boeing 757.

The plane crossed the New York state line on its way to Chicago. I sipped my complimentary bourbon and leaned back in the spacious First-Class seat Dansby had insisted on booking for me. I needed to check on my gallery, although Wes was doing a great job promoting it and keeping our artists happy. Dansby had generously upped my salary in the hope I'd find my way back to him. Time away would provide space for me to consider how I wanted to spend the rest of my life. Whatever I decided, I had a set of viable options for one of the few times in my life.

On the downside, lady luck, if she was indeed a lady, had left me at the altar again. Leslie and Kat were both gone, and I wondered if the face in the acrylic window covered a flaw where women were concerned, my luck preferring the dark side. Within a single year, I lost the two women I loved: one murdered and the other a killer on the run.

I finished my drink and searched the night sky. If I'd accomplished little else, I left New York's pundits a tad wiser, and possibly transformed myself into a better person. More gratifying, I secured the painting for Dansby and erased the fact that I had almost failed one of the most important people in my life. Perhaps he was right in that I had a special talent. A strange one to be sure, but one that had value. Twice in a lifetime I rescued two incredible pieces of art from obscurity. And possibly in the future, Lady Luck would turn her capricious face in my favor and find someone to share my good fortune.

I leaned back against the headrest and met the eyes of the brunette flight attendant. I raised my glass and she smiled and held my gaze. Whatever the future held, I decided another drink was definitely in order.

End

Note from the Author

Word-of-mouth is crucial for any author to succeed. If you enjoyed *Shadows of Leonardo*, please leave a review online—anywhere you are able. Even if it's just a sentence or two. It would make all the difference and would be very much appreciated.

Thanks!
Will

About the Author

Will Ottinger is an award-winning novelist who grew up in Savannah. He is a graduate of Emory University and Northwestern Graduate Trust School. Now living in Atlanta, Georgia, he and his wife owned a Chicago art gallery and wealth management training/consulting firm. Former president of Scribblers Ink, a Houston writers' group, he is now a member of the Atlanta Writers Club.

You can learn more about him and his work at www.ottingerauthor.com.

Thank you so much for reading one of **Will Ottinger's** novels.
If you enjoyed the experience, please check out our recommended
title for your next great read!

The Last Van Gogh by Will Ottinger

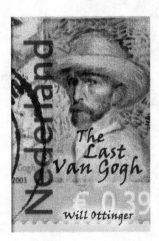

2019 Maxy Awards "Best Mystery-Detective"

"Ottinger is world class in developing characters, setting scenes, and building suspense as he weaves the story, ever-drawing the reader deeper into the mystery." –Ken Bangs, author of *Guardians in Blue*

CPSIA information can be obtained
at www.ICGtesting.com
Printed in the USA
LVHW030056021220
673097LV00004B/133